MONSTER OF THE DARK

MIRRORS IN THE DARK BOOK 1

KT BELT

RUBBER TREE BOOKS

ISBN: 978-954913-00-4

Cover design by: Jeff Brown

Visit KT Belt and sign up for the mailing list at:

http://www.ktbeltbooks.com

CONTENTS

1. Happy Birthday — 1
2. New Friends — 13
3. The Forging of 111724 — 37
4. Barriers — 57
5. The Mask — 71
6. Edge — 91
7. Clairvoyant at Last — 105
8. Carmen vs. Edge — 129
9. First Flight — 169
10. Why Live — 201
11. Alone in The Dark — 223
12. Numb — 237
13. Another Flight — 251
14. In the Clouds — 271
15. The Artemis Incident — 297
16. Darkened Future — 315
17. The Monster's Lair — 327
18. Edge vs. Artemis — 343
19. The Beginning of Hope — 357
Epilogue — 365

About the Author — 369

1

———

HAPPY BIRTHDAY

"They'll be here any minute."

Mr. Grey looked at his wife, Mildred. Her words sent a shudder reverberating down his spine. He had prepared for this since the day his daughter was born; he knew what was to come. Every parent who'd been told what they were knew what was to come. Some would say it was a miracle she hadn't killed them. He'd read the stories. But now, today, their rabid dog—their little girl—would be quite thankfully taken off their hands.

That was the reality of their situation. Reality, however, and his actual perspective were unable to match so coldly or perfectly. He glanced at his wife again and instantly knew she was also incapable of making the mental leap.

"Do you think she knows?" he asked.

Mildred paused for a moment. "I…I don't know," she muttered. "She knew we were going to throw her a surprise party, even though we said we weren't. She also knew she wasn't going to receive any presents, and that it would be a chocolate cake with vanilla icing." She looked at Carmen for a moment. "But she seems happy enough."

Mr. Grey watched the girl as well. She did seem happy—there were no qualms about that. She was watching her favorite movie on the holoprojector whilst amusing herself by making five of her dolls dance in time with the music. She giggled triumphantly when she managed to make Suzy, one of her oldest and most beat to death dolls, perform a backflip and land on her feet. It was quite obvious that Carmen was getting better at her…*talents*. It seemed less and less like the dolls were being manipulated by telekinesis and more and more like they were actually alive. That couldn't be an easy feat, though Mr. Grey couldn't speak from personal experience. Suzy finished her performance with a modest curtsy, which caused Carmen to clap with glee. Mr. Grey shook his head. *Rabid dog indeed*, he thought.

"What do we do?" Mildred asked.

"I don't think there is anything we can do."

"What if we run? My sister is on Earth. Perhaps we could stay—"

"It would never work," he said, cutting her off. "It doesn't matter where we go. Earth, Evonea…even if we lived on a starship, it just doesn't matter. They'll find us. They'll hunt us down. They told us as much when she was born."

"But they're almost here."

"I know."

"We'll never see her again!"

"I know."

"Damn the UTE! All these new rules, and none of them make any sense. Carmen could never hurt someone—I know she can't. They can't make her."

Mr. Grey heard her words, but gave no reply. He wouldn't say what he thought—for both their sakes he couldn't, not now. He'd heard many stories on what exactly children like his daughter were made to do. They made him shudder.

"What do we do?" she muttered again.

He took a deep breath. "I don't know."

She choked back a whimper. His jaw clenched tight. It hurt to talk and was agony to think. How Carmen remained unaware of their state was beyond him. He could only guess she was used to it. Her parents had lived in shocked helplessness for the whole of her six years of life. She'd probably look at them in utter amazement to ever find them genuinely happy. No wonder she liked her dolls so much—there were no demons in their plastic skulls. She could read into them whatever she wanted whenever she wanted. He remembered how she used to cry when they read her a bedtime story.

"What do we do?" Mildred repeated softly, more to herself than to him.

Mr. Grey unclenched his jaw just enough to speak. "We may as well join the party," he said. Carmen, at least, looked like she was having fun.

His wife nodded, and the two of them walked into the living room, where the movie was almost over. The end was always the same; he had to have seen it a hundred times himself. There is a ball at the castle. The prince grabs the servant girl's hand by some special mistake. He is surprised by the error, but they start dancing anyway. They fall in love by the end of the dance, and she becomes the princess. It was a cute, if typical, story, and Carmen loved it. She already had her dolls paired off to join in the dance.

Her parents stopped next to her. It was pointless to announce their presence, a lesson they had learned when she was just a few months old. She glanced at them over her shoulder and paused for a second or two. Then, all at once, her dolls wobbled and fell to the ground. Carmen didn't seem to really care as she sat there, completely still. No one knew what thoughts traveled her psyche in those instants, but then her composure became that of a frightened, cornered beast. She scurried a few feet away, wrapping her arms around her head as if trying to keep out a loud noise.

We have to try harder, Mr. Grey thought. He grabbed his wife by the hand. "Come on, Carmen. Let's all dance together."

He was completely out of practice, and Mildred was only going through the motions, but that was beside the point. Carmen, for her part, stood her dolls up, made them hold hands, and then rotated them slowly. She watched her parents with an expression best described as curious distress. She didn't move away from them, nor did she wrap her arms around her head anymore; she just stared at them and did nothing else. The attention made Mr. Grey feel like an incomprehensibly ugly painting in a museum.

"Smile at least," he told Mildred softly.

She looked up at him, and he wished he could take his own advice. She and Carmen looked so alike: the softness of the cheeks and chin complimented by sharp eyebrows, and blonde hair and blue eyes. He couldn't help wondering if he was staring at his little girl decades into the future. He would never know. He would never see Carmen go off to school for the first time. He would never see her fall in love or start a family of her own. His last image of her would be of a little girl who pitied her parents. Worse than that, it was a pity she knew deep down she had caused.

Mildred broke into tears. It was pointless to console her, so he buried her face in his chest so Carmen couldn't see. Of course, it was futile, and Carmen started to cringe again even before the crying began. There was nothing he could do for any of them, least of all himself.

The girl turned toward the door, and the doorbell rang a

second later. He didn't know whether he was relieved or sad when he heard it. Mr. Grey pulled his wife from him.

She had not cried just a single tear. She was not merely hurt and in need of time to recover. She did not look noble or strong in her suffering; she simply looked like a mother who would never see her child again.

"Are you going to be okay?" he asked.

"I can hold on. Get the door. That has to be them," she said.

"What about Carmen?"

"I'll take care of her. Go, before they break down the door."

Mr. Grey didn't think they were that urgent. They rang the doorbell again but did no more than that. Reluctantly, he did as his wife asked. His feet dragged as he walked, and his shoes may as well have been dipped in cement. His hands shook as he opened the door. ...He was unprepared for the world he saw before him.

Heavily armored soldiers stood on either side of the walkway that led to the street. They kept their rifles to the side. All the same, he didn't have to be a Clairvoyant to know they were tense. More soldiers stood in the street, taking cover behind several military aerocars whilst their weapons were trained on both him and the house. His neighbors nervously observed the scene. Their curiosity couldn't keep them from watching, but their fear only allowed them to steal a peek from behind nearly shut doors. In front of him stood a man in a relatively formal suit, flanked by two other men in rather basic black body armor. All three of their gazes seemed to knife through him.

"Mr. Grey, it's time," the man in the suit said.

They were plain enough words, yet they hit Mr. Grey like a blow to the guts. He couldn't speak. The three men stared at him in much the same way Carmen often did, yet this was harsher. It didn't have a child's innocence and instead carried —intent.

He looked into the house and saw his wife and daughter walking toward him. Mrs. Grey moved how he had earlier. Carmen, as always, seemingly flowed across the room. Even her first steps had been graceful. When his wife finally saw the force arrayed against them, she froze. When the force arrayed against them saw the little girl, they came within a hair's breadth of gunning her down right then and there. Every soldier jumped, save for the three men standing right in front of them. Mr. Grey grabbed his wife and held her close.

"Carmen, you have to go with them. They'll take care of you," Mildred said, no longer crying. If anything, her voice seemed to have found some hidden reserve, allowing her to speak in a calm that belied the situation.

The child offered no protest and began walking toward the aerocar at the end of the walkway. Its door was already open. The man in the suit walked beside her, and the other two men followed close behind.

Carmen could feel her parents weakening with each passing second, like their souls were being drained by their tears. It was a relief to be even this far away from them. They always made her feel bad, though she could never say exactly why. It was the worst today, but she looked forward to her favorite dinner tonight. Her parents usually cooked whatever she wanted when they made her feel especially bad. She just hoped she'd be back from wherever she was going before the *Scrimpies* came on the holo. She'd missed it last week and didn't want to miss it twice in a row. Just then, her mother called to her. She turned to see what she wanted.

"Stay good!" Mildred yelled. "No matter what happens, stay good, Carmen!"

Honestly, her parents were a pathetic sight. It was a wonder they were even able to remain standing. Tears streamed down their faces as they clutched each other, obviously trying their best not to cry. Carmen had no idea what her mother was talking about, but she nodded dutifully anyway and then turned and continued walking.

She always enjoyed being outside, especially in the daytime. She just felt more energetic to be out in the sun than cooped up in some dark room. The sun was certainly shining this day, and almost all of her neighbors were out. It was amazing to think that had nothing to do with the weather, though. She was the cause. She couldn't say exactly how she knew that; she just did. There was so much fear that she could almost taste it. The men with the guns were the most fearful. Most could barely look at her, particularly when she returned their gaze.

The men she walked with were different, though. She couldn't read their thoughts. Well, she could kind of read the thoughts of one, but his consciousness was distant at best. The other two may as well have been statues. That had never happened to Carmen before, and she didn't exactly know what to make of it. It wasn't like they weren't alive, like her dolls. In fact, the two men were more vibrant than any other individual here. Trying to come to grips with them, however, was like trying to gauge the direction of the wind in the middle of a tornado.

The four of them reached the aerocar, and the man in the suit gestured for her to get in. She did so without question, and then he sat next to her. The other two men sat up front. No one said anything, but Carmen didn't mind that. She often thought people talked too much anyway. What was the point when, most of the time, you already knew what they were going to say?

The aerocar didn't move right away as the soldiers still piled into the rest of the vehicles in the convoy. Carmen didn't pay them much mind; her attention was firmly fixed on the man in the suit. Why couldn't she figure him out? He was different from every person she'd ever met, that much was certain. He did nothing more than watch her casually out the corner of his eye, but she could swear he was fighting her. If he wasn't, there was resistance of some sort, whether it was produced by him or not.

As he drew more of her attention, this wasn't just a game anymore to her. Carmen thought she found a crack in his shell, but when she pushed through, the next barrier was even stronger. The frustration made her curl her hands into little fists, and it was then, and quite by surprise, that she heard a voice in her head.

"*Impressive,*" it said. "*However, it's more polite to ask permission first.*"

Carmen's mouth dropped open. Her parents always told her she was different from other people—that she was special. She wasn't so sure about the second part, but she already knew the first. The other kids were just *different* around her, wary even when she sat quietly in a lonely corner of the playground. They could look at her and somehow know she was not one of them. Yet, for all that, she never thought she'd hear voices in her head. Crazy people heard voices, and she wasn't crazy. She was just different, as she was constantly told.

The man in the suit looked at her and smiled. "*Don't be alarmed. You're not imagining this,*" he said telepathically.

Carmen now knew how those kids at the playground felt. She moved as far away from the man as possible while continuing to stare. Her breathing quickened. She didn't even notice the car had started to move.

"How…how do you do that?" she asked quickly.

The man smiled again. "*You are strong. Unusually strong. But it seems like you have yet to discover the full extent of your abilities. I shall correct that.*"

She had no idea what he was talking about. "Who are you?" she asked.

The man paused for a moment. "You may call me Janus," he said, using audible sound for the first time.

She considered her response for a few seconds. "My name is Carmen." Her mother and father would want her to be polite—and her mother did tell her to stay good, whatever that meant.

"No, it is not," Janus said sternly.

The change in his demeanor took Carmen aback. It was not that he was angry—at least, he didn't seem angry. He was just so…forceful.

"You don't have a name. Not yet. You don't have a name until we give you a name."

Carmen was scared for the first time that day. She liked her name and didn't want a new one. If she had to get a new name, she didn't want it to be from whoever this man was. She pressed even harder against the door.

"When do I go home?" she asked.

Janus looked at her and then turned his attention outside the aerocar. "We're almost there," he said simply.

The ground whizzing by outside was completely unfamiliar. She didn't know if he was lying or not. His mind was still completely unreadable, and his outward expression was just as impenetrable. Carmen didn't say anything. Maybe if she was good, she'd be taken back home sooner. Was that what her mother meant when she told her to stay good? This had started off as an interesting trip to somewhere Carmen didn't know, but now she just wanted to be back home with her parents. They didn't *always* make her feel bad.

Minutes passed in silence before the aerocar dove back down to street level. Carmen looked out the window once again, and her heart sank. They were nowhere near her house. Worse than that, she had no idea whatsoever where they were. She glanced at Janus, wondering if he'd give her an explanation, but he didn't notice her gaze.

The convoy rapidly approached a large building in the distance. She couldn't make out much of it from where she was sitting, but she could tell it was, at minimum, an imposing structure. Surrounding the complex was a large metal fence that was just as intimidating. Just looking at the place made her heart race. The aerocar pulled up to the fence and stopped at the guard post.

"Were there any problems?" the guard asked casually while he studied Carmen sitting in the back seat.

"Thankfully not," the driver replied. "We probably wouldn't be able to stop her otherwise."

The guard nodded glumly. "Let's hope our luck holds. You're cleared inside."

"Thank you."

Carmen had always liked car rides—even more than she liked being out in the sun. That was no longer the case, though. The building, whatever it was, loomed ever larger, and she would be quite happy to never see it again. For the first time in her young life, she was completely powerless. She didn't know what was going to happen, even distantly, and the adults here did not seem bent on keeping her happy. She was nearly hyperventilating when the car stopped at the front doors.

Janus got out of the car and walked around to her side. He opened the door and then extended his hand. Carmen just stared at it. This had to be a mistake. Why did they want her? What had she done? She just wanted to go back home. Janus just stood there with his hand out. If this was a mistake, he sure didn't act like it.

Her first instinct was to ask if they could take her home now, but not knowing what the answer would be made her lips tingle. Her mother had to be right—she was usually right about everything else. All Carmen needed to do was just be good enough, and they would send her home. Perhaps then her parents would be happier more often. Besides, even if they didn't send her back, her father was bound to come for her sometime soon. He was probably already on his way.

Carmen looked at Janus's hand again and smiled. This all made sense now. She'd be the goodest little girl Janus had ever seen if it meant he would let her leave sooner. Gently and thoughtfully, he helped her out of the car. They walked inside the building hand in hand, Carmen beaming the entire way. Janus glanced at her curiously but said nothing. The hallway they entered was cavernous. There was no decoration of any kind, and no one else was in the hall. She was surprised; she had assumed a lot of people would be in a building this big, possibly even people like her.

"You are here because you are an asset," Janus said. He didn't even glance at her when he spoke. His gaze was fixed straight ahead.

"What's an asset?" she asked, her young tongue tripping over the word.

"An asset is a monster much like myself, like all of us—a monster created for the sole purpose of giving other monsters who would do us harm pause." Janus was silent for a moment before he spoke again. "In time, billions will cower at the mere thought of your might, and they would be right to do so."

Carmen didn't understand. She was different—everyone knew that—but she was not a monster. She wouldn't even say Janus was a monster. He was scary, but there was no way he was related to those things that lived under her bed. The two of them rounded a corner, still hand in hand. This hallway ended with a door that was closed.

"I shall be your handler during the length of your stay. I shall care for you and provide whatever you need. In turn, you shall learn from me. Do you understand?" The door grew closer.

"Yes," Carmen said, no longer smiling. She didn't want to believe it, but she realized she may be staying here longer than she'd thought.

They walked through the door and into a large room with no other exit. The walls were padded and the floor was hard tile. There were no windows, but surprisingly there were people inside—quite a lot of people, in fact. They wore all white and doctor's masks, and they stood next to several machines. Carmen didn't know what the machines were, but she recognized some of them from the doctor shows her father occasionally watched.

Janus looked at the assembled group, and they all nodded in turn. He then turned his attention to her. "Nothing here happens in a straight line, nor is it easy," he said to himself as much as to her.

She hesitated for only one brief second before announcing confidently, "I'm ready." She could do this. She could be good.

The man casually pulled a pistol from his suit. Carmen had never seen a gun in person before. "Some rebirth is required," Janus said. He then turned the weapon on her as the girl's eyes grew wide. "I'm sorry," he uttered.

The last thing Carmen saw was the muzzle flash.

2

NEW FRIENDS

Subject: 111724 Age: 6 Status: Induction

Carmen awoke in a brightly lit room. Her entire body ached with a dull pain that left her notice only after a few seconds. She was wearing different clothes, although calling the gown she was draped in "clothes" would be a laughable kindness. The ugly gown, however, was barely a consideration in light of her current predicament.

Her young mind was still lost in a fog, perpetually going over and over one thing—one event. She touched her chest where she was shot…and there was nothing. Carmen could quite clearly remember the bullet tearing into her, yet there was no wound now. The perception hung over her like a whispered echo of dreadful tidings. She wondered hesitantly if it had even happened. It would be the most surreal nightmare she'd ever had, but it was the only believable explanation.

It was about then, as her consciousness moved beyond herself, that she noticed she was physically restrained to the bed she was lying in. She couldn't help but let out a small whimper as she studied the lock. She had no hope of undoing it.

"Momm—" she began to utter, but her words fell short as she took in the sights around her.

She was in a rather large, bright room with absolutely no windows. The walls were stark white, as was the floor. Everything seemed *clean* and purposely so. It would take her days to find even one speck of dust. These, however, were all trivial details. What had her complete attention, and what made her swallow hard, was that she wasn't alone. Other children lay all around her, also restrained to their beds. Most were older than herself, if only by a few years, but there were a couple of teenagers. On the other hand, so far as she could guess, none were younger than she. Why that was or what it meant, Carmen couldn't say.

Everyone was injured in some way. One little boy was covered in bruises. Another boy's arm was clearly broken in multiple places. A girl, one of the few teenagers, was missing her leg, which seemed to have been burned off. The sight made Carmen's hair stand on end, but the girl was sedated and thus spared from the view of her missing limb. Adults tended to the children. They wore all white and had face masks much like the people from the room where Janus shot her. Tears began to fill her eyes as she thought about her apparent death yet again.

"So, 111724, you're awake," one of the doctors said.

It took Carmen a moment to realize she was talking to her. There was nothing outwardly scary about the woman, but Carmen tried to move as far away as possible nonetheless.

The woman smiled. "Don't worry," she said softly, "I won't hurt you."

"I want to go home," Carmen whimpered, still crying.

The doctor forced a smile when she heard that. "Now,

111724, you have to be hungry. You've had a long day, and your body is still trying to grow up big and strong."

Carmen didn't say anything. She actually was a little hungry, and it was hard to not show interest at the indirect offer. All the same, she'd rather just go home and eat leftovers than stay here and have her favorite meal, if given the choice.

The woman smiled again. "What is it you Clairvoyants say? 'Mind and body are a team?' If you ask me, you spend too much time on the mind and not enough on the body. Here," she said, producing a lollipop from her pocket. "Just don't tell your handler that I gave your body a treat. It will be our little secret."

Carmen looked at the candy, hesitant. Her mother would say she shouldn't have a snack before dinner. She had no idea what Janus would say. Just thinking about him made her cry again.

"Now, now, now," the woman said. "Not that again. Take it. It's fine."

She took the lollipop meekly. "Thank you," she muttered.

"There. That's better, isn't it?"

Carmen stuck the candy in her mouth and nodded. She didn't really feel any better, but like with her parents, it was easier to pretend to be happy to make other people happy. The doctor seemed nice enough for the courtesy.

"Now, I just have to do some checks to make sure you're okay. No more crying, right?"

"…Right."

"Good."

The tests were simple enough. First, she did a physical examination like Carmen's doctor back home used to do. Then she asked Carmen to throw a ball in the air with her right hand and then her left. After that, she had Carmen repeat what she said word for word. The sentences grew more and more complex and were recited with increasing speed, but the girl got most of them right. Next, she repeated written sentences. Last, the doctor asked her to recall some of her earliest memories.

"All right. You seem to be completely intact," the woman said, but Carmen didn't know what she meant. "Stay here. Someone will be along to collect you shortly."

Carmen looked at her restrains. It wasn't like she'd be going anywhere. "Okay," she muttered softly.

The doctor smiled one last time and then departed with a nod. As she sat there, the girl wondered what she had done wrong to make Janus shoot her. She had tried to be good. She had tried her best—she was sure of it. Tears began filling her eyes once again. Why was she here? What had she done wrong? She had no idea. Perhaps it had something to do with why her parents were upset all the time. She had always known they were upset because of her. Had they just not wanted her?

She looked around the room and decided the other children didn't seem that special. She couldn't read most of them without some effort, but other than that, they didn't seem in any way peculiar. Quite a few were crying. For most, it was obvious that outright pain produced the tears. Still, she wasn't the only one who simply sat in her bed and cried for no immediately obvious reason. The adults didn't seem to care or even notice and just carried on with their examinations, moving on to the next child when they were finished. They all seemed nice, and some gave out lollipops like her doctor had. Their concern, however, extended no further than that.

Carmen's crying made her vision blurry, and the situation made it hard to focus, but that all stopped when her gaze came to rest on one girl across the room. She was the same age as Carmen, had dusty brown hair, and was most certainly not crying. If anything, she was actually staring back at Carmen while slowly shaking her head. The girl was covered in minor scrapes and cuts, which seemed to be bite marks upon further examination. She didn't know what kind of animal could produce bites like that, but she'd rather not know, truth be told. The girl had to be in some sort of pain, but there were no tears, no whimpers—nothing. Carmen looked down at herself in that moment and felt suddenly embarrassed. She had no injuries to speak of. In fact, she was quite comfortable physically. She even had a lollipop.

She looked at the girl again and was quick to realize she was different from every other child here. Carmen could read most of the other children in the room if she really, really tried, but that was not the case with this girl. If they were a mud puddle, then she was like the never-ending expanse of an ocean. She so completely drowned out her colleagues by just existing that it was almost absurd. As the girl stared at Carmen, she seemed decidedly unimpressed by what she saw. She sighed casually after a moment and then looked away. Carmen watched her for a few seconds more before she did the same.

Why am I here? she thought again. If there was anything these kids had in common, it was that they were hard for her to read or simply couldn't be read. She had never thought about it before, but perhaps she was hard to read too? Janus had said they were both monsters, whatever that meant, and he was hard for her to read. If that was the case, why had he hurt her? What did she do wrong? This was just how she was.

It was then that she noticed a man moving through the room. As she watched him, every fiber of her being knew he was here for her. She'd known it from the moment he entered. She sat up in preparation to leave before he even spoke.

Carmen planned to give both of her parents a big hug when she got back. They'd never believe her hell.

"111724, you are to come with me," he said.

The man wasted no words as he removed her restraints. Carmen didn't say anything either. Whoever he was, he wasn't a monster like she or Janus. She could read him quite easily, but she didn't waste her time trying. She was just happy he had come to collect her instead of Janus. She never wanted to see him again.

"Hold your hands out," he said firmly once her restraints were off.

Carmen did as he asked. He then took a pair of handcuffs off his belt and quickly placed them on her. All of a sudden, she felt a little lightheaded. The feeling passed relatively quickly, but everything seemed just a little different than it was a moment ago. The world seemed *less* than it usually was, if that was even possible. People around her weren't as vibrant as they were before, and she could no longer read this man. For some strange reason, she was also very, very tired.

"Follow me," he said.

He started walking, and when Carmen hopped off her bed to follow, she almost fell over. She took another wobbly step before she wondered, *What's wrong with me?* It took almost everything she had to just maintain her balance; it didn't just *happen* like it usually did. She also felt heavy, like she had eaten cement for breakfast. Carmen looked at the handcuffs for a moment then at the man. She was tempted to ask if he could take them off, but she couldn't read him and had no idea what he'd say.

She had trouble keeping up as he moved too quickly for her. She had never worked this hard on anything in her life. Slowly but surely her balance improved, but even so, each step had to be measured and planned out in advance. Carmen hoped there were no stairs along their route; if there were, she'd probably end up right back here with a new lollipop to suck on.

The man paused for a moment to sign some papers. She appreciated the break and took the time to survey the now strangely dull room once more. Like moth to flame, her eyes rested again on the brown-haired girl from before. She was watching Carmen too, shaking her head in disgusted pity. Carmen felt embarrassed all over again.

"Come on," the man said, placing his hand on her shoulder.

She hadn't been paying attention and was so surprised that she couldn't help a quick scream. She couldn't remember the last time she'd been surprised by anything, and it wasn't a pleasant sensation. Everyone in the room looked at her with equal surprise, and for the first time in her young life, she was glad that she had no idea what the people around her were thinking. Cheeks red, she wobbled out of the room with her new handler.

These halls were different than those from earlier today… or yesterday—whenever it was that she first arrived. There were actually people in the halls this time, and most were paired off. A child, much like herself, trailed their handler in handcuffs. The children seemed her age; the oldest she saw couldn't have been more than a year or two older than herself.

At any rate, Carmen was still curious about what had happened to Janus. He told her he was her handler. Maybe he wasn't supposed to shoot her and got in trouble? She couldn't muster the courage to ask this man. Her shyness wasn't rare —no other child here really seemed to be talking with their handler either.

"I've been looking for you," someone said behind her.

She didn't scream this time, but she did almost jump out of her skin. She could never get used to this. How could people function without knowing someone was there before they were, well…*there*?

"What's up?" her handler asked after turning to see who it was.

The woman was maybe a few years older than the doctor who had tended to her earlier. Whoever she was, she didn't have a child with her, and Carmen wondered whether she was a handler.

"This whole Space Force thing just got off the ground. Passed the vote earlier today," the woman said.

Carmen doubted the conversation had anything to do with her, considering she had no idea what "Space Force" was.

"So, what does that mean for us?"

"Actually nothing," the woman said. "The treaty says Space Force is only to be used for xenomorphic threats and policing. It will be a part of the UTE, but we'll remain and continue being administrated by the New Earth planetary government—though we are acting on the behest of the UTE."

The man sighed softly. "This whole United Terran Empire thing will never work. Space Force is an even dumber idea. I don't get it," he said. "We practically save humanity single handedly. Earth is finally weak enough that they have to listen to our terms and we don't have to listen to theirs, and we give it all up to start some grand terran alliance. Stupid, if you ask me."

"I don't know," she began. "If we were united, we may have been able to fight off the sortens before they enslaved us."

Carmen still had no idea what they were talking about. She vaguely remembered her parents talking about some far away war on other planets. She also recalled that all terrans came from a place called Earth and that New Earthlings were fighting to liberate it and the rest of the colonies, but she couldn't remember much more than that. They had never talked to her directly about it.

The man shrugged. "I still think the whole effort is a waste of resources."

"We'll see," the woman said. "Anyway, is this the new girl everyone's talking about?"

Carmen jumped again, if slightly, when the conversation turned to her. People of all ages had talked about her all the time. Usually the words were passed in whispers and tinged with fear. That was just how things were. The sun rose each day, and people in unseen corners would discuss the little blonde girl with the piercing eyes. For all that, however, Carmen found it hard to believe she was already known by enough people here for them to say anything worth mentioning.

"Has she given you any trouble?"

"No, she's been pretty compliant so far."

"You still put binders on her, though," the woman pointed out.

The man nodded. "No reason to take my chances, not that it would really matter. These were the highest resistance binders I could find. If the tests were right, she could probably bust them any time she wanted to."

Carmen took a moment to study her handcuffs when she heard that. She wished she could take them off. When she looked up, the woman was staring down at her with an expression that was as worried as it was accusing. At that, Carmen put her fermenting plan to bed and resigned herself to continue walking.

"So, how strong do you think she actually is? Ten percenter? Seven?"

"Don't know, but that's what we're going to find out."

"Hmm. You hear about 111720?"

"Yeah," he said without missing a beat. "Completely off the scale." He paused before speaking again and took a moment to glance at Carmen. "For some reason, these third-generation genetic-massaged kids are a great deal stronger than the gen twos. Earth reported a couple of days ago that they have a really strong one. He's a couple years older than 111720 and 111724, though."

The woman nodded. "Nobody even knows how any of this energy projection stuff works. Maybe the guys in the lab just stumbled upon something. Maybe I need an upgrade."

"We're both too old for that."

"I know. Just saying." The man nodded, and the woman continued. "Anyway, everyone is taking bets on how 720 and 724 compare."

She watched Carmen closely for a few seconds, and the girl returned her interest hesitantly. Even when the conversation was about her, she still had no idea what they were talking about. Now she felt like a vegetable in a grocery store. She hated this place.

"My money's on 720, definitely," the woman concluded.

"I don't know," the man replied. "It can go either way. Stuff like that is hard to guess."

"Right," she said. "But tell me how it goes. I have to get back to work."

"Okay, I'll see you later."

The two coworkers gave each other a parting nod, and then the woman left. Carmen didn't say anything. She wondered who 111720 was. What most drew her curiosity, though, was why everyone else was curious about them.

What made them so different or interesting? And why was everyone so interested in comparing them? What was the point? As always, she also wondered when she would be allowed to go home. She had done everything they asked.

Her handler gave her no clues as to what her fate would be. He just led her, completely and utterly stone faced. Carmen wished she were back in bed, all things considered. Even restrained, it was more comfortable to lie there than walk here in these blasted handcuffs. All of a sudden, her handler stopped at a closed door. He opened it, and the two entered.

The room was much like the one she had died in: large with padded walls, no windows, and a tile floor. The small door on the opposite wall was the only real difference. The room was completely empty. Carmen nervously looked at her new handler. She didn't think he had a gun on him, but there was no way for her to be sure. He glanced down at her, and she backed away. There was no place for her to escape to in here. As he reached into his suit much like Janus had, her breath caught in her throat. But instead of a gun, he held a key in his hand.

"Stay here," he said as he removed her handcuffs.

She grew lightheaded again, but the feeling passed faster than before. She sighed contently. It had caused her more trouble in her life than it was worth, and she had only gone a few minutes without it; nevertheless, she had missed what made her *her*. She had ached for it in the same way she would her sight if the lights were shut off. Carmen closed her eyes and took a deep breath. She could feel practically every air molecule rushing into her nose. She was also well aware of the moment her handler left the room, despite that her eyes were still closed and he didn't say a word in parting. Carmen smiled. She guessed, in a way, she was special after all.

When she opened her eyes, she studied the room one more time. She still couldn't figure out why, exactly, she was here. Perhaps every room was like this? If it wasn't for the small door on the opposite wall, she'd be hard-pressed to say she was in a different room than before. Yet, though the room was empty, she wasn't exactly alone. She didn't know who or even what it was; she just *knew*, and her best guess was that it was behind that small door.

She moved toward the door but got no further information as she did. She just knew there was something alive behind it. There was no handle or anything to open the door. There was, however, an obvious hinge, so it seemed like it could be opened. Carmen bent down and gave it a soft knock. The only response was the dull sound of her knuckle on the metal. She groaned softly. Maybe they'd stuck her in here to see how she handled boredom. She walked to the far corner of the room, sat down, and made herself comfortable. It wasn't like there was anything else to do.

* * *

The mood in the control room had never been this tense. First there was 111720, and now there was 111724. The odds of there being not one but two inductees at their level, and of them both being here, were astronomical. Just as long as 111724's prescreening was correct. It was rare when it was not, but there were errors from time to time. Whether 111724 knew that she could break out of the room any time she wanted was an ongoing debate. 111720 had almost succeeded in that. Everyone watched the beast on their display monitors as she sat in a corner of the room and did nothing.

"I don't think she's as powerful as her chart says. She's too docile."

Janus looked at the technician and nodded. It was certainly possible. "I don't know, though," he said. "The strongest ones are usually the most finicky." He stared at her in the display monitor for a long while before he spoke again. "There's just something about her that's hard to place."

"She's definitely a type three, if anything," the technician said before he looked at Janus. "Maybe you can get her leaning type two?"

"That would be the best combination," Janus agreed. "720 is type two leaning type one." He sighed tiredly and turned to a different technician. "Are we ready?"

"Almost. It will just take a minute to complete the calibration."

"And 724?" Janus asked.

"According to the biomed sensors, she is calm enough to give us an accurate read."

"Good," Janus said. "Send it in as soon as you're ready."

Carmen soon lost track of how long she'd been in the room. She honestly didn't care; it didn't make any difference. She would stay here until someone let her out. How long that would take was completely out of her control. With that in mind, she started doubting her father would ever come for her. If he or her mother were going to rescue her, they would have done so by now. There were only two explanations she could see. Either her parents couldn't come for her, or her parents didn't want to come for her. She had a hard time figuring out whether it was one or the other.

She closed her eyes and then lay flat on her back. Again, she wondered what these people wanted with her. They shot her and then gave her a lollipop, and now they'd stuck her in an empty room with nothing to do. She just wanted to go home. Why wouldn't they let her leave?

Just then, there was a sharp pinprick in her consciousness. Although the sensation was rare, she had felt it before. Usually it meant something had changed and quickly, if not violently. She opened her eyes. Nothing appeared to be different. The room was still just as boring and dull as before, and the small door was still closed…. But whatever was behind the door was more…well, *more*. It was hard for Carmen to place her finger on.

Whatever was behind that door, for whatever reason, was now more energetic, more vibrant, than it had been a minute ago. The thing had an aggressive, albeit simplistic energy. It came in waves, building upon itself before dying off only to build again to an even greater level. It, however, was also unfocused in its intent. It was raw, uncontained aggression and nothing else. She bolted to her feet a second or two before the door began to open.

Began was the operative term—the door opened at a glacier's pace, despite its small size. Carmen glanced at the main entrance behind her. She didn't think anybody would be coming to retrieve her any time soon. She didn't know how she knew; she just knew she would be stuck here for possibly a very long time.

When she looked back at the small door, it was fully open. She couldn't see inside; it had simply opened to a black void. She dropped to her knees to get a better look but still couldn't see anything. It was pitch black nothingness. That thing was still in there, but she couldn't see it, whatever it was. Its energy remained ever growing and aggressive. All was silent, but her nerves were shot just the same. Then a shriek reverberated out of the void.

No terran she had ever met could make that sound. It was

both ear-splittingly loud and high pitched. Her hair stood on end and her heart rate doubled. The shriek came again, and Carmen backed as far away from it as she could. The third shriek sounded quite a bit closer than the first two, and then she saw it—the creature.

The animal was like none Carmen had ever seen or heard of. It was four legged and came to about her waist in height. From head to tail, however, it was more than twice her size. Its scales alternated between dull yellow and green in blurrily defined tiger stripes. The head was crowned with a brightly colored frill that waved back and forth as the animal breathed. Its beak was armed with tiny though numerous teeth that could undoubtedly cause a good deal of damage.

She watched the creature, unable to move a muscle. It, however, moved quickly, although awkwardly, despite its size. It had almost shot into the room, but now it buzzed from one side to the other after first pausing to check its surroundings. It stopped and looked at Carmen before it hissed, the ever-growing aggressive energy she had felt before aimed right at her. The sensation felt as if the ceiling had fallen on her, and she staggered and dropped to her knees. She couldn't say it was painful—not exactly. It was more uncomfortable than painful, like being covered in mosquito bites. The pressure, however, made her groan. She fought against it, yet it continued changing, adapting against her. She closed her eyes and groaned again. Just thinking was a struggle. It was even getting hard to breathe.

She only barely registered that the animal was moving closer to her until she heard a shriek right beside to her. Carmen looked to her left and was greeted by the wall. When she looked up, the horrible thing was staring back at her. It shrieked; she screamed and then managed to dash out of the way before its beak could clamp down on her shoulder. There was no place to go. All she could do was run to the other side of the room. The pressure in her mind only grew worse when she stopped. She screamed through gritted teeth and couldn't help but fall to her knees again. The animal only glared at her as it gave an annoyed hiss. Then it ran along the wall toward her, its claws leaving finger-sized puncture wounds in the padded material.

Carmen tried to watch from her rather pathetic position. Conscious thought had left her long ago. She was too besieged to think and so scared that it wouldn't have made much difference anyway. She ran to the other side of the room, slipping and sliding on the tile floor the entire way, when the animal got within striking distance again. It jumped off the wall and scampered after her. When Carmen turned, it was right in front of her. She was cornered. Her breath could barely keep up with the machine gun beating of her heart.

The animal gave an angry hiss and stalked closer. It analyzed her every move—every quivering muscle. When she tried to run past, its strike was total perfection. Carmen let out a pained wail as its teeth tore into her.

* * *

"Got a big spike on that one," the technician said.

"How high?" Janus asked.

The technician took a moment to study his instruments. His eyes grew wide. "That…that can't be right," he muttered to himself. He glanced at Janus. The Clairvoyant stared down at him expectantly. "There's something wrong with my equipment," he said softly.

"Excuse me?"

"There is something wrong with my equipment," the technician said with more confidence. "Calibration check!" he yelled out.

"Calibration check!" came the reply from elsewhere in the room.

* * *

The creature had Carmen pinned to the ground, clawing and snapping at her at every opportunity. Her gown was a bloody rag by this point, and she had no real idea of what was going on. There was just the bloody beak coming for her yet again. This time, it clamped down on her arm as it rose to defend herself. Despite that her arm wasn't its target, the creature appeared to be satisfied anyway, and as it shook its head from side to side, Carmen's fingers went numb. She screamed and punched it in the eye as hard as she could. Her other hand went numb on impact as the animal gave a pained cry before backing off of her and scampering a few steps away. Carmen stood hesitantly.

She hadn't thought she'd be able to actually hurt the thing. Now that she had, it lit a fire in her that put stars to shame. What pain she felt fell away as she focused on her opponent. She wanted to hurt it—badly, in fact. She wanted to make it feel every ache she felt. She wanted it to suffer for her being brought here, locked up in this room with this *thing*. Most important, she wanted it to pay for her inability to go home. But no, she knew she shouldn't.

The creature recovered and approach her again, more cautiously than before.

* * *

Janus watched the display monitor along with everyone else. Only his eyebrow rose, however, at what he thought he saw. 111724 would be an interesting one.

"Check complete," one of the technicians announced. "Your readings are correct."

"That's just not possible," the first technician muttered to himself. "It's just not—"

"Yet it is," Janus interrupted, ending the argument. Everyone was silent as he stared at the monitor. "I think we've given her enough for one day."

Then he left the room.

* * *

The animal circled Carmen slowly. It snapped at her when the opportunity presented itself, but she was usually able to avoid the attack. The eye she had hit swelled over, leaving the creature blind out of it. Carmen didn't have much interesting in fighting back, though. Her left arm was a bloody mess, and her right hand was numb to the point of utter uselessness. In fact, she couldn't even move her right hand.

She was snapped at again halfheartedly, but she kept up her defense. The animal tried to dash behind her, and Carmen was ready. She easily dodged out of the way before its jaws could clamp shut. Then, it stood still for a moment and looked at something behind her. She paused too, not exactly sure of what to do. Whatever had been assaulting her consciousness earlier had lessened dramatically after she struck the animal, and she didn't even notice it now. She still, however, couldn't tell what had just entered the room. Carmen couldn't read it, other than to know she and her new pet were no longer alone. She didn't want to chance a backward glance to check.

"Carmen, move out of the way," a voice said softly. She recognized it as Janus's almost instantly, and a quick look confirmed it. "Carmen, move for me, please."

She did as he asked with no more hesitation. Then she waited as Janus casually stepped forward, stopping between her and the animal. It looked at the man and gave a defiant shriek in response. Janus looked down on it, decidedly unimpressed, and even took a moment to sneer. Seconds later, an unseen force lifted the creature into the air. Its next shriek took on a panicked edge as it struggled against whatever was holding it. A painful cry filled the air as the animal's neck was slowly crushed before the sound choked off to nothing. It fell to the ground, dead.

Carmen could only stare. Janus turned to face her, and her gaze shifted to stare at him. She still breathed hard, and she hurt all over. She half wondered if he was going to shoot her again, but in the end, she didn't care. She was so happy someone had finally come to rescue her from the monster that she didn't care that it was Janus. She ran to him and hugged his leg, crying desperately. All she wanted was to go home. That was it—she just wanted to go home and escape this horror of a place. Why couldn't anybody understand that? Her crying, however, choked her voice every time she tried to speak.

"Now, now," Janus said softly. "It's okay. It's all okay now. You're safe."

Carmen made no response. Janus gently pried her off his leg before he picked her up and held her close. She had stopped crying by this point, but she stiffened when he touched her. The feeling lasted for only a moment before she allowed herself to be comforted. She missed how her father had used to pick her up in much the same way. After closing her eyes, she tried to imagine that Janus was him.

"Come on, let's clean you up," he said.

He then walked out of the room with Carmen still in his arms. They didn't say anything to each other. It was only minutes before her blood soaked his shirt and pants, never mind the trail left in their wake. If Janus cared about any of that, he didn't let her know. Carmen didn't care much, either. Frankly, she didn't even notice, as her eyes were blissfully closed the entire trip. It was with some disappointment that they arrived in the medical wing in only a few short minutes.

He placed her in an empty bed, not bothering with the restrains. Instead, he sat next to her and, from time to time, spoke mild words of comfort. A doctor arrived in short order.

"Shattered," he said when his examination reached her right hand.

Janus nodded. "It's important that you learn to cushion your blows, 111724. We all remember our first shattered hand or foot."

Carmen noticed he no longer referred to her by her real name. She also realized her injuries were similar to those of the girl she had seen earlier. She wasn't here now.

"Okay," Carmen said simply, though she had no idea what he was talking about.

The examination and subsequent treatment didn't last long. Thankfully, she got a change of clothes—real ones this time. In any case, the animal's bites produced severe lacerations at worst, which were easy to heal. There was just her hand to be concerned about, which the doctor set in a few minutes before putting it in a cast.

Janus asked her questions about her family and her home throughout the treatment. Carmen had never really had any friends, so that subject didn't last long. She was a bit hesitant to answer his questions at first, but she opened up more once it seemed like he was genuinely interested in what she had to say. She recalled with muted glee the story her mother had always told her about when she was born: that she was so beautiful that three of the nurses fainted, and the lights went out after flickering wildly. She still didn't know why her mother always looked upset when she said that, but Janus only nodded seriously. Then Carmen told him how, almost a year ago, she hadn't been hurt when she fell off the jungle gym at her favorite playground, and that all the people there had just stared at her while she brushed herself off. Janus laughed at that one, and eventually Carmen did as well. She guessed it was kind of funny how everyone had made it into a big deal when it really wasn't.

"Okay," the doctor said. "She'll be all right. Just give her two or three days to fully heal that hand."

Janus nodded. "Right."

She didn't receive a lollipop from this doctor, though, if she was offered one, she'd probably refuse it. The doctor then left, and Janus turned to Carmen.

"Ready?" he asked.

I guess so, she thought. She had no idea what she was supposed to be ready for.

"Yes," she said.

He helped her out of her bed and then led her out of the room. Carmen still had no idea where he was taking her, but she was just happy he didn't put those handcuffs on her. They didn't talk as she dutifully followed behind him. While she walked, however, she couldn't help but notice his bloody clothes. He was nearly covered in her blood. He didn't seem to mind, though.

They entered an elevator, went down several floors, and continued on, still without saying a word. This floor was bathed in a softer light. The walls had a slight, almost organic curve to them. There were even plants here and there, and many, many doors. Each had a number, but other than that, the doors were nondescript. They passed dozens and dozens of them until they finally stopped at one that read *111724*.

"This is where you shall stay between forgings," Janus said.

Carmen looked at the door hesitantly and then at him. "What's forging?" she asked.

"You are little more than raw iron," Janus started, "but we shall heat you to the melting point, mold you into shape, shock cool you, and then, finally, you will be steel."

Carmen felt decidedly cold and all the more nervous when she heard that. She looked at the door again and, now that she thought about it, realized there was something behind it, much like there had been something behind the other one. She took a step away from it.

"But that is not for today," Janus continued. "Today, there is someone I'd like you to meet."

She didn't want to meet whoever or whatever it was, but he opened the door before she could protest. The next thing Carmen knew, she was knocked flat on her back by some...*entity*, and it was now on top of her. She screamed, but it was no use. Something big, wet, and slimy washed over her face again and again with no mercy. She reached out and felt fur, and it was at this moment that she opened her eyes. It was a puppy—a German shepherd puppy, upon further examination.

"This is Mikayla," Janus said. "She is yours."

Carmen could only giggle. She had always wanted a dog, but her parents never agreed to it. Mikayla continued to lick her face as Carmen struggled to her feet. Janus beckoned her inside the room. She entered, and the puppy bounded playfully after her. The room was easily as nice as her bedroom back home. There weren't any windows, nor was there a holoprojector, but there was a bed, toys, books, a couch, chairs, and a small table with a plate of food on it. She was quite hungry, now that she thought about it. She looked back at Janus and smiled.

"I'll come for you in time," he said.

"When do I go home?"

Janus paused for a moment. "111724, one day—maybe tomorrow, maybe years from now—you'll learn not to ask stupid questions."

He then closed the door and left her alone.

3

THE FORGING OF 111724

"I wonder why you're here?" Carmen asked.

The dog simply stared back at her and wagged her tail. Carmen knew Mikayla couldn't speak; she hadn't gone completely crazy. She'd never been able to read animals before, and until now she never really wondered why. The puppy had been only company for the past few days. She hadn't seen Janus or anyone, other than a doctor who removed her cast, but he barely said a word to her. It was hard to tell time; there were no clocks, windows, or even a calendar. A week could have passed for all she knew. Yet, even a week would feel like no more than an hour with her new friend.

"Everyone says I'm different. I guess they're right. That's why I'm here. But why are you here?" Mikayla barked and then licked her face. Carmen laughed. "I was being serious," she said, still laughing lightly. "Why would you want to be in here with me? I bet you'd rather be outside, running and playing in a forest somewhere."

Mikayla made no response. Carmen waited for a moment, half expecting at least a whimper. She sighed and leaned back to rest against the wall when it was obvious that nothing was forthcoming.

"I used to go to the park all the time. I was always able to run the fastest. Even some of the older kids couldn't keep up. I bet they couldn't keep up with you too."

Mikayla wagged her tail. Carmen took that as a "yes" and smiled. She then leaned forward, stopping just short of the dog's lethal, ever-licking tongue.

"I wonder what your home was like?" she asked. "You can't be from here. You're too nice. You saw Janus—he's my handler. He's real mean. Believe it or not, my first day here, he actually shot me," she said, dropping her voice to a whisper. Mikayla inched toward her with head cocked to the side. "Yeah, he really did."

She paused before she continued. "My mother said, if I 'stay good,' they'd let me go, but let me tell you a secret." Carmen's voice was now just barely audible. "I think I'm going to run away. If I can get out of here, I'll try to find a policeman. My parents always said that, whenever I needed help and they weren't around, I should go to the police. You should come with me.

"My parents would like you," she continued. "You're so pretty and well behaved. My mother always said we couldn't have a dog because it would leave...*accidents* all over the house, but I don't think you would do that. I could even take care of you. ...How would you like that?" she asked.

The dog gave no reaction, which made Carmen nervous. Shortly after, though, and for no apparent reason, Mikayla looked at the door, barked, and then rose to all fours. Carmen looked at the door just as it began to open.

"You're so smart," she said to the puppy under her breath.

She hadn't sensed anybody coming. It would be a little

stupid to plan her escape with someone listening over her shoulder.

It was Janus. "It's time," her handler said simply.

Carmen had no idea what, exactly, it was time for, which was par the course for this place. She didn't complain, though; she didn't have any choice. She said goodbye to Mikayla with a kiss on the dog's head and then left the room. Janus started walking immediately. Carmen followed, staying close to his side. There were a few people in the hall, but the combination was never different: one child was always paired off with one handler. Boy or girl, from no younger than she was to, at most, a few years older, it made no difference—no child wandered the halls unattended. Everyone's movement was purposeful and direct. She received a brief glance of curiosity from a passerby now and then, but that was the most attention anyone was paid. There was virtually no talking as well.

She looked at Janus in that moment. She had never met a person like him before. When compared to his peers, though, he wasn't all too different or even unique. Physically, he was powerfully though subtly built. He was quite different from the heroes her father used to watch on the holo all the time. Janus's muscles seemed more...*useful*. He, like his peers, appeared to be about her parents' age, but their energy, like their outward manner, was something else entirely. Her parents had always been expansive, open, and warm, albeit depressed. With most of the handlers, she'd sensed no such thing. They were trim, focused, and intense. Janus notwithstanding, she couldn't really say they were *bad* people, at least by their energy. They were simply...fire.

"For now, 111724, we shall communicate through telepathy," Janus spoke.

"How do I do that?" Carmen asked aloud.

She didn't even know what the word telepathy meant! She guessed it had something to do with hearing Janus's voice in her head—something she hadn't even known was possible until she met him. When she wanted something to move without touching it, it just happened. It always had, but how do you speak without speaking?

Janus glanced down at her while her eyebrows scrunched together.

"In the end," he began, *"you will realize that, ultimately, there is very little I shall directly teach you. You already know what you already know. If you need to speak to me, stop thinking about it and just do it."*

She thought about what he said until she realized she shouldn't be thinking about what he said. She should just do it…somehow. Carmen looked at her handler then thought and then not thought about her task. When that proved impossible, she simply thought the words in her head.

"Like this?" she thought…spoke…said, whatever it was.

"Good," Janus replied. *"A Clairvoyant doesn't have to be taught their abilities. They simply decide whether they use them or not."*

"What's a Clairvoyant?"

"A Clairvoyant is what I am and what you shall realize you are after you stop fooling yourself."

Carmen glanced at him, but he didn't bother looking down at her. He simply walked on, not seeing just how flummoxed she was. How was she fooling herself? She thought he'd said they were both monsters. Were Clairvoyants monsters, or was she a monster and needed to be a Clairvoyant to 'stay good?' This was all too confusing.

"But…but—"

Janus cut her off. *"I do not mind your questions, 111724. I promise you that I shall answer everything you ask to the best of my knowledge, even if you won't understand the answers. However, you get ahead of yourself."* He paused for a moment. *"Your question is not a simple one. A Clairvoyant is the end state, and to understand what makes a Clairvoyant clairvoyant, you have to understand the perspective from which a Clairvoyant derives his or her clairvoyance."*

Janus was right: she didn't understand anything he said. Her parents always told her she was smart, and she guessed they were right, but everything he said was quite simply beyond her. At least he was answering her questions, though. Carmen was on the verge of asking him to elaborate when Janus continued.

"Most people have it wrong. We are not technically clairvoyant. We do not see the future, and we are not aware of things that no one else can perceive...per se. We are simply more sensitive. We are more sensitive to the Dark."

"What's the Dark?" Carmen asked.

The two of them entered an elevator, and Janus pushed the button to the floor they were going to before he answered. *"The Dark is the source of your power. It is the generative force of everything about you. It is your master, but you are not its servant."*

"But what is the Dark?" she asked again.

She was pretty sure he hadn't answered her question. His explanations were so dizzying that she only really understood half of what he said, if she were being generous. Worse, she could only care so much about the source of her power. After all, she didn't even know she had *power* until now. Power to do what; what did that even mean? Her parents had sent her to bed without dessert at least once or twice.

"It is the chaotic part of your psyche," Janus said matter-of-factly. *"It has had many names throughout history, but I will refer to it as the Dark. It cannot be defined. It cannot be*

given dimension, though many have tried. It is not tangible through the senses. It simply…is."

Carmen still didn't understand. "*But—*"

"*111724.*"

"*Yes?*" she spoke hesitantly.

"*What is your favorite flavor of ice cream?*" he asked.

"*Coffee.*"

"*…Why?*"

Carmen had never really thought about it before. She'd always like coffee ice cream the most. "*I don't know. I just like it.*"

"*Why?*"

"*I guess I just like how it tastes.*"

"*Why?*"

Try as she might, she couldn't come up with a reason. "*I just do.*"

"*Exactly,*" Janus spoke. "*The Dark is what makes you* you. *And as you just proved, it makes you* you, *even if you are consciously unaware of it.*" The elevator doors opened and the two began walking again. "*Your ignorance, however, will not last. Your Dark is strong, easily within the top one percent of everyone who has ever lived. Consequently, you are closer to it than most. I do not know when it will happen, but one day—and I assure you it will be a day you remember—you will become self-aware. Then you will be a Clairvoyant, a monster of the Dark.*" He was quiet for a few seconds. "*Do you understand?*"

"*I guess so,*" she spoke. It was probably the biggest lie she had ever told in her young life, but it was also the easy answer. It wasn't like he hadn't warned her. "I don't want to be a monster," she muttered softly to herself.

Janus heard her anyway. "*You will have no active choice in the matter. What order you wish to impose or chaos you wish to embrace is dependent on you and your Dark. What conscious will you wield also serves the same master. Fight yourself if you wish; just remember the only reason you'd do so is because you want to."* He allowed a moment for his words to sink in before he asked, *"Do you have any other questions?"*

"No."

He said nothing else, and they continued on.

This floor was more heavily trafficked than the previous floor had been. The organically curved walls were gone; instead, this place was more machined and purposeful. The pattern remained the same, however: one child for one handler. The children were still around her age, but they weren't like the kids from the previous floor. Most had minor bruises here and there. In a few cases, a child was laid out on a stretcher. Most often, the child was still alive, but Carmen was acutely aware that several were not. She wondered if that was how she'd looked after Janus shot her. In the rarest of instances, it was the handler on a stretcher and not the child, and more often than not, the handler was dead. The child didn't follow obediently alongside in such cases—at least not of their own accord. Instead, they were suspended on a moveable platform encased in a disgusting orangish brown foam. The mass of goop reminded her of a melted marshmallow. Only the child's head remained uncovered so they could breathe. Janus gave no reaction to any of this, so she guessed it was normal as she nervously watched it all.

He stopped suddenly at one of the several doors lining either side of the hall. Carmen didn't know what was inside the room, but if it was like all the others rooms she'd been in, she could make a pretty good guess. What would it be this time? Would they have a terrasaur try to eat her? Would Janus shoot her again? Would there be another one of those terrible creatures from before? Would they set her on fire and be done with it? Would there be an endless plate of vegetables for her to eat? Her future, while unknowable, was undoubtedly terrible.

She didn't sense anything alive on the other side of the door, but that didn't really mean anything—not in this place. Carmen's young imagination could think of plenty of horrors that weren't alive. Enough people had to have been killed here that ghosts were certain to be lurking somewhere. She didn't think she could sense ghosts. If she could, she didn't think she'd want to.

Janus opened the door, and she had nowhere near enough time to make her peace. Her breath was quick and her heart raced. The lights began flickering all around her, and no one cared. Janus entered, and she followed a half-step behind. Her obedience stood in stark contrast to the near panic she felt. She would do as Janus asked her—follow him wherever he went. She wouldn't complain. She'd try to stay good, even if a very real part of her screamed for her not to enter that room. Carmen was used to such…*intuitions*. In fact, they were some of her earliest memories. But now it was a different; it was irrational, unsure. Everything felt like danger, and more than likely, she was right.

There was nothing immediately ominous when she walked inside. This room was almost exactly like every other room on this floor: large, square, and with padded walls. Thankfully, there were no small doors housing who-knew-what. The room's only unique feature was that the floor was covered in sand. Carmen had no idea why it was there, but sand itself wasn't immediately menacing, so she really didn't care. Her gaze darted around the room. There was nothing she could see with her eyes or any of her other senses. There was nothing here, other than her, sand, and Janus. She looked at her handler and then backed away. He was the most obvious thing that would do her in.

"You have a difficult task before you, 111724," Janus said orally.

Carmen shuddered when she heard that. If this would be difficult, what had everything else been?

"There are trillions upon trillions of particles of sand on the floor," he continued. "My report tells me you are familiar with telekinesis. Considering your potential, any natural aptitude you show for anything will have quite staggering results. This is the test. I want you to lift every last grain of sand into the air and hold it there until I tell you to stop."

Carmen looked at the floor. Her task was sobering. Making her dolls dance, while fun, wasn't exactly easy, and this would be like making all the aerocars on her block dance. She wasn't sure if it was possible…except, perhaps it was. Janus wouldn't give her something she was utterly incapable of doing. She didn't think he would, at least. What would be the point?

Janus walked a little ways from her, and Carmen took a deep breath. She figured there was no method to this, so she focused on a small clump of sand and lifted it into the air. The effort was almost unnoticeable; the concentration, however, was quite high. At home, she had at most a dozen individual dolls. Currently, she was supporting several thousand individual grains of sand, if not more. The effort to add a few hundred more made her gasp. It also made her once again doubt that this was actually possible. Maybe it was meant to test her sanity. She wasn't sure she'd pass.

She was tempted to add another small clump to her pile but stopped short. There was no point—she was dropping the sand she was already suspending faster than she could possibly add more. Her grasp on each particle waned as her concentration slipped. Every attempt to catch the falling sand only made Carmen drop more. Eventually, the very last particle fell back to the floor, and she was holding nothing.

She breathed hard, and looked over at Janus in her brief moment of rest. The Clairvoyant stared back at her like a statue. What was she doing wrong? He said this would be difficult, but she thought she should still be able to do it. Carmen looked away from Janus and surveyed her sandbox once more. The only conclusion she could make was that she wasn't focusing hard enough, so she took a deep breath again then gritted her teeth. Once more, a clump of sand rose into the air. She levitated another before the effort began taking its toll. She added a third clump and had thus far managed to clear a nearly unnoticeable spot in the room. It was about this moment that her plan went awry. Janus coughed softly, and that was enough of a break in her concentration to lose all the gains she had made. The sand fell to the ground; seconds later, so did Carmen, in a mixture of frustration and pure mental exhaustion.

She looked at her handler again and wondered if he had coughed on purpose. He had to know it took almost all of her focus to maintain the pathetically small pile, let alone the entire room. She wouldn't put it past him—even if that would make it the gentlest thing he had done to her since she stepped into that car. He wasn't doing anything now, though. He simply watched her. Carmen turned back to the sand.

I want to go home, she thought yet again as she rested on her knees. The desire was just as true now as any other moment she'd been here. Sand—she was trapped in a room with sand. First guns, monsters, and now sand. She grabbed a big clump of the stuff and let the sand slowly seep between her fingers. It was hard to think she'd used to like this stuff at the playground. Life was so much simpler when you were just running through it or building stuff with it.

Carmen ran her hands through the sand again. Then, slowly but surely, an idea came to her. She had to be going about this the wrong way.

She got to her feet. The answer was obvious. She just needed something to focus on—that was her problem. She was concentrating harder than she ever had in her life, but she had nothing to aim at. Carmen looked at the sand and raised her arm. A large clump levitated into the air at the same time, like the mass was in the palm of her hand. It was still arduous but manageable. In fact, it was considerably easier than before. After moving her arm to the right, an even larger clump of sand joined the first. Carmen gasped from the strain, but she wasn't close to giving up. She could do this—she knew she could do this. All she needed to do was focus, be tough, and be strong.

I can do this, she thought after a groan. Just then, she heard laughing. All the sand dropped in a flash and Carmen looked at Janus. He chuckled while slowly shaking his head.

"Why do you toy with yourself, 111724?" he asked. "We are not wizards. We are not mystics. We do not wave our hands and expect *magic* to happen. I will never tell you that you need to keep the world in balance. I will never tell you what herbs, sacrificial babies, or words you need to use to manipulate your power. You are a Clairvoyant—such nonsense is beneath you. You will simply walk into a room and bend it to your will. Heat, light, minds, sand…it makes no difference. It will happen simply because you exist."

She didn't really care about anything he was saying. "It's too hard," she whined.

"It's hard because you want it to be hard," Janus said. "I

do not know why. That's a question you have to ask yourself. But if you want to levitate the sand, just do it."

"It's too hard," Carmen whined again. "I can't do it. It's impossible."

"Why is it impossible?"

"I can't concentrate hard enough," she said, now on the verge of crying. "And…and you keep distracting me."

Her handler was silent for a minute or two. "Concentrate?" he finally asked. "Why would you need to concentrate?"

It was now Carmen's turn to be silent. The answer was obvious to her. "How else am I supposed to do it?"

"Do you concentrate when you walk down the street?" Janus asked after a brief pause. "How much conscious thought do you use to control your thousands of nerves and muscles to simply stand still?"

"But…but this is different," Carmen whimpered.

"How?" he asked, letting the question hang before he spoke again. "What you are has very little to do with what you see when you look in a mirror. You're a Clairvoyant, a monster of the Dark. You take in the energies around you, harness them, and change your environment based on what you desire. You do the same thing with your physical shell, your body. So, once again, how is this different from anything else you have done in your life?"

She thought about his words and didn't have an answer. Part of that was because she didn't really understand anything he said, as usual, but his logic seemed to make some sort of sense. Just thinking about thinking how to walk made her head hurt. It was nice how it always *just happened.*

"Try again, and don't concentrate this time."

Carmen nodded and turned back to the sand. She didn't bother getting up, though. She'd just collapse again after another bout of frustration. Surely Janus would clap his hands or shoot her or something if she actually started making headway. She wished they would have given her a nicer handler.

She lifted a small clump of sand into the air for a moment and held it there. Nothing was different; she had to concentrate just as hard as ever. Carmen dropped the sand without trying to add any more. She was right—this was pointless. When she looked at Janus, though, he merely looked back at her. She turned away and took a deep breath. This test really was meant to drive her mad. No one could lift all this sand. She wanted to see Janus do it, if it was so easy. She glanced at him again, opened her mouth, and then looked away just as quickly. The man was entirely too scary an individual to seriously ask that question. Carmen instead closed her eyes and sat there. He couldn't punish her for just sitting.

It was then that she thought about a similar problem from not all that long ago. When she had to use telepathy, she *just did it*. She didn't think the two skills were related—they probably weren't. Her brain felt like it was about to melt. Perhaps she was just thinking too hard?

She kept her eyes closed and focused on the room for a moment. There was Janus. As always, it was hard not to notice him. He just, well…was. She guessed all Clairvoyants were like that, but she didn't know for certain. There was also the sand, all that wretched sand. There was nothing really to it; it was just there, albeit in a completely different way than Janus. It wasn't alive and it wasn't dead. The grains were just objects—trillions upon trillions of objects—and she had to move every last one.

She thought about what Janus said about how she didn't think about walking while she was walking. That was true. She couldn't remember the last time she had consciously thought about it. The question was how would she think about moving sand without thinking about moving sand? She wasn't exactly sure. At first, she simply imagined the sand levitating—not each and every grain, but a large clump. At the same time, Carmen felt a very odd type of strain. It wasn't exactly uncomfortable, but it reminded her of standing up from a chair really fast. There was resistance. In fact, there was considerable resistance, but it passed quickly. Now there was just a very small but noticeable weight. She took a deep breath. She could live with it.

Let's try some more, Carmen thought.

This time, she didn't imagine the sand rising. Instead, she simply wished for the sand to rise, allowing it to happen. She felt that odd discomfort from before, though it was even more insignificant in intensity and passed even more quickly. Carmen was encouraged. She had already cleared more than she ever hoped to and had yet to even break a sweat. Maybe her efforts would even be noticeable? She couldn't help her curiosity, and after opening first one eye and then the other, she studied her new surroundings.

Her mouth fell open. At best, she'd hoped to see a hole maybe the same size as herself in the sand, but half of it levitated above her. The sight was so unbelievable that the floating material bobbled and then fell. Carmen caught it just before it hit the ground, but still this was ridiculous. Before, she'd struggled to support a few hundred grains of sand, maybe even a few thousand if she was being generous. How many were in the air now? A bazillion gazillion? And she wasn't even *that* tired! Eventually, Carmen smiled as she stared at the spectacle.

I can do this.

She stood then and looked at the remaining pile of sand, her smile unabashed. The test was almost trivial now. She raised one insignificant speck of sand without thinking about it. Then she added another and another. The rate increased from single grains, to dozens, hundreds, thousands, till at last, trillions of grains of sand flowed into the air like a river until there was nothing left on the ground. Carmen held the sand over their heads, as Janus had told her to do, and looked at him. There was some effort involved in just holding the sand in place, but she could manage it.

Her handler, however, remained unmoved. "For however powerful you may be, 111724, it seems you still have to learn attention to detail," he finally said.

Carmen was dumbfounded. What was wrong now? What did she possibly miss? Janus took a few steps forward before she could ask, revealing the sand under his feet.

"Oh yeah," she muttered.

Then, without pause, she lifted that sand into the air. She looked down to find sand underneath herself as well. When she levitated that, her task was complete. Janus didn't say anything as he watched the sand above them. After a few seconds, he turned his attention to Carmen. She smiled nervously.

"Good," he said. "Are you tired?"

She smiled outright. "No." It was somewhat of a lie. She was a little tired, but no more exhausted than if she had climbed a flight of stairs.

Janus nodded. "Always remember that the use of your abilities will be tiring. Channeling the energies around you will never be completely efficient. The resistance of the world before it submits to your power is fatiguing, but it is nothing that could kill you. At most, a Clairvoyant will pass out after overexerting themselves."

Carmen already knew this. Her parents had remarked more than once on how much she could sleep. In turn, she often wondered how anyone could not sleep as much as she did.

"There isn't much you can do about this," Janus continued, "but always know that your mind and body are a team. You must feed your mind and discipline your body to ever reach your full potential. A disciplined body can reduce the need for you to rely on your other abilities, even if the effect is ultimately minor."

"Okay," Carmen said simply.

Her handler nodded again. "All right, you can put the sand down."

She nodded as well and then did exactly as he asked—sort of. She more dropped the sand than put it down. The error was obvious just as soon as she let it go, but she made no attempt to catch anything; she just covered her head and hoped for the best. Carmen never noticed any of the sand actually hitting her, though. It had covered the entire room like a cloud, but she was certain it never touched her. She looked up at Janus when the deluge was over, hands still over her head and smiling warily. It was kind of funny. Janus only shook his head. Then he walked toward the door after a soft sigh. Carmen followed in his wake.

After they left the room, not a word passed between them. She no longer really noticed that she was more or less forgotten between her episodes of torture. It just seemed… well, normal at this point. They didn't talk as they walked down the hall, nor as they entered an elevator, exited a floor below, and continued on. This floor looked just like every other. It was long and there were no decorations, just doors on either side of the hall. There were more people here too, and they were more beat up than those on the other floor, as hard as that was to believe. Carmen didn't really notice it anymore, though, either. There was no question whatsoever that she had gotten off lightly with the sand. It was unlikely that her next test would involve something as gentle as bubbles. She was on borrowed time, and there was nothing she could do about it.

They entered a room with nothing inside—no sand, windows, furniture, nothing. It was just like every other room, and Carmen couldn't say that surprised her. There was a door on the opposite side of the room, however, the same size as the one she and Janus had entered through. Carmen looked at it cautiously. She didn't have the best luck with doors.

She looked at her handler. "What am I going to do here?"

The effort just to utter those words more than matched her trial with the sand. Fear had choked her voice to almost nothing.

"This," Janus said as he pointed toward the door.

A man walked into the room. It wasn't some terrible monster she had never seen before, and he didn't have a bomb, a gun, or even a knife. It was just a man. His clothes were simple, and he himself looked simple with hair trimmed short and no distinguishing facial features. There was nothing distinguishing about his appearance. Despite this, he was different from every other man Carmen had ever seen. There was just *nothing* about him, almost like he was...*empty.* Every other living being she had ever sampled had been dynamic and ever changing—in short, full of life. In that measure, this man would be dwarfed by a house fly. How that was possible, she didn't understand. He may as well have been the sand she had lifted earlier; there was no difference. Carmen couldn't look at him anymore. It was too sickening.

Janus walked toward him. "This is a Construct," he said. "Every aspect of him has been carefully genetically engi-neered as needed for their specific purpose. They are not clones," he said firmly. "Fundamentally, they are a robot made of flesh."

As she watched the man, it was hard to disagree with that assessment. Janus circled him, and the Construct simply stared straight ahead. The only time he moved was to blink every now and then. He was a rather impressive robot, at least —more muscled than any man she had ever seen, including the heroes on the holo programs her father watched.

"They feel no pain," Janus continued, "have no hopes, and have no dreams. They will be your principal opponents for most of your stay here."

Carmen looked at the man, unsure of whether she should be happy that Janus indirectly indicated her stay would one day end or worried that this thing would be her opponent in something she probably wouldn't like.

"A Construct will never be your equal. They can press you—they can even kill you, if you get careless—but a Clairvoyant drowns them in every measure. As I said, in your case, of all the beings that have ever lived in the galaxy, only about one percent of them can ever be your match," Janus said. Carmen couldn't say she was comforted by her handler's words as she studied the Construct. "This is why you must always fight to the death."

She shuddered when she heard that.

"When you kill your opponent, you give them your highest respect. Anyone challenging you is either a fool or seeking death. Why they would want this shouldn't be any of your concern. These people, animals, whatever they'll be, will know what you are just by looking at you. If they *choose*"—Janus emphasized the word—"to stand in front of you, it is only fitting that you honor their choice with their ultimate and inevitable end. This is why every death you deal must be both clean and complete. Never let there be a person maimed by a Clairvoyant; let there only be the dead remains of those who have fought you and the lives of the people smart enough to never try."

As she looked at her handler, tears began to fill her eyes. "I don't want to fight him," she whimpered.

"You will," he said simply as he stared down at the little girl.

"I don't want to," she muttered again. "I…I want to go home."

Janus sighed at her usual request. "Does your constant bellyaching over going home give you comfort?" he asked.

Carmen didn't say anything. She doubted he even wanted an answer.

"Know this, 111724," he continued. "There is no *home* for Clairvoyants. We are consciously aware of more than most. Some would say we are aware of everything. In either case, and as a consequence, we are part of nothing. That is the great gift and burden of our perspective. You know this as well as I do. I tire of entertaining your self-delusion. Do not ever say it again in my presence," he finished casually.

She swallowed hard, but there was still a lump in her throat. "I don't want to fight," she said meekly.

"Yes, you do."

Carmen paused for a moment, wondering how that logic worked. Of all the things in the world, she was certain she didn't want to fight this person or anyone else.

"You say you don't want to fight him, and in the strictest sense that may be true, but both you and I know it is not completely the case. Your heart is beating faster, is it not? Your pupils are dilated. Your hands are shaking. You're not even looking at me anymore. Instead, you're focused on your opponent, analyzing him for weaknesses and formulating your strategy. Your mind may say it doesn't want to fight, but your body—*the Dark*—knows it is inevitable. And it wants to win. My desire is only to get you in greater touch with this force while dispensing with all your superfluous aspects. This is the most complete and effective way. I am sorry."

Carmen took a half-step away from him and the robot. "No."

Janus looked at her before dropping his head for a reflective moment. He pointed at the Construct and then at Carmen. "Kill her," he said, calmly.

The Construct wasted no time and minced no words. He assumed a guard and started walking toward her.

"No," she said, backing away. It was only a few frantic steps until she was against the wall. The Construct cocked his arm back. "No!" Carmen said more urgently.

A second later, she couldn't speak anymore. She vaguely registered the punch, much like how she vaguely remembered raising her hands to defend herself. Now the entire side of her head where she was hit felt numb. She couldn't move her mouth anymore, and it was growing increasingly hard to breathe. Carmen coughed and then watched the blood spew forth and fall to the ground moments before she joined it.

It was hard to say that she was in pain; it was more like she had been unplugged from the world. She didn't even feel connected with her body anymore. She couldn't feel her fingers, and then her toes went numb. Her arms and her legs soon succumbed after a brief shudder in protest. Last, she grew very, very cold. Her breathing stopped, and the last thing she saw before everything went dark was Janus.

4

BARRIERS

Carmen ran frantically across her room, sliding and tripping as she went. Mikayla playfully barked and bounded after her.

"Quiet, this isn't a game!" Carmen hissed. The dog didn't understand, though.

She rushed to pile the meager books she had been provided on top of the pillows and blankets already haphazardly blocking the door. She'd been at it since she awoke in her usual cold sweat. Thankfully, her door opened into her dorm instead of the hallway. Nevertheless, she didn't think her barricade as it currently was would be enough to deter Janus. *I need something heavier*, she decided.

Her eyes came to rest on her chair, and once again she darted across the room. It was obvious after a few grunts that she wasn't strong enough to pick it up, so she slid it across the floor instead. The effort produced a horrible screech, and Mikayla howled in response.

"Quiet, quiet!" Carmen yelled. "I have to stop him from coming in!"

She went to her table next and pushed and strained, but it was no use. She got behind the table, pressed her shoulder into it, and screamed as she pushed with everything she had. Her feet lost grip and slipped out from under her several times, and every muscle burned. Mikayla ran around her, barking wildly, but the girl ignored the dog as tears began streaming down her cheeks.

"Please," Carmen cried, as she tried to get the table to even budge, but it didn't yield. "Please!"

Eventually her body could give no more, and she fell to the ground, utterly spent. Her dorm room seemed to shrink to the size of a coffin as fear gripped her. Her mouth and throat were completely dry. The lights flickered, bathing them in periods of remorseless dark while also painfully illuminating her situation. Her whole body trembled as she thought of how Janus might kill her again. Her hand went to where his bullet had ripped into her, but there was no scar. She felt the side of her face where she was punched, but there was no mark that could tell what happened. There were only memories and nightmares. Mikayla licked her wet face; it was meager comfort.

Carmen heard a clicking sound. It was only after a minute or so that she realized it was the sound of her chattering teeth. She paid it no mind. What was more concerning was how hard it was to breathe. She gulped the air rapidly, almost in pants, but to no avail. Her skin tingled as the room spun. Mikayla may have made some noise. She didn't know for sure, as she was groaning too loudly from her twisting stomach to hear much of anything. Yet, in her horrible wretched state, she remembered the room of sand.

She raised one of her hands slowly. Her limb shook involuntarily to the point of uselessness, but as she stared, feeling slowly came back to her. After wiping away the tears from her wet face, she looked at the table again. A thought sent it careening into the door with a loud bang, and a startled Mikayla jumped.

What else is there? Carmen thought as she hurriedly looked around the room.

Her work desk was the next obvious reinforcement. She didn't know how she could be so stupid as to forget her obvious gifts before. She was gentler with the work desk, telekinetically placing it so softly that it was hard to tell when it touched the ground. Then she looked at her bed. She could sleep on the floor. It rested against the door only a few seconds later. After that, there was nothing else to move.

"Mikayla," she called, and the dog obediently responded to her summon. Unable to think of anything else to do, Carmen sat in the center of the room and held the puppy close.

Mikayla whimpered. She had been squeezing her too tightly.

"Sorry," she muttered before her eyes fixed on the door. Such was her focus, she had to think to even blink. "Everything is going to be okay," she said softly as she petted her. The texture of the dog's fur was distracting. "Everything's going to be okay."

It was only belatedly that Carmen realized her food entered through the same door she had barricaded. She didn't care, though.

"Everything's going to be okay."

Mikayla was so comfortable that she began to fall asleep. Carmen, by contrast, could hear the rapid-fire beats of her heart while her temples pulsed. She stroked the dog faster. There was nothing she could sense or feel, but Mikayla suddenly perked up and lifted her head. Carmen swallowed hard. Someone was at the door. Whoever it was tried to open it, but her barricade held firm.

"Everything's going to okay," Carmen muttered imperceptibly as fresh tears welled in her eyes.

"111724," Janus called. "111724, open the door."

She could make no response other than a small squeak.

"111724, open this door right now," he commanded, sounding more annoyed than angry.

Carmen was unable to even pet Mikayla coherently. Her shaking hand skipped along the animal more than caressed her, and her tears began to soak her shirt collar. "Everything is going to be okay."

"I will not ask again," Janus said.

The girl swallowed hard. "Everything is going to be—" she started to say, but her voice caught in her throat when the door opened a crack. Another push from Janus turned that small crack into a sliver. "Leave me alone!" Carmen screamed.

Her handler gave no reply. The door opened slowly, and she screamed and cried with each ever-widening inch. Eventually, she was able to see that he wasn't opening the door physically; he stood in the center of the frame and simply stared at her while it opened seemingly by some horrible magic trick. Janus's gaze froze her soul, yet it contained no wrath that she could discern. He didn't even seem annoyed anymore. Nevertheless, Carmen screamed and kicked her legs until she had propelled herself firmly into the opposite wall. The door opened fully, and Janus walked calmly inside. She cried hysterically and raised her arms to protect herself, as if he were going to boil her alive.

He still didn't speak. He looked at her and then turned and looked at the remains of her makeshift barricade. With no prompt or ceremony, the items of her barricade levitated and slowly flew back to their proper places. Carmen watched the scene in trembling horror. She had spent all morning on what he had demolished and corrected in seconds. Mikayla, the traitor, even went to him and licked his hand.

"111724, it's time," he said simply.

Carmen's throat was too paralyzed for her to speak. Her legs felt like they were made of mush. The best she could manage was a few squeaks and quivering moans. Janus took a few steps toward her, and her eyes grew wide. He paused after that, watching her for a few seconds in silence as the girl's terror remained unabated.

"You can be tiring," he finally said, more to himself than to her. He then abruptly left the room.

Surprised, Carmen was just about let out a sigh of relief when some unseen force lifted her off her feet and out of the room. She gave an earsplitting cry that could have shattered glass, but it was no use. She looked at Mikayla, who barked and jumped at her. It was hard to tell if the dog was trying to aid her master or if she thought this was another game, but it made no difference either way. The door to Carmen's dorm closed, and she floated after Janus, crying the entire way. He placed her on her feet when they reached the elevator, not completely ungently. She cried on the floor.

"Stop it. The noise is growing bothersome," he said nonchalantly. It only made her cry louder than before. "111724," he said firmly, looking down at her.

Carmen glanced up at him. She stopped crying out loud, though there were still tears in her eyes.

Janus didn't seem to care. The elevator door opened, and he looked down the corridor and then at her again. "Will you walk?" he asked. Carmen, well aware of the alternative, nodded meekly. "Good," he replied. He then exited the elevator. Carmen followed obediently, albeit on shaky legs.

This floor seemed the same as all the others, though it was hard to tell with her swollen eyes. Her whimpers were reduced to a few choked off moans that Janus didn't seem to mind. The trail of tears in her wake, however, remained. Her feet felt impossibly heavy. It was no small wonder that she was even able to trudge behind him. Janus entered a room, and Carmen followed. Neither handler nor charge said a word.

The room was empty, save a small desk in the center. Other than that, it looked the same as the room in which the Construct killed her, the same as the room of sand, and the same as the one in which she was shot. Janus said nothing. She began to hyperventilate. He glanced at her with a raised eyebrow.

"No," she squeaked weakly as she backed away from him.

Janus sighed loudly. "111724," he began, but Carmen started screaming before he could say anything else.

She just couldn't help herself. Her legs gave out from under her, and she became a crying mass on the floor. Janus stood over her but didn't speak. He sighed again, loudly, when it was obvious that she wouldn't be stopping any time soon. Once again, that unseen force lifted her off the ground, and she shrieked. She was sat at the desk, calmly and gently, despite what her hysterics implied. Then Janus pulled out a small object she couldn't see, and she rose her shaking arms in a futile attempt to keep whatever it was at bay. Her handler rolled his eyes before placing the object on the desk. Carmen shrieked again. She didn't know she could scream so loudly, and it made the door to the room vibrate as her vision blurred. It abruptly stopped, however, when she finally saw what he was going to attack her with. Unless her guess was wrong, it was a Personal Data Device, or PDD. For a fleeting second, she wondered if it was a bomb that was just shaped like a PDD, but when she picked it up, she realized it was indeed genuine. She had played with or at least used a PDD since as far back as she could remember. She looked at Janus, curious what this new devilry would mean.

He placed his arms behind his back and started walking slowly. "Mind and body are a team, 111724," he said. "For the moment, your mind will be our focus. Unfortunately, how intelligent you are or are not is a potential neither you nor I can affect. Wisdom—true wisdom—is, regrettably, also beyond our ability to engineer. Its chief architects are knowledge and experience. Experience comes with time and exposure to the vagaries of life, and I do my best to craft your experiences. It is knowledge that we must busy ourselves with and which provides the most value for effort."

Carmen looked at the PDD and then back at Janus. "What do you want me to do?" she asked hesitantly.

"This is a simple knowledge assessment. A test, if you will."

Carmen activated the PDD to find he wasn't lying. As she scrolled through the assessment, there were math problems, passages to read, words to spell, and other minutiae. She felt suddenly lightheaded.

"That's it?" she asked after shaking her head.

"How shall I teach you if I don't know what you already know?" he asked back matter-of-factly. "We are monsters, 111724, but that doesn't mean we are stupid monsters," he added.

Carmen took a deep breath, and tears welled in her eyes again. "That's not what I meant," she said. "I thought you were going to have me—"

"Have you what?" Janus asked, cutting her off.

She hesitated. It was hard to speak. "I thought you were going to have me fight again," she finally eked out.

"All of life is a fight, 111724. Every second of every day,"

Janus said. "Indeed, every test you take, except this one, will be graded only as pass or fail. To pass is to live another day to be tested yet again. To fail…"

"You'll kill me if I fail a test?" Carmen asked with watery eyes.

Janus paused a moment. "Is every failure lethal?" he asked simply. "If you fail to tie your shoes, will it kill you?"

She thought about it before answering, "No."

"Correct. But, if you fail to tie your shoes, it may be difficult to walk or run. In short, you have to deal with a hardship."

"What will happen if I fail a test?" she asked.

Janus opened his mouth, as if he were about to answer, then closed it slowly. "You will find that out in time," he said. "But enough of that. This is your knowledge assessment. You have as much time as you require. You may begin."

Carmen swallowed hard and then got to work. The beginning of the test was quite easy. On and on it went, though, and the further she advanced, the harder it became. She didn't know how long she spent on the assessment. Janus was even lenient enough to allow her to take a few short breaks. After a while, she had to skip a question or three to make any progress. Eventually, she could do no more and stopped. Janus picked up the PDD and studied the results.

"Did I pass?" she asked nervously.

"As I already said, this test will not be graded," he replied with minor though noticeable annoyance. He then nodded slowly. It was hard to tell, but he didn't seem displeased. "If you have no more questions, we may go."

"Where are we going?"

He never answered; he just turned to exit the room. Carmen was well aware that resisting him was pointless, so she followed him out feeling decidedly cold. They were in the elevator soon enough and deposited on yet another floor. The hall here vibrated from an oddly muffled rumbling noise, like a continuous thunderclap. She looked at Janus, tempted to ask him what the sound was and, more important, what it meant to her health, but her handler seemed completely oblivious to his charge. It started her young mind thinking.

"Why are you my handler?" she asked meekly.

He glanced down at her with an expression she thought was as close to confusion as he could show. "That is not a question assets are in the habit of asking."

"Please," she begged.

She didn't think Janus even liked her. At times, it seemed like he outright hated her or at least wanted nothing to do with her. Her parents were always sad around her, but she didn't question whether they loved her; they just had to. But Janus....

"I was assigned to you," he said simply. "There are more factors than I care to mention, but suffice it to say it was not my decision. Does that answer your question?"

Carmen brought her hands to her shoulders, hugging herself slightly. She stopped walking as an idea turned over and over again in her head. Janus eventually stopped and looked back at her. She couldn't even look in his general direction.

"If there is something you'd like to say, 111724, let's hear it. You are wasting time."

She hesitated. "Do you hate me?"

Janus said nothing at first. "Hate?" he muttered as he considered the concept. "I can see why you would ask that. Indeed, some handlers don't particularly care for their charges. There are some who can be said to even hate their charges. As for myself, no. You can trust that I don't hate you." Carmen felt no fondness behind his words either. "You are my charge. You are here to learn from me. Whether I hate or like you is of no great importance to the fulfillment of that task, nor is your affinity for me of any great importance."

Carmen hugged herself tighter. His words were about as comforting as sleeping on a bed of porcupines, but she had to admit that, on second thought, Janus didn't seem to outright absolutely, utterly, and completely hate her guts. She sniffled as she tried to comfort herself with the idea that at least she had that.

Janus began walking again and she followed. They entered a new room and, for once, it was completely different from the others she'd been in. It wasn't very wide—she could easily walk from one end to the other—but it was long. At the far end of the room were targets.

"How often did your parents touch you?" he asked.

Carmen was so taken aback by him asking about her parents that the best she could manage were a few incomprehensible sounds. Finally, she asked, "What?"

"How often did your parents touch you?" he asked again. "A hug or even a simple pat or kiss."

"Not very often," she said.

"Did they say why? Especially when they touched you by accident, or when you weren't expecting it."

Carmen thought back to them, even though she usually tried not to. She was still certain they were going to come rescue her, but now it was harder and harder to believe as much, except on the coldest and darkest lonely nights. She couldn't even say it out loud anymore.

"They said it hurt. Like getting shocked."

Janus nodded slowly. "Do you know why that is?" Carmen shook her head. "Then let me educate you," he began.

"Surrounding you and every other living being is a

bioelectric field. I will not describe it scientifically. No one has yet been able to do so, though many have tried. Anyway, your bioelectric field is unique to you and only you, like a fingerprint. As a Clairvoyant, you can sense another person's bioelectric field and get impressions from it. For instance, you can know when someone is lying to you, their mood, or even at times exactly what they are thinking. Most of these impressions will be imparted to you subconsciously, like reading a facial expression."

She nodded, though she really didn't understand what he was saying. She always felt so dumb around him.

"I'm sure you always knew your parents were around, even when you didn't see them or hear them," he continued.

Carmen nodded again. That was true. She had just figured everyone was able to do that. "Why did it hurt when they touched me?" she asked.

She remembered how they winced almost every time she made contact with them. Eventually, she just stopped doing it to spare them the pain. She had figured that was normal as well, but even so, she hadn't liked it. It was hard to say why.

Janus held out his arm. "Try touching me," he said.

Carmen looked at him, not sure if he was serious. The sincerity in his eyes, however, told her he was. She hesitantly reached out, her hand shaking a little. After a few wavering seconds, her finger touched his hand and she yelped. The surprise of the pain was more than the reality of it, and she cradled her finger for a moment before thinking nothing of it. Janus slightly rubbed the spot where she touched him, and a small part of her was surprised he was able to feel pain.

"It hurt when you touched me because of the interaction of our bioelectric fields. For an average person, the bioelectric field of a Clairvoyant is so overpowering that they can be affected by it *without* physical contact, if the Clairvoyant is in a high state of charge."

"So, no one will ever be able to touch me?" she asked mournfully.

Janus shook his head. "You can be touched. You pet Mikayla, don't you?"

"Yes," she replied with a small smile. She hadn't thought about that.

"You are relaxed with Mikayla and have a low state of charge, though you are consciously unaware of it at the time," he continued. "Your state of charge can be consciously controlled to the point that you can touch anyone, even another Clairvoyant, with no discomfort."

"How do I do that?"

Janus shook his head again. "A lesson for a different day, perhaps. You are not here to learn how to hug people. You are a monster. This is why you are here."

He raised his hand and pointed a finger at one of the targets. A shaft of bluish-white light shot from his finger toward the target at the other end of the room. The lights in the room flickered just before it happened, and Carmen jumped from the thunderous noise. The impact on the target was no less dramatic. At first, it began in an explosion of bright light that was hard for her to look at. Janus extinguished the beam a second or two later, and all that remained of the target was white-hot, half-melted slag.

"Essentially, this is radiation from a Clairvoyant's bioelectric field. Its most tangibly felt quality is extreme heat," he explained.

Carmen looked at him and the target, her eyes large and unblinking. She nodded slowly.

"You try," he said.

"I…I can't do that," she muttered, shaking her head.

Janus looked at her hard, and she knew instantly that had been the wrong thing to say. Instead of protesting further, she took a few steps forward and aimed her finger at a target. Her hand was in the shape of a gun, and she thought she looked ridiculous, so she quickly changed to just point at the target like Janus had. Then she stopped.

"How?" she asked before adding, "Please."

"How does a bird fly?" he responded. "How does a bat use echolocation? How does a dog wag its tail?"

"But that's different," she whined.

He waved away her words with a hand. "Not at all. For a Clairvoyant, creating beams of heat or even walking on the ceiling is as natural as flying is to a bird." Carmen opened her mouth to protest, but Janus spoke again before she could say a word. "111724," he began, "in time, much that you consider impossible will become mundane. Much that you thought you'd never be able to do shall summon not even a second thought. The limits you possess now are only the beginning of your potential." He took a deep breath. "Now, try again. I don't want to hear any more of what you can't do. There is much to accomplish today."

Carmen shuddered. "Will I have to fight again?"

"Eventually."

"I can't do that."

As Janus looked at the quivering girl in front of him, his eyes narrowed. "We will see."

5

THE MASK

Subject: 111724 Age: 8 Status: Forging

It was all so easy now. There was no thought—not consciously anyway. There was only will, force, pain, and submission. Her every opponent had fallen to her with pathetically little effort. This had to be her seventh or eighth today; she had lost count, as she tended to do. For their part, however, she did sport a bruise or two from when she grew careless or, as Janus would say, when she allowed it to happen. He always argued semantics, but his constructs never stayed in her mind for very long. The here and now always took precedence over his nonsense.

She took a casual step back, and the Construct's foot passed where her face had just been. She hadn't seen it coming and reacted faster than any terran was capable of; Carmen had just known it was coming. She didn't know the future—no Clairvoyant did. She wasn't even a Clairvoyant according to Janus and his semantics, not yet anyway. It wasn't even extrasensory perception that kept her a step ahead. The body could move in only so many ways, and a kick to her face or at least some part of her was the only move the Construct had left. She'd engineered as much about three to five seconds prior. A block here, a dodge there, a feint, a blow, a counterblow—she may as well be pruning roses. It was all so easy. Once you knew a thing, it was easy to predict.

This Construct was slightly better than most of his peers. She'd noticed over the years that, just as Janus said, there were slight variations from Construct to Construct, even if they largely looked the same. She could only assume they were intentional variations, though she didn't see much point in them. Pure clones would probably be easier to make, although that was merely a guess. At this point in her life, however, guesses were her only refuge from the certain horrors of the next day.

Today would be especially terrible. She had math class today—a math test specifically. She hated algebra. What was the quadratic equation again?

She reeled back, and her face stung as the Construct slipped a punch through her defenses. She glared at the make-believe terran. That was no fair! She hadn't been paying attention. This *thing* had no worries. It had no family either, though she had long forgotten what hers looked like. It was just a guppy bred and trained to be good sport before it was killed. It barely even provided that.

A small rage ignited within Carmen, and suddenly this particular fight, at this particular moment, had a purpose. What it was exactly she didn't know or really care, just like she ultimately didn't care about most things now. The feeling surged through her, though, and she allowed it. She even conjured more to add to the fire—a bad memory here, a shattered hope there. She was young, but there was quite a lot to draw upon.

The Construct hesitated for a second. They were dim beasts, no doubt about that, yet even they occasionally realized what she was and gave pause, especially now. The lights flickered and a spark ran along her arm, but she restrained herself to that. There was no reason to go all out; this would be over soon enough.

It started with a light blow to the Construct's chest. She punched with all of her physical might, which wasn't much. Her body had been disciplined, as Janus would call it, by years of fighting, but she was still a little girl against a full-grown man. The next hit, however, wouldn't be nearly as gentle. Her body could be read like any other person's, and her planted feet and twisting hips gave away that she was going to throw a left punch. It was all too obvious—even the Construct knew it was coming. Just as she hoped he would, he raised his arm to protect himself, and the trap was set.

Her telekinetically-amplified punch broke his arm and continued on to graze his chin. Constructs didn't feel any pain —she knew that better than they did. She didn't fully hit him, but there was enough force to make him stagger and fall to his knees, just as she'd wanted. Carmen glared at him for a very short moment before she punched him in the throat. The Construct didn't die, though; not yet, anyway. She had crushed his windpipe, and he fell to the ground, choking. His body gave spasms, but he didn't die.

"111724!" Janus started.

"I know, I know," Carmen muttered as she turned around. Her handler always watched her fights, but there were distinct times she wished he didn't. "Every kill must be definite and clean," she finished for him.

Janus stared down at her. "Yet?"

She shuddered. Although she couldn't read him, he was extraordinarily gifted in seeing right through her. She may as well have been made of glass around him; she was at least as brittle. Carmen didn't know if he read her or if he was just good at guessing what was on her mind. Either way, it was pointless to lie to him. He always knew.

"He hit me," she said.

"So what?"

"It was no fair. I was distracted."

Janus nodded and then asked, "Did it hurt when he hit you?" The question didn't seem to be born out of any concern for her wellbeing. He could have just as casually asked her for the time.

"Yeah, I guess so."

"So, you drew your own attention to induce a sting that forced you to refocus on the fight. There are more efficient techniques, but it was effective. The fight ended soon after. Still, that doesn't explain why you were so harsh."

Carmen rubbed her bruised cheek. "He hit me."

"Because you allowed him to," Janus retorted. She opened her mouth to speak, but he cut her off. "111724," he began, "are you suggesting that he made you angry?"

She glanced at the now dead Construct and then looked back at her handler. "Yes," she said simply.

"That is beneath you," Janus remarked. "Always remember that mind and body are a team. We are not unthinking brutes. Use your emotions—cherish them, keep them close, and allow them to reach their full expression— but never let them rule you. Your emotions are part of the Dark, just like everything else about you. They are illogical and largely subconscious, which means they make an excellent motivating force for whatever aim you wish to achieve. Channel the explosion, focus it. A Clairvoyant is never more powerful than when their conscious reason is united with their subconscious desire. But *do not* cheapen yourself as you just did," he said firmly. "Do you understand?"

My conscious reason and my subconscious desires want me to run away, she thought, but she didn't dare say it out loud. Carmen always had half a mind to protest. She never did, though.

"Yes, I understand," she said, even if her voice was a bit hollow.

Janus looked at her sidelong. "That's it? 'I understand?'"

Carmen looked him in the eye before glancing away quickly. "Yes."

"You don't have anything else to say?"

"No," she said, trying to keep herself from shuddering again. "I understand."

"Perhaps you do," Janus said softly to himself. Handler and charge were quiet for a brief moment before he spoke again. "But with you, it's always the same: just enough and no more."

It was hard to tell if he was disapproving, complimenting, or just stating facts. She had no idea what he was talking about, anyway. Typical.

Janus watched her for a few seconds longer before he sighed and started toward the door. "That's enough death for now," he said. "It's time for school."

Carmen swallowed hard. She'd rather stay here and kill Constructs than take her test. One was wholly easier than the other. Despite that, she followed him out the room as obediently as always. She wasn't bad at math, as far as she could tell, but she had no one to compare herself to, as all of her classes were one-on-one. She passed most of her assignments, but she eventually learned what a failing grade meant.

Failure usually meant she went a day or days without food.

By now, she gathered that bringing her back to life each time she died wasn't simple, cheap, or even certain. Janus often scheduled a high calorie day the day after she failed a test. His comments were that the high stress would either shape her into a more fearsome monster than she was now or break her. Either outcome seemed like it would do. If she survived intact, that was good. If she was broken, she could be put back together again into a stronger whole, which was just as good. Carmen, however, had yet to be broken. Janus never said much about that, other than revealing a quick flash of surprise at her resiliency during one of his rare unguarded moments.

All the same, she was now a different little girl than when she first arrived. Her blonde hair spent most of its time bound in a ponytail. She'd used to like styling her mother's hair and her own, but that joy had been sacrificed early for sheer practicality. The word "why" was all but exorcised from her vocabulary, why or how only mattered in very specific instances. On the rare times she met someone new, her first thought was usually how she would beat them if they had to fight. Her body and her mind were now hard, focused, and disciplined. She didn't bother with anything else—there was no reason to.

Carmen and Janus walked to the classroom in silence as usual. It was hard to remember the last time he or anyone else had asked her a question as simple as "How are you?" Well, the doctors asked whenever she was nursing a broken bone or four, but Janus hardly ever showed any open concern for her welfare. When he did, a lesson was always contained within. She'd gotten used to it long ago. It was just how it was here. You didn't talk to your handler, or anyone else for that matter.

When they exited the elevator, she began growing anxious. Her life had devolved to constant testing, constant battle, and constant stress. Mental or physical, there was never any difference, she fought in both realms—mind and body were a team. But then there were math tests. She hated math tests. Janus opened the door to the classroom. Carmen dutifully entered, but only because she knew she had no choice.

The classrooms were all the same and had no windows. There were never windows in any room Carmen had been in here. Trees and clouds were practically a figment of her imagination at this point.

Around the solitary desk and PDD were her distracters for the day. They were a relatively new addition, and there were four this time. As usual, they wore body armor and were armed with rifles. Their sole goal was to try to shoot her at random intervals throughout the test. The distracters were never Clairvoyants or even Constructs; they were just average, normal people. Carmen could easily read them all, which made them quite purposefully a minor issue, albeit one that sapped some of her attention, of which she had little to spare. She felt her cheek where the Construct had punched her. Little attention to spare indeed.

Janus nodded at all the distracters in turn. He then looked at his charge. "You have two hours, pass or fail."

The soft sigh of an eight-year-old girl filled the room. This was a hard test. Every test was hard. Most of the questions weren't exactly beyond her; they just took an inordinate amount of concentration to solve. She sighed again and doubted she'd have dinner today. Her time had to be getting short, but she needed to take a second to sit back and regain her focus.

One of her distracters took a shot at her in that moment. It was the worst time he could have chosen, as her attention was fixed on nothing in particular, causing his thoughts to rattle in her head like boulders in an avalanche. She didn't kill the distracter—she never killed the distracters. Janus had always been strict on that point, and she never complained about it. This time, she spoiled the shot simply by holding the trigger open telekinetically. She then turned her attention back to the test.

Almost done, she thought—hoped. There were just a couple questions left. They were mind-numbingly, soul-destroyingly hard, but their number was few. She leaned back and a bullet just missed her. Carmen's lips pressed together in a sneer. The distracters were annoying, but they were just a fact of her weird, violent life.

Janus had told her their purpose. A Clairvoyant just existed like a hurricane just existed. She wasn't supposed to focus her thoughts on any one thing, at least not consciously. He preached that conscious thought was inefficient and caused doubt or hesitation. Such weaknesses would never do. The distracters forced her from that state of being. If she focused too much on the test, they'd kill her. If she focused too much on them, she'd never pass. It was all nonsense. If he explained it to her fifty times, she'd still think he was blowing smoke.

She hunched over the PDD. She could solve this problem. Perhaps, if she just…. But Carmen's thoughts were broken as she stopped a bullet in midair just before it hit her. She tried to not let it faze her; her mind was already running in circles, trying to remember how to solve the problem. It was then that one of Janus's earliest lessons came to mind. It was about doing without thinking about what you were going to do. He was usually referring to telekinetically snapping a man's neck as opposed to solving math problems, but whatever worked. She smiled as the answer appeared in front of her like magic. Then she casually batted one of the distracters' guns away with her hand. He fired anyway and just missed hitting one of his colleagues in the foot. Carmen didn't notice that part, though; she was on to the next problem.

This one was pretty easy, and she solved it in only a few seconds. The next was a different story. Her heart sank as she tried to comprehend it. It was only by minor miracle that she managed to avoid being shot again. She started tapping her finger against her desk. There was nothing else she could think to do. Carmen was well and truly stumped.

Well, maybe if I just... she thought, but then two of her distracters tried to take a shot. She ended that by telekinetically aiming their guns at each other. Then she gritted her teeth. It was hard enough to think as it was. Her head hurt so much from concentrating on the problem that she half wished the distracters actually would put her out of her misery. Seconds later, one attempted just that. Carmen foiled the shot by again holding the trigger open. She was a bit sick of them. They were just doing their jobs, but enough was enough.

A different distracter tried to shoot her, and she made her move. Her method was nothing sophisticated as she pressed all four distracters against the wall and held them there. They struggled against her power, but it would be no use; she could hold them for hours if she needed to. She sighed contently. Scratching a hard-to-reach itch was always satisfying. Then Carmen got back to work, never noticing her handler's raised eyebrow.

Minutes passed. Carmen sat hunched over her PDD as the air filled with the groans of the distracters struggling against the unnatural and tangibly felt will of an eight-year-old girl.

Janus glanced at his watch. "Time," he said.

Carmen leaned back and pushed the PDD away. He picked it up.

"You passed," he said.

She smiled broadly for the briefest of instants. The expression died, however, when Janus looked at her. She glanced away and then stood. He only shook his head, which prompted a quizzical look from Carmen.

"What about them?" he asked casually, pointing to the distracters.

Oh, yeah, Carmen thought. She released them without pause and then turned to her handler, not registering their groans and muttered curses.

"If you do that, it kind of defeats the point," Janus said. It was as much a question as it was a statement.

"The point is to pass the test, right?"

"In a manner of speaking," he replied.

Carmen nodded. "Well, I needed to concentrate harder on the test, so I dealt with them. They shouldn't have pointed guns at me in the first place or gotten in my way. They know what I am," she said, quoting his nonsense back at him. She didn't believe a word of it, but if luck was on her side, it would at least shut him up.

Janus looked at her hard for a long while before he spoke again. "Indeed," he said simply. "There is one more lesson for you today then."

He left the room with no further words. Carmen, close behind, had to fight a smile. It worked! In fact, he didn't even offer a counterargument. She wasn't foolish enough to think this would be the start of a trend, but she'd take what she could get. She made sure, however, to wipe any elation from her face before Janus could notice.

The two of them entered an elevator and dropped off on the floor they had been on previously. Carmen knew that meant only one thing: there was more fighting in store for her. Each floor seemed to have a dedicated purpose. The fighting rooms were on one, the classrooms on another, and the dorms on yet a different floor. She really did hate fighting. It was a waste of time. Unfortunately, it seemed like she'd have to put up with more of it before she was done for the day.

They entered a room that was the same as every other fight room. Janus didn't say anything; he just walked to a corner of the room to observe her. Carmen got ready. As usual, she had no idea what would come for her. The door burst open, and two terran Constructs ran toward her. She sighed as she wondered what the point of the exercise was. They couldn't beat her. They couldn't even really press her—not anymore.

The Constructs covered the distance in all of two seconds, but it seemed like an eternity to Carmen. She nonchalantly raised one of her hands. To the outside observer, the movement happened in a flash. Carmen, however, took a moment to revel in the energy gathering in every fiber of her being before it was focused and finally unleashed through the palm of her hand. The raw power was only slightly reduced by her internal resistance, and the beam of heat was a dull red. She didn't need much; the Constructs weren't wearing any armor. The beam hit her first target in the chest and burned a hole straight through him, continuing on to ablate the padding on the wall. The Construct fell over, his momentum sending his body sliding a few feet before finally coming to rest.

Her attack couldn't be carried on to his counterpart, as he was too close to her. It wouldn't ultimately matter, though. The Construct lashed out with a punch. She dodged out of the way, and he broke every bone in his fist against the wall. The damage to his hand didn't slow him down, and as he grabbed her with his other hand, Carmen could only shake her head. This was an especially stupid Construct.

Any other time, she took in the various energies of the world around her, enjoying them and using them as she saw fit. Now the process was reversed. She allowed her inborn discipline and reserve to fail. There was no focus to her power anymore; there was just power. Arcs of electricity rippled across her body, and her eyes glowed a bright silvery blue. The room filled with the rancid smell of the Construct being cooked alive as her current flowed through him. His grip on her tightened, a byproduct of every muscle in his body seizing. Then, all at once, it stopped. The Construct fell to the ground, dead, and Carmen looked down at his twitching body. She always hated doing that. The inefficiency grated on her nerves.

Just then, three more Constructs ran into the room. She punched the first in the head, her remaining charge causing a large spark on impact. It was a dramatic display, though of moot consequence, as her fist struck with enough force to send pieces of his skull flying across the room. Carmen frowned. She didn't mean to be so messy; it just happened from time to time. She telekinetically cleaned the blood off her hand before breaking the leg of a Construct as he tried to kick her. She answered back with a kick of her own to the head. The force was a bit more modest this time, granting death not by crushing his skull but by simply disconnecting it from his spinal column.

The third Construct gave no pause at the fate of his comrades. His dim mind probably wouldn't even notice or care if he was set on fire. She was tempted to do just that. She hated them—hated them all. They were such pathetic creatures. She may as well be fighting her dolls. The Construct tried to punch her, and she moved out of the way with almost playful ease. Then Carmen ended the contest with a single blow to his chest. She sighed. Her fist had penetrated a good inch or two into his body and was again covered in blood.

She kept that in mind as yet another wave of Constructs rushed toward her. She felled the first two by telekinetically snapping their necks. The next two she smashed together in midair. The last she finished by physically throwing into the wall behind her. His momentum, combined with a few hundred thousand pounds of telekinetic force, was enough to create a crater on impact. This came as a bit of a surprise. She'd been banging on the walls for years and didn't think they could be damaged. When she turned to face her next opponents, she got an even bigger surprise when there was only one Construct to offer a challenge. Didn't Janus see that they'd have to send dozens upon dozens of those things for her to even break a sweat? Yet a part of her, deep and largely forgotten, screamed a whisper that went unheard.

The Construct approached her in a tight guard. Carmen didn't waste her time with such things—not with Constructs. It was then that she noticed this robot was different from all the others. His eagerness waned as he paused and surveyed the death in the room. Horribly broken and mangled Constructs were strewn about, the usual result after an asset like herself exercised in one of the fight rooms. She didn't know what to make of his countenance. Constructs didn't have countenances. How was she able to sense a mood that wasn't supposed to exist?

The realization was off-putting. She could practically taste his anxiety. He moved closer, tentative and cautious, like he was trying to feel her out. Unlike him, all the Constructs she had ever fought had been stuck on kill mode from the gate. Her unease seemed to bolster her opponent, and as he tried to punch her, confidence gathered behind the blow. The

Construct's spirits rose ever higher as a kick grazed her cheek. *Spirit?* A Construct having spirit was like a ghost trying to buy a suit.

Carmen soon had enough. This was almost embarrassing. The Construct tried to punch her again, but she blocked it hard, and his arm fell, limp and broken. She followed up with a punch to the face. It wasn't as forceful as she could have made it, but it was enough, and the Construct staggered backward from the impact. Then she felt something new.

It had been a while since she had sensed it in another person, but she was certain what it was: fear. She was also certain she was the cause. Her every move caused the feeling to ebb and flow like a kite on the wind. The Construct could barely move now, let alone defend himself. She watched him in curious amazement. No other Constructs appeared to be forthcoming, and Janus made no move to intervene. She had a bit of time.

Her opponent didn't say anything. She had long been of the mind that Constructs couldn't or didn't know how to talk, yet he groaned from time to time as he cradled his rather grievous injures. No one had ever hit her that hard, so she didn't know how she'd take it herself. The Construct appeared just short of crippled. She raised her hand to scratch her nose, and his anxiety increased tenfold. *Strange*, she thought. She dropped her hand, and that same anxiety lowered as well, though not by much.

When she cocked her head to the side, she felt his fear burble. She took a few steps back and it dropped. She took a step forward, and it rose so quickly that it was almost an explosion. She didn't exactly know what to think. He was like a puppet on a string. Everything she did or even didn't do affected him to magnified level. She couldn't say she was unaware that she caused as much in the world around her, but she had never noticed it so clearly before. Carmen decided she'd had enough of this and prepared to put him out of his evident misery.

As she walked toward him, he tried to slink away. It was no use in his condition, though. His thoughts were wild and raging to the point that she found it hard to focus through the noise. He slouched in a pathetic heap, trying to stay live for just a few seconds longer. He spat blood and his legs wobbled under him, and in that moment, he looked at his soon-to-be killer. The Construct didn't speak, but in his biologically engineered eyes was a plea. Carmen knew it without even reading his thoughts. She was sure she'd given the same look to Janus on more than one occasion.

The soft whisper, there and not there, like voice lost in howling wind, redoubled its efforts, but she ignored it. Then she telekinetically closed his eyes and snapped his neck without a second thought. What happened next was not just a pinprick on her consciousness; it was more like an atom bomb. She saw white, and her fingers went numb for a moment or two. The Construct was dead, yet he remained in her mind like a bad smell. Carmen's stomach churned as she grew nauseous. She clenched her teeth and fought against it, and it slowly ebbed away, though not completely.

Janus walked toward her. "You seem troubled, 111724."

"No," she said defensively.

"Hmm, interesting," he muttered. "Well, if you're not troubled, I require you to remember one thing. The power you wield is extraordinary. Accordingly, the consequences for using it are equally extraordinary. If this is not borne by you, it will surely be by others. There is nothing you can do to prevent this, just like there is nothing an elephant can do to avoid trampling flowers underfoot. You should always be mindful of this."

Carmen nodded glumly.

"Are you sure you're not bothered?"

"No," she said more forcefully. "The flowers should move out of the way if they don't want to be trampled," she said, trying to repeat his mantra back at him. "Nothing you're saying is my problem."

"It's not?" Janus asked.

"No."

"You are powerful, 111724, but you are no match for the entire galaxy, nor even a small town that has decided it doesn't want to be trampled. Even if you were, you could not continue completely unmarred. There are few who can, and trust me, you don't want to be like them.

"I assume you saw something like a flash when you killed the last Construct," he continued. Carmen didn't say anything. "He was different. I'm sure you've realized that by now. He felt pain. He was self-aware. He had hopes, dreams, so on and so forth, like any other person. You can consider the flash you saw as sort of a psychic shockwave or one last scream. It grows in strength in proportion to the mind that produces it.

"Remember your lessons of thermodynamics, 111724," he said. "Mentally, we are all energy, just like a stick of dyna-mite or a star. When we're snuffed out, we don't just stop; the explosion is perceived as grief. There is no defense against it and no avoiding it as a Clairvoyant. Our abilities put us closer in touch with others whether we want to be or not. The effects are cumulative, like a building repeatedly bombed. You will remember each and every death or hurt you cause, probably for the whole of your life. And sometimes the weight of one can be too great to bear. It takes a very…*special* type to not be affected by it. Most refer to them as sociopaths, but we call them type ones. You, at least according to your personality profile, are a more sensible type three. And it didn't affect you?"

Carmen was quiet for a short moment. Her skin tingled. She didn't know her face was pale as well. She looked at Janus until she noticed one of his eyebrows rise. She turned away sharply. It was then that she realized there was a tear in her eye.

"What about all that stuff you say about *taking care* of someone who gets in my way?" she asked. "And bending the world to my will?"

"Everything has its price, 111724. We all create our own worlds, whether we realize that or not. That's your choice, just like it is mine. There is no choice, however, as to whether we live in it. Even Clairvoyants must account for their actions. Your power simply magnifies the outcome of your will to more than your immediate environment. And that power will set the course for many."

Carmen turned around. She was always loathe to show him her back, but in this case it was better that than him seeing her tremble. "That's..." she started, but her voice quivered.

Carmen looked at all the constructs all around her and the *different* one at her feet. It was at that moment that she also noticed the smell of burned flesh and their bloody entrails splayed all over the floor. She had seen this before, but not when everything was quiet and she could really stand back and look. She wiped her face then turned to face Janus, who looked down on his charge. His eyebrow rose again.

"That's not what I meant," she said, her voice steady.

"What did you mean, 111724?"

"Why didn't you tell me?"

Janus slowly shook his head. She knew she shouldn't have asked. "Why didn't I tell the Clairvoyant that she affects more than what is in her small bubble? That other people and things can affect *her* as well?" he asked, though his questions were more statements than anything. "Now that you're aware, does it bother you?"

She looked at her handler, unsure of how to answer the question. It was hard to determine exactly what he wanted. When Carmen closed her eyes, she could still clearly see the vision of death all around her. She shook her head, pushing the image to the deep dark depths of her mind, where it could be forgotten. She hadn't done this. It wasn't her—it couldn't be her. Janus had made her do everything. Slowly, the revolting feeling that had gripped her ebbed away.

"No," she answered, opening her eyes.

Janus looked at her hard after she said that, but she remained stone faced. He nodded slowly, obviously considering something deeply. "Well, I think you've had enough for the day," he said after a quick grimace.

He then left the room, and Carmen followed close behind. They walked in silence as usual, but Janus seemed a bit different. He took an increased interest in her, glancing in her direction every now and then. She didn't know what he was looking for, but it couldn't have been anything good, knowing him.

After entering an elevator, they exited on the dormitory floor, as expected. They reached Carmen's room soon enough, and Janus opened the door. Mikayla leaped on her as soon as she could fit through, which was also typical. The German shepherd was as big as she was now.

"Down," she said harshly, pushing the dog to the ground. Mikayla whimpered.

"I'll come for you in the morning."

Carmen nodded, and the door closed. After a brief pause, she undid the tie in her hair and let it fall free. She then sat down and called Mikayla to her. She hugged the dog tight, as she often did at the end of her day. Her friend knew the routine, giving a sympathetic whimper and resting her head on Carmen's shoulder. The dog was always there for her, for however long she needed. Today was one day…it was every day. She was sure she would not remember it.

6

EDGE

Subject: 111724 Age: 12 Status: Naming

Janus had no particular like or dislike for most of his coworkers. They tried to make the most out of a job that was unfortunately as gruesome as it was necessary. The majority of the personnel who weren't Clairvoyants had wives, husbands, kids, or pets and could even be called good people, despite everything they did here. Janus wasn't sure where he fell in that measure, but most of the people he knew here were inoffensive. That most certainly wasn't all of them, though, and it always amazed him how they seemed to sniff him out.

"Everybody wonders," one of the dolts began. "Even you have to wonder, Janus. 111720 or 111724?"

"720 has been named. I think she's Artemis now," a different moron replied.

"Artemis?" the first imbecile said to herself. "That name doesn't fit at all."

Janus looked at them for a short while and couldn't help rolling his eyes. They weren't Clairvoyants—Clairvoyants didn't ask questions that were as irrelevant as they were stupid. In any case, the two were romantically involved in some way, and everybody knew it. They were inseparable, except whenever their legitimate partner stopped by for a visit. Janus didn't know their entire story, but he didn't care to learn it. He barely knew their names—Isabelle and Larry?

"So, what do you think, Janus?" Isabelle asked again.

Janus stared back at her. The gaze of a Clairvoyant usually caused the average person to wilt, but not this one. She was either too stupid or just didn't know better. He sighed. They were his pain at least once a week.

"I do not care," he said simply.

"I don't believe you," Larry replied.

Janus sighed again. Clairvoyants lied from time to time, just like everyone else. Lies could be helpful when the situation called for them. All the same, it was a bit much for these people to suggest they were worth the trouble.

"Everyone has wondered about them since they got here," Larry continued.

"I do not care if you believe me or not," Janus said. "I am not here to pit children against each other like wild dogs."

"But you shoot them, right?" the man more said than asked. "You torture them, keep them in cages, isolate them from everybody except their handlers, and force them to fight constructs. What difference does it make if they fight each other?"

"Yeah, besides," Isabelle added, "just think of the bets. Everyone wants to know who's better. It's not like they wouldn't fight each other—that's what they do. We wouldn't even have to prod them."

"Clairvoyants fight to the death," Janus said.

Larry shrugged. "So?"

Janus stared at them. "You two disgust me." He then stood and began walking toward the door.

Although Clairvoyants were the majority of the population in the facility, whenever one moved, attention was drawn to them. He, like all Clairvoyants, had learned to expect as much.

"No, wait!" both Isabelle and Larry said before he could leave the dining hall.

He turned to face them. "You may see no difference in what you suggest and what we do. Admittedly, we ride a very fine line. Everything that happens here, however, has a purpose."

"And what would that be?" Isabelle interjected with a dismissive tone.

Janus looked at her quizzically. "How can you work here and not know?"

"Yeah, yeah, we know," Larry began, answering for her. "To create an embedded and controlled population of Clairvoyants as a deterrent to invasion. We all know. But all you handlers do is hammer them all day. It won't make a damn difference if they fight each other. It won't mean anything to them."

Isabelle agreed, making an argument Janus paid no attention to. Larry's statement, idiotic as all of his statements were, got Janus thinking. But before he could make any conclusion, though, this conversation, such as it was, needed to end.

"I will not allow you or anyone to satisfy your curiosity at her expense," he said.

"But, Janus—"

"Do not speak to me again on this matter," he said firmly. Then, without waiting for a response, he left the room.

He walked down the hall, wishing he had a glass of water to clean the bad taste from his mouth. The dolts, however, weren't on the forefront of his mind.

"Won't mean anything," he said softly to himself.

The business here attracted all kinds, the noble and ignoble among them. Even those two understood the purpose of the facility, its mission. He wholeheartedly agreed with it, yet its meaning was a barely remembered fog. In this place, the halls and fight rooms, like everything ever created, were as much a servant of the Dark as the Clairvoyants trapped within them. And if the Dark did anything, it clouded its meaning and perpetuated itself.

He shook his head. There were times he wondered if it was the assets or their handlers who were really being tested. The assets were young; they just grew used to it after a while. The carefully constructed madness the handlers created was only Tuesday to their charges. The handlers were fully aware of every step along the path. The pitfalls and perils along the way served an ultimate purpose, but to whom and in what way? It was undeniable that the feedback loop from handler to charge was reflected back from charge to handler.

Janus focused on 111724 for a moment with that in mind. She wasn't very special. She was frighteningly strong, and a lot of people talked about her in conjunction with Artemis, but she wasn't all too unique or different. At least, that's what he thought, which made his task over the past year or so difficult. There was nothing about her for him to grasp onto in what would be one of his most unique responsibilities as a handler. She was smart; she knew her role and played it as well as she could. 111724 always gave just enough for what he needed and no more. Sure, she broke character every now and then, but it was an almost perfect performance. And that, in retrospect, could do.

He was almost to her now and could sense her power more and more with each step. It was subtle; even a Clairvoyant could miss it. All the same, there was no denying its potency. It was like watching the ever-darkening sky before a hurricane.

Janus arrived at her room now and opened the door. There she was, sitting quietly on her bed and reading a book. Mikayla lay beside her as 111724 casually played her fingers through the animal's fur. She was different from the little girl he had met more than six years ago, which was of course the point. But he remembered what she was, and the contrast between then and now was striking. She was in transition from what she was to what she'd eventually be, and for this one singular moment, he could actually *see* her.

She gave no reaction to the door opening. She could never sense him coming, and he had no idea why. Regardless, she seemed so calm and peaceful, if a little sad. She sported a few bruises from a hard fight the day before. The stress of her battles had long since morphed her body into that of a toned and athletic predator. Yet in her face, there was only a soft echo of the horrors of her life. His wasn't the only forging she was suffering either. Nature had its purpose, just as he did. Janus had even reduced the stress on 111724 to allow the onset of puberty. All things considered, nature looked like it would make her potent in more than one realm.

The girl in front of him, however, appeared to have no interest in the power and influence she'd eventually wield at her leisure. He didn't know if that was strange or not. There were adults who would kill to be half of what she was as an adolescent. Just then, she looked up at him and the moment was shattered. There was no visible change in her demeanor, but to Janus, it was like someone had turned off the lights in the room.

"111724," he said, "it is time."

She never complained, at least not anymore. What she did do was tie her hair back in a ponytail, and just like that, her facade was complete. She was focused, disciplined; there was nothing free or extraneous about her now. 111724 was exactly as he wanted her to be: an indestructible monster that only knew purpose. He wished he could break her of that. In linear time, he knew her better than even her parents did. He had been around her all day, every day for the past six years. Few in her life would ever be able to boast as much. Janus, however, didn't *know* her—not really. She hid from him, and all he could see were glimpses of her here and there. He tried not to think about it for the moment, though. Today was a special day.

He left the room, and 111724 obediently followed him out as she always did. The lights shut off behind them, and the two conducted themselves in their normal routine. 111724 knew well what was expected of her. That knowledge had penetrated nearly every aspect of her psyche, coloring how she spoke and directing how she moved. It was subtle yet quite apparent for someone who knew what to look for.

She was graceful. All Clairvoyants were graceful, but she was slightly more subdued than her peers, and Janus always found that curious. She never seemed to be a shy or with-drawn personality by nature, and there were distinct fits and spurts in which she was anything but. Most of the time, though, there was no swagger in her movement. There was no bounce, vivacity, or anything that could be considered distinctive. Janus had tried for years to coax that out of her. At this point, he figured he'd just have to live with it.

They entered the elevator as usual, but this time they exited on a floor 111724 had never been to before. It wasn't all too different from any other floor. The lack of decoration was par for the course, as was the lack of windows and most other things. 111724 knew something was different, though. She looked around the corridor before glancing hesitantly at her handler. Her display was a bit more inquisitive than normal, at least outwardly. She put a lid on it immediately, despite that Janus never said anything.

There was, however, one thing she didn't or couldn't hide. 111724 was nervous—maybe even scared. It would be hard for just anyone to tell, as it didn't appear on the surface. He probably wouldn't notice if he didn't know her so well. Her energy, even as she tried to diminish it, was a storming rage. She may as well be on fire. Now, though, it was vibrant in a different way. When someone walked past her, it didn't ignore them as it usually did. Instead, it nervously rose in almost violent protest before falling to its previous level once the person was safely out of sight.

Janus produced an effect in her that was just as pronounced but exactly opposite in magnitude. His every glance and even his every breath caused that same energy to shy away. 111724 shied away herself every now and then when she couldn't help it. Janus never thought he'd have such a hold on her at her age, but everyone was unique and responded differently. Some Clairvoyants were complete psychopaths; others were housecats. 111724 was a person just like anyone else, but for one of the most powerful beings in the galaxy to actually be frightened? Taken at face value, it was hard to believe.

111724 only grew more nervous with each step as they neared their destination. It was amazing how she could never read him, yet in the back of her mind knew when they were getting close to where he was taking her. He opened the door and they walked inside. 111724 was immediately pinned in place. She gave a questioning glance to Janus, unable to keep her composure. He couldn't remember the last time that had happened. She looked at the room again and then back at Janus. He waved for her to continue. Of all the things he'd told her, he never said curiosity was a bad thing.

There were hundreds upon hundreds of different rooms at this facility. They were all mostly the same, but not this one. This one was unique. It was hard to tell exactly how big it was at a glance. The room was purposely made to get lost in. Multiple paths, irregular and only rarely arranged in straight lines, wound through row after row of weapons. Janus had toured the place for hours and still found new secrets.

111724 probably knew all of that in the back of her mind. She took a moment to study a rather gruesome looking set of brass knuckles. She moved on after only a short moment. Her steps were tentative, yet, as amazing as it was, he'd say she had actually forgotten about him, if he didn't know better. She seemed to have no clear aim or destination, nor did she walk very quickly. Janus simply shadowed and watched. He doubted she had much interest in weapons; this was probably just the simple pleasure of seeing something new. The life of an asset followed a routine, even if he tried to mix it up and keep her off balance as much as he could. In that, this was not only something new but also something new that couldn't kill —unless, of course, static weapons could leap out of their display cases and attack her.

Her progression took her to a wall of axes. No single type of axe repeated itself, yet there were hundreds on display. Some had handles that approached and, in some cases, surpassed the length of her body. Different axes were far shorter. Their heads showed easily as much diversity. Carmen didn't know anything about axes, but she winced when she saw the head of one and thought of what it could do to a person's body. She had her fill of them about then and continued on to the clubs.

The first few were pretty straightforward: just wooden

sticks that were heavy on one end. They slowly got more and more sophisticated as she went. Like the axes before them, there were hundreds of kinds. Some were studded with spikes while others were surprisingly small. Either way, they were rather unimpressive weapons to her. Such brute force just didn't seem sensible. Perhaps, after years of killing scores of Constructs, she'd lost all respect for it?

She left that section without as much as a backward glance. Then she went on and on. The collection was almost unending. There were no clocks in the room and, for all that Clairvoyants innately knew, their sense of time remained pedestrian. Nevertheless, to say that hours passed was all too easy to believe. There were just so many and such different weapons. Some of the gathered arms were elegantly simple. A few were gruesomely exotic. None were ever repeated. Many she would be hard-pressed to describe if she were asked to. Then there was a transition from uniquely terran instruments to the alien.

The sorten weapons were the most savage of that group. They nearly approached their terran counterparts in some cases, but just nearly, and only here and there. Their most horrific implement, in her opinion, was what could best be described as a spear with many hooks well suited to turning internal organs into external ones. She didn't have to guess that either—the written description next to the weapon was quite clear on that point, and there was even a picture of a victim for further clarification.

The collection of alien weapons wasn't as exhaustive as it was for terrans, despite the standouts. The arms of the terrasaurs and Eternals weren't even included. Or perhaps, considering their respective cultures, there weren't as many alien weapons simply because they didn't make as many as terrans did?

Carmen was back in familiar company soon enough. The study piece was knives this time. She had some experience with them, always from the business end. Next to guns, they were the most popular weapon used against her, and like with being shot, she didn't think much about being cut anymore, even though it happened rarely. Usually, it didn't take much for her to turn the knife against whoever was wielding it— broken arms or wrists often preceded that. The body could only move so far in one direction.

She continued on after a quick backward glance at Janus. He still shadowed her, and she noted that he was being rather quiet today. It wasn't like he was ever a chatterbox, but now he wasn't saying anything at all. *Maybe this is some sort of test?* she thought. He didn't usually speak when she was being tested, but there was nothing here for her to be tested on. As a matter of fact, the room seemed rather meaningless to her. Still, she wasn't complaining. It was somewhat interesting in its own way. She had no particular care for weapons, but she'd never thought there were so many different kinds.

Next were swords, though several blurred the line between what could be considered a sword and a knife. She had long figured there was some purpose for each weapon to be the way they were. It would be hard to believe there wasn't some overarching reason as to why some weapons went from broad, blunt tips to narrow, tapering points and back again and why some axes required two hands and others only one. The variations between one weapon and the next were just as distinct and indistinct as faces. On the surface, or even far away, they all looked the same. Conversely, upon closer inspection, sometimes it was the subtle differences that gave each its character. Janus had taught her long ago that few things existed to simply exist. There was some reason for their design, even if she, or anyone else for that matter, didn't know it.

Carmen took the time to survey most of the many swords, not because of an abundant interest but because the more time she spent in here, the less time she spent elsewhere. She had never liked fighting, school, or pretty much anything else she did here. Some of the swords were honestly weird. She didn't think a wavy edge would contribute much, but what did she know? Her eyes rested on hundreds of the things. After a while, she no longer noticed the nuances of each; they simply blended together. At this point, she was just walking through the room to walk, but she still made a heroic effort to look at everything. Janus followed closely behind, and she'd rather not leave. Then she stopped.

What drew her attention for the moment was a longsword—more than one. It was hard for her to say why these weapons caught her interest more than the others, as longswords were simple looking devices. It wouldn't be a stretch to say they were little more than sharpened steel bars. But they were more than that. Like their peers, there was purpose in their design. She didn't fully know what that purpose was, but she could sense it faintly. They were so very simple yet utterly sophisticated at the same time. That aspect of their character was quiet—most would miss it upon first glance. She would be the first to admit that she couldn't fully grasp it, but it was plain as day in front of her. The weapon was perfectly made to do what it was designed to do and nothing more. That was the dominant trait of all the weapons in this room.

Janus walked up beside her. When he pulled a footlong metal cylinder off his belt, Carmen's first instinct was to move away from him. Anything he produced usually had an ill effect on her health.

"This is a Taper," he said, "the preferred weapon of a tele-kinetic."

Carmen looked at it and was unimpressed. It didn't even look like a weapon. Janus seemed to sense this, but he didn't say anything. Instead, he telekinetically held the weapon away from his body. He then spun it until loud cracks graced the air, and the weapon extended to its full length. He stopped it spinning, and she could see it was now almost as long as he was. Each end of what had been the cylinder, which was now a shaft, tapered to a sharp point. Janus raised the Taper over his head, guiding it with his palm, and then spun the weapon again. As before, there were several loud cracks, but the sound blended into one loud noise after a short moment. He finished his demonstration by placing the weapon back on the ground. All throughout, he never physically touched it.

He motioned for Carmen to extend her hand. She did so hesitantly. When he placed the weapon on her open palm, she would have dropped it if but for telekinesis. It was ridicu-lously heavy. At its widest point, its diameter had to be no bigger than her forearm, but she wouldn't be surprised if it outweighed her significantly. Physically, she didn't have the strength to hold it. Telekinetically, however, it was no great task. She levitated it above her palm and spun it slowly, just to see what it was like. As she did, she thought about her physics classes. The Taper was heavy, but there was no real limit to how fast a Clairvoyant would be able to wield it. She considered those two aspects and then cringed when she thought about the potential damage from a full-speed hit. She handed it back to Janus, who telekinetically collapsed it back to its original size and put it away.

"As I said, the Taper is the preferred weapon of the tele-kinetic, if they wish to use a weapon." He gave a passing glance to the swords. "But your personality profile said you'd prefer a long-sword…. I guess it's no surprise you found your way here."

Carmen looked at the swords as well for a brief moment before turning back to her handler. Janus didn't look at her. Instead, he slowly scanned the room.

"When we were being trained by the sortens, they didn't know what to make of us," he began. "They didn't exactly know what they were dealing with, much like we still don't. They knew nothing of human nature. They just knew that if they were especially brutal to terrans, a small number of them would manifest a curious control and understanding of energy. Understandably, their methods were harsh—unnecessarily so. I won't bore you with stories, but suffice it to say the first of us didn't last long. They were either driven insane or suicidal by the training, or their bodies simply failed."

He looked at Carmen in that moment and she felt uncomfortable under his gaze. There were few times when she was ever comfortable around him. It was hard for her to think that he had gone through the same thing she had—and that it had been worse. She'd never really thought about it before; she just assumed Janus had popped out of an egg, or something, exactly the way he was now. It was a bit much for her to think that her handler had been *created*, so to speak. At some point in time, he could have been crying in a cell of a room, much like she did.

"They never called us Clairvoyants either. We were referred to as 'Energy Projectionists' or as 'Special Terrans.' 'Clairvoyant' was a term we coined for ourselves. At times, I guess it is a true descriptor. I think it helped us to believe we knew more than our masters—that we had some power over them, even if we never did. Few of us knew our real names. Much like you, we were separated from our families at a young age, and much like you, our masters gave us numbers, not names. Out of necessity, we had to give each other names for the brief times we were allowed to socialize. It is difficult to describe a person or even a thing with just a number."

He looked around the room again. Carmen looked too, but she wondered what she was supposed to be watching for.

"There are thousands of weapons in this room," Janus said. "They are shaped by purpose and function, and that shape—that reason they were forged in their unique manner—gives them their history. They cannot escape the roles they were literally cast in. It defines them. Each and every one has a name, save one." He looked at Carmen as he spoke. "You hide from me, 111724. At least, I thought you were hiding from me. You are one of the most powerful Clairvoyants to have ever lived, yet you barely use that power. Or, at least, I thought that was the case. You are difficult because you are exactly what you appear to be. I assure you that is rare. You know the limits and give exactly that and no more, not because the limits are yours but because no more is required. I don't know if you do this consciously, or if it's an intrinsic part of your character, but in either case, you know the Edge, and that can do as a name."

7

CLAIRVOYANT AT LAST

"She's like a machine."

That truth was so obvious that no one bothered to nod in agreement. Edge, as 111724 was now called, took to her new toy well. Like all Clairvoyants, she needed no formal training; the knowledge to kill just came naturally. It made no difference if was death by fist or the long-sword she was now wielding, and no one knew how or why that was. The end results, however, were painfully obvious for all to see.

Carmen never thought about any of that. She winced as another Construct fell before her. Janus had been true to his word. After that horrible day, each and every one of her challengers had a full psyche, and she felt each one cry out just before she ended them. The feeling was unpleasant enough to buckle her legs when it caught her off guard. At minimum, her fingers would go numb. She shuddered to think of what a *real* person's death would feel like.

The sword did make a Construct's passing quicker, though, and it did more damage than her fists could ever hope to. The weapon was odd in a way. It wasn't a part of her, and there were distinct times that it was annoying to have to work around its natural limitations, yet she could feel her energy working through it. There was always a small grin on her face as she swung the sword, momentum gathering on the tip of the blade. The simple physics of her instrument magnified her power almost like magic. Sure, the sensation of the Construct's death shortly thereafter couldn't be described so lovingly, but everything before that was gravy.

Her fingers still tingled as technicians entered the room to remove the bodies of her victims. She didn't watch the process. She didn't even think about it, or much of anything else. Really the only thing on her mind was how many Constructs it would be today before they'd let her leave. These trials had long become a ridiculous routine to Carmen. All she was doing was going through the motions.

When she heard a technician vomit, she sighed. This cleaning would take longer than usual. Her fingers impatiently tapped the wall, now that she was able to fully feel them again. How the technicians were routinely unable to stomach the gore was beyond her. She saw it and was sometimes literally covered by it every day, and she was perfectly fine. Carmen couldn't help rolling her eyes when her thoughts went to how Mikayla would sometimes shy away after sniffing her. She didn't know what the problem was; she cleaned up before going back to her room, for all the good it did.

Her eyes turned to her handler, who never said or did anything, as usual. He just watched her work. She couldn't remember the last time he'd even given her any pointers about her performance. He told her to start and he told her to stop; there was nothing in between. It was hard to guess why that was. She didn't think she was perfect, and Janus had said as much more than once. Nevertheless, the criticism had dropped sharply since he named her.

Edge. She couldn't say she hated the name. She liked her real name better, of course, even if she hadn't heard anyone say it in years. All the same, if it came between being called Edge and 111724, she'd rather not be a number. The reason was hard to give words to.

The technicians finished clearing the room, and her next opponent appeared. She sighed again. He was wearing hard armor and was also armed with a knife. Janus had said it was only proper for a Clairvoyant to use a weapon if their opposition was also armed and to fight barehanded otherwise. It was something about respect and blah, blah, blah, nonsense factor times three. She truly didn't care about the reason. But armor, particularly hard armor, she couldn't stand. Her sword was quite useless against it, and aiming for the ever so small gaps was such a pain.

Her raised hand sent of beam of heat straight through him without a second thought. Out of the corner of her eye, she saw Janus nod, which didn't mean much coming from him. Tea leaves were less cryptic. Approving or disapproving, it was always so hard to tell. Her analysis would have to wait, though, as two more Constructs were on her, also in hard armor.

She had less than a second, which was more than enough time. Carmen raised her arm and sent another beam of heat racing across the room. When the energy found its mark, however, it splashed off the Construct like water. She swore. Not only were the Constructs in hard armor, they were also shielded. She couldn't help giving Janus an annoyed look, despite the axe swinging toward her face. Unsurprisingly, there was no reaction on his part.

Fine, she thought. Her entire life had been nothing more than a game. Janus and everyone else said she was being tested, but it was just one big game. They'd change the rules and she'd adjust. They'd change the rules again and she'd adjust again. All day, every day, it was one big game. If these were the new rules, she'd play along. Even they knew she was just playing along. It wasn't like there was anything else she could do.

She dodged out of the axe's way easily enough, but the other Construct, also armed with a long-sword, required a parry to avoid. This would be difficult even for her. Sure, she could just telekinetically crush their heads, but that would be *disrespectful*, as Janus often said. No, no, no, not that! Killing them was fine, but not playing by the rules? Sacrilege.

The Construct with the axe came at her again while she contemplated that piece of pointlessness. She wasn't exactly ready for him. A forward flip corrected that, though, as well as put both Constructs on one side of her. The maneuver wouldn't have been possible without telekinesis, as she was off balance, but thankfully not all of her natural abilities were considered cheating. She needed them. The axe-wielding Construct's weapon was quite small, requiring only one hand. It was faster than her weapon could ever hope to be, but it did trade away reach to gain the advantage. Carmen had no qualms about exploiting that either.

She worked to keep that Construct at a distance while she fended off the powerful and accurate strikes of his counterpart. There wasn't much margin for error—she didn't wear any armor. She rarely did, and in those times its principal purpose was to stop bullets.

It didn't take long for her to tire of being on the defensive. Her first attack was a simple if violent affair. From the start, she had never used her long-sword the way non-Clairvoyants did. Most of the stances were the same, as were most of the cuts and thrusts, but beyond that, everything was different. She held the weapon weakly, not out of meekness but because she didn't really need to hold it at all. With telekinesis, the sword whirled around her with such speed, power, and precision that actually holding the thing was secondary. This time, the intent of her attack was not to kill, at least not to kill the Construct. His shield, however, was not long for this world.

The attack lacked any semblance of sophistication. She swung her weapon with every joule she could telekinetically apply. Her target was the head of the Construct armed with the long-sword, and to say she found her mark would be an understatement. The shield resisted the impact calmly enough. There was a loud bang when she hit, but it wasn't from the shield, which only flashed. The sword didn't fare as well. She hit as squarely as she could, but the weapon still bent and strained from the impact. If it was made from any material other than infinium, it would have snapped. Carmen gritted her teeth. She felt everything as the force of her own attack flowed back to her through her weapon. She couldn't be harmed by her own energy—no Clairvoyant could—but physics were physics, and its laws couldn't be broken. Well, sort of.

She had done exactly what she had set out to do and was now in a very bad position. The Construct's shield had fully blunted her attack. He wasn't even rocked. Worse than that, his shield wasn't down. Even worse yet, she was completely motionless. For one brief instant, her sword rested against the Construct before she could retreat and reset. She'd been in enough fights by this point in her life that the mere thought of being stationary produced an almost instinctual dread. The fear was well warranted. The other Construct exploited the opportunity, leaping on her without a moment's hesitation. Once again, she wasn't ready.

The Construct was coming from her left side, and the only way she could possibly defend herself was to lift her sword off the head of the Construct she had just attacked and then try her best to move it across her body for a badly positioned parry. There was another option, though. She could just go the other way around; a simple spin would do it. Clairvoyant or not, it was something she always loathed doing. She always *knew* where the Constructs were, but she preferred to use her eyes, and for a brief moment both Constructs would have her back as she spun. It was all a question of timing. Inches and fractions of a second were all she had. If it came down to her muscles, it would be hopeless. Then again, what hopelessness she suffered in her life had never been due to any shortcoming in ability.

She telekinetically lifted herself just off the ground and then spun in place. The room blurred and she let out a groan as, for one brief moment, she became a living gyroscope. Fighting against her own energy was never fun. All Clairvoyants hated it. And that was just the beginning.

Carmen stopped spinning just as quickly as she'd started. That was a mistake. She'd never had much that she could call her own. Sure, she was the one of the most powerful beings in the galaxy, as she had been told over and over again, but to say she had many great possessions was a joke. She had never wasted the time to think about it before. That was, until her little maneuver made her lose her balance. The room continued spinning, even though she was not, and the struggle to keep from falling over was only overshadowed by her outright war to not throw up. The move worked, though, and the rampaging Construct's axe was batted aside. She even took a moment to counter thrust. It wasn't the best idea either.

The Construct's shield resisted her attack so completely that the only thing she accomplished was pushing herself backward the length of her outstretched arms. Honestly, it was kind of comical. Two grown men hatched from test tubes were trying their best to kill her. If they succeeded, she'd be revived for them to try again a different day. She was almost completely unable to hurt them, and her attempt to stab one sent her sliding backward, as if she were standing on ice. Yeah, laugh riot of the century. No wonder they made her play this game.

Now, most hilariously, the other Construct's sword was rushing to remove her arms from her body. It was a simple counter. She physically let go of the sword while telekinetically holding it against the other Construct to keep him at bay. She didn't even have to step out of the way of the attacking Construct. His sword hit nothing but air, and now the tables were turned. She pointed both palms at his head and unleashed everything she had in two searing beams of heat. The roar was deafening, like a continuous clap of thunder. Their bright white light was blinding as well, but Carmen didn't notice. Clairvoyants couldn't be directly affected by their own energy. She also didn't notice that the temperature in the enclosed room was fast approaching the boiling point. Despite that, her opponent's shield held firm. She cursed the devices. It was no small bit of mercy that they were relatively rare.

The effort to sustain the onslaught started taking its toll. To date, she had never passed out from any fight. She'd been close, but no more than that. It wasn't like being knocked out or getting a torn muscle—those had happened quite a few times before. No, at best it could be described as trying to keep your eyelids open when you're very tired. It always began slowly. Her heat beams soon cooled to a very bright orange, though she didn't notice. Moments later, it became increasingly difficult to hold the Construct off with her sword. Those were all the clues Carmen needed to come up with a new plan of attack. She extinguished the heat beams as one would turn off a water faucet. Then she grabbed her sword and charged the Construct full on. He never saw her coming; her beams had been so bright that they melted his retinas.

An odd tickle coursed through her. At the same time, the room cooled faster than what was naturally possible. She was feeding on herself, gathering that which she had just spent, and focusing the energy on the tip of her sword. She screamed as she did it. This would hurt. Just before impact, Carmen lifted her target slightly off the ground. The shield would absorb most of her momentum, as it was designed to, but now it wouldn't stop her in her tracks.

The tip of her sword met that barrier with a bright flash, yet the drama was incomplete. The sword failed to penetrate anything, as she expected. What momentum she had left served to carry her shoulder into a thunderous collision with the Construct's chest. Carmen cried out. The shield provided no give, stopping her dead in place. But she wasn't done. Another telekinetic thrust sent she and the Construct sailing across the room. In that, she needed to be careful. Too much force would be blunted by the shield. Yet steadily, if quickly, it built. She glanced at the rapidly approaching wall and winced. This would hurt too.

The padding on the wall counted for nothing. Carmen, even with all her senses, didn't notice it. The wall crumbled as their two bodies slammed into it. The padding held mostly together, but the concrete behind it was violently ejected as the wall cratered. She groaned. She felt everything through her body. When she punched or kicked, she normally cushioned the blow with a wall of air. It had become a habit after several broken fists. There was no blunting this impact, however. She wanted to inflict maximum damage, and that had its price.

She momentarily went numb. Then there was a sharp pain. Something was broken somewhere. It wasn't the first time, of course, but breaking bones was never pleasant. Her vision blurred and her ears rang. She couldn't help falling to her knees afterward. The Construct fell over too. He was uninjured, but there was something different about him. … His shield was down.

Carmen wasted no time in getting back to her feet. She had wanted to end this before it even started, but he was still wearing that pesky hard armor. It also didn't help that she was so spent she felt very much like the twelve-year-old girl she was. He came at her, and it was by luck that she managed to parry the blow. Then it built. As Janus said, mind and body were a team. Admittedly, her mind wavered every now and then, but her body was a forged disciplined machine by this point. The pain fell away to nothing, and in seconds she returned to being the monstrous beast that had slain thousands.

The Construct's next attack she batted away with pathetic ease. He was literally swinging blindly, and a simple flick of her wrist almost ripped his sword from his hands. A hard hit to his head made him stagger. It was possible that a very hard telekinetically-amplified thrust could have penetrated his armor, but she didn't need all of that. She showed the Construct her palm and, moments later, burned a hole through him. He fell to the ground and soon died, and all that remained was his counterpart.

He still had his shield and was fresh, and his weapon was faster than hers. Moreover, she didn't want to go through all that nonsense again, so she chose guile instead of power. It would all happen so quickly that even her observers would be hard-pressed to say what, exactly, happened.

She rushed the Construct full on. Just running with her

muscles was a refreshing change after all that work with the prior Construct. Her opponent was waiting, braced, perhaps thinking she'd tackle him like she had his counterpart. The predictability of the attack also gave him an opportunity. His axe began rushing down to strike her head when the moment came, and she averted it by moving her sword across her body. That modest act also moved the Construct out of position. Unfortunately, she couldn't counterattack, but that wasn't the intention. In fact, she even let go of the sword. Then Carmen jumped—almost flew. Her momentum carried her behind him as she twisted in the air to face the opposite direction before telekinetically stopping her momentum to land behind him. Her sword flew back to her hand and, just like that, was pressed against his throat.

You could shake the hand of someone who was shielded. The system was smart. It wouldn't perceive something so innocent as a threat, just like it wouldn't perceive a relatively slow-moving piece of metal as a threat, even if it did have an edge. Thankfully, there was a gap in the Construct's armor just large enough for her to exploit. She held the sword against his throat in one hand, his head in the other, and pushed. The edge did all the work.

* * *

The group watched the monitors with held breath. It was hard to comprehend what they had just seen. It wasn't her cleanest fight, and there were times in which she was clearly pressed. But it gave them a glimpse. For several brief moments, Edge unleashed everything she had. Most of the readings were off the scale.

"Incredible…" one of them uttered.

More Constructs entered the room, and she dispatched

them with almost comical ease. She was like an earthquake or a tidal wave, inevitable and devastating. Janus could only shake his head as he watched.

"How does she look?" he asked through the intercom.

He preferred to be in the room with Edge whenever she was working, but there were advantages to being in the observation booth. Being able to see all the readouts was one. It took a moment or two for the technicians to get back to him.

"Off the scale," one of them finally said. "A bit inefficient, but still impressive."

"She's toying with us," Janus said after a few seconds of thought.

"What do you mean?"

He paused for a moment as Carmen killed another Construct. He doubted it ever crossed her mind that she wasn't the only one who felt them die. She was particularly brutal with that one, cutting him in half with her long-sword. And, unless Janus missed his guess, he swore he saw her smirk at the accomplishment. *She's never done that before*, he noted.

"The inefficiency," he said, trying to ignore the aberration. "She's not really trying. She's toying with us."

The technicians in the observation booth shared looks among themselves. Janus knew his charge better than anyone, but if she was holding back, just how much was left to be uncovered?

"Why would she do that?" one of them asked him.

Janus looked at one of the cameras that dotted the room, seemingly staring at whoever asked the question. He sighed. "Because Edge likes being particularly stubborn. That's just how she is."

"But Artemis had more trouble with two shielded and

armed Constructs. Edge can't be *that* much stronger than she is."

Artemis. Always Artemis, Janus thought. It had to be the biggest rivalry that never actually existed. They didn't even know each other. He could easily point out opponents that Edge had greater trouble dispatching than Artemis did, but what would be the point? At times, he wished they could fight each other just so everyone would shut up about them.

"I don't think she is," Janus said. "They're just two different people. According to her handler, Artemis toys with us by being excessively violent when we want her to show restraint. Edge holds back when we want her to *not* show restraint. It's nothing special. Lock someone in a cage their whole life and they'll think up small ways to defy you. Besides, they're getting to that age," he said.

He was happy he didn't have kids, let alone teenagers. Why people bothered was beyond him.

"So, what should we do?"

Janus's own words echoed in his head while he thought of his charge. *Edge holds back when we want her to* not *show restraint.* Except being "limited" was as much a part of her personality as water was wet. Even that small smirk, if he saw what he thought he had, was limited. It made her what she was. He'd even named her after it. She did what he expected her to do and no more. Until now, though, he had never really wondered why. Did one of the most powerful beings in the galaxy actually not know how powerful she was? He couldn't tell either way.

He watched the girl effortlessly slay a man twice her size, but this time the handler could only marvel at the thinly veiled vulnerability of her deadly machinations. No one else saw it— the two halves, each unknowingly in the service of the other. It was, however, the eternal quandary that had vexed Janus during the entirety of his time with her. He doubted she was even aware.

He thought about it. Then he thought about it some more. As his monster felled more Constructs, he was reminded of a kitten toying with a mouse. So unnoticed was her effort, he could almost see her eyes drift off into daydreams as her claws were soaked with blood. In the end, he guessed she just needed to grow up. His eyes fell in that moment. It was something he never wanted to do, but sometimes the method superseded the means.

"Send her in," he said.

Edge glanced in his direction at that. She even held it for a few seconds, which was rare for her. When he returned her gaze, she looked back at the door and waited patiently for whatever may come.

Carmen stared at the door and tried to forget what she had just seen. She swallowed nervously. She just couldn't believe it. If she didn't know better, Janus looked sad. It didn't appear to be sadness from pain, shame, or regret. He didn't seem depressed either, just sad, for one crystal-clear brief moment. Carmen didn't know what that meant. She'd always figured Janus's parents were stones; he certainly shared many of their traits.

Just then, there was another energy just outside the room. Constructs were dull, lifeless husks. Even the Constructs she fought that felt pain and fear and cried out when she killed them were barely more than that. This energy was greater than a thousand Constructs. It was vibrant, as all truly living things were, and it was growing ever greater.

The energy outside the room only increased in strength,

becoming more and more excited. Carmen's skin tingled. She glanced at her handler again and thought of all the times she'd been in this situation. A small fear was lit. A lifetime of torture, neglect, and hurt poured into every aspect of her psyche, making her feel suddenly weak. *This is it*, she thought. Whatever was behind the door was going to kill her, and this time they were going to leave her dead.

The door opened ever so slowly, creaking as it went. Three Constructs ran toward her. Carmen paused. She'd expected more, but that thing—that energy, that feeling—was still there. This time, the Constructs wore soft armor, a minor annoyance. She thrust through the first one with such force that he may as well have been protected by paper. As the construct fell away dying, she decided she'd had enough. There would be no more rules. Everyone in this facility wanted to kill her. They had always wanted nothing more than to kill her and break her—to end her as she knew herself. And she would do her best to make that goal very, very difficult. What could Janus do to her, anyway? Send her to bed without dinner? That would certainly bring her to tears.

She dispatched the other two Constructs by smashing them together and then flinging them into the nearest wall. A solid crunch filled the room when they hit. She dropped the next score by telekinetically snapping their necks. Yet more Constructs came. Perhaps she didn't sense one great energy. Maybe there were thousands upon thousands of Constructs hidden behind the door, and the mass was like one great cloud.

Either way, the arms and legs of Constructs that got too close quickly littered the ground. These ones could feel fear —she could almost taste it. With that in mind, a part of her hoped that, if she were gruesome enough, they would just leave her alone. Thus far, her theory was proving incorrect.

She felt a twinge of pity for them. It was a wonder exactly how they compelled the Constructs to attack her. The business of the fight rooms seemed to be a forgone conclusion by all involved, though. She had never seen it questioned or challenged by anyone. Indeed, the thought was quickly pushed to the back of her mind and forgotten.

She ripped a tooth out of one of the Constructs and used the hard little piece of enamel as a makeshift bullet. It zipped around the around the room at a speed too fast to see as dozens of Constructs fell over dead after a puff of blood from their head or chest. One Construct was lifted off his feet by the impact of the tooth hitting him square in the chest. It shattered and the fragments went on to imbed themselves in the Constructs unfortunate enough to be standing next to him. Carmen didn't mean for that to happen, but she'd take it. Even so, they kept coming.

She gave the lead Construct of the next group a hard look. It would be enough to make any normal person stop in their tracks, but not this one. A mere thought crushed him into a ball no bigger than the palm of her hand. The blood sprayed from his rapidly shrinking body like a fountain, and the entire room was painted with it, except for Carmen and Janus. The splash flowed around them to splatter the wall behind. Upon seeing that, the other Constructs did give pause for a moment. Her sword permanently ended their hesitation.

* * *

"Holy shit. She's like Artemis in there," one of the technicians uttered under his breath.

"Yes, it's quite impressive," Janus said, sarcastic. He doubted anyone picked up on it.

For all her power and all this fury, it was violence just for violence's sake. She was as aware of what she was doing as a boulder tumbling down a mountain. This was beneath her.

"Are you sure about this, Janus? Do you really want the two of them in there? If Edge goes all out, there may not be anything left," a different technician said.

He didn't give much consideration to the warning. That was the point. Besides, safeguards were in place. They always were.

"Is our girl ready?" he asked.

"Yeah. We'll be sending her out in just a few seconds."

"Excellent."

* * *

Carmen crushed a Construct's head, causing his eyes to pop out. It was always a rather disgusting side effect. In any case, that energy was still behind the door, undiminished despite all the dead Constructs. She slit the throat of her next opponent before slicing another in half. She didn't have much time to worry about the energy, whatever it was.

The door opened again, and she was ready. A Construct carrying a baseball bat rushed her. She let him hit her. There was a thunderous clap as the bat hit a wall of air, but her hair didn't even move. She responded by hitting him in the face with the hilt of her sword. Then, as the Construct staggered back, she cut him from shoulder to hip, splitting his chest open. The next Construct would have tackled her if she didn't telekinetically flick him out of the way. He hit the wall head first and slumped to the ground, never to get up again. A flick of her wrist disemboweled another. A kick, stepping in with her shoulder, and then another flick of her wrist cut a different Construct's face off. Another lunged at her. This one was fast; all she saw was the blur of its movement. But a half-spin on her part moved her out of the way and brought her sword down on the back of its neck. It was all so easy. She barely even saw the last one, and now its body and head were sliding in two different directions across the floor.

Just then, Carmen noticed the energy behind the door was gone. It wasn't dissipated or someplace else, it was just gone. *Odd*, she thought. Something like that didn't just disappear without a reason. As she thought back on the last few seconds, nothing stuck out to her. She did what she always did in these rooms: kill Constructs. Now that she was thinking about it, she wondered about that last one. It was very fast, and she never did get a good look at it. There was just a blur, and she reacted as she always did. No thinking, no worrying, and no hesitation—she had simply killed him.

As she thought about it more, Carmen was hard-pressed to say that the brief flash had even been a person. There was a growl from her subconscious and then a thought. It was of when she'd been trapped in here with that monster. Just thinking about it made her shudder. Janus had killed it, but who was to say there weren't more? They could be bred like the Constructs.

She turned around to make sure that it was truly dead. What she saw was far worse. Her entire body seemed to seize while, at the same time, she felt very weak. An odd pain rotted and festered in the pit of her stomach, and the sensation spread throughout her with each beat of her racing heart. She tried to speak, but her tongue was dead. The only sound she produced could best be described as a cross between a wail and a groan.

"Mi—" she tried again, but the festering rot had reached her throat, choking off her voice. It hurt to breathe.

She said it again, but the word was too quiet for anyone to hear.

"Mikayla," she finally muttered. "No…" she said softly as she went to her dog. "How…. How did this—"

There was nothing Carmen or anyone else could do. Mikayla was well and truly dead, and no magnitude of science or hope could change that fact. It had been a masterful strike. With one blow, she had severed the German shepherd's head from her body. The wound was frightfully clean, its effectiveness obvious for all to see. One of Mikayla's paws twitched at random intervals, but that was the only thing marring the utter precision of the girl's craft.

She fell to her knees and reached out to touch what was left of her former friend but stopped short. She wanted to— she desperately wanted to—but part of her feared what would happen. Her parents, the Constructs, Mikayla…. Intentional or not, Carmen had destroyed everything she had ever touched. The taint from her fingers could cause what was left of the dog to burst into flames, disintegrate, or who knew what. For the whole of her life, she had always wondered why people were wary of her, if not downright fearful. She had never had any friends, not really. She had always hoped that people just weren't used to what she was and that it would pass over time. It never passed, though, not even for her parents. As Mikayla's blood spread across the floor, Carmen began to understand why.

"Do you remember what I told you when we first met?" She looked up with a start to see Janus standing over her. "I said there is nothing that I will teach you. And I haven't. I can't even say I ever actually tested you. If I did anything, I merely gave you choices."

It didn't take Carmen long to realize that the reason she was in this room today had nothing to do with actual fighting. Tears welled in her eyes.

"You planned for me to kill her all along," she said. "From the day you gave her to me."

"I planned nothing," Janus said dismissively.

"But—" she tried to protest, but her handler cut her off.

"I engineer the situation. You ultimately choose how you respond to it. And that has and will always have nothing to do with me."

"But—"

"Edge, I have a specific purpose that serves one mandate," he said. "You are a monster created to give other monsters that would do us harm pause. Those were some of the first words I said to you."

"I'm not a monster," Carmen said quietly.

Janus sneered. "Yet…."

He looked at her and then at the bloody sword still in her hands. She didn't realize she was still holding it and dropped the weapon immediately. Her handler then looked around the room, and her gaze followed his, a half-step behind. The walls were painted red with her opponents' blood. Body parts were strewn about the floor. Bodies lay everywhere. There was no blocking the construct from her mind—not this time. She couldn't grit her teeth and ignore it. She couldn't fight and vanquish them all.

"Who was it that decided to use lethal force against your own dog? It was not I," Janus said as he walked slowly behind her. She heard his voice like an echoing whisper.

"You never needed to even fight back—not once in any of the fights you've ever had. You could have ripped the door off its hinges and walked straight back to your room if you wanted to. Few in this complex would have the means to actually stop you. Or you could have simply let them kill you. There's nothing I could do to take that choice away from you. I wouldn't even waste my time trying." He took a long pause before he spoke again. "You fight yourself, Edge. I have never known why, but you do. Still, you can't deny what you are. You are a monster like me, like all of us, and you always have been. Your choices over the years have only served to illuminate that fact."

Carmen closed her eyes and shuddered. He was right. As sure as she was breathing, he was right. It was obvious from the day she was born to all who had ever known her. She had kept her parents prisoners in their own home before she could even walk. Everyone in her neighborhood was terrified of her, even though she knew absolutely nothing about them. There may as well have been a sign in the front yard that said, "Beware of Clairvoyant."

She began to cry again. And the rot—that festering, ever constant rot—grew worse. In the back of her mind, she had always known. She had tried so hard not to be, but it never made a difference. Carmen remembered a time when she was younger and a boy her own age had been terrified after he accidently bumped into her. No matter how many times she said she didn't mind, he ran away from her. His parents ran with him. She could never be rid of all her talents and her ability. She reeked of them. That was their price, and it was too high. She hated herself for it. She always had.

"What happened to me?" Carmen whimpered softly, closing her eyes. "How…how did this—"

"Nothing has happened to you," Janus replied.

"No," she said sharply. "I…I couldn't have done this. I wouldn't do this. I don't hurt people. All I want is to go home. All I have ever wanted was to go home!"

Janus sighed before he spoke. "You should know more than anyone, especially now, Edge, that there is no such thing. There is no rest or relaxation. There is no salvation. There is only power and desire. And, considering how much power you have, if you ever truly wanted to go home, you would have by now. There is nothing standing in your way."

Carmen thought about what he said. At the same moment, her fingers tingled and she felt decidedly hot. "There's you," she said. She opened her eyes and stared at him. They glowed. "It has always been you. I may make the choices, but you don't give me any choice," she added as the lights in the room flickered wildly. She got to her feet. "You're my *handler*. You've known that all I wanted was to leave, but you kept me here. This is all your fault."

Janus looked completely unmoved. "If I have anything to do with you and your self, then remove me from your path as you did your dog," he said simply. "A lie will always remain such, no matter how much you believe it."

Carmen winced. His words stung. "Shut up!" she yelled as she hit him as hard as she could in the face.

It just happened. One minute, she was sitting on the ground crying; the next, he was staggering before her and her fist was throbbing. Carmen's mouth hung open in surprise. Janus had never lied to her; she had to give him at least that. When he said he was a monster, that was the straight truth. He was an unfeeling, inhuman, evil monster. She had lived in terror of him almost from the day she met him. And now, hard as it was to believe, she had actually managed to hurt him.

It was as if the sun turned black, water flowed uphill, or bricks had learned to fly. And in that unending quagmire, one last untouched piece of her let go. Until this point, she didn't even know it existed, but now, watching him, it screamed. The room cooled and even grew darker. A spark rippled along her arm, followed by another and then another until her body was consumed by them. The hair of people half a mile away stood on end. Nearer, several vomited. Scores of people outright fainted in the observation booth. Carmen, however, noticed none of this. Her sole attention was on Janus. She'd hurt him. It was a drop in the bucket compared to what he had caused her, and she wasn't finished.

"How do you like it?" she screamed. "Let's see you pass this test!"

She rushed him. There was no technique or focus to her attack; she simply leapt on him, bringing them both to the ground. Her hands wrapped around his throat.

"I hate you!" she yelled.

Janus didn't fight back. He didn't even try. He simply stared at her. Carmen stared back. She could have popped his head off with a thought, but she wanted her muscles to do the deed. She squeezed as hard as she possibly could. She'd never get her life back, but she wanted to feel his drain from his wretched body with every fiber of her being.

"I hate you!" she yelled again. "I hate you! I hate you! I hate you! Why me? Why did you have to do this to me? I didn't have to be here!"

Out of the corner of her eye, she saw the body of a Construct and then Mikayla. She focused in on Janus and tried to ignore them, but she couldn't completely. He was almost gone, and realizing that filled her spirit with joy. The feeling washed over her like warm honey. She wanted to kill him. She wanted to hurt him—badly. Yet there was another part of her, long unseen and almost forgotten. She was surprised it still remained in her. It whispered one thing so softly that it was a miracle it could be even be heard. But hear it she did, and it reminded her of one important thing she was terrified to admit. That, while what she was feeling was devil-ishly sweet, it was not a flavor that was meant to be enjoyed. No matter how much she wanted to outright kill her handler, and no matter how easy that would be, she couldn't. She wouldn't allow herself to—not anymore. She couldn't blame this all on him. She couldn't innocently say it wasn't her fault. This would be her choice, and for the first time, Carmen was aware of it.

Janus was right. He'd never lied to her. There were no obstacles in front of her. At least, the obstacles were not this place, the Constructs, or Janus himself. It was just her. It had always been just her. No matter how long she lived, how many excuses she came up with, or how many opponents she slew, her one and only obstacle would always be herself.

Her grip on Janus's throat began to slacken. Suddenly, the door burst open and several armed soldiers ran into the room. They pointed their guns at her and fired even before her telekinetically amplified reflexes could react. Their weapons, however, didn't fire bullets. Instead, a thick, sticky foam struck her with enough force to blow her off her handler before nearly entombing her to the adjacent wall. She struggled against it, but it wouldn't budge.

"Are you all right, sir?" one of the men asked.

Janus coughed a few times before he answered. "Yes, I'm fine."

But the men didn't pay him much heed. They swapped out their foam guns for guns that did fire bullets and leveled them all on Carmen, who still couldn't move.

"What about her?" one of them asked.

Janus looked at Carmen. She stared right back. Neither wavered, withered, or made any reaction at all. They just stared. He was sure that had to be the first time she didn't shy away.

"She won't give you any trouble," he said. "Take her back to her room."

8

CARMEN VS. EDGE

Days, weeks, months—Carmen had no idea how much time passed. The hours blended together into a never-ending loop she could not escape. She spent most of the time crying. Try as she might, she just couldn't stop. She'd have a respite of a few seconds every now and then, until an old memory or unwanted feeling got her started again. After a while, she cried just because she was crying, and then she no longer knew anymore. It was like she'd been lost in the dark for so long that she'd forgotten how to see the light. Her only rest came when she was too exhausted from it all and passed out from the effort.

* * *

Janus sat in the dining hall alone. The idiots hadn't graced him with their presence for quite some time. He did not know why; until recently, he couldn't escape them, even to the point that he considered making threats of bodily harm so they'd leave him alone. But lately, nothing. It was possible they thought the question of who was better, Edge or Artemis, had been answered. He had finally broken his charge, and what remained couldn't be called impressive. Maybe everyone had forgotten about her? He hadn't. Janus had not seen her since that day, but he never could forget her.

* * *

Carmen felt so weak. Even sitting up in bed was a struggle. Her captors weren't completely inhumane and brought food regularly. She hadn't had the heart to eat any of it, though. Most of the time, she didn't even notice it was there, let alone that someone came in to drop it off. She had perceived the room and everything in it only faintly. Food was the furthest thing from her mind, but now she could eat a few bites. The effort took her all, and she threw it up more times than not, but she could eat. Each morsel always tumbled down her throat, echoing as it went. It was in those moments that she was perversely aware of her own body. It was a wonder if she even existed at all.

Now that she thought about it, her room was deserving of that same question. There was nothing in here that she had ever asked for or wanted. Her books, toys, couch, and table were merely ornaments meant to sooth her nightmare of a life. All of it had nothing to do with her. She remembered what her old room had been like, if barely. It wasn't much, but it had been hers, decorated how she wished, stocked with what she liked, and given character by the limited means to fulfill her growing tastes. Her present living quarters were as much a construct as the shells she constantly fought.

She sat in bed with her head spinning and face wet. She was too weak to stand for more than ten minutes without falling down, yet she crushed her chair into dust with no more than a thought. She telekinetically threw her table into the wall hard enough to turn it into splinters. It was dark in her room, yet she felt each falling particle like they were crashing boulders. Her attention turned to her toys and they were burned to ash. Her books became confetti. On and on she went until there was nothing left. Now her room was properly empty, as it had always truly been. She looked in the dark where Mikayla usually sat, yearning for the comfort of her resting on her shoulder. But Carmen had to reminder herself —the room was empty.

* * *

Several people left the dining hall all at once. Janus did not know why, but he didn't care. He was still lost in his thoughts. If there was one day that would forever be seared into his memory, it was when he first met Edge. She was not what he expected. The briefing he'd gotten beforehand and the personality profiles could only say so much, especially at her age. What exactly he had expected was hard for him to remember. Everyone feared something more violent and savage than the average Clairvoyant. Maybe a child that bordered on the inhuman; perhaps some kind of beast? All that power had to have colored her psyche in some way. It certainly did now. But the reality of Edge and the figment of everyone's imagination that predicted what she would be couldn't have been further apart.

It had started before he could even see her house. Her power had manifested itself faintly in the distance, like a star that was only a point of light in the night sky. Clairvoyants had no command of gravity, but to say they weren't falling deeper and deeper into her well as they went would be a stretch. The Clairvoyants that had been with him were weaker than himself, and their hair stood on end miles away. The sensation was blunted for Janus. If anything, the girl's energy was a curious thing. The spectacle was much the same as watching a waterfall or an erupting volcano. It was power—raw power. Even the non-clairvoyant members of his team, who were dim to such things, could sense it on the approach.

He remembered wondering what could remain in the face of such destructive potential. It was not that Edge's personality profile implied that she was inherently violent, but she was a child, and the potential was always there. A bath unwanted or a cookie ungiven was all it took to make tempers flare. There were all kinds of monsters.

* * *

Isabelle couldn't help a small smile. It had taken months and months and months. There were countless bribes as dozens of people were shuffled to new jobs to ensure that only those who wanted this to happen remained. Now the day had finally come. Her plotting surely rivaled that of Admiral What's-His-Name—Carsono Wright, or something? It was such a weird name. Anyway, the last and hardest piece had always been getting that watch dog, Janus, away from Edge. Monetary coaxing aside, almost everyone else was onboard from the start, even Artemis's handler. He went as far as to say that he didn't know what Janus's problem was and that the *assets* wouldn't care either way.

She was apt to agree. It also helped that she was set to make quite a bit of money from the endeavor. Artemis was a killer in the truest sense of the word. The facility never went on lockdown whenever Edge was moved. Sure, she was strong, but at this level it all came down to instincts, and Edge's would make her nothing other than dead meat. It was possible Janus knew that and that was the real reason he didn't want them to fight. *What difference does it make?* Isabelle thought. Clairvoyants died all the time in forging. Sure, not all of them were able to be reanimated, and it would be a pity if that happened to Edge. Still, it wouldn't be out of the ordinary for this place.

Isabelle sighed. Janus could be so stupid sometimes. She'd even say that to his face if he wasn't a Clairvoyant. On second thought, he probably knew what she thought about him anyway. She tried not to think about *that* and its implications. Instead, she thought on how she'd spend her winnings. She smiled again. It wasn't going to be just in bets either. She planned to sell the video to the highest bidder if the fight was a hit. Even the UTE would probably want it. No one had ever seen two Clairvoyants with this level of power fight each other before. Some of the scientists in the facility salivated at the thought of studying the data.

Just then, the thought of those riches, not to mention fame, didn't produce the warm, tingly feeling it usually did. She felt decidedly uncomfortable in her own skin all of a sudden. Sweat beaded on her forehead. It became ten times worse when the elevator opened to the dormitory level. Isabelle had never been on this floor before, as it was usually reserved for each asset's respective handler and the janitors. Edge's room wouldn't be too hard to find, though. And it didn't take a bribe to get a key to her room, just front row seats.

Walking down that hall may have been the hardest thing Isabelle ever did in her life. A small pit in her stomach felt heavier and heavier the closer to Edge's room she got. The sensation made no sense. Even so, she slapped her hand to her mouth several times to keep from throwing up.

"I was fine this morning," she muttered to herself. *It has to be something I ate*, she thought.

The feeling didn't get better. Instead, it got much, much worse. She felt weak, and her legs seemed like they were made of rubber, as if some force had sucked the energy right out of her. It was only the knowledge of all the money she'd make that kept her from running back into the elevator and never coming back. Her hand practically shook as she opened Edge's door. There was nothing she could think to do to stop the tremors. Her fingers were numb. Her hand, if not her entire body, felt more like some sort of ghostly aberration than something she consciously controlled.

Her breath caught in her throat when the door opened. For a few seconds, she could do nothing more than stand in the doorway and stare. She wasn't a handler, just a technician. Most of her time was spent with computers, calibrating instruments, and of course Larry. In all honesty, she didn't know much about Clairvoyants, despite working here. She would have never guessed this was how they lived.

The lights in the room were off, but the destruction was quite easy to see. Edge's room looked like it had been literally ground to powder. Isabelle knew the assets were given some meager possessions to occupy their time between forging, but none of that was here. Nothing at all remained, other than a fine dust and splinters on the floor with ashes dispersed between. A cold, dry air crept toward her. It was hard to tell if the facility's ventilation system was malfunctioning or if it was just her nerves. Truth be told, goosebumps riddled Isabelle's body as she looked at the, well…emptiness. Then she looked at the room's occupant.

Edge sat on her bed and leaned against the wall. Her arms rested loosely on her knees. She didn't move at all, other than the ever so slight tremble of her breathing. Isabelle took a small step back without even realizing it, and her arms went across her chest almost as if she was hugging herself. Edge looked at her in that moment. Isabelle didn't know how she knew that, since the girl's face was obscured in the dark, but there was no denying it.

Her hand found the handcuffs on her belt on their own accord, and with it a small measure of confidence.

"Lights," she said, squinting as her eyes adjusted. Edge made no reaction to the brightness. "I'm your handler now," Isabelle said, stepping back into the room. "You're coming with me."

She tried to make her best show of it. She had no idea how handlers were supposed to act, but she doubted they were scared out of their minds. All things considered, she may as well be in here with a rampaging terrasaur or an anti-matter bomb. Perhaps Larry should have retrieved Edge instead. It didn't help that Isabelle felt sick to her stomach. Each step made the room spin. It grew worse the closer she got to the Clairvoyant. The girl made no reaction, though. She simply watched.

Isabelle stopped at the foot of Edge's bed. She pulled the handcuffs off her belt. "You're—" she started to say, but her words were cut short as she choked back her rising bile.

Isabelle looked at the twelve-year-old and wondered what she thought of her. Did she know what she intended? If she did, did she care? Was she simply waiting for the opportune moment to strike? Why would a Clairvoyant of her power even need to wait?

She took a deep breath. "You're not going to give me a hard time, are you?"

Edge sat still, but just then she leaned forward and tied her hair in a ponytail. Isabelle swallowed hard. She had no idea what that meant. When the girl was finished, she presented her arms. Isabelle slapped the handcuffs on her.

"Good," she said softly to herself. She held the links

between the handcuffs and smiled. The sickening feel was gone and the room was no longer spinning, but neither were the cause of her joy. "Good," she said again. Carmen shook her head a few times, but Isabelle didn't notice her discomfort. She pulled her to her feet with the handcuffs and almost dragged her out of the room. "Come on," she said roughly.

Carmen was in no position to protest. Janus never used the handcuffs with her. She could barely remember the one and only time she'd been subjected to them. This set was quite different. They were more...complete. Absolutely nothing of what made her *her* was left. She wondered if she'd even be able to put out a candle by blowing on it in her state.

Isabelle beamed. This was a special occasion. She gave a hard pull on the handcuffs just because she could and smiled when Edge's body jerked forward in response. Here she was, the great monster, the one-percenter, the terrifying Clairvoyant, Edge, and with just a small piece of technology, Isabelle had her at her whim. She steered the girl into a nearby wall and smiled again when Edge winced from the pain.

"Ahh." This felt good.

The terror of the galaxy was no more fearsome than her niece. It was hard to remember why she was scared of the girl to begin with. They drew so much attention as they went that Isabelle may as well have had an exotic beast in tow. Edge herself was nothing new. It was hard for most to ignore her, but she was a well-known entity. It wasn't her that made everyone curious; it was that she was subdued in chains and being led along by the decidedly average Isabelle. Only flying pigs would be a more incredible sight.

There were relatively few people in the halls, though, which was expected. Everyone had staked out where they were going to watch the fight by this point. They knew what was going to happen. Isabelle guessed the stragglers in the halls simply wanted a closer look at one of the contenders.

Carmen just walked. She didn't particularly like her new handler, whoever she was, but she'd rather have her than Janus. She was just so rough, though. It had a crudity her previous handler could never possess. Janus was inhuman in his cruelty, yet there was purpose behind it that Carmen couldn't deny even if she didn't agree with it. This woman had none of that. They were ultimately minor slights, but she hurt her just to hurt her. Carmen couldn't really say what the difference would mean in the long run. Both handlers were deplorable people in their own way. She tried not to think about it. Doing so would draw comparisons to Janus, and she hated thinking about him.

Her new handler gave another hard jerk on the handcuffs, and Carmen was content to just walk. With the handcuffs curtailing her abilities and with her still a little weak from her stint of not eating, walking was enough. The halls were near empty, save the few people gawking and staring. She didn't know why they were so deserted, but she didn't complain about it. She typically received a fair deal of attention by just existing, and there were times it was downright annoying.

She closed her eyes. Her handler made quite a job of leading her, so she didn't need to see. With her other senses dulled to almost nothingness, Carmen took a moment to bask in not being what she was. So much of her life had been influenced by that which she had no control over and didn't even want—*most* of the time, anyway. She was a Clairvoyant; she hadn't become one. The few seconds of no sight, limited sound, and not knowing that which she should have known provided an interesting peek into a world that she rarely glimpsed.

When she wasn't wearing handcuffs, she was faintly

aware of the people around her. She also knew their general moods. At times, she even knew specific things about them, though she often wished the information could be kept private. Now, under the specter of the handcuffs, she felt isolated. She was so very alone and such an insignificant speck that she may as well have not existed at all. It made her wonder if she actually had to take the handcuffs off. In and of themselves, Carmen didn't hate her abilities, but she'd prefer to just be ignored, given the choice. If that meant she had to be less of what she was, she had no problem with that—at least, not anymore.

* * *

Where did everyone go? Janus wondered.

There were no staff meetings or anything else he was aware of. If he didn't know better, he'd say the building had been evacuated. He could still sense the presence of other people in the facility, though, even if he couldn't see them. He considered what that meant for a moment. It probably meant nothing. He'd be summoned if he was needed.

Janus instead thought about his charge, as he usually did. There would be no more fighting for her. She had seen enough of it in her young life, by his reckoning. There was no more forging that could be done on that matter. She'd been broken, and now the task was to put her back together again properly. That was the hardest duty for any handler, and he wasn't sure he'd be able to manage it. What made Edge *Edge* was a delicate balance that even he could only catch hints of on rare occasions. It was a difficult thing to understand.

As he started toward her dorm, he thought perhaps he'd start with her first flight. All Clairvoyants remembered that choice, though he hadn't been given much of one by the sortens. He stopped to consider for a moment that he may never see her again. On more than sparse occasion, a first flight turned into the final flight. There was nothing he could do about that. It would be completely up to her. He didn't like thinking about it.

* * *

Isabelle frowned. Edge slowed her pace for some reason, and it was suddenly difficult to drag her along. *Why now of all times?* she thought. They were almost there.

She pulled on the handcuffs hard, nearly making the girl trip. "Come on," Isabelle said.

She looked down on Edge. Edge glared back at her. Isabelle's breath caught in her throat. Edge was dangerous even handcuffed; there was no denying that. There was also no denying that Isabelle didn't exactly subdue her. Edge was allowing herself to be led. It was intoxicating to be in charge of such power, but she really didn't want a reminder of who was actually in charge.

"We're almost there," she said sheepishly. Edge made no response, and the two of them continued on.

There was positively no one in the hall now. No surprise, as the halls weren't the place to be for this spectacle. The observation booth was the front row, center stage. If not that, the numerous rec rooms that would be streaming the fight were just as good. Either way, Isabelle looked forward to when she'd be rid of the little terror. She didn't know why Janus and some others fussed over them so much. Yeah, they were people just like she was. Sure, even she herself could be a Clairvoyant if she wanted to, but they were just so strange. The way they moved was a fluid, graceful mess that seemed more suited for a fish than any real person; so effortless, so purposeful, yet so unnatural. Even restrained by the handcuffs, Edge moved like a dancer. Plus, just being around them was uncomfortable, like being boiled alive. Isabelle could never get past it.

She looked down at the girl just before she opened the door to the fight room. She held Edge's arms up with one hand and held the key to the handcuffs with the other.

"You're not going to give me any trouble, are you?" she asked once more, looking the Clairvoyant in the eye.

Isabelle had never really done that before. Whenever she was around Clairvoyants, her thoughts were usually focused on getting away and not on taking a long look at what she was trying to escape from. She was unimpressed. Edge's pearly blues were muted—almost lifeless—belying the girl's otherwise sharp features. If the eyes were the window to the soul, hers was a dullard. How this person was one of the strongest beings that had ever lived was hard to believe. The fight could end before Isabelle had a chance to even get to the observation booth. Edge casually looked away, which Isabelle took as assent to continue.

Good, she thought with a suppressed smile.

She cautiously removed Edge's handcuffs before placing them back on her belt. She also took a step back without even realizing it. Edge made no indication that she was going to strike. She only blinked several times, and a hand went to her head to steady herself. She looked like she was dizzy. Then she looked at Isabelle.

The woman took several more steps back. "Oh my," she muttered to herself.

There were no lights flashing, sparks of electricity, or any of those dramatics. Edge didn't telekinetically rip her to shreds. Actually, she didn't move at all. She just stared. She stared as only a Clairvoyant could, penetrating as well as any dagger or bullet. Isabelle was utterly naked before it. She didn't think Edge was mad at her. It was more like she'd gotten the Clairvoyant's full attention. She'd rather not have it. She swore each individual atom of her being was being studied, like how a lab technician would study mold in a petri dish. Just then, Edge shook her head slowly. Isabelle didn't know what that meant. It was the same kind of disapproval one would give an ugly piece of art.

Isabelle swallowed hard and then opened the door, wondering what happened to all the dullness she'd seen earlier. Edge looked in the room, paused a moment, and then looked back at her new handler. Isabelle was about to open her mouth when the girl entered the room without a word or backward glance.

Carmen wasn't surprised to find herself in another fight room. She also wasn't surprised that it was the same as almost every other fight room she'd ever been in. It was empty, save for one soul, a brown-haired girl about her age. She didn't think she was a Construct. She'd never fought female Constructs; there would be no point. Besides, this girl was more than a simple machine made of flesh. She stood in the center of the room with such quiet confidence that it was almost intimidating. Her back was to Carmen, but when she turned, there was something familiar about her face. There was even something familiar about her energy. Everyone's was unique, and if Carmen didn't know better, she'd say that she had sensed this girl's energy before. She couldn't read her, nor did she remember when they could have met. Whatever the case may be, the girl, whoever she was, studied Carmen just as curiously. She seemed to be just as surprised to see Carmen as Carmen was to see her.

The two girls took a few curious steps toward each other. Carmen noted that the girl didn't move like a Construct. The ones she faced were what they were designed to be: athletic with incredible balance and precise, well-coordinated movements. They paid for their incredible performance with short lifespans and extreme caloric requirements. By contrast, there was weight and power behind this girl's actions. They were also deliberately graceful, like she could walk through a brick wall for all the effort of stepping on ants.

Carmen grew anxious as they moved closer to each other. There were only two types of people in a fight room—handlers and opponents—and since it was doubtful that this girl would be her new handler, there was only one possibility left. Carmen didn't want to fight her. She didn't want to hurt people anymore, especially not someone who looked like she was as much of a victim of this place as Carmen was.

Except the girl made no action against her. When she tried to walk behind her, Carmen turned to keep her in full view. She tried again, and Carmen turned again. She could only guess the girl's intentions. Though, on second thought, she didn't think she was trying to gain any sort of advantage by moving behind her. She was walking too slowly for that to be a serious goal. Did she simply want to study all of her counterpart? Carmen tested the theory by turning around the long way when the girl tried to move behind her again. For one brief, instant Carmen's back was to her, and nothing happened. She returned the favor by walking behind the girl, who stood still as she did so. There was even a confident smirk on her face when Carmen appeared in front of her again. Carmen didn't know why. Then the girl took one solitary step toward her. The action didn't seem curious or exploratory in nature, at least not to Carmen. She took another step forward, and Carmen took a step back to keep the same distance between them.

* * *

Isabelle practically ran down the hall. Her pulse beat through her like fire. If anyone had actually been in the halls, she would have crashed through them like a wrecking ball. She'd be justified in doing so; missing even a second of this long-awaited showdown would be blasphemous. Of course, the thought of the credits she'd earn from the endeavor buzzed in her brain, but what was the point of putting in all this hard work if she wasn't able to sit back and enjoy the show?

For that reason alone, she should have gotten Larry to do it all, if she could have. He and all their friends were able to relax while they watched the fight of the century, yet she had to do all the dirty stuff. How was that fair? He'd probably screw it up somehow if it was up to him, though. He wasn't the fastest minnow in the pond, as both she and his wife agreed. *Thankfully he has other virtues,* she thought with a contented sigh. But that was for later tonight.

She got in an elevator. It would be a short trip. She'd only barely caught her breath when the doors opened again. *Now which booth is it?* she thought. Why did everything in this place have to be so nondescript? If she could find a better paying job, she wouldn't think twice about leaving, if just for better scenery. The thought produced a knowing smile. Money? She wouldn't have any problems with money very soon—especially after Artemis killed or at least beat the little blonde milquetoast.

"Ahh, life is good," she said to herself as she opened the door to the observation booth.

The place was packed. She never really spent any time in the observation booths herself. Consequently, she had no real idea of how they normally operated. Nevertheless, it was obvious that they were never designed to hold this many people. Only sardine cans approached this level of meat packed density. There were so many chairs on the floor that mice would have had trouble walking through. Thankfully, some very wise soul had raided the mess hall for several kegs of beer and food. Those items rested on a table, but other than that sacred area, the tables were covered by people standing on them. There was no room to sit. There were, of course, the technicians, scientists, and even the odd handlers one would expect to see in an observation booth, but now they were joined by security guards, cooks, program managers, and probably half the janitors that worked here. Isabelle figured she'd have an easier time trying to count who wasn't watching the fight. She knew of at least one person. In any case, in that moment, they all looked at her.

Isabelle beamed. Their stares were like the nourishing rays of the sun. Aside from the money, this was what made the effort worth the trouble. No one ever thought they'd see Artemis and Edge standing toe to toe, at least not when Janus was Edge's handler. No one ever thought anyone other than their handlers would be able to wrangle them and bring them together. But she had done it.

It started slowly, but the lot of them began clapping. Isabelle walked slowly forward and embraced the applause. Arms reached out to pat her on the back. She heard "Good job," and "Way to go," more times than in the whole of her life up to this point. She soaked as much of it in as she could. Isabelle smiled again as she wondered if this same scene was happening throughout the facility. She'd find out later. For now, however, this was the best moment of her life, and to think it was only the start for her. Nothing would ever be the same after today.

She continued to walk through the booth. At the end of her journey was Larry, and the two embraced in a kiss.

"Is Edge dead yet?" Isabelle asked. If she had missed all the action, that was the most important thing to know.

Larry shook his head. "No," he said, and she groaned. "It's really strange. They're just walking around each other and stuff."

"What?" Isabelle said, dumbfounded.

"Yeah. They haven't even slapped each other or started pushing and shoving or anything."

She looked away for a moment and began worrying that maybe they wouldn't fight each other. It would be just her luck that she went through all this trouble for naught. Just then, someone shoved a beer in her hand and put his arm around her.

"Who cares about all that shit?" the person said loudly. "We're here, they're there, and they'll start killing each other eventually. Let's have fun."

Isabelle couldn't really argue with that logic. She downed the beer with a smile. Larry then led her to a chair that had been reserved just for her, and they sat down and awaited the show. Silently, she hoped this would be like watching storm clouds. They would roll in and build all day, and you wouldn't know when it was going to rain, but you knew it was inevitable. Then, when you least expected it, there would be thunder and lighting.

* * *

Carmen took another step back. Her eyes were wide, and she was near panting. It was then that she remembered her first ever fight. She didn't want to fight now, just like she didn't want to fight then. But she also remembered what Janus had said—how her body, her Dark, wanted her to fight and prepared itself to win, despite what she consciously thought.

All the reactions were the same as then, as when she killed Mikayla, and as when she tried to kill Janus but couldn't. As probably every moment in her life, she was set against herself.

She took another step back, and her hand brushed against the wall. Her heart rate ratcheted up twenty beats. The girl shook her head in pity. It was at that moment that Carmen realized who she was.

"I know you," she said. "We've met before."

The girl took another step forward, but it was smaller than before. "I doubt that," she said simply. "I'm sure of it, even."

"Why?" Carmen asked.

"Because I've killed everyone I've met, other than my handler."

Carmen winced but remained undeterred nonetheless. This girl seemed a bit…extreme, but she didn't think she was crazy. Reason had to work.

"But we've met before, sort of…years ago, when I first came here. I was crying in the hospital, and you looked at me from across the room."

"I don't remember," the girl said. She then assumed a guard and took another step forward.

"Okay, well, we don't have to fight. My name is Car— Edge. What's yours?"

"Artemis," she said, with none of Carmen's hesitation on what to call herself. "And you're right. We don't have to fight each other."

Carmen smiled and nodded. "I'm sure we can be friends. I don't have any friends…not anymore. I'd like to get to know you."

Artemis shook her head again. She also smirked before she took another step forward. "I don't think you understand, Edge. You were right. We do not *need* to fight. I, however, want to." She then laughed lightly in a childish way. "And I think we're going to get to know each other rather well, for however long it lasts."

"No, wait!" Carmen yelled, holding her hands out in a feeble attempt to hold her off.

Artemis shook her head once more. "Do you always talk this much?"

Carmen paused a moment, surprised by the question. "No, I don't think so," she said as she considered her answer.

"Good," the girl said slowly.

She barely heard her, since, as soon as she finished speaking, her fist was rocketing toward her chest. Carmen had fought countless Constructs up to this point. Artemis's attack was like nothing a Construct could ever muster. There was a snap and velocity to the movement that constricting muscle fibers could never match. It was also very, very precise. The impact point was dead center on Carmen's heart.

She remembered when she'd been in this situation before. She remembered how inevitably surreal it all was. Carmen had just been a kid and was fighting for her life against some guy who seemed to be ten times her size. Her legs had felt like they were made out of cement and she'd been too paralyzed to move, until she keeled over, dead. This time, however, she simply turned her shoulders, and Artemis's fist hit the wall with a soft thud.

Carmen took a hesitant step out of the way. Artemis gave her an annoyed glance over her still outstretched arm. She would have more luck guessing the fate of the universe by studying grass billowing in the wind than by reading this girl. Nevertheless, it was a pretty fair guess that Artemis hadn't expected her to move.

"We can tal—" Carman tried to eke out, but it was in vain.

Artemis's outstretched arm soon turned into a well-aimed back fist. Only a block on Carmen's part prevented it from connecting. Another punch was behind it, but she would have never known it was coming if she wasn't a Clairvoyant. She'd felt it moving through the air, and it ultimately ended up shaving her cheek. Carmen ended the exchange by stepping in and forcefully pushing Artemis back with one hand.

"Stop it!" she said.

Artemis glared at her. "It will be a lot easier for you if you stop fighting back," she snapped.

The words stung Carmen more than any punch ever could. As Janus said, she really didn't have to fight. The decision would ultimately kill her in this case, but there was no power in the universe that could take that choice away from her. She didn't have much time to contemplate that as Artemis sent a jump kick her way.

Fine, she thought. She wouldn't fight. She had other means.

A mere thought flung Artemis into the nearest wall. Then Carmen held her there. It wasn't an easy task. She'd never had another Clairvoyant resisting her telekinesis before. It was a strange sensation, like pushing two repulsing magnets together. But she was able to manage it. She gave a satisfied nod over ending the contest before it really got started. Perhaps Janus was right. She didn't have to fight if she didn't want to.

"So, can we talk now?" she asked the girl still pressed against the wall.

Artemis gritted her teeth as she strained against the invisible force. She didn't say anything, but all of sudden she looked right at Carmen. Just then, Carmen felt something lifting her off her feet, and she gave a yelp. The fight rooms weren't very big—a fact she had known far too well whenever her back was pressed against a wall—and now she was flying across the relatively small room at high speed with no way of stopping. The result was inevitable. She hit the wall with a thunderous crash and gasped as the wind was knocked out of her. Her focus on Artemis was broken in that moment, causing the girl to fall to the ground. Carmen didn't notice. What she did notice, however, was that the force holding her against the wall was now trying to twist her head off.

Carmen screamed again, but whereas before she did so out of surprise, now it was filled with the ear-splitting terror of her imminent doom. Her neck muscles just didn't have the strength to be of any use, so she had to hold her head in place telekinetically. The two forces pressing against each other made her skull feel like it was in a vise.

Out of the corner of her eye, she saw Artemis smiling triumphantly up at her. Carmen sneered back and then telekinetically sent her sailing into the nearest wall without a second thought. Artemis's hold on her waned upon impact, and she dropped to the ground. After several quick gasps, Carmen looked across the room at her opponent, who was in a similar state.

The two glared at each other for a quick second before springing to action. Carmen didn't waste her time in trying to use reason. At this juncture, reason would get her killed. No, her goal was to be first on the draw, and she managed to make par. The two girls zoomed around the room under the thrall of the other, crashing and bumping into walls, the ground, and the ceiling as they went. After a while, Carmen just didn't have the concentration to hold onto Artemis anymore, and she dropped her much like the sand so many years ago. Artemis dropped her as well only a few seconds later.

Carmen was literally seeing stars. Her entire body ached.

In that moment, she vaguely remembered Janus saying something about never using telekinesis on another Clairvoyant. At the time, she thought it was just another in his long string of stupid, pointless rules. Now, considering the blood she was spitting out of her mouth, she had to admit it was probably a good idea for both parties to limit themselves in at least that way. She glanced at Artemis across the room. Unless Carmen missed her guess, she'd say the girl had come to a similar decision not to use *every* weapon in her arsenal. At least Carmen wasn't whipping across the room again.

Artemis came to her feet hesitantly. Carmen shot to hers, which was a bad idea. She had yet to get her equilibrium back, and she fell back to the ground with a plop. Her opponent looked down at her and slowly shook her head. Carmen sighed. Was she really that pathetic, or was Artemis just suffering from a stiff neck? All things considered, if she could see herself, she'd probably shake her head too.

She got to her feet again, albeit slower than before, so she wouldn't fall down again. Artemis assumed a guard and began walking toward her. Carmen unknowingly took a step back.

"I assume we can't talk this out," she said.

Artemis took a few steps closer. "That would be a good guess."

"Why do you want to fight me?"

"Boredom."

"What?" Carmen asked, dumbfounded.

"I don't know about you, but I'd rather not go back to my room. Reading and coloring books get dull really fast."

Carmen actually rather enjoyed her coloring books—that was, until she burned them. "Yeah, but—"

"Yeah, but...I don't know what you're so worried about. I'm sure they'll revive you or something after I beat you."

"That's a bit beside the point," Carmen replied after swallowing hard.

Artemis chuckled lightly. "Yeah, I guess it is. Anyway, I do have to thank you for being a good sport up to now."

Carmen stared at her for a moment, unable to think of a response. "Umm, well, you're welcome," she finally muttered.

The other girl chuckled again, but it was short lived. She closed the distance with a lunging punch Carmen was able to easily avoid. The next few moments after, though, were more pressing. There was no doubt in Carmen's mind that Artemis wanted to kill her. The reason for that was dubious, but the intent was clear, and now all the more so. It seemed, after those first few almost exploratory strikes, she adjusted to Carmen's level of ability. She adjusted to Artemis's ability as well.

This was no Construct. A Construct could never match a Clairvoyant's ferocity and precision. Carmen barely had enough time to think about what she was going to do; she could only react. It was then that all of Janus's sermons on the Dark, conscious or subconscious desires, and acting without worrying about what you were going to do and how you were going to do it made sense.

Artemis's foot sailed toward her head, and Carmen's arm rose almost automatically to intercept it. The girl's opposite foot shot out right after it, and Carmen sidestepped out of the way. More punches, more kicks, and to Carmen, she may as well have been sleep walking. A growing fatigue began taking its toll, but for now it couldn't break her trance-like focus. That was, until Artemis made a mistake. It was slight —almost too small to capitalize on—but to Carmen, the elephant in the room wore a pink tutu while singing opera.

Her fist started out until she stopped it short. She didn't

want to kill Artemis. She also didn't want to beat her or even hurt her; she just didn't want to die again.

The moment of indecision came at a price. Artemis managed to slip a punch through Carmen's defenses. It was a glancing blow, but it still stung. Another blurred her vision. She didn't allow a third. She telekinetically flew backward for a quick breather before Artemis was on her again, this time even fiercer. Carmen figured her opponent must have sensed the blood in the water. The best she could do was use that aggression against her.

Matching it force for force, while possible with effort, was a losing battle. It was an unstoppable juggernaut that had more in common with a tidal wave or meteor strike than a person. Carmen wanted no part of it, nor did she want to conjure a similar beast to defeat it. No, she could redirect it— refocus it. Artemis attacked, and Carmen made her miss. Artemis rushed her, and Carmen allowed her to overextend. Except, it just wasn't enough; Artemis was simply too great a dynamo to stave off. If anything, she seemed to be getting stronger or at least gathering more momentum.

Carmen flew out of the line of fire once again, and Artemis followed like a shadow or reflection. Carmen watched her, trying to predict her movement, but reading the girl was impossible. She was unknowable and unfathomable. She was a creature of such endless depths that even the greatest scholar who'd ever lived wouldn't be able to come to grips with her. Carmen bobbed, weaved, and danced to escape her, but it just couldn't be done. There was no going around it, no reasoning with it, and no intellectualizing it away. It was just there, blazing before her in a blinding, scalding light, pressing her to the limits, and accepting nothing but surrender.

She dashed out of the way once again and evaded it. In

the back of her mind, she knew she could only keep this up for so long. A punch just missed over her shoulder. A kick just grazed her cheek. Another punch was stopped short by a block. Carmen slipped and danced behind Artemis…and then it happened.

Carmen never saw the punch. It connected with a thunderous clap, but she didn't hear that either. As a matter of fact, she didn't even feel pain. There was a white flash and then, all of a sudden, she was strangely disconnected from her body. She could still think, but she couldn't feel. She couldn't really sense her surroundings anymore. No taste, no sound, no sight—it was as if the world had been ripped from her with that one punch. The only thing she was aware of, and even then only dimly, was that she was falling toward the ground like a log. It was that and that alone that let her know she was not dead. Nevertheless, in her dead-like state, her mind raced. No one thought stood before her, front and center. Millions buzzed by, leaving only brief glimpses of what they were. She knew only seconds had to have passed, but in that eon, one thought repeated itself over and over again. *No!*

The Clairvoyant's limp body came to attention with a snap. She never even hit the ground. Telekinesis supplemented her lost balance, holding her in place just long enough for her to get to her feet. Then her attention turned to Artemis. Fire burned through Carmen's veins as sensation slowly came back to her. Why Artemis didn't try to escape was as perplexing as it was foolish. She would make her pay for that.

Carmen's punch was not born of any great technique. Swung wide and wild, it was sloppy in its movement. In spite of that, it contained so much power that a Richter scale would be needed to properly measure it. Only missiles approached its velocity, leaving Artemis little choice but to block the blow. Her block, however, was just as sloppy; she didn't have time for finesse. The best she could do was raise her arm and try to meet force with force. Unfortunately for her, the attempt only resulted in her groaning as the bones in her arm broke under the strain. Teeth flew out of her mouth on impact. Blood soon followed, and Artemis fell to the ground in a heap.

Carmen stared angrily down at her.

* * *

Isabelle knew she would remember this day for the whole of her life. There was no memory, amplified or even outright fabricated, that could ever recall the amount of fun she was having. Now, though, her eyes glazed over and her mouth hung open. The knot in her stomach echoed the silence in the room. Quite simply, the planet had shifted. Before this…*debacle*, watching the fight was like watching a sun rise. The event was utterly beautiful and awe-inspiring in its scope, but the outcome was an expected certainty. Yet now a fluke of cosmic mischief was moving that great celestial juggernaut in the wrong direction.

"This is not happening," she muttered to herself.

The soundtrack had been perfect until this moment. It was almost as if the girls were playing for the audience on purpose, or at least just for her. Some stupid people had bet the other way. In any case, Edge would run and she'd get hit. She tried to run away again, and she'd get hit again. The melody was masterful in its execution—five stars, two thumbs up, utterly perfect. The knockout solo was killer, but why did Edge have to go and change the tune? How was it even possible for her to change the tune? A knockout was, well, a knockout. Isabelle saw the hit. The lights weren't just out; they had been blown out of their sockets. She hated Clairvoyants.

Isabelle's fame was assured at this point. The fight had thus far lived up to its billing, even with Edge unable to effectively fight back until now. But the money—all that beautiful money—was utter smoke. The only thing worse was the tension. For who knew what reason, Edge had yet to finish Artemis off. The little blonde, formerly considered milquetoast just stared at her. Isabelle wanted to yell at her to get it over with.

* * *

Carmen's blood boiled. Artemis was totally at her mercy. It was quite certain that she'd receive none if the situation was reversed, but Carmen couldn't act. She desperately wanted to. She wanted to smash Artemis's head in and then go back to her room and never come out. When she looked at the girl, though, violent retribution was the furthest thing from her mind.

Carmen couldn't help wondering if she ever looked as helpless. She could feel the girl's fear and pain despite that she still couldn't read her. It was palpable. She had little doubt in her mind that even a non-Clairvoyant would notice. For some reason, it struck a chord. They were counterparts, or at least the closest Carmen had ever met. There was no real difference between them or their circumstance. And here she was, this indomitable force of nature, poised to wash over the pathetic, quivering mass. It was so vulnerable, so weak—a hurt, pathetic nothing. She resented the thing almost as much as her heart broke for it. Parts of her, in equal measure, wanted to both hug it and stomp it out of existence.

"Shit," Carmen swore under her breath.

Nothing was ever what it seemed. After today, she'd never argue with Janus about what the Dark was or whether it existed. She fought it with everything she had, yet there was no way to win. Every battle pained her. Nothing had ever made her feel so small or lost, and that was all the truer as she stood over Artemis.

She looked at her counterpart. Their battle—contest, war, whatever it was—had no real meaning. Nonetheless, she could feel the last six years surge through every blow, every block, every move and countermove. It made no kind of sense. She'd always been fighting—fighting to live. But what was her life? She thought back to her now empty room. All she had left was the battle. She didn't want to surrender. That, for some reason, seemed worse than death. Resistance, however, that immediate, unending reflex that was her only real company, seemed as strict and narrowminded of a friend as a straitjacket.

Artemis slowly recovered. Carmen took a couple of steps back as her opponent looked less and less pitiable. The arm her punch had plowed through hung lifelessly at the girl's side, bent at an awkward angle. Artemis soon rectified that, however, by snapping it back into place with telekinesis. Carmen winced at the sight. Artemis winced and groaned as well as she brought both hands into a guard, telekinetically manipulating the busted limb.

Carmen sighed. "Do we have to keep fighting?" she asked.

Artemis said nothing but spat a wad of blood onto the ground. Then she took a few steps forward. Carmen sighed again and prepared to defend herself. This time, however, a quiet voice in the back of her head decided she wouldn't *just* defend herself. The same voice wouldn't allow her to outright kill Artemis, but it wasn't content with simply being a target either.

Artemis came at her, but cautiously. Either way, Carmen was ready. Her opponent made a soft, hesitant punch, and Carmen let it connect. A surge of confidence filled the room in that moment. Carmen even saw it in Artemis's face as worry and apprehension gave way to calm and focus. The girl's next punch reflected as much, and she batted it out of the way. A third punch was coming. It wasn't on its way yet, but Carmen *knew*. Maybe Artemis attacked in a pattern she was only aware of subconsciously. Perhaps she was becoming more able to read Artemis after being so intensely confronted by her. Whatever it was, Carmen was so sure the punch was coming that it may as well have been printed on a bus schedule.

If she had time for it, she would have closed her eyes and sighed contently. There was just something so satisfying about knowing the seemingly unperceivable. It was much the same as when she'd walked in the sun when she was a child, or when she stood on the ceiling. She was reminded of when a sparrow showed off its flying skills just because it could, or the times Mikayla had seemed to just enjoy being a dog. In any case, Carmen stepped to the side and nailed Artemis with two quick punches. Then she stepped away and waited.

Artemis stared at her. It wasn't a look of pain; even Carmen would admit she didn't hit her that hard. It was enough to sting, but no more than that. If anything, Artemis's gaze was as much accusing as it was shocked. Carmen swore she heard her mouth, "But you can't do that!" Whether the girl had actually spoken or not, Carmen couldn't help a small smirk. Artemis frowned.

She tried to attack again, but Carmen was first on the draw, staggering her with a kick to the head. From there, that small voice in the back of Carmen's mind told her not to stop. She was quick to heed the advice. Another blow landed home, followed by two more. Artemis's back collided with the wall and, for one brief second, she was cornered. The quiet voice in the back of Carmen's head screamed, but she hesitated. She still attacked, but her punch was halfhearted and arrived to finish the job a hair's breadth too late. Her fist cratered the wall on impact, leaving Artemis none the worse for wear.

Her opponent was breathing so hard that she panted, blood leaked from her brow, and her arm was still broken. Nevertheless, she gave no indication that she was going to back down. Her firm, unwavering step forward proved that. Carmen prepared herself. Nothing happened, though—at least not at first. The two girls danced around each other, but both refused to commit to anything substantial. Then, all of a sudden, it ended.

Carmen threw a punch and then a kick and hit nothing but air. Artemis responded with a kick of her own, and Carmen caught her foot in her hands before she flung her across the room. Carmen attempted to take advantage only to have her fist graze the top of Artemis's head, but everything went wrong after that. Somehow, Artemis maneuvered behind her. She grasped Carmen's ponytail, yanked, and Carmen screamed as her scalp felt like it was on fire. She didn't put up much fight as she was brought to the ground. The hand grasping her hair let go, balled into a fist, and clocked her in the jaw. Carmen barely felt it. It wasn't a soft punch, but the hair pulling had been so painful that a punch to the face was a welcome distraction. In the same realm, she didn't notice the kick flying toward her face until it was almost too late. The best she could do was to raise her arm to block the blow.

Tenths of a second turned to hours as Carmen watched

her arm bend under the strain of the attack until it snapped like a twig. Her mind screamed; she, however, uttered no sound. It hurt too much to do so. The most that escaped her lips was a gasp. It was a minor miracle that Carmen maintained the wherewithal to pull her head back as Artemis's foot just missed her chin.

Her opponent didn't continue her attack. Carmen didn't know why. Nevertheless, her arm fell limp and lifeless beside her, and she noted that she couldn't move it without telekinesis. When she glanced at Artemis, the girl smirked down at her. Carmen sneered back once she connected the dots. Despite that she had never really intended to break Artemis's arm, she guessed turnabout was fair play.

She telekinetically snapped her arm back into place. It wasn't the first time she'd done it, and she only winced sharply. Then Carmen stood and assumed a guard. Artemis did nothing of the sort. She just smiled.

"Sure we can't talk this out?" she asked sarcastically.

Carmen gritted her teeth. She had been waiting for Artemis to say such reasonable words since the start of this contest, but she didn't have to be telepathic to know when she was being mocked. She replied by raising her arm and blasting the girl with a beam of heat. Artemis did the same. Their two scorching, white-hot pillars of radiation, however, never touched each other. Carmen's mouth fell open in shock as the two beams flowed around each other like two repulsing magnets, completely missing both girls before continuing on to ablate the wall behind them. She didn't think it was possible, but with the unbelievable staring her in the face, Carmen was forced to reassess that view. They stopped their beams at the same time. After that, some unheard signal sent them both on the offensive.

* * *

"Holy shit!" about eight people in the observation booth said simultaneously.

Isabelle figured that was an understatement. This wasn't a fight; it was a collision of an unstoppable force and an immovable object. It was the struggle of an infinitely strong being trying to lift an infinitely heavy rock—eternal night meeting everlasting day. At this point, it was tough to even following their movements.

The noise in the room didn't help, as everyone constantly screamed. She couldn't blame them; she screamed too. This was just too exciting not to. The milquetoast would get rocked, but then she would answer back *hard*. Artemis would stagger and then respond with a blow that would cripple anyone else. Isabelle was almost to the point of not caring who won anymore. This display was priceless. The play of energy between the two Clairvoyants made her hair stand on end. Really, everyone's hair was standing on end.

A visible spark had arced between her and Larry when she accidently touched him. The best way to describe it was that she felt like a kid again. It wasn't because of how excited she was—it wasn't that simple. She just had so much energy. It would probably be a few weeks before she was tired enough to sleep. Until then, she could probably run a good three or four miles between breaths. Being around Clairvoyants was weird.

Isabelle took a moment from watching the carnage to survey her surroundings. Larry was yelling so much and at such volume that she would have trouble speaking to him even through an amplifier. The lab geeks were babbling amongst themselves in squeaks and squawks—something about being "off the scale" on the new *modified* scale. She didn't care enough to listen more than that.

At any rate, everyone winced as the little milquetoast suffered another kick to the midsection. The sound was intermixed with the dejected yelling of the "stupid" bettors. Isabelle looked at them and smiled. There was as much beer on the floor as had been consumed, and people were falling over each other to try to get a better view. The walls practically vibrated, and the equipment beeped so often it was almost smoking.

Isabelle smiled again. Today was a good day.

* * *

Janus paused for a moment. He did not know why he did—even as a Clairvoyant, things weren't always clear—but the momentary hesitation brought all of his senses to the forefront. Nothing was immediately apparent.

What could it be? he thought with a sigh. There were no clues.

This was one of those moments in which being a Clairvoyant was more trouble than it was worth. Nobody knew everything, and sometimes *knowing* without actually knowing anything at all was like having an itch that couldn't be scratched. He'd never particularly liked the faux ignorance. It may be related to how he was currently feeling about Edge. Either way, he didn't feel very comfortable—almost sick to his stomach, in fact. If he wasn't certain before, now he was. Edge's first flight would be today. His Dark had spoken, and her time had come. He just needed to collect his charge first.

Just thinking about her made him nervous, but the reason was annoyingly difficult to place. He wasn't scared of her. If she wanted to kill him, she would have done so when she had the chance. Besides, he wasn't worried about dying anyway. Like unexplained pinpricks on the consciousness, the notion that he would have a short life and that it would end violently was just something he accepted. His Dark produced no anxiety from that truth.

Maybe his state was simply because he didn't know what he expected. That, of course, was no different from any other day. This next step, however, could be the end—her end. The choice would be hers to make. Just thinking about her dying permanently made Janus quake. He was not ashamed to say he was somewhat fond of his charge. There were no rules that said a handler should or should not be, and after six years of almost daily direct contact, it would be inhuman not to develop some kind of attachment. It was a unique pleasure to silently cheer her on during every challenge he gave her. Her triumphs were wholly hers and hers alone, but to watch her revelry, in the rare times it appeared, was sweet.

As the elevator dropped off on the dormitory level, Janus took a deep breath. Something was different, though—he should have been able to sense her by now. The lights were flickering, so it was probably just his nerves. Lights flickering around a Clairvoyant of her power was as common as thunder with lightning. Then Janus noticed the walls seemed to vibrate.

He opened her door, but there was no one inside. His eyebrows furrowed. The only people who would remove Edge without his knowledge were the medical staff, and if they had done so, they would have informed him by now.

The walls vibrated again. At this point, it was more of a tremor.

Janus studied the room, but there was no evidence he could discern. In fact, there was hardly anything in her room at all. He had no doubt Edge had thrown a temper tantrum at some point, but that didn't explain why she wasn't in her room. He felt sick again, and as the wall shook once more, it dawned on him.

* * *

Carmen couldn't really think anymore. She didn't feel the pain from her body either. She wasn't numb; it was just that each injury was perceived distantly at best. If anything, it was like she was speaking to her body through a radio. She'd call down to the engine room for more power, and a few seconds later she'd have it. She'd call again and receive again. Each time, however, she was given less and less over longer and longer intervals. She didn't know if Artemis was suffering in the same way, but she knew she wouldn't be able to keep this up much longer.

She was cartwheeled across the room from a particularly hard kick. It was harder to move and focus for a moment until the engine room could properly respond. Even so, it was ultimately no use. Fighting back was only delaying the inevitable. She wouldn't say it was because Artemis was stronger or better than her. In fact, she barely even noticed Artemis at this point. Carmen just didn't want to manage the effort anymore. Deep down, from the very beginning, she'd known this day would come. She was tired of it all. Even the whispering of her Dark was silent in this matter.

She had been feeding off herself for so long that there was nothing left. For years, every challenge, every poke and prod by Janus, spurred some furnace buried deep inside her to burn that much hotter—to up the pressure to what was needed. Now it was spent. There was still ferocity in her action. She still wanted to stop Artemis if she could. But the question remained: "Then what?" What about the next time? How long could she go on doing this?

Whatever the answers were, she picked herself up off the ground yet again and stood, ready and waiting. Artemis hesitated. Carmen didn't know why. It wasn't like she was any greater of a threat now than she had been five minutes ago. Artemis breathed hard. Her face was bloody and bruised, and her clothes were ripped. There was silence between them as they stared at each other. Artemis slowly shook her head while she looked Carmen in the eye. Carmen's only reply was to raise her guard. After no more than a few seconds' pause, Carmen's war started once again.

* * *

Janus moved with such speed that his passing was marked by a streak followed by a gust of wind. He didn't just run or fly —it was a combination of both. He flew down a hall until he came to a corner. With no hesitation and without slowing down, he ran along the wall and ceiling before vaulting into the air once again. He groaned as his inertia fought against him. All Clairvoyants hated that.

He didn't know exactly where they were. Edge was so strong that sensing her exact location wasn't easy. The best he could do was follow the tremors. It seemed like the entire building was being rattled to pieces. Any other being would give pause to the fact that the tremors were growing stronger, but Janus was heartened by this. If there was ever a time he wanted Edge to fight, it was now. She would need everything she could muster, simply to hold Artemis off. He was somewhat surprised she'd been able to last this long.

The thought made him push even harder. She was his charge. He had killed her more times than he could count, but his primary responsibility was her wellbeing. Live or die, he shuddered to think what would be left of her after this. He felt another shake, and it was hard to tell if it was the building or that overworked muscle in his chest. The lights flickered, though, so he guessed it was the former.

Janus slid to a stop. He was close, but he knew, through no apparent means, that they weren't on this level. He looked up. Seconds later, the Clairvoyant emerged from the melted hole in the floor. The lights didn't flicker on this level; they had been blown out. He was getting closer.

He wasn't sure where to go from here, but he didn't waste his time thinking about it. Instead, he stood very, very still. His hand rose and then pointed at the wall. After a pause and a breath, his beam set to work on one wall, then the next, and the next. Edge could probably do the work in half the time, but he would have to manage with the more limited strength he could wield. When it was done, he bolted through the hole, mere moments from his objective. That didn't comfort him, however. For some reason, the tremors had stopped.

The door to their fight room was flying across the room before he even realized he had ripped it off its hinges. Then he saw them. Both girls were a bloody mess. It also stained the floor and walls and was dripping down from the ceiling. Fist-sized craters and large scorch marks also colored the walls. They noticed he was there in that moment.

Artemis held Edge in a headlock and seemed just one wrench away from twisting it clean off. It was a curious predicament for a Clairvoyant to be in. If Janus had the time for it, he'd wonder why Edge didn't just shock her. You could only touch a Clairvoyant if they allowed you to, after all. Artemis glanced at him, and her gaze held enough wild viciousness to freeze even a Clairvoyant. Edge's demeanor, however, was hard to describe. She seemed tired if anything, like just existing took a great deal of effort. She barely even looked at him.

Artemis must have guessed his intent as her arms tightened around her prey. Janus was first on the draw. He ripped her off Edge telekinetically and then sent a beam of heat through her before she could respond. His spirits fell in that instant. He didn't want to hurt Artemis just as much as he didn't want any harm to come to Edge. She was just as innocent in all of this as his charge. But he didn't have a suppression team at his disposal, and he had no hope of fending off even a weakened Artemis. He didn't like it, but he didn't regret his action as she fell to the ground, dead, a look of surprise frozen on her face.

Janus paid her no further mind. His attention was on Edge. The girl fell in place, not even attempting to telekinetically cushion her fall. One of the most powerful beings in the galaxy was now a pathetic, bloody mess. He shook his head slowly as he walked toward her. Edge's breathing was labored, and it was obvious she was suffering from several broken bones. Nevertheless, she recoiled as best as she could —no more than a few inches—when he approached. He shook his head again, and a quiet voice in the back of his mind came to a conclusion. He didn't like it, but he had long ago given up fighting with his Dark when it made a decision. The argument was over before it even began.

He fell to his knees before his charge and scooped her up in his arms. She stiffened as he did and let out a pained moan. Janus was wise enough to know that the sound had nothing to do with any physically malady, though. Tears welled in his eyes as her blood soaked his clothes once more.

"I'm so sorry," he said slowly, repeating it again and again.

When Carmen heard him the first time, her eyes grew

wide before they sealed shut in disbelief. Breathing became even more difficult, and she coughed blood. She'd been in this situation enough times to know what was next. She feebly placed her hands on his shoulders, and as Carmen died one last time, she tried her best to push him away.

9

FIRST FLIGHT

Subject: Edge Age: 12 Status: Tempering

Carmen opened her eyes slowly. The sight was familiar. She was in the medical wing again. The place may as well have been her second dorm for as much time as she spent in it. The room was near capacity, as was typical. Her body ached, which was also not out of the ordinary. One thing that was different, though, was that she was handcuffed to the bed. Another change was that Janus was not with her. She didn't miss him.

She knew she had died once again. She'd lost count of how many times it had been, for what that knowledge was worth. She was casually aware that each time was a chance. She'd seen other assets, during her stays in the medical wing, that simply couldn't be revived. Carmen often wondered what would happen when her luck ran out. She had learned about Hell and similar places. It was a persistent worry, just before her last breaths, that she'd be there or someplace worse when her eyes opened again. Perhaps this facility *was* her ultimate damnation. She could certainly think of more terrible things than fire and brimstone.

She wasn't very distressed about it for the moment, though. If this was Hell or not, all she was concerned about was how many days she'd been out. That was often the most annoying thing. Carmen looked around the room for a few minutes, but she knew it was futile. There were several clocks, but they didn't say what day or week it was. Just then, her eyes fell on an old friend.

Artemis stared at her from across the room. Carmen nonchalantly stared back. Just as she was, the girl was hand-cuffed to her bed, had no handler to accompany her, and appeared to be in no ill health. Carmen was quite certain their masters were worried the two of them would go at it again, not only because of the handcuffs but also because a suppression team waited nearby. She thought it was a wasted effort, at least for herself. She didn't want to fight Artemis or anyone else, for that matter. Artemis, as Carmen guessed was the norm, didn't seem as reasonable. She was quite certain Artemis would have spat on her if she was in range.

Carmen didn't think much of it, though. She sighed, and remembering the first time they met, slowly shook her head in a manner that let Artemis know exactly what Carmen thought of her. The girl sneered back, which prompted a small smile on Carmen's part. She guessed that constituted the last laugh in their little contest. Either way, that supremely rare facial expression lived up to its billing and soon no longer graced Carmen's lips.

She sighed again, and then sat…and sat…and sat for hours. Artemis's handler eventually came. He was quite easy to read. Actually, she didn't even need to be able to *read* him to know what he was thinking. He was nervous, if not scared. A suppression team was also with him, and Carmen would say Artemis actually enjoyed the fanfare, as strange as that seemed. Still, the girl didn't resist going with them. What she did do was give Carmen a pointed glare before she was escorted out. Carmen gave no reaction, other than to hope she wouldn't have to see her again. Once every other lifetime was more than enough.

Carmen wondered when someone was going to come by and collect her. She looked for Janus at first and was even worried that he may have forgotten about her when he didn't appear promptly. She scanned the room for a few intense minutes with every sense she had before she was forced to conclude that she would just have to wait.

More time passed, and eventually her time came. It was a man who sparked her consciousness from the moment he entered the room, despite her diminished awareness from the handcuffs. He had a suppression team with him as well. He didn't say anything as he unbound her from the bed, other than that she was to follow him. She did so dutifully. They left without a word, and the suppression team followed them back to her dorm. Throughout the journey, she was tempted to ask where Janus was. She ultimately didn't care that much, though. He wasn't here now. Maybe he was busy and would be by to collect her in the morning. It made no difference.

The man wordlessly opened her door when they arrived. There was a plate of food on a brand-new table inside. The debris from her prior destruction had been cleaned, and they'd even taken the time to outfit the room with some other bare necessities. It was tempting to destroy everything again just because. That would have to wait for tomorrow, though, as she was hungry. She walked inside, hardly noticing the door closing behind her, and sat down to eat.

The food was fresh and warm. It wasn't her favorite, but she wasn't in much of a mood to complain. She took her first bite and then paused. The food tasted like chalk. She looked at it, utterly confused though strangely not surprised. Her meal didn't seem to be prepared badly. She'd had similar before, and it always tasted just fine. But something was decidedly different. Her appetite seemed to have left her just as her teeth closed.

She looked around her empty room. Everything seemed oddly dull, almost lifeless. Her body felt weak, probably from the hunger she was not experiencing, or because of, well… just because. Carmen looked at her new possessions. She had crushed her old ones to bits and, just like that, they gave her new ones. She'd been killed and, just like that, she was alive. Worst of all, she was back in this room again—trapped in this room for now and always. It didn't matter how many desks she obliterated or how many times she was revived. It would never end.

She looked at the food again and her eyes narrowed. How many times had she had that meal before? She forced herself to take another bite, and it tasted even worse than before. She pushed it away. Then she went to her bed and tried to sleep. If this wasn't Hell, perhaps she was simply dreaming and would eventually wake up.

* * *

Carmen didn't know when she finally nodded off. Now, however, her eyes snapped open with a flash. She wasn't saved by a nightmare, as far as she could recall, she hadn't set an alarm clock, and Mikayla wasn't slobbering all over her face. She had simply awoken. But why? Her eyes scanned the room, but she saw nothing.

Strange, she thought. It felt like there was someone else in the room with her. There quite obviously wasn't, but the presence was too significant to deny. It wasn't some great power like Artemis, but it caught and held her complete attention anyway. Now that she was more awake, she realized it wasn't in the room; it was approaching her room. Carmen sat still for a moment, unsure of what to do. She knew her track record in this place. This wouldn't be anything good.

"Lights," she said. She wouldn't face this new horror in the dark, but she didn't bother to get out of bed either. Crushing whatever it was with telekinesis as soon as it got in the door would be less work.

Closer and closer it came. Her brain shifted through the ether, and eventually she determined this thing had to be a Clairvoyant. The person's dynamism couldn't be pinned on anything else. Carmen looked up as whoever it was reached the door. Her breath even caught as they turned the handle.

There was a long pause before the person entered the room, and one of Carmen's eyebrows rose when she finally saw her new company. It was a woman maybe a year or two younger than Janus. She was Asian with raven black hair, cut short, and tidy. She wasn't very tall—perhaps only a few inches taller than Carmen, if she had been standing. And while this woman wasn't all too much shorter than Janus, for some reason she had none of his overbearing, ogreish presence. She was almost twig-snappingly skinny, which probably had something to do with it, but it was more in how she carried herself. There was a quiet, nearly arrogant style of fierceness to her movement, like her every action was a laughing, face-slapping challenge. There was so much grace to it, though, that she seemed downright gentle if not serene. Carmen had never encountered an energy like it before.

No one said anything. Carmen could read her—not well, but it could be done. At first pass, this person was nothing that gave her pause. Still, it was hard to tell exactly what she wanted. Carmen's mouth opened to more directly satiate that curiosity, but at the same moment, the woman looked at her sidelong and raised an eyebrow. She shut her mouth almost instantly. Then the woman turned and walked out the door without saying anything. She didn't even beckon for her. Despite that, Carmen felt prompted to follow. Her shoes were on in seconds, but there was no time for her to change her clothes, nor was there time to tie her hair in a ponytail. She just got off the bed and out the door as soon as she was able. After walking briskly to catch up, Carmen was walking side by side with her like she used to do with Janus.

The woman, however, still didn't say anything. Carmen stared at her, which was met by a quick glance. "If you are wondering who I am, my name is Kali," she said.

"Are you my new handler?" Carmen asked.

Kali smiled for a moment. "I prefer to think of myself as more than that. But if you want to consider me your handler, I have no problem with that," she said.

Her words fit together in the same effortless, gear-like fashion as every other Clairvoyant Carmen had ever met. Yet there was a welcoming if not warm aspect to her voice that Janus could never match. It caught her off guard.

"I don't want to fight anymore," Carmen muttered.

Kali smiled again, but she didn't say anything. Carmen didn't know exactly what that meant. Why was this so weird? She opened her mouth to protest, but Kali raised a hand, silencing her. Her new handler said nothing, though, and simply walked on. Carmen stopped in place. She was tired of being led who-knew-where to do god-knew-what.

"I said no."

Kali didn't stop walking, choosing instead to slow her pace. She casually glanced at Carmen over her shoulder with a bemused smirk. To Carmen's surprise, she didn't look angry. She didn't even seem annoyed. If anything, she seemed expectantly patient. She said no words. In fact, all she did was turn forward again and continue walking.

Carmen just looked at her. An argument was coming—it *had* to be coming. Part of her was even steeling for one. But now she was so deflated that she actually gasped. How could she respond to that? She'd never been at this point with Janus before. He usually just said something she only barely understood and then went on with whatever she was protesting against. Kali skipped the explanation. She didn't even give any indication that she would wait for whatever Carmen decided to do.

Weird, she thought as she considered her options. Her reticence continued for a few seconds longer before she decided to follow…for now, at least. Besides, she was a little curious about Kali. There was something so alluringly different about her manner that Carmen would be hard-pressed to say she didn't enjoy being around her, if just for the contrast.

The two of them got in the elevator. Carmen didn't see what button Kali pressed, but it didn't matter anyway. She had little doubt as to what floor it would be. The fight rooms, always the fight rooms. Her mind ran in circles, trying to figure out how to avoid the painfully familiar place. Unfortunately, nothing came to mind. The appropriate floor came… and then it went. The elevator didn't stop. Carmen glanced in Kali's direction. Her new handler made no reaction. It was at this moment that Carmen noticed the floor for the fight rooms wasn't selected; it didn't seem to be a mistake. Janus never made mistakes. Kali seemed at least as competent.

Where is she taking me? Carmen wondered.

There was no way of knowing. When the elevator opened again, Carmen was quite certain she had never been on this floor before. The unlikelihood of a mistake was confirmed when Kali stepped out of the elevator without a second thought. Carmen followed.

It was dark here. The lighting was minimal and, as was usual for this place, there were no windows. The hall stretched on for a respectable distance as a kind of dimly lit tunnel. A door was at its end. Carmen could make out a sliver of light from under it even at this distance. She looked at Kali, who unsurprisingly had no reaction. Carmen looked at the door again, not liking whatever her prospects were on the other side of it.

"Where are we going?" she asked hurriedly. Her eyes had adjusted to the point that she could make out Kali's smile.

"Nowhere in particular," her handler said simply.

"What's through that door?"

"That's completely up to you."

"What?"

Kali sighed softly. "It's difficult for me to explain now. But you'll find out."

Carmen stopped in place. "No!" she said. The words flew out of her mouth with such force that they may as well have been a punch.

Kali didn't say anything, but she did stop walking. Then she turned slowly. Carmen swallowed hard. She was going to get it now. She took a few hesitant steps back and subconsciously balled her hands into fists. Kali didn't look angry, though. She had that same serene air about her as when they first met. Janus wasn't a madman. He'd never even raised his voice at her—sort of. But Kali was just...*odd* in her calm. It was off-putting.

"Edge," she said, looking down at her charge, "there is nothing I can say to you to make you trust me." She paused before she spoke again. "I don't even expect you to. But trust me when I say I will never do you harm. I will never hurt you. I will never do anything—*anything*—that isn't in your best interests."

Kali was right. There was nothing she could say that proved she was sincere. Carmen knew that better than most. People mixed the truth and lies together so effortlessly that they may as well have been ingredients for a cake. Even so, Carmen could read her handler well enough to know she was telling the truth, for what that was worth. There was no conscious prompt on Carmen's part, but the knowledge made her defenses fall.

Her handler saw as much, and she smiled and then nodded at the sight. "You asked me what's behind the door. And I'll tell you I honestly don't know. It's up to you. But, if you'll let me, we can face it together," she said, holding out her hand. Carmen stared at it and stepped away. Kali only smiled again as she pulled it back. "Whatever you like," she said simply. Then she began walking again.

Carmen followed slowly. All she could do was stare at her. Eventually, they were walking side by side, and she continued to stare. Who was this person and where had she come from? One thing was certain: she didn't belong here. Kali was like a flower in cow manure or a snowball in Hell. But as Carmen stared at the impossibility before her, the less and less she questioned its existence.

After a while, Carmen tired of studying her new handler and instead looked toward their destination. She took a deep breath. It wasn't that she didn't appreciate, on some level, Kali's offer, although it was just as unbelievable as Kali herself. It was more likely that unicorns would run in and carry her to safety, all things considered. In any case, if her fate was solely up to her, she wondered what it would be. Nothing immediately came to mind. If it came down to what she wanted, however, she guessed she could look forward to some peace…for whatever form such a thing would take.

As Kali's hand went to the door handle, Carmen's tension rose to the boiling point. The door opened, and the girl's mouth dropped and her eyes grew wide. She was outside! Her mind went blank in that instant, and she couldn't move. As a reflex, she raised her arms to shield herself from the long-forgotten rays of the sun. Her eyes didn't hurt when they adjusted to the brightness, but the warmth on her skin felt like acid. There was no time she could remember being overly hot or cold. She wouldn't say it was hot now, but the sensation was so strange that the only thing she could think to do was suppress it to avoid being overwhelmed.

"Come on," Kali said over her shoulder, not slowing her pace.

Carmen did her best to comply. She even took a moment to lower her arms. She probably looked a bit ridiculous with them held up, but no one was watching. She looked and looked and looked, but there was no one else around. The shock almost pinned her in place again. If she ever managed to escape—and she'd planned as much more times than she could count—she expected at least one if not several armed guards to intercept her the moment she stepped outside. Kali gave no reaction, so Carmen assumed the present circum-stances weren't unusual.

Armed guards or no, the facility did have defenses, though. A relatively imposing concrete wall seemed to ring the compound. It was also topped by barbed wire that faced outward. She remembered there being a metal fence when she was younger, but she couldn't see it now. Perhaps the wall had been an upgrade, but it wasn't much of one if that was the case. To her or really any Clairvoyant, it was about as impregnable as a sieve. She could fly over it without a second thought. If she had the time, she could just burn through the concrete. She glanced at Kali and felt the strong urge to choose option one. Kali glanced back, seemingly knowing what she was thinking. With that, Carmen put the fermenting plan to bed.

They passed a corner of the building, and Carmen received another shock. Just a short ways away were other children. They were about her age, certainly no younger, and were Clairvoyants. They weren't in the middle of some escape attempt, though; they were just quietly playing some game she had never heard of. Frankly, she thought they looked very awkward. Sure, they moved with all the grace and poise one would expect from a Clairvoyant, but it was like they didn't know what they should be doing, and it had nothing to do with their game. They glanced in Carmen's direction for a moment before once again paying her no mind. She did the same, moving on to study the more interesting trappings of her surroundings.

The compound was larger than she'd ever thought. She had only seen it from the outside once, and that was years ago. The fact that the facility extended several stories underground only added to that mass, and Carmen was immediately reminded of her lessons about icebergs. On the outside, it didn't resemble a prison as she expected it would, concrete wall notwithstanding. People moved freely. There was a calm if distant atmosphere to their demeanor, more from the students than from the handlers. If pressed, she would even admit the place came across as *open*, if such a thing could exist in this horror.

Behind her, in the far distance, loomed the skyscrapers of a city she didn't know. Local geography was never in her lesson plans, and she always assumed it was a calculated play to limit her options if she ever did escape. If so, it had worked. She had no idea where she was or even her orientation. The facility, for all its size, was an insignificant speck compared to that metropolis, and that was all she knew about it. The sight was impressive. Just looking at the middles of the buildings disappear in the clouds only for their tops to reappear and then stretch on and on made Carmen nauseous. Even so, she had never been one to be all too interested in brick and steel, especially after being submerged in it for most of her life. And it was now that she relaxed enough to become reacquainted with an old friend.

She sighed contently, but even that couldn't do what she was feeling justice. It was hard to believe she'd almost forgotten. The big burning ball in the sky bathed her with energy, and every fiber of her Dark soaked it up, letting it course through her and playfully letting it go only to absorb yet more. Locking a Clairvoyant underground was like blinding an artist or hobbling a Thoroughbred. As far as she was concerned, it was another in the list of crimes she was a victim of.

Kali kept her same pace, which was another crime. Carmen had so much energy under the sun that she could run a marathon on her hands while singing opera. In due time, though, they crossed the courtyard and exited one of the gates in the wall. Carmen looked back at it. She'd dreamed of this moment—the day, the exact second, she was finally out of that place. Yet it passed with no ceremony, even on her part.

She looked forward without a second thought. There were no more buildings in front of her. The air was moist and warm, and as they went, she began to hear an odd noise. It was rhythmic and gentle, but there was a dull crash every now and then. She'd never heard the ocean before, and she could even feel that great body of water churning. They followed no path, despite their track being a straight line. The land was tended here, just like in the compound, leading Carmen to think it was all the same property. She groaned softly. *I still haven't left.* But she knew, as she always did, that they were almost to their destination.

Their journey ended at a bluff overlooking the water she had sensed earlier. Kali stopped walking, but Carmen couldn't help taking a quick glance over the side. It was a sheer drop to the water below. Waves crashed into the jagged rocks of the bluff, but ignoring that, it was a rather calm precipice. Sea birds hovered on nearby thermals, and the sky was clear, giving a good view of another shore far in the distance. Carmen looked to Kali after parting a lock of hair from her face.

Her new handler didn't speak at first. Instead, she took a moment to look over the side, which prompted Carmen to do the same again.

"You asked me where I was taking you," Kali finally started. "I told you I don't know—it's not up to me. I am merely giving you a choice."

She didn't speak again for a few minutes as she looked at the water below. Her eyes fell, and Carmen was hard-pressed to find that same serene air Kali commanded so confidently before.

"Clairvoyants lead…interesting and very unique lives," she said, pausing again as she swallowed hard. "You've only had a taste of it, but I'm sure you've had your fill," Kali added with the slightest hint of bitterness. "But there is one thing we can experience that no one else can. We can let it all go, completely and utterly. For a moment, we can know what it's like to be completely free. What you do with it is up to you, but it's a choice you have to make. No one—not me, not Janus, *no one*—will ever be able to take that away from you."

Kali looked over the edge more intently. "Jump." Then she took a few steps back to give Carmen more room.

"Jump?"

"That's the easy part. What happens next may be the hardest, most defining moment of your life."

"What did you choose?" Carmen asked.

Her handler looked away and glanced at the ground, but she said nothing. On the list of traits she didn't share with Janus, Carmen noted that she had never seen him uncomfortable before.

Carmen peered back over the edge and took a deep breath. She had no thought or feeling for her next few seconds; she simply closed her eyes and stepped off.

She figured this was probably the most pleasant sensation she'd experienced in recent memory. Her bonds to gravity were broken, and she didn't miss them. It was so calm, so peaceful. She suffered no control over anything and thus no burden. She was just a falling projectile with no care or worry for the first time in her life. Only the rising volume of the airstream hinted otherwise. She didn't worry about that, though. Truthfully, she didn't care about much of anything for the moment. Not about being brought to this place. Not about being forced to fight. Not about being tricked into killing Mikayla. Not about anything. As the rushing wind grew louder, Carmen felt nothing. She penetrated the air like a bullet, subconsciously moving it aside while leaving enough for her to breathe. There was no more drama in it than in being within a womb. Time seemed to pass in eons. Then she opened her eyes.

She was far closer to the bottom than she'd thought. Carmen didn't feel fear. Not at first. She was simply surprised. When Kali told her to jump, she'd never thought she would be falling to her doom. Now that she was faced with it, the reality produced little more than a shrug. She wasn't scared of dying. Not anymore. She'd been dead too many times already for that. There was no doubt in her mind that there would be no resuscitation from this. The rocks she was hurtling toward would rip her body beyond repair, and that, all things considered, wasn't so bad. She had nothing to live for, really. She had no friends and no family. She didn't even have a dog anymore. There was just hope. A small, unspoken hope.

* * *

Kali glanced at her watch. As all Clairvoyants, she lacked any extra sensory perception of time. She could only shake her head when her stopwatch timed out.

"Too bad," she muttered to herself.

She now knew why Janus was so hesitant about bringing her here. Edge had a great deal of potential; that was undeniable. Kali checked her watch again to make sure she'd done the math right and then sighed. *Such a pity*, she thought, noting that Edge could now be considered a total waste.

"Oh well," she muttered.

Then there was something. Kali had just enough time to notice the hairs on her arm were standing on end before a streak about the size of a twelve-year-old girl zoomed past. Her new charge was soon just a small dot and then nothing. Kali allowed a hint of a smile.

This will be interesting, she thought, preparing for the wait.

* * *

Carmen hurtled upward with no particular destination, care, or concern. Then she let herself fall, giggling the entire way. Her jump off the bluff had been too short. Now, however, she fell for thousands of feet. As the water rushed up to meet her, she could only smile at it. Kali was right. This was a state utterly unique to Clairvoyants and Clairvoyants alone, completely out of control but not powerless. She stopped her descent at the last possible second and then skimmed across the water before shooting upward to do it all over again.

The air battered her, and it became more and more of an effort to consciously move it aside as her velocity increased. Her inertia, the eternal enemy of every Clairvoyant, fought against her as she playfully tumbled through the sky, even graying her vision when she pushed too hard. Then she let it all go and fell. For some reason she'd probably never know, she felt the overwhelming urge to flip onto her back. She did so without hesitation and calmly watched the sky leave her. Carmen felt a small yet growing anxiety, but she ignored it. As the ground approached, that anxiety redoubled its efforts to be heard. In spite of it, Carmen could only marvel at the sky.

It had been years since she'd seen it. Pictures did that great ocean no justice; it was far prettier than any static image could convey. It billowed and churned almost like it was alive. Indeed, Carmen could feel its energy, and she had danced among it like she belonged there. But now no longer. She shot across the surface of the water again at the last possible moment, taking no time to correct her orientation and instead allowing a lazy finger to skip along the glassy surface beneath her while she sky-gazed.

Then, all at once, she became more sensible. After turning right side up, she thought about what she was going to do next. There was no pursuit that she could sense, but that didn't mean it wouldn't be coming. For now, though, she was sure she wasn't being hunted. The distant shore she saw earlier was now less so, and she increased her altitude to get a better look.

It was no grand metropolis like the one that overlooked the facility. There was no great hustle and bustle that she could see or sense, nor were there great buildings of ingenuity and science rising into the sky. It was just a town, albeit a very large one. Throngs of aerocars scurried between the two population centers, leading her to assume they serviced each other. At any rate, houses dotted the land in front of her and stretched far into the horizon. Streets wove between the buildings, placing everything in neat order. At least, it seemed that way from the air.

Carmen looked at the city behind her. She'd rather hide there if she could. It would be hard to even find a starship in that mess. To go there would mean she'd have to overfly the facility, though. They certainly had to be looking for her by now, and that would be too big a risk. She looked back at the town.

"This will do…for a little while," she said to herself.

Then she dropped back down to wavetop level and shot across the water. As the shore and town fast approached, a large building, possibly the town hall, caught her eye. There was no one near it that she could sense. Nevertheless, a young girl flying through the air like a bullet was sure to draw attention. She slid to a stop behind the large building and then took a deep breath.

Her fingers were tingling. This was probably the most exciting moment of her life. She'd done it—she'd finally done it! Carmen had finally managed to escape. This was more than just getting out the gate. Even if the building wasn't in the way, she doubted she'd be able to even see that hellhole now far in the distance. She had never even dreamed of putting this much space between her and that past horror so quickly.

Now, however, her concern turned to her present surroundings: bushes and trees. She began walking. It wasn't like she could take refuge in a treehouse. The streets were clear, with just a few parked aerocars here and there. Aerocars also overflew the town high above, but she paid them no mind. There was no way anyone would know who or what she was from way up there. No, Carmen had a different problem. She had dreamed for years about getting out, but now she was acutely aware that she had never considered what she'd do if she ever actually escaped.

All she could think to do for the moment was to walk aimlessly. It was hard for her to get her bearings; everything looked the same. It wasn't that every house and every street looked exactly alike, but each fit quite neatly into a few broad categories with only small variations between them. In a way, it kind of reminded her of the empty corridors and boring sameness of the facility. It wasn't that the town was uninteresting or even dull; it just didn't live up to her expectations of what the outside world would be.

She could sense people all around her, even though she couldn't see them, and that made her nervous. There were so many people that pinpointing one individual took a bit of effort. In that moment, Carmen realized just how exposed she was in the open. As she turned to run behind a nearby house, she was immediately knocked on her back.

"Ow," she muttered, but it was more out of shock than any real pain. She looked up to see a hand in front of her.

"Excuse me, I didn't see you," the person said.

Carmen looked up from the hand and found a man

standing over her. He was holding the hand of a little girl who was maybe four or five.

"Daddy, is that one of those kids from the school?" she asked.

"I think so," he said. "She's dressed like one of them. Let me help her up and we can ask."

Carmen glanced at the man's hand and then scampered away from it without any real thought. It was simply her first instinct. She somehow came to her feet and was running away before she knew it. Distantly, she heard the little girl wonder aloud why she was running away. Carmen didn't really have a reason herself, but she darted into the next available alley and then hid behind a tree. There was no pursuit that she could see or sense, but it was about then that she realized how idiotic that would be.

"Stupid," she said, chastising herself.

She didn't think that guy, whoever he was, could help her in any meaningful way. But she'd definitely drawn more attention to herself than she would have liked. She took a quick glance out from the alley. The man and his daughter were just down the street, and it didn't seem like they were looking for her. She couldn't sense any concern for herself either. In fact, it seemed like they had no real concern for anything at all as they took a nice walk, hand in hand.

Carmen paid them no further mind and tried to think about what she'd do next. The first thing was to actually look where she was going next time. Thus, for the moment, her attention was on the alleyway. It was a relatively dark, dank cocoon, and she had no care for it. A few quick steps brought her to the other end, where she stopped short. There was a large number of people here, and she couldn't help watching such an oddity.

Their clothes swayed and moved about them freely; belying the drab but highly functional attire she shared with all other assets. Such colorful outer expression would be ripped to shreds in any real fight. Carmen was glad that, for all the indignities she'd suffered, she had yet to fight naked. The movement of these people was heavy and aimless. Not aimless in the way Carmen was—she simply had no idea where she was going—but it was a lack of direction more akin to a leaf in the wind. The stumbles, pauses, pointless starts and stops, and looking one way and then the other for no reason were so common that it reminded her of the background static on the facility's intercom system. Yet each person's arms swung about as if they were trying to control the mess. All they seemed to manage with the effort was to throw their bodies off rhythm to their own steps. Carmen had never seen anything like it. She didn't even know people could be so…uncoordinated.

She moved out into the crowd, trying her best to not be seen, like the almost imperceptible thrust of a shark gliding through the water. When someone happened to notice her, she darted behind a nearby tree before their eyes could fix on the anomaly. Currently, she hid from one particularly observant little boy. It seemed that awareness was inversely proportional to age. Patience, however, followed the opposite formula. The boy quickly tired of looking for her and soon enough paid her no mind, leaving Carmen to focus on her objective.

"This is close enough," she muttered to herself as she eyed the ice cream stand.

It would turn out that the first thing to come to mind during her great escape was how hungry she was. She remembered ice cream from long ago. That seemingly ancient memory contained no recollection of how it tasted, just that she liked it. A few books she'd read mentioned how it wasn't very healthy. Nevertheless, she figured she could stand whatever damage it gave her. Besides, she didn't have many options for what to eat. It was just a matter of how she'd pull it off, as there were a lot of people at the stand.

She could feel her Dark quietly yet persistently let itself be known. Anxiety washed through her veins, and she made no attempt to stop it. In fact, she used it, embracing its heightened perception and hair-trigger focus. The opportune moment came like an atom bomb, and Carmen flew into action. She telekinetically retrieved the cone from the vendor's hand, even taking the time to *politely* pull his fingers from it so he wouldn't be ripped from his feet. She then disappeared behind a nearby building before anyone could follow the wayward ice cream cone.

With her prize held triumphantly in hand, Carmen sat on the steps of the house she hid behind. The ice cream was red —whatever flavor that equated to. She hesitantly leaned forward and took the smallest, most glancing lick possible. It wasn't enough to tell her anything, though. Truth be told, she probably hadn't even touched the cone and spent the last few seconds pondering the taste of air.

Her next attempt was bolder. When her tongue retreated back into her mouth, she smiled. She bit into the ice cream and then laughed as she messed her face. It didn't take much for her to suppress the instinct to telekinetically clean herself. Instead, Carmen took another bite and giggled at her messy result. She licked the ice cream after that. Biting devoured it too quickly.

It wasn't long before she got a headache, but she didn't care. Each lick washed her body in raw pleasure, sinking into every pore and igniting fires within her she didn't know she had. Her full attention bent to consuming the sugary goodness before her. How or why this was bad, she didn't know.

"Excuse me?"

Carmen leapt to her feet upon hearing the voice behind her. She'd been so enraptured by her cone that she didn't even notice the door opening. She turned to face whoever it was, and out of reflex raised one of her fists. It was then that she realized how ridiculous she must look. Her face was an ice cream-caked mess, as was her hand which held the now half-melted, half-eaten cone. Her clothes were no better. And here she was, trying to pick a fight.

"I…umm. I…" she muttered.

She managed no better than that and, partly out of embarrassment, and partly because she didn't want to explain what she was doing on the person's doorstep, Carmen fled to the street. There were still people around, and now she had no way to avoid their interest. She was amazed to note that she didn't garner too much of it. A few people smiled her direction and a couple others even politely waved, but that was it. There were no nervous stares or hurried steps to get away. It wasn't like they didn't know what she was—she could read them well enough to tell that wasn't the case. But, strangely, that truth brought no drama.

She turned to the right and saw the ice cream man walking toward her, a hand behind his back. Carmen dropped her cone and stopped just short of assuming a guard. He was on her before she could sense what he was holding. He stopped in front of her, and she looked up at him.

"Why do you guys never ask first?" he said with a chuckle.

Then he produced another ice cream cone from behind his back. This time, the flavor was vanilla. He handed it to her and, after a short chuckle, messed her hair before walking away. Carmen couldn't help a bemused smirk as she looked through the hair that fell in front of her face. She'd read enough of his intentions to know the gesture was some small measure of retaliation for stealing the ice cream, but she'd thought she would suffer worse. She shuddered to think what the punishment would be if she stole back at the facility. Of course, she never had any opportunity to.

Carmen figured she'd keep her punishment for now. Besides, her hair didn't really get in the way. Even if it did, she didn't need her eyes to see or navigate. She licked her new ice cream cone and noted that she preferred the red ice cream to vanilla.

In any event, it was convenient not to have to hide from everyone. It also helped that no one was afraid of her. It was strangely refreshing. This almost seemed to be the normal state of things, even if it was utterly abnormal.

She walked slowly and enjoyed her ice cream cone in her new peace. She finished it after a few minutes, having savored every morsel. She wasn't hungry any more, and she still had a slight headache, but that was okay. Carmen's base problem remained, though. What would she do next? It was so pleasant here. It wasn't a question she was too keen on answering, at least not immediately.

Odd as it was, she thought it a fun game to try to be like everyone else—to move like they did. It was difficult. It wasn't any one singular aspect, but the fact that they seemed to be connected. The stiff action and lack of balance made it challenging for her to concentrate on one without neglecting the other.

The hardest aspect to copy was how rushed they were. It was haste without any clear purpose or direction. It was rushing to stay in place—sacrilege to any Clairvoyant. There was so much anxiety, so many small inconsequential details that held total sway, and so many boulder-sized observations they never even took note of. It was hard for Carmen to believe such a state was even possible. A man's hand flew to adjust a loose shirt cuff before he was tripped badly by an unnoticed street curb. A woman eating several candy bars complained loudly about how difficult it was to lose weight. On and on it went. The more she tried to emulate them, the more attention she drew, and it was hard for her to say why.

She gave up the game after only a few minutes. It was too tiring to play for very long. With that change, the other ducks no longer paid her any more undue attention, and as before it was a welcome feeling. She moved through them unnoticed or, if noticed, acknowledged politely. Nevertheless, she still didn't have a destination, and it was time for *that* to change. Someone or something had to be after her by now.

She touched her face and then glanced at her ice cream covered fingers. *This won't do at all*, she thought. Her first instinct was to remove the ice cream telekinetically, but she spotted a water fountain a short walk away and chose the more fun option.

The fountain was quite large with three distinct levels, and the top towered over her. Designs were carved into the stone of each level. She didn't know what they meant, if they even meant anything, but they were pretty to look at. She even took a few seconds to study them when she got a little closer. The water flowing from the top didn't shoot into the sky like a geyser; it clung to the etchings in the fountain, subtly enhancing their appearance before emptying into the large pool below.

Carmen sat calmly on the edge of the pool. A few others rested quietly around her, but she paid them no mind. Instead, she wondered why someone would make such a nice fountain and not stock it with fish. *Oh well*, she thought. Then she dunked her head in the water. That move garnered her so much attention that, instead of announcing itself as a soft pinprick on her consciousness as such things usually did, it came as a bolt of lightning. Carmen, however, was in no position to care. The novelty of her new sensation was worth it. It was hard as a Clairvoyant to really touch anything—a grand irony, she thought. Falling leaves, rain, and dust flowed around her just as people parted her path.

She concentrated on the cold water pressing against her face before pulling her head out and savoring the feeling of the water sliding down her features. A little ice cream remained on her face, so she dunked her head in again. There was still one small speck left when she pulled her head out yet again, so she took care of the blemish telekinetically. A quick head shake stopped the water from dripping all over the rest of her, but it soaked everyone around her instead.

She looked at them sheepishly when she realized and then muttered a soft, "Sorry."

A young girl looked at her and giggled. "This one is silly," she said. It took Carmen a moment to realize it was the same girl she saw earlier. Her father was still with her.

"Yeah, she certainly is," he said sarcastically while he rung out his shirt.

Carmen guessed that may be true and smirked. She then noticed the girl had a coin in her hands. She tried to skip it along the water, but it sunk to the bottom after a loud plop. Carmen looked at the coin through the glassy surface. A thought came to her as she gazed at the many others. She had never skipped a coin before. If only she had some money. She thought about it then was struck by the obvious.

She held her hand over the pool, and a coin from the bottom leapt into her palm. The proper technique to skipping coins escaped her, so she just chucked the thing. As it impacted the water, anyone watching had no doubt that the coin would be skipping to the bottom of the pool. A Clairvoyant didn't have to play by the rules, though. A small tele-kinetic thrust sent the coin back into the air; another continued the motion upon contact with the water. The other side of the pool fast approached when a third thrust curved the coin around the outside edge of the rim to come back toward her. Everyone took notice as the impossible happened right before their eyes. Carmen simply raised a hand, which the coin popped into when it was close enough. Then she flicked it back into the pool.

She looked again at the little girl, whose amazement was about as obvious as a continent from space. Carmen smiled at her and then looked at the "magic" coin at the bottom of the pool. It was then that she noticed something else: her reflection. It had been years since she had seen herself. It wasn't that she'd forgotten what she looked like; it was just that, when faced with it, the ghostly apparition staring back at her was…striking.

Her face was just so different from what she remembered. The markers that made her *her* were eroding away. They were transitioning, becoming sharper and more refined. Her knife-like eyebrows now looked like they could cut steel. Her face was thinner. Years ago, it would be hard for anyone to say she had cheek bones. Now they rested quite attractively where they should. She stared and noted how hard it was to spot the child from long ago. Even her hair was a different color—darker, though still quite blonde.

Her attention drew her to the little girl again. Carmen watched her, but she paid her no mind. At any rate, she couldn't help wondering what the girl would look like when she was older. There were traces of her father in her face—even in her movements and some of her speech. Her mother wasn't here, so Carmen only had half of the picture, but it was still interesting to guess.

She looked back at the water and realized she had no information to make much of a guess in her own case. She couldn't really remember what her parents looked like. It was hard to even remember having parents at times. Carmen presumed there were echoes and shadows of them in her, but there was no way of knowing what they were. It was doubtful that she moved, spoke, or thought like them, though. She was different. She was unique. She was *special*. She looked at all the people around her, noting their seemingly alien dress, their utterly unfathomable perspective, and their completely inaccessible lives…at least for her. *So special indeed*, she thought.

She stepped away from the fountain, telekinetically tying her hair into a ponytail as she went. As she consciously and calmly walked away, those in her path stepped aside, almost as if by instinct. Carmen didn't notice them. She instead reflected on the bland sameness of the town, trying to remember the one she'd come from. It was long lost to her; she could recall nothing in particular. Perhaps every town was like that after a while. They just *were*. Everything else was simply reflections of a mirror in the dark. She didn't know for certain. What she did know was that it was time to go. She'd wasted too much time here. Carmen looked upward and leapt back into the sky.

* * *

The hair on Kali's arm stood on end. "Right on time," she said to herself.

She still couldn't see her new charge, but the effects of her approach could be increasingly felt. Eventually, she could see a speck in the far distance. It rapidly grew. In moments, Carmen slid to a stop right behind her.

She stood in place for a long moment after that, saying and doing absolutely nothing. Kali waited for the girl to make some sort of acknowledgement until it became obvious that she'd have to ask the question.

"Why did you come back?" Kali asked over her shoulder, though she already knew the answer.

Carmen turned to face her but remained mute. Kali doubted she'd lost the power of speech during her short time away. If anything, it looked like she was chewing something hard. Her mouth would open, nothing would come out, and then she'd close it only to repeat the process a few seconds later. Kali couldn't read her at all. Edge was far too strong for almost anyone to do that. She didn't know what was on her mind.

Carmen looked at her handler, who stared back expectantly. She didn't know why this was so difficult. She knew exactly what she wanted to say, but for some reason, she was unable to give voice to it. Kali continued waiting, and Carmen soon tired of the attention. She walked past Kali and sat on the edge of the bluff. She just couldn't take her gaze any longer. A few seconds more and it would have made her burst into flames—at least, it felt that way. Kali sat down next to her.

Carmen ignored her and simply looked at the horizon. As she had assumed, the town could only barely be seen. She pondered the events of the day, and that seemed a fitting circumstance.

"You know," she started softly, but in truth she wasn't really speaking to Kali, "when I was younger, I used to think that, if I was *good* enough, they'd let me go home." She nervously glanced at her handler, who looked back, expressionless. "Pretty stupid, huh?" Carmen muttered.

Kali smirked and then gave a quick nod. "I guess so."

Carmen looked back over the water before she spoke again. "…There's no going back, is there?"

"You can try," Kali said after a brief pause. "I don't recommend it, though."

"Why?" Carmen asked out of curiosity.

"Hmm. Figured you'd know. But, anyway, I don't need to tell you that you're different. I'm sure you realize that."

"Damn near since the day I was born," Carmen said after a sigh.

Kali smiled for a moment. "But do you know how?"

"That's simple. I'm a Clairvoyant."

"Anyone can be a Clairvoyant," Kali said. "Most choose not to be, but either way, it's not very unique."

Carmen considered her words for a minute or two. She remembered Janus saying something similar. Nevertheless, she made no response. It was obvious Kali was going to elaborate.

"What makes you, me, and every other Clairvoyant here different is that we never had a choice. Our Dark wouldn't allow it."

"What do you mean?" Carmen asked.

"When you were in the town, what did you see?"

"People," she replied simply.

"And what did you notice about them?"

"Well," Carmen began, considering her response.

"It should have been obvious," Kali said.

"Well, they were kind of disjointed." Her handler nodded slowly, and Carmen continued. "I don't really understand it, but big things sometimes meant nothing to them while little things caused them distress. Or they'd be rushing, rushing, rushing with no place to go. I guess the best way I could describe it is that their right hand didn't know what their left was doing. I don't know how they could live like that. It's…meaningless."

"Nor can they fathom how you can't," Kali said. Carmen looked at her quizzically, and she laughed. "Edge, not everyone is consciously aware of when someone is lying to them, or happy, sad, or depressed in casual conversation. Not everyone knows what they want. More important, not everyone is consistently motivated to get it. There are also few incapable of deluding themselves positively or negatively whenever it suits them. We're clairvoyant not because we know that which is unknowable but because we constantly face and engage with reality. We're too sensitive to just ignore it and go on about our days. That would drive us mad."

"But what about the Dark?" Carmen asked.

Her handler didn't answer right away, instead pausing for a moment to think. She motioned with her head to the town far over the horizon and then turned back to Carmen.

"The difference between you and them is not that you have a Dark. Everyone has a Dark. It's merely a question of volume."

"I don't understand," Carmen said.

Kali leaned close before she spoke again. "Let me whisper in your ear," she said, doing just that. "Let me talk to you each and every day. Let me tell you things you need to hear, even if you don't want to listen. Now, how long will it take for you to ignore me, if you can even hear me in the first place? How steady would your nerve be if, the moment everything was quiet or calm, you heard me from out of nowhere? Would that make you disjointed, as you say?"

Carmen nodded.

"Good," Kali said. "Now let me SCREAM!" she yelled. The transition caught Carmen so off guard that she almost fell off the bluff. "I will yell and shout at you every second of your existence! I will only get louder the more you try to ignore me! I will not give you a moment of peace. I absolutely will not stop…EVER, until I get my way! And that," Kali said after a brief pause, "is the difference between you and them. You can't be like them. You won't allow yourself to."

"So then what do I do?" Carmen asked, trying her best not to sound forlorn.

"That's up to you. Janus had you fight simply because it is the best way for you to learn how to use that energy effectively. I know you won't believe me when I tell you, but it broke his heart to have you do it. He loved you. That's why he resigned after your fight with Artemis. He couldn't take it any longer."

Carmen didn't know he'd resigned. Either way, Kali was right. She didn't believe her. That monster didn't have a heart to break.

"Are you going to have me fight?" she asked.

"No," Kali said. "I have a more difficult task. Janus taught you how to live. I'm here to teach you why."

Carmen looked at the water below. That was a question she asked herself more and more frequently. She didn't say anything as she sat very still. Kali sat with her, seeming to enjoy the view. A few minutes passed in silence before her handler ended the moment.

"Would you like to go?" she asked simply.

Carmen had been thinking just that, but she still didn't speak. Instead, she stood, and Kali stood with her. Carmen glanced at her handler, thought about it for a moment, and then put her hand in Kali's. The woman smiled, and they walked off, hand in hand.

10

WHY LIVE

Carmen sat in her bed, ready and waiting. The items in her room, static and unchanging as always, were her only company. She looked at the spot where Mikayla used to lie. It was hard to imagine that had been only a few days ago. Now there was no sign that her friend had even existed. Her room had been cleaned so thoroughly when she was away that not even the smell remained. Her eyes turned elsewhere as she tried not to think about it.

Kali said she would come for her in the morning, though she didn't say for what. Carmen didn't think it would be anything very bad—her handler did say yesterday that she wouldn't be fighting anymore. Perhaps it would be a different kind of test.

Several more minutes passed, but her new handler still didn't appear.

Carmen sighed loudly. Although there were no clocks in her room, she was quite certain Janus had come to retrieve her at the same time each day. It was only now that she realized just how accustomed she was to his schedule. No matter how sleepless her nights ever became, she was ready for him come in the morning exactly when he needed her. Now? She guessed Kali had more trouble getting out of bed. She sighed again and got out of bed herself.

She paced slowly around the room. She knew every inch of it—she'd had six years of unremittent study. *Six years...* she thought. Carmen closed her eyes and touched the wall as she had countless times before. She knew every millimeter, each and every surface imperfection, and could describe such with the same ease as reciting the alphabet. Yet, when she opened her eyes, she was greeted by her distorted reflection from the brushed metal wall. That she didn't know. Her monstrous reflection didn't even look human. It was certainly her, what else could it be? She looked again at the spot where Mikayla used to lie, and then her eyes turned away. Her handler was coming.

Kali opened the door and extended her hand. Carmen smiled, went to her, and took it. Then they left the room, and the lights shut off behind them.

"What are we doing?" she asked casually.

Kali nonchalantly let her hand go after a moment or two. Carmen didn't mind. She welcomed the gesture, but she didn't need her hand held everywhere they went.

"Today, we are going on a field trip," the woman said.

"Field trip? What's that? What's it for?" Carmen asked as they got in the elevator and stood side by side.

She watched her handler intently, but Kali wasn't looking in her direction, nor did she answer her question. After a time, Kali glanced at her out the corner of her eye. Carmen noticed she wore a slight smirk.

Like a shot, Kali's hand flew towards Carmen's face in a backhanded slap. Carmen easily blocked the blow and then reflexively raised a hand to vaporize her handler's head. She stopped only when she consciously registered that Kali wasn't actually attacking her.

"I'll let you guess what a field trip is for."

Carmen didn't speak, but the young Clairvoyant's confused face said more than a thousand poems. Kali laughed lightly upon seeing it.

"Edge, you have been conditioned to a very fine point for only one thing. You would have killed me without even thinking about it until it was all over," Kali said without the slightest hint of concern.

Carmen looked at her still raised hand and felt oddly embarrassed. "Sorry," she said meekly.

"Good, good," Kali said. "It's good you apologized without me informing you that you should. That is what a *field trip* is for—to dull that point slightly."

"I...don't understand."

"Edge, not everyone everywhere you go will be seeking to fight you. In fact, very few shall. You and I can talk, and you can talk to the other assets here, but that won't give you enough experience in how to interact with the many varying personalities you'll have to engage in day-to-day life. You need practical experience. So, we go on field trips."

"That's it?" Carmen asked, wondering about the catch that was sure to exist.

"In so many words," Kali quasi elaborated.

Carmen nodded slowly. "I really am sorry," she said. "I didn't mean to do that."

The elevator door opened, but the two of them remained still. She didn't really know Kali. Honestly, she didn't fully trust her. But she didn't want to her hurt her; even the idea of it made her feel sick. Her thoughts began to stray back to Mikayla when Kali unexpectantly patted her on the arm and smiled. The contact produced a brief shock in both of them from the interaction of their bioelectric fields.

"Don't worry about it," the woman said, seeming not to notice the pain.

Then she beckoned her charge on. Carmen nodded, and they exited the elevator. They were outside in seconds. Carmen couldn't help closing her eyes and sighing in sheer bliss as the warmth of the sun washed over her. She thought she heard Kali chuckle but wasn't sure. She didn't much care either way. After taking a few steps forward that were more like skips, Carmen flew around Kali in lazy circles just off the ground. Kali casually watched her charge but didn't join in her youthful exuberance.

"So, are we going to that town?" Carmen asked.

"You mean the one you flew to yesterday?"

She soon had enough of flying and once again walked next to her handler. She did wish Kali would walk a little faster, though. "Yeah," she answered.

As they slowly approached the concrete wall surrounding the facility, Kali shook her head. "That town wouldn't be appropriate."

Carmen gave her handler a curious look. "What do you mean?"

"Assets often fly there for their first flight," Kali explained. "The townspeople are used to Clairvoyants. We will go there for other field trips, but that town will never give you a...*realistic* example of what you'll encounter when you're released from here."

Carmen wasn't really sure what her handler meant by "realistic example," but she nodded anyway. She figured she find out soon enough. Besides, she had a more important question.

"When will I be released?"

"When you're eighteen," Kali replied.

"That's it? I don't have to do anything? I don't have to pass some test? I just turn eighteen and I'm released?" Kali nodded, and Carmen's eyes shifted rapidly back and forth as she considered the new information. "That means I'm halfway through."

Kali glanced at her over her shoulder. "If that is what you like to think."

Carmen didn't see how what she said could be interpreted any other way. She'd arrived when she was six, she was twelve now, and she'd be released when she was eighteen. Sure, in this place, an hour felt like an age and a day an eon, but she could count.

They were at the wall now, and Carmen stared up at it while Kali talked to the gate guard.

"Why don't we just fly over it? Why do they even have a wall?"

"The wall isn't meant to keep assets in; it's meant to keep non-Clairvoyants out," Kali said without glancing in her direction.

"Why would they want to come in here?"

"To harm you or destroy the facility," she answered nonchalantly. "There have been several protests...some violent."

Carmen looked at her handler, not sure if she was being serious. What had she or any other Clairvoyant here done to anyone? Kali had to be exaggerating. She looked at the top of the wall again.

"Come on, let's go. This is taking too long," she said, already levitating in place and ready to bound over the wall with a single thought.

"Edge!" Kali yelled harshly.

Before now, her handler had only given her fleeting

glances here and there. Now Kali stared at her hard. Carmen couldn't say the woman was angry, but her feet came back to the ground and stayed there as if she were nailed in place. Kali's eyes narrowed slightly as a silent period on the matter. Carmen knew she was saying "Don't challenge me." The guard Kali had been talking to was as frozen in place as she was, but she noticed his hand hovered over some sort of button. Kali turned her attention back to him and, after letting go a long-held breath, he moved to pick up the papers he had dropped.

"I apologize for my charge," she said, her voice returning to its normal soft, caressing tone. "There will be no problems," she added.

Other handlers and assets were starting to queue behind them by this point. Carmen even heard a few of them discussing the incident from an instructive standpoint. Her cheeks turned bright red in embarrassment.

"That's good," the guard said, visibly relaxing further. "I don't think the suppression team could get here fast enough. You're cleared through."

"Thank you," Kali said. She then looked down at her charge. She wasn't *that* much taller than her, but Carmen felt two inches tall anyway. "Edge," Kali called before stepping through the gate.

Carmen dutifully followed her handler out of the compound. They appeared to be walking toward a bus, and other assets and handlers also went in the same direction.

"Why aren't we going to fly to where we're going?" Carmen asked with muted glee compared to a few minutes before.

"Flying is too tiring," Kali replied.

Carmen nodded as they got on line for the bus. Just then, she heard someone scream.

"I'm not going again! You can't make me!" some girl yelled.

Everyone turned to see what the commotion was about. It was an asset about Carmen's age. Most of the assets she could see were about her age or a little older. The girl didn't seem to notice all the attention she was receiving; her focus was fixed on who was presumably her handler.

"I can't take it anymore! No more field trips!"

Confused, Carmen looked at Kali. Field trips didn't sound too bad from how she'd described them. They sure seemed better than fighting. Her handler didn't notice her curiosity, though. Instead, her eyes narrowed like they had on Carmen earlier. Even when Kali's annoyance wasn't aimed at her, it still gave her pause.

The girl shrieked in response to something her handler said, but Carmen didn't hear what it was. "No! No! I'm not going!" she screamed.

The girl continued screaming, but her words became more and more incoherent. No one moved against her, not even her handler. That seemed to provide no comfort for her as she backed away from everyone. Carmen noticed a suppression team running toward them. The girl didn't see them coming, nor did she seem to sense their approach as she continued screaming. Now that Carmen thought about it, she couldn't sense them either.

The girl turned to face her attackers right before it happened. With no words and no warning, the suppression team hit her with a foam cannon. The sticky, brownish-orange goo hit her in the face first before encasing the rest of her body in muck. A muffled scream could be heard as she fell over. Carmen's eyes grew wide as she turned to her handler, but Kali showed no apparent concern for the suffocating girl. The foam bulged but refused to give way. They could hear more muffled screams, but no one did anything. Carmen's nails dug into her palms. A few seconds later, a member of the suppression team freed the girl's face from the foam while the rest of the team leveled rifles on her. She gulped the air in sharp pants while fresh tears rolled down her face. Carmen let go her breath in a relieved sigh.

"Thank you. I will take over from here," the girl's handler said.

The leader of the suppression team nodded, and the squad returned to the compound in perfect military order.

"I hope I never see you behave like that," Kali said without looking at her. Carmen glanced at her handler, whose eyes were still fixed on the girl. "Clairvoyants are the some of the most powerful beings in the galaxy. They should act like it." Then she turned to get on the bus. "Come on," she called.

Carmen followed her. The bus driver wasn't a Clairvoyant, and when she looked him in the eye for a brief second, he was near trembling. She could almost taste his fear, and it wasn't palatable. She did her best to ignore it, but the feeling stuck in her consciousness like an ice pick between her eyes.

She sat by the window and busied herself with watching the girl. It was as good a distraction as any. She was still mostly encased in the foam as her handler spoke to her. It was impossible to tell what was being said, for what little it mattered.

"What is that foam made of?" Carmen asked. She well remembered the one time it was used on her.

"I can't honestly say," Kali replied. "Effective, isn't it, though? It dampens a Clairvoyant's bioelectric field, rendering them largely powerless. Binders work the same way. Both were invented by the sortens."

As usual, Kali's words were as abrasive as silk. But Carmen was quite sure she heard some bitterness in her handler's voice when she mentioned the sortens. She looked at her with a raised eyebrow.

"The sortens?" she asked.

"Yes. What of them?" Kali asked as the bus started on its way.

"Janus told me he was interned with them when he was a kid—before the revolution."

"And?" Kali asked.

Carmen swallowed hard. Perhaps this wasn't the wisest question to ask. "Were you interned with them?"

"Every Clairvoyant my age was," Kali said nonchalantly.

Carmen nodded. "What was that like? Janus said several of the training methods used on Clairvoyants came from them."

Kali didn't answer at first. She leaned back in her seat and got a faraway look in her eye. She then closed her eyes for a few seconds and took a deep breath. Carmen was transfixed. She'd never seen her handler—or really any handler—like this.

"I'll simply say it was quite horrible," Kali replied. Carmen opened her mouth to ask another question, but her handler spoke before she had the chance. "Your focus shouldn't be on me. Relax. Take a deep breath. This will be a long day," she said gently.

Carmen nodded but couldn't help showing concern for her handler. Kali smiled when she saw it but said nothing more. In any case, the trip wasn't very long; the bus floated to a stop after only a few minutes. Most of the assets and handlers stood to get off. Carmen stood as well.

"Not here," Kali said. "This is a Haven City stop. We will eventually go to Haven as well, but for now it will be too overwhelming for you."

Carmen had no idea what she meant but sat back down.

She nervously rubbed her hands together. She had no idea why field trips were such a big deal. After all, she flew to that other town just yesterday and was none the worse for wear. She'd certainly rather be here than fighting, but perhaps she was just ignorant?

In short order, the bus was on its way again for another brief trip. Carmen was quick to realize they were just in another part of Haven City, and she didn't get up to leave this time. She instead marveled at the forest of skyscrapers all around her. She'd never seen anything like it, nor had she ever felt anything like it. Cities had people in them—lots and lots of people. She knew that intellectually. The knowledge of it, however, and the reality of how their mere existence assaulted her Clairvoyant senses was something else entirely. Despite her best efforts to ignore or block out the sensation, it was like someone was constantly screaming in her ear. It was about now that Carmen realized what Kali had meant by the experience being too overwhelming.

The bus began moving again, and Carmen breathed a sigh of relief as they got farther and farther from the heart of the city. After several minutes, they were well clear of the city and she was able to relax a little, despite the annoying bus driver. He wasn't as bad, though, now that most of the Clairvoyants were gone. After a time, the bus stopped again. The suburb they had arrived in gave her flashing memories of her own neighborhood, but she could recall little to nothing from that time in her life. She looked at Kali, curious if it was time to get off. Her handler shook her head, though, so Carmen got comfortable again.

The bus took to the sky, joining the air traffic far overhead. Carmen looked at the ground moving briskly past underneath them. She didn't think Kali would take her somewhere this far away, but she didn't know the half of it.

Minutes passed—tens of minutes, maybe even a couple hours. Eventually, the bus dove back to ground level and came to a stop.

"Here?" Carmen asked, dismally wondering if there was yet another leg to their journey.

Kali nodded. "Yes."

The woman and the girl then stood and made their way out of the bus. Carmen noted that other Clairvoyants still had yet to disembark. *Where the hell are they going?* she wondered as she looked at them. But that was neither here nor there. Carmen looked at the bus driver again. She could still sense fear, but it was mixed with a muted joy, and she was well aware that it was because there were now two fewer Clairvoyants for him to contend with. The bus driver experienced a quick shot of elation as he closed the door behind them, and Carmen wondered why it was such a big deal. They had all sat calmly during the trip. They hadn't even spoken to him.

She tried not to think about it as she stood next to her handler and slowly looked around. The bus stop was on a small hill, which gave a good view of the lay of the land. The town wasn't very big, and the fact that it seemed quite in the middle of nowhere only enhanced that perception. There were no cities to be seen and no other nearby towns. When Carmen looked up, she saw few if any aerocars flying overhead. The most dominating feature wasn't really the town itself but a large forest nearby that extended far into the horizon like a badly kept blanket. Her parents had never taken her hiking, and woods then and now were of little interest to her. The forest was forgotten after only a few seconds when Carmen looked at her handler.

She didn't understand why they were here specifically. She agreed that Haven City was a little overwhelming, although she'd convinced herself that she'd get used to it. But this place? There had to be more squirrels than people here. She could only guess that Kali didn't have much confidence in her and wanted to start small.

"So, what now?" Carmen asked.

Kali looked around for a few seconds more before she turned to her charge and shrugged. "I don't know. You tell me."

Carmen was expecting any answer but that. "Me?" she muttered. "I don't know."

Kali looked at her expectantly, but when it was obvious that Carmen had nothing else to say, she shrugged again. "Well, I'm hungry. Let's get something to eat," she said as she started walking. "I think it's this way."

"You...don't know?"

"I don't know everything, Edge."

"Sure seems like you do," Carmen uttered under her breath as she began following her handler. Kali heard her and gave a wry smirk.

The town, at least this part of it, was very quiet. No one was on the streets. There were also no businesses for as far as Carmen could see—just rows and rows of houses. She looked around curiously. It felt to her that they were being watched by unfriendly eyes. When she looked in the window of a house, she saw its drapes sway back and forth. She looked at another house and found the same thing. When her eyes fell on a third, she caught a woman watching her intently. When she noticed Carmen watching her just as intently, she moved out of view like a shot and closed the drapes. They swayed back and forth as their colleagues had in the other houses.

"People are watching us," she pointed out.

Kali looked at her charge over her shoulder. Carmen motioned toward a house with her head where a man watched them from a window. He didn't shy away, however, when the Clairvoyants glanced at him. Carmen couldn't sense exactly what he was thinking, but she was completely aware of how anxious he was. He seemed to find some comfort in a cold metal object in one of his hands that she couldn't see. It had to be a gun.

"So they are," Kali replied without the slightest hint of concern.

"Why?"

"They aren't used to seeing Clairvoyants in person. They're curious."

"Curious" wasn't the word Carmen would use. Her head darted around, and everywhere she looked were dozens of eyes, watching everything they were doing. A few disappeared when she turned in their direction, but she could sense everything they were feeling or thinking. Carmen gave a subconscious shudder.

The eyes followed the Clairvoyants every step of their way downtown. People driving by stared, and it felt like someone threw a bucket of ice on her each time. A woman across the street gathered her children, who had been playing outside, into her house as the Clairvoyants approached. The children offered no protest as they called to their mother with squeals of panic and terror that the Clairvoyants were getting closer. Carmen shuddered again as their fear washed over her. A man maybe twice her size stood in front of them, trembling. To Carmen, his thoughts were as clear as a fireworks display. His wife's name was Ella, and he wondered if he would ever see her again. Kali smiled at him and nodded. Carmen looked uncomfortably at the sweat on his brow while she held herself. He gave a loud exhale once they were well clear.

"There. Let's try there," Kali said, pointing.

Carmen said nothing. Instead, she looked at her handler in utter disbelief, amazed that she seemed unaffected by everything around them.

She glanced at Carman over her shoulder. "You don't like it?" she asked.

Carmen's eyes grew wide as she stared at her insane handler. Then she subconsciously shook her head. "I…I don't care."

Kali shrugged and then casually motioned for her to walk across the street. Carmen, at a loss, followed. The restaurant was a generic diner. She could barely remember the like from when she was younger. It held none of her focus now, though. She didn't want to focus on anything. The thoughts and feelings of people she couldn't see but knew were present whispered in the back of her mind, threatening to drive her mad. She groaned out loud when she saw the restaurant was almost completely full. The people inside looked their way, and it felt like they were throwing daggers.

Kali stepped forward to get in line behind a young couple. Carmen stayed right beside her. She couldn't help biting her lip. She knew what was going to happen. She didn't know how she knew; she just did. Each agonizing second before the inevitable made her teeth grind down harder, to the point that she was almost tasting blood.

First, the woman slowly turned. Perhaps she realized someone was behind her and was going to offer a polite greeting. If so, the greeting never came—at least not a polite one. The woman looked at Kali and then Carmen and gave a startled shriek.

"What? What is it?" the man she was with muttered as he also turned. He saw the two Clairvoyants and shrieked as well before grabbing the woman and pulling her away. "Excuse me, excuse me. You can go ahead," he said nervously. "Let's get out of here," he said to his companion.

Kali gave them a reassuring smile but said nothing. Carmen said nothing either as their thoughts rang in her skull like church bells. *I'm not going to set you on fire. I'm not going to rip off your arms and legs. I haven't done anything to you. I'm just following my crazy handler to get something to eat,* she reflected.

Kali glanced at her charge. "Looks like we're next."

"Yeah, I noticed that," Carmen remarked under her breath.

If her handler heard her, she gave no response, and the two approached the hostess Her face was white with terror.

"All right, go ahead," Kali said.

It took Carmen a few seconds to realize she was talking to her. "What?"

Kali rolled her eyes. "Tell the greeter how big our party is. It's normal etiquette."

Etiquette!

"Two!" Carmen barked.

Her handler pursed her lips but didn't seem especially annoyed. Carmen felt two inches tall again nevertheless.

"Please excuse my charge," Kali said. "This is her first time out. Anyway, that table, right?" she asked, pointing.

The hostess swallowed hard. "Clairvoyants?" Kali nodded, and the hostess gave a disbelieving nod in turn.

"Thank you," Kali said as she started toward the open table. "Edge, say thank you."

"Thank you," Carmen muttered as she tried to forget the horrific ways the hostess was sure she was going to kill her and everyone else in the restaurant.

She took hesitant glances at everyone as they walked to the table. Those she glanced at moved as far away from her as they could while clutching belongings or loved ones. A waiter dropped his food tray but was so frozen in place by the sight of the Clairvoyants that he didn't seem to notice. His thoughts wafted toward Carmen like a bad smell as he wished he'd gotten up early enough to see the sunrise if this was his last day. He had always wanted to see a sunrise.

When they sat down, Kali busied herself with the menu. Carmen wrapped her arms around herself and rested a weary forehead on the glass. She didn't need to sense the people rushing out of the restaurant—she could hear them. For those who made it outside, she'd never sensed such relief. For them, the experience seemed akin to waking from a nightmare.

"Edge, what's wrong with you? You were rude," Kali said, and Carmen looked at her. Her handler glanced at her over the menu but seemed otherwise unconcerned.

"Rude? Everyone hates us. They're terrified of us," Carmen said as if it was obvious.

"Of course they're terrified of us," Kali said, now looking at the asset fully.

"Why?" the girl snapped.

Then she shuddered as their waiter approached. She'd fully sensed him before he even entered the room, such was his state.

"May I take your order?" he asked, quaking horribly between each word.

"Edge," Kali offered.

"I don't want anything."

The woman shrugged and then made her order. The waiter more ran than walked away.

"Why shouldn't they be terrified of us?" Kali asked, turning her attention back to her charge.

"We haven't done anything to them," Carmen pointed out.

Her handler nodded a few times. "No, we haven't. But, if you wanted to, you could kill every single man, woman, and child in this town, and no one could stop you—not even me. They don't know that last part, but it doesn't matter much to them, as I could also kill every man, woman, and child, and they couldn't stop me." She took a deep breath before she spoke again. "It is a bit of a risk to take you here."

Carmen looked out the window, now understanding why they'd come to such a remote town. If she went berserk or tried to escape, there were less people in the way here. She closed her eyes and took a deep breath. She'd thought Kali trusted her. It had been nice to have someone to talk to who wasn't keen on the most effective way to beat someone to death. She missed Mikayla.

"I don't want to hurt anyone."

"They don't know that," Kali said, and Carmen looked at her sidelong. "Edge, you may know what everyone is thinking and feeling, but no one can read you. *I* can't even read you. Put yourself in their position," she began. "How comfortable would you feel around someone who knows everything about you at all times when you know nothing about them? Someone who knows you better than you know yourself—who could kill you or hurt you whenever they pleased, for whatever reason. How would you consider such a person?"

Carmen stared at her handler defiantly. She didn't know why she was so mad at Kali all of a sudden. She didn't really care about these people or their feelings. She was constantly bombarded by them. Why was that so hard for Kali to understand? Yeah, she could kill them all, but so what? What about her? Did they care about her at all? Did anybody? Did *they* care that, by the end of the day, she'd be locked in some room deep underground? Did they care that no one was able to read *her* thoughts or feelings on anything and that it would never change?

Then, everything hit her like an anvil. A tear rolled down her cheek. *We really are monsters*, she realized. She covered that side of her face so Kali couldn't see. If it was true that her handler couldn't read her, she was especially thankful for it in this instance.

"There have been several incidents," Kali continued. "They're not frequent, but they aren't rare either."

Carmen stealthy rubbed her cheek of the wayward tears and took a deep breath. "How does everyone know we're Clairvoyants?" she asked.

"How do you know someone's a Clairvoyant?" Kali asked back.

She looked out the window and saw several townspeople giving the building a wide berth. They spoke to each other, advising any passerby against entering. She glanced at her handler just as the food arrived.

"I can sense it," Carmen said. "But…normal people can't do that."

"Maybe, maybe not," Kali said with a shrug. "Anyone can become a Clairvoyant. As I said to you yesterday, it's all a matter of volume. Perhaps, on some level, they can sense subconsciously what we are. I can't really say."

Carmen's eyes dropped as the thoughts of an older couple came to her attention. "You can't say?" she asked, trying to distract herself.

Kali cocked her head to the side. "Edge, I'm not a *normal* person. I can know what they are thinking, but I don't think like them. Neither I nor you ever can. Our perspective is too different. If you really want to know, you can just ask. In fact, it would be good if you started talking to people. We'll work on that next."

Carmen shuddered just from considering the prospect. *They'll run away from me first*, she thought.

"Why does what they're thinking not bother you?"

"It bothers you?" Kali asked, and Carmen nodded several times. "I mostly ignore it."

"How?" she asked, longing and pain evident in her voice.

Her handler sat back in her chair and thought. She looked out the window for some time. "It's been so long that it's hard to say how I consciously do it. I don't really think about it most of the time. That's part of the reason we are here: so you can learn how to block out the thoughts or feelings of others, if you wish to."

"But how?" Carmen begged. She groaned out loud when the waiter returned to drop off the bill. "Please."

"Edge, it honestly pains me to see you like this, but there is really nothing I can do. I can tell you what worked for me, but you are not me. You'll have to suffer through it until you figure it out." Carmen looked at her handler with pleading eyes. Kali sighed softly. "For me, I guess it was a change in my mentality."

"What do you mean?"

Kali looked down for a second and took a deep breath. "Eventually, I accepted that everyone hates me—everyone is terrified of me. They always will be. They have reason to be. I largely filter it out, though. It's unimportant. There are things worse than people hating you."

Carmen's mouth hung open as she stared at her. "That it? Just accept that everyone hates me? But there are other things worse than that!"

"Essentially, yes," she remarked. "As I said, that's what worked for me. Personally, I think it's an act of compassion."

"An act of compassion?"

"Yes, compassion," Kali said firmly, annoyed by her

charge's raised voice. Carmen reined herself in but only just, and Kali continued. "Remember what I told you earlier. You are one of the most powerful beings in the galaxy. You should act like it. Yes, almost everyone is terrified of us, and that terror drives some to hate us. Yet, you've seen me. I could crush them to fit in the palm of my hand," she said, holding her hand out for effect, "but I smile at them. I'm polite. If that is not compassion, what would you call it?"

Carmen said nothing. She looked away from her handler and brought her arms around herself again in a hug. Kali stood when it was obvious nothing else was forthcoming, and then she looked down at her charge, who couldn't return her gaze.

"Enough of that. Let's continue. Maybe we can try talking to some of the people outside. I also think I saw an ice cream shop."

"What's the point?" Carmen muttered.

"You can't stay at the facility all your life. Come on," her handler said, looking around for where to pay. "It's time."

A shiver reverberated through Carmen's body upon hearing those words. She stooped over as her gaze welded itself to the table before her. Her mind was blank as the thoughts of the town echoed throughout her. None were comforting.

Kali paid and began walking toward the door. Carmen hadn't moved.

"Edge? Come on." She still didn't move, so Kali walked back toward her. "Edge? What's wrong with you?"

Carmen stood reluctantly. Her handler eyed her up and down but said nothing as Carmen actively avoided looking her in the eye. Kali eventually sighed and then made her way toward the exit. Her charge followed slowly. When they exited the building, it felt like Carmen was hit by a tidal wave. Even Kali grimaced slightly. Everyone looked at them when they came outside. A few people were already running down the street to get away.

Kali surveyed the area. "What about them?" she said, motioning toward a group of girls about Carmen's age. "They might be a good start."

She knew why Kali picked them. They were about her age and surely had something in common with her. But Carmen looked at their bright, colorful clothes compared to her drab, functional attire and their well-kept and styled hair compared to her ponytail, and she concluded something entirely different from her handler. Carmen took a subconscious step away from them and Kali while slowly shaking her head.

"I…I can't," she said softly as she looked at them.

"Edge?"

Carmen looked at her handler with a start, seemingly having forgotten that she was there. She took another step back. "I can't," she barely eked out while taking another step back. She shook her head again. "I'm sorry. I just can't. I can't take any more."

"Edge?"

Carmen backed farther away, words failing her. Her face contorted in a hopeless attempt at holding back tears. "I'm sorry," she said.

Then she started running. She heard Kali call to her, angry and disappointed, but her handler made no pursuit. Carmen's emotions were such that all coordination was sapped from her movements. She tripped over herself several times until she took to the air and skimmed along the ground. Everyone watched and cowered as the young Clairvoyant streaked through the town. Carmen nearly drowned in their mass panic.

She didn't know what she was doing; she just felt an overwhelming urge to get away. The only thing she was certain of was that she didn't belong in the town she flew to yesterday, she certainly didn't belong here, and the facility was becoming disturbingly comfortable. She was almost at her destination now. It was crazy and stupid, but it seemed the most logical choice. It was the one place that felt just as alone as she did every day—the only place that seemed appropriate for someone like her.

Without a moment's hesitation or doubting thought, the Clairvoyant, Edge, flew into the forest and disappeared. No one followed her.

11

ALONE IN THE DARK

Carmen didn't venture far from the edge of the forest. There was no reason to tire herself out in a futile attempt to get away. She was quite sure, for the past few hours, that a suppression team would come for her at any moment. They never came, though. By now, the sun was setting.

She could see the town through the trees and could run to it in a breath, yet it seemed a sea away. She could sense it just as distantly. It was refreshing, considering her ordeal earlier in the day, but it was also strange. The townspeople had no care or concern for the marauding Clairvoyant now. She seemed completely forgotten. She could somewhat sense Kali, so she had to be somewhere in the town, but no one seemed too concerned about her either, as far as Carmen could tell.

She rested her hand against a tree as she looked at the town, taking a step forward before she realized it. Then she retreated deeper into the forest. She couldn't go back—she couldn't face Kali. The thought of it was worse than enduring the town and even worse than killing Mikayla. She hardly knew her handler at all, but one thing was certain: Kali, unlike Janus, had expectations for how she was to conduct herself. As Carmen thought about it more, she had to admit that Janus had expectations too. The difference, however, was that his were about what she *did*. Kali had expectations about what she *was*, and she had failed them all. It was hard to say why that meant so much to her.

The sun was quite beyond the horizon now and its light was receding with it. *Kali's not coming*, she thought. She might be a rebellious asset, but frustratingly she was still a dutiful one. If not a suppression team, surely Kali herself would come to collect her. It didn't make sense to further infuriate her handler by being elusive.

Carmen waited a while longer as her surroundings grew darker. Eventually, she was in total darkness, but her company remained the animals and insects of the forest. She swallowed hard but was able to keep herself from taking another step toward the town. Instead, she turned, fell to the ground, and began pulling her hair.

"What should I do? What should I do?" she muttered to herself over and over again.

She pursed her lips, annoyed that she hadn't eaten anything when she had the chance. She was quite hungry now. Carmen turned to look at the town again, now dimly lit by the street lights. She also sensed Kali. She turned back around and was no longer tempted.

When she looked forward, the long dark of the forest lay before her. It wasn't the most welcoming sight and, if anything, made her shiver, but in her current situation, it would do. She stood and began walking slowly. Her feelings and mind—almost everything about her—was numb. The only thing Carmen was certain of was that, with every crunch of her feet trampling the undergrowth, she was another step farther away.

The forest was wild and untended in its growth, even this close to the town. There were no paths that she could see, though she was walking in the dark. Nevertheless, it seemed like no one in the town ever journeyed to the forest. Indeed, she'd been at its edge all afternoon and sensed no one come close.

Ultimately, the lack of any path was of little consequence. She maneuvered around trees, thorns, and other hazards of the wild with all the grace and poise of her kin. She never once stumbled or tripped. She had no idea where she was going, but she didn't really care. She didn't walk in a straight line, but she didn't meander either. As she went, she never came to a branch she had to stoop under to clear or a thicket that blocked her way, and the serendipity of this never crossed her mind. Clairvoyant through and through, each decision was no decision. Hesitation only came through conscious thought, and she wasn't thinking. Annoying leaves and small branches parted in her path seemingly by magic. Only when the undergrowth occasionally caught her pants did she notice the semiconscious telekinetic impulse that freed her. Even then, she was aware of it only on the same level that she was aware of her calm and steady breath.

Deeper she went until Kali could no longer be sensed. She couldn't sense anyone from the town either. She could sense but not see animals all around her, but they were no great concern to Carmen. For whatever reason, she had never been able to discern the consciousness of animals, not even with Mikayla. She could tell they were alive but nothing much beyond that. They were too raw. All the same, the animals hurried out of her way much like the townspeople had earlier. Perhaps they also knew she was a Clairvoyant.

As she glided nimbly down a ravine, she felt something at the edge of her perception. She walked toward it for no real reason at all. Whatever it was, it was more interesting than the endless sea of trees all around her, and there was no reason to worry about it. As Kali said, she was one of the most powerful beings in the galaxy.

The forest canopy gradually opened as she went. It was a star-filled night—New Earth had no moon. She'd never been good at astronomy, and it held no interest for her, but Carmen was pretty sure she could see New Saturn. It wasn't a very bright planet, so it was hard to know for sure. Fog parted around her and swirled in her wake. With her eyes prompted by no conscious direction, Carmen looked until, at last, her gaze came to rest on what looked like a fire in the distance. There was a figure next to it.

Carmen stood still as she considered what to do. The person had no idea she was here and could be bypassed with little difficulty. That, however, was not her first instinct, and she began walking toward them, curious. The irony that she'd come here to get away from everyone only to find someone was not lost on her. As she reflected on her kindred spirit, however, she was well aware that no one would be out here if they wanted to be around people.

Eventually, she got close enough to see that it was man. He was built like a bear and even made the Constructs she'd fought look small. He hummed quietly to himself as he sat by the fire. Carmen considered leaving him alone in his peace before she thought better of it. She deliberately stepped on a twig, and its snap echoed through the forest.

"Who goes there?" the man said with a start as he stood. Carmen said nothing, and he gave another small jump of surprise when his eyes found her. "What are you doing here, girl? Are you lost?"

Carmen took a few steps forward and shook her head. "I don't know where I'm going, but I'm not lost."

The man looked at her with an eyebrow raised. His hair was trimmed short, and his body had the look of an athlete who had only slightly gone to seed. By the fire, he had set up a small camp with a tent, a pot, and a few bags. She didn't think he had been here very long. A pile of wood had yet to be placed in the fire. As she moved a little closer to him, he felt none of the fear the rest of the townspeople did—surprise and confusion yes, but not fear. The contrast struck Carmen as unusual, but she didn't dislike it.

"You hungry, girl?" he asked after a few seconds of silence. "I've got some beans. It's not much," he added with a shrug.

Carmen was so hungry that he could have offered his boots and she would have accepted. She nodded several times before taking a seat on the opposite side of the fire. She'd never seen fire out in the open like this, and she stared at it while the man sat back down and got comfortable.

"Name's Eli," he said.

"Edge," Carmen replied as she studied the flames.

She could feel the heat, sure, but she could also feel the chemical bonds of the wood break down and change in the inferno. It was a strange sensation.

"Edge, huh?" he muttered. "You a Clairvoyant?" Carmen nodded and wondered, as usual, how people always knew. "Now, now, don't get too close! You'll burn yourself!"

Carmen smiled at that. Then she placed her hand on top of the flames. Eli marveled at the fire flowing around her hand, seemingly like water, to no ill effect.

"It can't hurt me," she said as she waved her hand slowly from side to side in the fire. "Our bioelectric field means it never actually touches us." Her eyes shot open in shock as her shirt sleeve caught fire. "Shit! Shit!" she yelled as she moved to pat out the flames.

Eli broke out in uproarious laughter. Carmen could admit it was somewhat funny, but she didn't even smile. Instead, she cradled her arm. She had been burned a little, and that sensation was also new. She grimaced from the pain. Eli noticed.

"A girl as pretty as you shouldn't have such ugly words come out of her mouth," he said.

Carmen couldn't help smiling. No one had ever said anything like that to her before. To Janus, Kali, and everyone else at the facility, her face may as well be a block of wood.

"Here, let me see if I have something for your arm."

Then he turned around and rummaged through one of his bags. Carmen walked over to him, still holding her arm. It didn't hurt that much, at least not compared to other injuries she'd suffered, but this was all so fascinatingly new that she went along with it just to see what would happen. He eventually produced a small bottle.

"Let me see."

Carmen sat in front of him and held out her arm. He slowly rubbed whatever was in the bottle into her wound.

"Old herbal remedy," he said. "I never trusted all the dermal-whatever stuff, even when it was used on me."

His hands were quite rough, but his touch was gentle. He looked at her and smiled, and it was so genuine that she could feel it radiating through her like ripples in a pond. She smiled back after wincing when he touched a sensitive spot.

"There. Now how does it feel?"

"Better," she half-lied. Then she went back to her place on the other side of the fire and sat down.

Eli turned to get something else. "I'll get started on those beans."

Carmen nodded but said nothing.

"Where did you even learn words like that?" he asked casually as he poured the beans into the pot.

She glanced between him and the stars. She hadn't seen them since she was a little girl.

"They give us books to read."

"Makes sense," he muttered. Then he noticed her looking at the sky. "Pretty isn't it?" Carmen nodded. "I found this place a few years ago. No one knows about it. I remember the first time I saw the night sky here."

"Is that why you're here now?" she asked innocently. After a second or so, however, her eyes narrowed on him before he even spoke.

"Uh…ah, yes," he stuttered.

She knew he was lying, but she didn't know what the lie was. His thoughts weren't completely clear to her, which was odd. They were muddled, not straying to any one thing as most people's thoughts did. She didn't pay it much mind, though.

"How do you know I'm a Clairvoyant?" she asked, changing the subject. "Seems like everyone does just by looking at me."

"You kind of can tell just by looking at you."

"What do you mean?"

Eli shook his head slowly and seemed amused by the question. Carmen groaned softly. It was mildly frustrating that the answer was so obvious to everyone but her.

"It's how you move. You're almost like cats or…or water flowing over rocks," he said, searching for the right words. "You probably wouldn't make a sound running on dry leaves, unless you wanted to," he continued. "It's even how you speak. 'I don't know where I'm going, but I'm not lost.' Only a Clairvoyant can talk like that. And then the eyes…." His voice trailed off, and he appeared lost in thought.

"What about the eyes?" she asked to get him back on track.

Eli glanced at her and then gave his head a small shake. "They look right through you. It's like you don't even see me—like you're studying my very soul."

Carmen looked away as her thoughts turned inward. She never realized that even how she looked at people was different from everyone else. It really was true. She was a Clairvoyant, and every single thing about her reflected it. She wrapped her hands around her knees and shivered.

"I *am* a monster," she said softly to herself.

She glanced at Eli in that moment. She knew he'd heard her. His eyes widened slightly, and then his face became very dour, but he didn't say anything. Just then, Carmen felt suddenly uncomfortable, like her skin had been turned inside out. She winced as she resisted the feeling, and was unable to help a small moan.

"Edge, you all right?" Eli asked quickly.

Carmen took a deep breath as whatever she was being assaulted by suddenly went away. "I'm fine," she said. "Maybe a little hungry, though."

He nodded sharply. "Beans should be ready by now. You can have them all, if you'd like," he said, handing her the pot and a large spoon.

"Thank you," Carmen said.

She took a few spoonsful and sighed contently, unaware of just how hungry she was. Eli watched her but didn't speak. She glanced at him, trying her best to make her eyes not look right through him.

"Why are you so nice to me?" she asked softly. "I know you're not afraid of me."

"Clairvoyants can read minds. Why don't you just read mine for the reason?"

"We can read minds, but it is a matter of degree, and I can't fully read yours. If I focused on it, I probably could. But…it seems like you're distracted."

He met her gaze for a second and then looked at the fire. As he rubbed his hands roughly together, she felt uncomfortable again.

"Why are you being so nice to me?" she asked again.

"I know Clairvoyants don't like repeating themselves," he said, prodding a few embers with a stick from his wood pile. He still didn't look at her.

"Yes, it is a little annoying," she admitted. "But why?" she asked, focusing back on her question. "Everyone from the town was utterly terrified of me."

"And that's a damn shame," Eli said, finally looking at her. "You seem like a nice girl."

"Thank you," she said.

She remembered from long ago that her mother told her to say "thank you" whenever someone said something nice. She blinked a few times, surprised that the reflex had stayed with her. Carmen still considered what he said curiously, though.

"My handler said it was because the townspeople weren't used to Clairvoyants."

"Handler?" Eli asked in a disgusted tone. "They give you a handler like a beast in a zoo?"

"Not exactly," she said, shaking her head. She had never thought about it that way. "Do you have experience with Clairvoyants?"

He held completely still for a long while. Carmen's hands were on her knees, and squeezed them hard to keep from moaning again as she felt her question race through his mind.

"Yes," he finally said. "Once."

His thoughts were crystal clear now, but they didn't

coalesce into any one thing. Part of him wanted to say more while, in equal measure, he also wanted her to leave. He ultimately said nothing. Despite his silence, Carmen was besieged by flashing images and feelings of pain. Her heart raced as Eli's memory slowly took hold. There was also something else. It was hard to identify at first, until at last she knew. It was shame.

"But that was another lifetime ago," he muttered, throwing the stick into the fire.

"It doesn't feel like it," Carmen said softly. He looked at her and paused, his face betraying shocked defensiveness. She hadn't meant to say that. She was even tempted to pretend she hadn't and drop the subject. Yet she felt tasked to continue. "You want to tell me about it," she remarked, well aware that he also didn't.

"It's not a story worth telling," he muttered, looking away.

Eli picked up another stick and started poking the fire again. The motion of the stick was rigid and hesitant. He seemed more like he was trying to distract himself than accomplish anything constructive.

For Carmen, her skin felt like it was on fire while daggers stabbed her skull. Even so, she looked nowhere near as uncomfortable as he did. Actually, she decided he seemed more at war with himself than uncomfortable, and in this war, there was no victory, only causalities. His demeanor now as opposed to when she first arrived took her so aback that the only thing keeping her from walking away and leaving Eli in peace was that, despite it all, he really didn't want her to go. Carmen looked at this giant bear of man maybe three times her age and eventually understood that she needed to take the lead.

"Tell me…. Please," she said, forcing herself to give him

a reassuring smile. It seemed like the most...*compassionate* thing to do.

He chuckled lightly then, but there was no mirth in the noise. "Everywhere I go, everyone knows," he said. He chuckled again. "Figures I would meet someone like you here who doesn't."

Carmen opened her mouth to say something, but Eli continued.

"I was a Phalanx Trooper during the Sorten War, all the way from the beginning. It's hard to think we had no idea what Clairvoyants were. It wasn't even twenty years ago. There were rumors of sortens training terrans to have special abilities, but they were too fantastic to believe."

Carmen listened closely. His words were clear but monotone—a forced lack of emotion. She bit her lip, well aware of the thoughts and feelings underneath Eli's words.

"I was with a battalion sent to secure Earth's moon. Luna was the effective high ground for the invasion of Earth. Reconnaissance passes showed that the sortens had a small base there," he continued. "The base had no defenses, no soldiers. We didn't know it until we landed, but it was a remote Clairvoyant research and training base."

He seemed unstressed as he spoke, but Carmen's mouth was dry and her hands trembled.

"In a panic, their scientists set them upon us." He paused for a short moment before he continued. "Most were about your age. Some were...." His voice trailed off. Despite that, Carmen knew exactly how young the younger Clairvoyants had been. "We were trained for every eventuality of battle. On Luna, though, it was like we were hit by a force of nature.... We did everything we could to survive."

Eli stared straight ahead and spoke evenly, seemingly lost in the memory. Carmen remembered every detail with him.

The wounds and stress of the battle lived with him still, no longer visible but all-pervading nonetheless. She held herself, her face fixed in sorrow as she listened.

"I remember every Clairvoyant that attacked us. I can still see their faces," he said slowly, looking off in the distance as though he was doing just that. "How they looked right through you…. I remember how we killed each one of them too." He took a deep breath. "Out of the twelve hundred troopers in the battalion, less than fifty survived. The Clairvoyants fought to the last man."

Carmen shut her eyes and groaned to keep the image from her mind, but it didn't work.

"When we attacked the sorten base, all the scientists there immediately surrendered. That was when we read their training methods—how they compelled the Clairvoyants to do anything they wanted. We forced the scientists to bury our dead and the Clairvoyants—what was left of them." He paused again for a few long seconds. "There are rules in war…between civilized honorable people. These scientists," Eli reflected as he shook his head. "It would be like accepting the surrender of maggots. We went slowly with them. Every time they begged for mercy, we made them read aloud what they had done to their research subjects. When we were… finished with them, we destroyed the base and all the research," he said, finally looking at Carmen.

"Why?" she asked.

He choked something back, which made her shiver. "After what we'd seen, we didn't want anyone to continue their work."

A chill spread from the pit of Carmen's stomach to every inch of her body. Eli could no longer look at her, and she watched him as he shifted uneasily.

"Everyone called us heroes after the battle, but we knew

we were not. We were monsters," he said. "There are only a few of us left now. A long time ago, people believed there was a supreme being who could forgive you for your sins. I beg every day. I get no reply."

Carmen had no words. Her mind and body were frozen. As she closed her eyes and brought her hands to face, his words, the images—everything—existed before her like a waking nightmare. When she looked at him again, he was fiddling with the fire. He still didn't look at her.

"I'm sorry," she said, at a loss for what else to say.

Eli didn't acknowledge her, but he did stir up the fire with slightly more vigor. "It's getting late," he finally said. "I've got a sleeping bag and some blankets, if you'd like."

"I don't need them. I'm not cold."

His look said he didn't believe her, but he didn't challenge the statement. "You should go to sleep at least. It is late."

Carmen had no idea what time it was. She opened her mouth, but Eli cut her off.

"We can talk in the morning. I need some time by myself."

She nodded slowly and then lay down, facing away from the fire. He said nothing to her and she said nothing to him while she tried in vain to purge the memory of the past few minutes from her mind. There was no sound at all, other than the crackling fire. Yet, once or twice, she was sure she heard him weeping.

12

NUMB

The young Clairvoyant slept through the night, though not serenely. Her normal nightmares, which caused her usual fidgets and whimpers, were bolstered by her conversation with Eli. She had never been to Earth's moon, fought Phalanx Troopers, or met a sorten, but from his memory, the sights, pains, and even smells from the battle could be recalled with disquieting accuracy.

She knew sortens didn't look like Janus, but he appeared as one in her nightmare, and it was strangely fitting. He didn't speak to her via voice or by thought; nevertheless, she knew her mission, and she resisted.

"It's time," he said, and she felt pain.

The pain couldn't really be described, but it still made her scream. She knew she was sleeping, but she was also well aware that no one could hear her. She was desperate to wake up—to be rid of her reality.

"It's time," Janus said, and there was more pain.

The next thing Carmen knew, she was on the surface of the moon. The vast, desolate expanse extended as far as she could see. Somehow, she didn't need an excursion suit. Kali was with her, but it wasn't really Kali as she knew her. She looked the same, but she was younger, about the age Carmen was now. Her handler—now her peer—had none of her usual confidence and poise. Everything about her was weak, like a beaten animal. The two were flying just above the surface with dozens of other Clairvoyants. Their army seemed about as fit to fight as a rented mule. Most were covered in bruises, and she could see burns on several, as well as missing limbs. Kali's cream-colored skin was bubbled, and her black hair was on fire. She laughed out a pained wail like a banshee as the fire slowly consumed her, but she didn't die.

Carmen brought her hand to her chest, and when she looked at her fingers, they were covered in blood from a gunshot wound. She screamed again. It felt like the bullet was still ripping into her—like it was doing so continuously. But she hadn't been shot at, not yet. She could see the army arrayed against them, though, and it was ready.

"It's time," Janus said, and there was more pain as the attack began.

They swarmed the troopers like bees. The troopers' shrill, pained cries somehow carried over the airless void of the moon. She killed, reveling in each death. Kali was right with her, on fire and covered in blood but having the time of her life. Each trooper felled looked like a Construct, her parents, and the nice man who'd mussed her hair and given her an ice cream cone.

Then, at last, she came to Eli. In his eyes she could see terror and her own reflection. He begged for his life while his comrades howled in pain all around him. His thoughts longed for the quiet comfort of home, for a long-lost girl-friend, for his father who'd advised him against volunteering, and for his mother he would never see again. But before Carmen could strike, he raised his rifle and fired. She gasped as she was torn apart. The bullets didn't hurt—not exactly. Each impact seemed to deaden where she was hit until, at last, she fell to the ground, limp and unable to feel anything at all.

Kali flew over them, shrieking like a demon but completely oblivious. Eli came to her slowly. He had dropped his weapon. He scooped her limp body into his meaty arms and cried.

"I'm so sorry," he said over and over again.

She had heard that before, but she couldn't remember when. The only thing Carmen could remember was that the words had seemed as impossible then as they did now. When she looked at Eli, she got another shock. It was Janus! Worse, the transformation seemed as fitting as when he had been a sorten.

Carmen tried to scream, but it became harder and harder to breathe. Kali danced and played around them, still burning and killing everyone, even other Clairvoyants. Carmen grew dizzy. Her world began to spin quicker and quicker with each failing attempt to draw breath. Then, at last, everything went dark and she was alone.

She opened her eyes and groaned softly as she sat up. Eli had been kind enough to throw a blanket around her, despite that she had said she didn't need one. She wasn't just being modest—she really didn't need it—but Carmen appreciated the gesture nonetheless. She looked at the tent and paused, then raised an eyebrow. She couldn't sense Eli at all. Her first thought was to call to him, but she decided against it. She still had no idea why she couldn't feel his presence, but if he was still asleep, she didn't want to wake him.

She gave a small shrug and then winced from a sharp pain. Her makeshift bed was as comfortable as a rock—because there were several rocks among the grass where she had lain. She stretched and messaged her body while telekinetically cleaning the dirt out of her hair and clothes.

Eventually, it didn't feel like her shoulder was about to fall off anymore, so she went to the tent and opened it, being as quiet as she possibly could. Eli wasn't inside. She pursed her lips as she looked around the camp. All of his belongings were still here. She didn't know what time it was. Perhaps she awoke before he expected, or after? Her best guess was that he'd gone for a hike or something and would be back later. He had said they could talk in the morning, so he at least expected them to spend that time together.

"Eli," she called. She didn't know if her voice carried farther than her Clairvoyant perception, but it was worth a shot. "Eli," she tried again. If he heard her, she had no doubt she'd hear him. There was no reply, though.

She let go an annoyed sigh as she considered what to do. She had planned to part his company after the morning. It wasn't too much of a bother that he was gone, but she did want to thank him for his hospitality. Eventually, Carmen decided a proper thank you and goodbye was worth the effort. She had nothing else to do anyway.

She stood up and looked around. "Where would he go?" she wondered out loud.

Carmen had read stories about people tracking someone by a slight bend in a blade of grass. Those people must have been far more powerful Clairvoyants than she, as she had no idea how to track someone like that.

"Where?" she muttered again.

She tried to think it through before she eventually realized she couldn't. She had no idea how Eli thought, or really how any normal person thought. Kali was right, as handlers routinely seemed to be. The perceptual frame of reference between Clairvoyants and non-Clairvoyants was too great a gap to easily surmount. Carmen closed her eyes as she sighed loudly and decided to handle this as a Clairvoyant.

The air was cool, and soft fog still covered the forest floor. Other than that, it was a picturesque day. Carmen paid attention to none of it, though. She didn't think. She stood very still. She'd never done this before, but she'd lived it every day of her life. The intuition couldn't be rushed; it just happened.

She opened her eyes and began walking. After a few steps, she turned slightly and walked in a different direction. The camp was almost out of sight now, and it made her wonder if she should just stay and wait for him to come back, but that didn't feel right. It was hard to say why, but the feeling didn't go away, even after she redoubled her commitment to trying to find Eli in the wild. Her body even wilted slightly. It reminded her of what she had felt when she talked to him last night. In time, the feeling lessened to just an annoyance at the edge of her consciousness. With more time, it passed to the subconscious and joined her other hurts that she paid no heed to but that were still part of her.

She left the clearing and was back in the forest proper. The direction in which she was walking wasn't very difficult terrain. Eli seemed to be an experienced woodsman and would certainly have no issue with it. The forest canopy blocked out most of the sun, leaving darkened shadows for her to traverse. The forest was quiet—disturbingly so. She was aware of life all around her, but none of it made itself known, not even as a warning caw or chirp that she was coming.

Her eyes scanned back and forth as she looked for Eli. Her ears strained to take in all available sound. Her Clairvoyant perceptions took in the entire world around her and fed the most relevant bits to her conscious mind to digest. But there was nothing. Absolutely nothing.

Carmen stopped in place, on the verge of giving up, when she felt prompted to walk in a slightly different direction. She felt the uncomfortable sensation from before and crossed her arms to hold herself. She didn't know what it meant—possibly nothing at all. She bit her lip, well aware that that was hardly ever the case. She changed course again. She hated the feeling, but it drew her like a moth to flame. It was all she knew. It was all she had to look forward to. The only time she could recall not being in its company in some way was when she jumped off the bluff.

On and on she went with slight course changes here and there, even once doubling back. There was no Eli, though. Then, once she suspected she was walking in circles, Carmen noticed something on the periphery of her perception. …It was nothing, yet not completely. It wasn't the absence of what was supposed to be; it was an emptiness in that which was already there.

Her meandering path became a straight line, and she even increased her pace. The fog and the brush made it hard to see, so she telekinetically uprooted whatever got in her way. The feeling only grew worse the closer she ventured to it, as well as the longer she delayed. Her steps turned into a slow run, and she was no longer able to think about herself. Invisible clocks counted down, hastening her, their alarms set to ring.

She could see him now. He stood still in another small clearing, appearing to be looking at nothing at all. She was heartened by the sight and moved faster for no reason that made any sort of sense. Then she slid to a stop. He held a pistol in his hand.

Carmen's breathing came short and rapid, and her heart pounded. She slowly shook her head.

"What are you doing, Eli?"

"You know what I'm doing. You know why I'm here. You always have," he said simply.

His back was to her. She couldn't see his face, but she could read all of his thoughts. It wasn't chaos or rage. There was unremitting order—a definite sense of things. Yet there was also pain…and shame.

Carmen found it suddenly hard to speak. She mouthed the words several times before they actually came forth. "I can stop you," she said.

Eli half-turned to look at her. "You can, but you won't," he replied. "You won't take this away from me. You're probably the only person who ever actually understood."

Carmen slowly shook her head again. A tear slid down her cheek. He was right, but she desperately wished he wasn't.

"I wish you hadn't found me. I didn't want to do this in front of you," he continued.

She swallowed hard. "I know." She took a deep breath before she spoke again. "I wanted to thank you…for last night."

He looked away from her for a moment and considered something. There were so many thoughts flooding through his mind that it was hard for her to focus on any one.

"You're a nice girl," he said matter-of-factly. The hand holding the pistol trembled slightly, a small aftershock from the earthquake in his mind. "I saw lots of girls like you on Luna," he remarked. His voice was hollow and full of regret. "I didn't even know their names. No one did. No one ever will."

The memories were called forth again, and his head dropped as each took root. Carmen felt a tear roll down her other cheek.

"It's wasn't your fault," she said, trying to come up with some comfort. "It was war."

He looked right at her then, and for one solitary moment, she knew what it was like for someone to look right through her—right into her soul.

"Nothing justifies what we did," he said firmly. He looked away from her again. "I've thought about this a long time. Came close a couple times…. Figures I would meet someone like you now. Has to be some sick twist of fate."

Carmen opened her mouth to say something, but Eli spoke first.

"Can you forgive me? For what we did to your kind—to kids?"

Carmen breathed in hard and swallowed. "I forgive you," she said. The words weren't hard to find at all.

Eli nodded several times as he looked away. He didn't look especially heartened by her answer, but she could tell it provided some comfort. His thoughts remained in the deep, dark depths where she was afraid to venture yet lived within every day of her life. The small meadow they were standing in was strewn with flowers. Colorful insects darted between them. To Eli, though, the scene seemed a hellscape. Everything did now.

"You shouldn't curse. It's not becoming. Promise me you won't."

Carmen looked at him through fresh tears. "I promise."

Eli nodded a few more times and smiled. As before, his smile was so genuine that she could feel it flow through her. She wasn't heartened by the sensation, though.

"Don't let them do it. Don't let them turn you into what they want," he said. "You're a nice girl…. Stay good."

Carmen froze in place. She didn't think Eli was a bad person, but she wasn't so sure about herself. She had easily killed more than he ever had, by several orders of magnitude. Her thoughts went to Mikayla and to his battle on the moon. If the circumstances were the same, would she have attacked all those troopers as her doomed peers had? It was hard for her to say she wouldn't.

He looked at her and waited for her response. She saw distress mount in his features when she was unable to give him one. "If you promise me anything, promise me that," he said, desperation creeping into his voice.

Carmen stood still, quivering like a cornered animal. She looked away a time or two. In each instance, she took a deep breath and swallowed hard.

Her mouth trembled open. "I…" she began, but despite her best efforts, she could utter no more.

Eli's eyes grew wide and then finally fell in despair as he watched her struggle. Carmen hated herself totally and completely in that moment. She wished she could have simply lied, but she couldn't—not now and not to him. The hand holding his pistol gave a quick tremor.

"Don't tell anybody about this," he said. "Don't tell anyone where to find me. I just want to be left here—I don't want anyone to know. It's what I deserve. I'm not a hero."

She nodded sharply to his command, no longer able to hold back her tears. Eli's every thought and feeling passed through her mind. Her body shook, yet his became still. His voice was calm, while she was barely able to speak. She'd never felt such pain before. How he stood before her and didn't shatter from it was beyond her. She swallowed hard again.

"Carmen."

"What was that?" he asked.

"My real name is Carmen. I wanted you to know."

"Carmen," Eli said, trying the name on for size. "I like it. Suits you better than Edge. Thank you for telling me."

Then Eli brought the pistol to his head and fired.

Birds flushed into the sky. A pair of spotted deer bolted in the other direction. The Clairvoyant, however, stood still. She cried no more tears as she stared at the body in front of her. She had seen dead bodies before, hundreds of them. They were usually worth no more than a passing glance. Yet now she stared.

For the first time, she felt absolutely nothing, like she'd been dipped in ice. Eli had fallen like the lumbering bear of man he was. She hardly knew him, but she knew almost everything about him. Carmen continued to stare, unable to process what she was looking at. Her synapses didn't fire, her heart didn't beat, and she took no breath. Eventually she blinked, and color came back to the world.

She walked toward him slowly, her breath shallow to the point of being almost ghostly. She stood over his body and wiped her wet face clean. Then she dropped to her knees. The pistol was still in his hand. She removed it carefully and held the weapon. She had held many weapons. She herself was a weapon. But Carmen had never held a gun. She considered the instrument for a second and then threw it away with all her physical might.

Then she looked at Eli. His eyes stared back at her in pained horror. She leaned forward and gently closed them. Next, Carmen looked around until she found a piece of wide, flat tree bark that seemed study enough. She could have done the job telekinetically in a matter of seconds, but for some reason she wanted to feel the pain and sting of the physical exertion.

After picking up the bark, she got to work on the grave. The ground was soft and yielded to her, as most things did to her might, but that was just the top soil. As she went deeper, the goings became harder, seeming to actively resist her every attempt at making headway.

* * *

"Yes, Captain, I assure you she is in the forest," Kali said.

"Sorry, ma'am," the leader of the suppression team said. "I've had my team search the forest and have found no trace of her. The place is wild—there are no paths or anything of the sort. But our scanner didn't indicate that she's there. She may have gone into the forest and then flown off."

"She's there," the Clairvoyant repeated in an annoyed tone. Every member of the suppression team stiffened when they heard it. "I know my charge. She wouldn't go anywhere else."

Kali didn't say out loud, however, that she was surprised Edge hadn't come to her yesterday. She knew her charge had spent most of the day at the edge of the forest, seemingly waiting for something. Kali had assumed she was simply waiting to muster the courage to face her and the town again, but that was certainly not the case now. Perhaps she'd overestimated how well she could anticipate Edge's reaction? She didn't think the girl would ever run away—she didn't seem bold enough for that. Maybe she had flown off?

The captain took a deep breath and looked at his tired men. Right as he was about to give his orders, his communicator beeped.

"Home base, this is Alpha Two."

"Alpha Two report," the captain said.

"She just came out of the forest, inbound your position. Shall we intercept?"

The captain looked at Kali, who shook her head. "Negative. Take observation position and report any change in her course."

"Yes, sir."

The captain turned to the rest of his team. "Take defensive positions. If she makes a hostile act, take her down. We will only get one chance at this. This is Edge; I don't need to remind anyone how powerful she is. Stay sharp. We've trained for this. Mitchell."

"Sir?" Mitchell said, stepping forward.

"Is the dead man switch active?"

"Yes, sir. The bird's overhead. Should we use it? We haven't completely evacuated the town."

The captain shook his head. "No choice. Better a town than a rogue Clairvoyant on the loose. Move out!"

The team ran to positions on either side of the street where the makeshift command post had been built. Kali ignored them and walked to the center of the street. By now, she could see Carmen. Her mouth dropped open. Her charge's clothes were covered in dirt, her hands were raw, and her fingertips were bloody.

Carmen walked slowly. Every part of her ached. The tree bark broke and she'd had to resort to her hands. She could sense the townspeople watching her as before, but now guns also followed her every movement. She didn't much care. It all seemed so trivial in the grand scheme of things. She could easily block them out. She walked toward her handler, who watched her in a state of shock.

"Edge? What happened to you? Where did you go?"

Carmen stood in front of Kali and said nothing, remembering her promise. She grabbed the woman in a desperate hug, suffering the shock of their bioelectric fields. She buried her face in Kali's chest as the surprised members of the suppression team vacated their positions and approached.

Kali brought her arms around her charge to provide comfort just as Carmen began sobbing. No one knew how long they stood there. Nothing was ever said between them about that day. Her handler never asked, and Carmen never offered. Eventually, they went for an ice cream as Kali had originally planned, though the suppression team stood by just in case. Then the lot of them loaded a transport and returned to the facility.

Carmen looked at the forest as they flew by. She wouldn't forget.

13

ANOTHER FLIGHT

Subject: Edge Age: 16 Status: Tempering

Carmen's eyes narrowed.

"I can't believe you're making me do this," she said through clenched teeth.

Kali glanced at her and smiled. Carmen glanced back. She had long since matched her handler in height, and they now stood eye to eye. *She would find this all amusing,* Carmen thought dismally. Janus, at this point, only visited her in vaguely remembered nightmares. Her memories of the man were more mythical now than accurate recollections. Still, he was certainly less annoying than Kali could be.

"Oh, what's wrong?" her handler asked, aping real concern.

Carmen shook her head. What was wrong should have been obvious. "I look like an idiot!"

"What makes you say that?"

Carmen glanced at her again and then pointedly rolled her eyes. There were times she wished Kali could read her thoughts. Her dress had to have been made by an idiot. Worse than that, it looked like it had been sold in a store for idiots in a land of idiots. Who knew—maybe these were considered regal robes in Idiotatopia? On Carmen, though…. Well, she looked like an idiot!

The dress was light pastel pink in color. It wasn't that she necessarily looked bad in pink—in fact, it complemented her skin and hair tones rather well. It just wasn't her taste. The failure that was her dress, however, went beyond simple preference in color. Oh no, this was not merely limited to her subjective judgment. Its horridness was as plain as day and night. The thing was a mess of ruffles arranged in what could liberally be called a pattern. Just looking at them gave Carmen a headache. It had gold trim here and there, though why gold she didn't know. It did nothing to help. Neither did the dress do anything to help her natural figure. If anything, it gave her curves and bulges she didn't even know she had, making it rather uncomfortable to wear. She wouldn't be surprised if the dress had been tailored for a mutant.

The two of them looked in the bathroom mirror. They were alone for the moment, even though the music from the party could be heard through the walls.

"Well, it's not that bad," Kali said. Carmen shot her a disbelieving glance. "I even think a few boys were looking your way."

Carmen rolled her eyes again and looked back at her terrible reflection. "The dress probably turned them into stone," she muttered under her breath. "They *couldn't* look away."

"Oh, you," Kali groaned. She rested her arm on her charge's shoulder. "Go out there and have fun—mingle. That's why you're all here. I'm not asking for much, just that you learn how to be around other people."

"No," Carmen said simply. Her handler groaned again.

"They're almost all Clairvoyants anyway," she added, noting a flaw in the entire reason for this get together.

She and Kali had taken several other field trips over the past few years, even to Haven City. They practiced casual conversation and etiquette, but the endless practice never amounted to much of anything. Outside of field trips, Carmen was also encouraged to socialize with her Clairvoyant peers. That amounted to even less of anything. They didn't shriek and run from her like normal people sometimes did, and she got along with most of them. She just doubted that associating with her peers was good practice for much. Kali often preached that, deep down, there was no real difference between Clairvoyants and normal people, and in a way Carmen guessed she was right. But dogs and cats were both mammals and had four legs, and, well….

"Edge, it's not like I'm torturing you or anything. Just go out there, talk to your peers, and, you never know, you may actually like it."

Carmen stared hard at the mirror. "Dressed like this?"

Kali groaned loudly this time. She stopped leaning on her charge and took a step back. "I happen to think you look very pretty. Just one thing, though. What's with you and ponytails? Always ponytails," she said as she began undoing the hair tie. Carmen glared at her. "You have such pretty hair. There," she said, loosening the last of it. Then Kali gently aimed Carmen's head at the mirror and leaned in close. "Now you tell me, do you really think it looks so bad?"

Carmen said nothing, but suddenly her reflection began to bubble. The glass cracked and the mirror warped. Soon, all that was left was a half-melted mess.

Kali stared at her charge. Carmen returned an innocent smile that bordered on a smirk. The expression was her best guess. She hadn't seen real innocence in any form for more than a decade.

"It wasn't me. The dress is just that ugly," the teenager said sheepishly.

Kali shook her head in exaggerated fashion and groaned once more. "Rebellious little scamp," she uttered before giving her a playful push. Carmen laughed. Kali then moved toward the door. "You're coming back out here, and that's final," she said firmly.

There was no arguing with that tone. Carmen had already given it a game try on more than one occasion.

"Fine," she said softly.

Kali nodded and walked out the door, but then she stopped all of a sudden. She frowned. "If you make yourself invisible, so help me," she warned before finally leaving.

Carmen nodded obediently and took a few seconds to gather herself before she followed her handler out. The past few years were definitely an improvement over her first six, but there were still downsides here and there. A big one was parties. She hated parties. It wasn't that she was shy or wanted to be alone. She rather enjoyed her time with Kali, and the two could and did talk for hours. What she didn't like was how awkward it was to be around anyone but her handler. She just didn't know what to do or how to act. More than anything, she *hated* being reminded about that.

She wasn't the only one either. It didn't take long for her to see why Kali had said that about turning invisible as a suppression team quite obviously hunted for a Clairvoyant that couldn't be seen. Each member of the team held a scanner, and they spoke loudly to coordinate their efforts. Carmen shook her head with a wry smile. It had to happen at least once every party, and it never worked. The wayward Clairvoyant was always found. Janus had mentioned to her long ago that Clairvoyants could bend light to make themselves invisible. She had no idea how to do it, but for situations like this, it was very tempting. She shook her head again when the now cornered Clairvoyant revealed himself. Unfortunately, what would probably be the most interesting goings-on of the night was now over.

Carmen briefly surveyed the room. It was easy to divide it into three groups. There were the handlers, who mingled quietly if coldly among themselves. There were the assets, who simply stood alone wherever they happened to be in the room. Then there were the children of the various support staff for the facility. She didn't know whose bright idea it was to include them in all this. They talked fluidly and openly to other people like them with no apparent wish to engage any Clairvoyant. There were also the suppression teams armed with foam cannons and rifles, but they didn't count.

She watched the normals with an odd tinge of envy. She could walk along the ceiling, dance among the clouds, and read minds, in some cases like a book. But thus far, Carmen had been unable to do what the non-Clairvoyants were presently doing without conscious thought or anxiety. She well knew why Kali wanted her and her peers to mingle, but it was so difficult. She hated parties.

Her eyes fell on her handler in that moment. Kali stared right back—disapprovingly. She motioned toward a group of assets standing close enough to each other that they could be considered together, even if they really weren't.

Carmen glanced at them. *"Why me?"* she asked telepathically, looking back at Kali.

There was no reply, which made her sigh. Her handler had a quiet yet violently unforceful way of getting her to do whatever she wanted. It was so effective that, at times, Carmen felt like she was a marionette. It was certainly different from the methods Janus had used. It was less overt —the difference between a growling dog and a barking one. She liked Kali very much, but there remained a part of her that was wary around her handler. It didn't even come as much of a surprise when she learned that most everyone at the facility, even other Clairvoyants, gave Kali a wide berth. She was like a thorny flower.

Carmen looked back at her peers and then began walking. Her stride matched that of someone going to their execution. *This will be easy*, she told herself. *All I have to do is just not think about it, and it will come just like everything else.* They noticed her approach. She always drew slightly more attention than the average Clairvoyant.

"Hi," she said when she was close enough.

"Hello," one of them replied.

"Edge," the other two greeted.

Carmen didn't know their names, but almost everyone knew who she was even before she actually met them. Personally, she had no real care for her minor celebrity.

She gave a friendly smile, which her counterparts returned when they remembered such a gesture would be proper. Then there was silence. Carmen looked at them expectantly, hoping she wouldn't have to do all the work. One of her peers looked away. The other two shifted in place uncomfortably. Carmen felt like a thumbless, blind monkey fumbling with a banana.

She glanced over her shoulder at Kali. Kali stared right back.

"Okay, so what do we do now?" she asked the group.

"I think small talk is next?"

"Oh, all right," Carmen said. "What do we talk about?"

"Well…" one of them began. "It's been nice weather, hasn't it?"

She could sense one of them sigh before he actually did. "Please," he muttered. "It could be torrential downpours and we wouldn't get wet."

"Yeah, maybe we should talk about something else," Carmen said. "What are you into?"

"I don't really know what I'm *into*," one of them began. "I was kidnapped as a child and then basically locked in here with coloring books and puzzles to occupy my time. For all I know, the greatest thing in the world could be knitting. Now, I'm trying to pretend that I'm a normal, well-adjusted person so, when I *graduate* from here, I don't freak out people who are actually normal and well-adjusted."

There were grim nods all around.

"Tell me about it," Carmen muttered under her breath.

"Maybe we can just pretend we're communicating telepathically. All we have to do is smile and nod every now and then," someone else suggested.

Carmen looked over her shoulder again, and now several other handlers were watching them with Kali. "I don't think that will work," she said. "We'll be caught as soon as they start asking us questions about the conversation we supposedly had."

"Well, if we hash it all out right now, that shouldn't be a problem. We just have to make sure we give them the same story."

"Okay," Carmen said.

Everyone nodded, and the plan was set in motion.

The first topic they pretended to discuss was everyone's favorite color. Carmen said neon green. It wasn't her favorite color, but that was completely beside the point. Remembering everyone else's choices wasn't that hard. They took a few minutes to make sure they remembered each other's preferences, just in case their handlers decided to compare notes.

The next topic was dogs versus cats. Carmen didn't really want to participate in that pretend discussion. She simply said dogs and helped the others remember the conversation they didn't have. After that, the pretend discussion went to balloons, or clowns, or some such thing. Pretty soon, the sheer mass of the make-believe became hard to keep straight. Her head even began to hurt.

"All right, is there anything else we should think up?" a sensible person asked about a half hour later.

"I hope not," Carmen said. No one responded, and she figured that was the end of their little ruse. "Nice to meet you. Thanks."

Everyone nodded, and she went on her way. Her destination was the punch bowl. All that talking had made her thirsty. She had company even before she finished pouring her first cup.

"So, how did it go?" Kali asked.

The question was casual. All the same, Carmen did her best to act enthused, though not too much. Overt eagerness would tip her hand.

"It went fine," she said.

"Really? What did you talk about?"

Carmen didn't answer right away. She was actually a bit surprised that her handler's tone wasn't as accusing as she expected. Perhaps that was just her guilty conscience. Either way, no answer came readily to mind. She couldn't really remember any of the script now that she needed it. After a few seconds, she could only sigh.

"We spent our time making up a pretend conversation so, when you asked us what we were talking about, we could use that instead of making it up on the spot," she said dejectedly.

Kali stood very still. Carmen was sure she was in for it now. But then her handler nodded slowly. "So, your conversation was…pretending to have a conversation. That's a bit unorthodox, but at least it's something," she said after a shrug.

Carmen thought about it for a moment. "Yeah." She smiled but then muted the expression in anticipation of her next question. "Can I leave now?"

"Oh, no, no, no, Edge," Kali said, waving her finger. "You don't get off that easily. Now go. There are other conversations to pretend to have," she continued, gently pushing her charge on.

Carmen groaned but offered no other protest. Unfortunately, her luck grew worse. Her next attempts were only met with blank stares. It was an event when someone even returned a hello. Kali spurred her on despite the hopelessness. At least her handler was right about one thing, she realized, as more than a few boys watched her. It wasn't just them, either —the spectacle drew quite an audience. Every time she walked across the floor, heads swiveled to follow. Carmen had no doubt that they weren't just interested in her ugly dress. She had to be the most entertaining clown for fifty miles; she sure felt like one. And that made it final. She hated parties. She absolutely could not stand them.

She found a chair and immediately sat down, fed up with the whole thing. She wasn't going back out there; she didn't care how mad Kali got. For now, her handler watched from a ways off but said nothing. Carmen only assumed she realized this would be a battle she wouldn't win.

Carmen closed her eyes and sighed, reveling in her moment alone. When she opened them again, they went straight to the clock. *Good*, she thought. There were only a few more hours of the marathon left. All she needed to do was stay welded to the chair and not move for anything, and she'd probably emerge unscathed. It was then that she noticed some of the security personnel had deliberately moved closer to her. *Strange*, Carmen thought. She wasn't doing anything belligerent. Even Kali wasn't looking at her anymore. Instead, she looked at something just behind her charge.

"Why did you stop? I was enjoying myself."

She turned around to see Artemis. The other girl looked… well, striking! Her dress was a deep blue and constructed in such an elegantly simple manner that it captured attention even while it seemed like it wasn't trying to. *Figures*, Carmen thought. The two of them didn't interact very often. It seemed the powers that be had made certain of that, lest they reprise their prior battle.

Carmen kept her eyes locked on the fellow one-percenter but didn't move otherwise. Artemis calmly sat next to her. Her entourage of security guards took station nearby. Carmen glanced at them before looking back at her. Whenever they did consort, it was usually only in passing. They were never alone in such instances, as security always followed a half-step behind Artemis wherever she went. Carmen was quite certain she got a kick out of the whole escapade.

"What do you want?" she asked dismissively.

Then she half-turned in her chair to show Artemis her back. Her position didn't allow her to see the other girl's sneer, but since that was the point, Carmen just used her imagination.

"I just want to talk. That's why we're at this party, isn't it? Besides, you're the one who made a big show out of 'Let's just be friends,'" Artemis said, adding a touch of venom to the last bit.

Carmen rolled her eyes. "That was years ago…and then you tried to kill me."

"Yeah, I guess I did," Artemis said after a light chuckle. "But that was then and this is now. I just want to talk." She paused, and Carmen didn't know she was looking around the room. "It wouldn't be polite to trash the place after they went to all this trouble."

"Well, at least you're more sensible now," Carmen responded sarcastically. She swore that girl took crazy pills in the morning. She didn't know Artemis smiled at the comment. "So, what do you want to talk about then?" she asked after a sigh.

"Oh, I don't know," Artemis began. "You seem to be the expert. When you were talking to those others, my handler said 'See? You should try to be more like *her*.'" She groaned. "Years and years and years. You have no idea how often people compared me to you and said *I* was lacking. I know it was just to get me to do something or behave a certain way or whatever, according to my personality profile. But whatever it is, I really, *really* hate it."

Carmen glanced at her over her shoulder. "Should I apologize?" she asked, half-sincere.

"Oh no," Artemis began. "We don't want the great Edge apologizing to little old me. I just want you to go back out there and make a fool of yourself again. It was quite fun to watch."

Yes, very sensible now, Carmen thought after rolling her eyes again. She turned to face Artemis, who smirked at her.

"You know, I really don't like you," she said simply.

"Yes," Artemis said, sarcasm bleeding into her voice. "Like I look at you and think rainbows, puppy-dogs, and roses." Carmen opened her mouth to respond, but Artemis cut her off. "But what are you going to do about it?" she asked, her tone more hopeful than not.

Carmen said nothing. She really couldn't think of anything to say. Her state only made Artemis smile. She opened her mouth but closed it again, as the words wouldn't be enough. It was soon obvious that only one response would do. She stood, bitter at what she was forced to do. Artemis didn't move; she just watched her expectantly. The security guards stiffened. As Carmen began walking toward the door, she could hear the other girl laugh.

"By the way," Artemis shouted between chuckles, "that's a real nice dress you're wearing!"

Carmen groaned. There was a difference between adding insult to injury and simply being cruel. She was out of there in moments. No one, not even Kali, tried to stop her—not that it would have made any difference. Parties were bad, Artemis was bad, and the two together were monstrous. She would *not* be staying.

In any case, when she stepped out, she wasn't exactly sure where she was going to go. She wasn't in any mood to return to her room. So, there was only one other place. Her trip across the courtyard was lonely if peaceful. When a guard spotted her, she waved to him and he waved back. The walls of the facility soon approached. Carmen flew over them without a second thought and continued on.

The bluff grew near. She could sense the edge without her eyes, but it helped nonetheless that there was enough moonlight to see. It was a nice night, the sky clear and the air calm. The view was captivating, as always. She often found herself here whenever she wasn't with Kali. Sometimes she wasn't alone, as the spot was popular with some of the other assets, but no one ever said anything to each other. There was no sense in spoiling the scene with idle banter. At most, they'd offer a polite nod in acknowledgement and then good if silent company. Carmen was the only person here now.

She didn't mind. The entire reason she'd left was to get away in the first place. She sat on the edge like she usually did, unconcerned with how dirty her dress got. It wasn't long for this world anyway—she planned to burn it at her earliest convenience. Other than that, there was nothing set in her future. She would stay here until she was ready to leave, which was usually a few hours. Sure, it was already late, but it wasn't like when she was first brought to the facility. She wouldn't miss the lost sleep.

With her mind on tomorrow, the day after, and the day after that, she leaned back and got to thinking. She would graduate when she turned eighteen, which was less than two years away. Just thinking about life outside of here made her nervous. Somewhere, somehow, she'd just gotten used to it all over the years. That was a bit hard for even her to believe.

She pondered for a moment where she would go and what she would do. Most Clairvoyants, she'd learned, became mercenaries of some sort. There were even recruitment posters all over the facility. Another option was to join Space Force or the New Earth Self-Defense Forces. Both choices held little appeal. She wasn't all too eager to hurt people again, even if that was her best, most marketable skill. Carmen closed her eyes and sighed. She used to think this place had stolen her life. It was a bit disconcerting to think that, really, it had yet to begin.

Just then, she realized she wasn't alone. Someone was coming toward her. It wasn't a Clairvoyant—the energy was too tame for that, despite its anxiety—nor was it someone she'd met before. A person's energy was as unique as their face, and this one wasn't familiar. She turned to see who it was.

It was a boy about her age and maybe a little taller. He wore a rather plain black suit, and she guessed he had come from the party. There was no doubt he was coming in her direction, though his first instinct seemed to be to hide when she turned. He jumped and then paused when her eyes rested on him. Carmen didn't say anything. He was too far away for anything but a shout anyway. He didn't speak either. Even so, she could see his hands if not his entire body shaking.

Why is he so nervous? she wondered. There was no obvious clue she could see. She probably could have read him if she wanted to, but doing that was usually more uncomfortable than it was worth. Her curiosity would remain unsated for now.

He gathered his courage, for whatever reason he needed it, and began walking toward her again. This had to be the most curious event of the night, as far as Carmen was concerned. He was close enough now that she was able to make out facial features. His hair was well tended, probably for the party, and he had the first signs of a mustache. He was a bit on the skinny side, but no more so than the rest of his peers. And he most certainly was not a Clairvoyant. There was purpose to his movement, at least in this case, but none of the measured precision or grace she and her cohorts wielded.

He stopped in front of her, and she stared up at him. He didn't say anything. It was obvious, though, that he was trying hard to. He swallowed hard.

"Hi," he muttered.

Carmen looked at him sidelong. She'd expected something a bit more…well, significant, given all the effort. "Hi," she said back.

He didn't speak again, at least not immediately. "Ho-how," he stuttered. "How are you?"

"I guess I'm okay," she said. "How are you?"

Long ago, her mother told her that asking them the question in return was the polite thing to do. Kali reiterated the same.

"Fi-fine."

She gave him another curious look. "Are you okay?" she asked plainly.

He paused for a moment. "Yeah. Yeah, I am," he said with a bit more confidence. "Can I sit with you?"

Carmen had no problem with that. It was just that no one had ever asked her for permission to sit here. She came to the bluff often, but it wasn't like she had any authority over the place. Now that she thought about it, though, no one ever asked to sit *with* her. It was a subtle yet noticeable difference. She motioned beside her and nodded.

The boy smiled and then sat down. "I'm Michael."

"Edge…or Carmen," she said. "You can call me either."

"What do you preferred to be called?" he asked.

"Carmen," she said quickly. The response required no real thinking. "I don't think anyone has called me that for a very long time, though. Maybe like five years, I guess?" she added with a shrug.

Michael stared at her. Carmen wondered why. Every other Clairvoyant here would say the same. However, his expression was practically raining disbelief.

"Well, I'll call you Carmen, then," he said after another swallow.

She couldn't help a small smile, which made Michael smile in turn. Hearing someone call her by her own name was refreshingly pleasant. It was as if, for that one brief moment, she ceased to be a Clairvoyant and was just another person. She looked away quickly and prodded the expression to fade. It was always a bit uncomfortable to keep a smile for too long. They tended to draw too much attention, and in this place, that could be lethal. She looked out over the water. The reflected moonlight gave it an eerie glow. Carmen usually wasn't out here this late. It was an unusual though not unwelcome change.

"You come here often?" Michael asked casually.

The question was pointless in scope, like he was speaking just to speak or biding his time. Carmen didn't care.

She replied, "Whenever I can," which was rarer than she preferred. She took a second to think. "I like it here. It's quiet."

"Yeah, I guess so."

"It's also fun to jump," she continued.

"Jump?"

"Jump off," she said, as if it was obvious. She looked down at the churning water below. "They bring us here to jump off the bluff. It's where we make our choice. ...It's very hard."

He stared at her, completely still, as if his entire existence was set on pause. The countenance broke when he laughed lightly. "My parents said Clairvoyants can fly. I guess that would be hard to do."

"Oh no, flying isn't hard, just tiring. What's hard is the choice."

"How is that hard?" he asked casually.

Carmen didn't answer right away. She had to have had hundreds of lessons on her Dark from both Janus and Kali by this point. The Dark permeated everything everyone did, even if they were unaware of it. It could be consciously perceived only dimly, even by the most powerful Clairvoyant, yet it needed to be constantly heeded by all. His question, innocent and naïve, was a quiet reminder that he had received no such instruction.

"It just is," she replied, not wasting her time trying to explain. He wouldn't understand.

Michael waited a few seconds before speaking again. When he realized she wasn't going to elaborate, he asked, "And what did you choose?"

Carmen sat still for a moment and thought. It was a difficult and strangely personal question to answer. She reflected on how Kali acted when she asked her the same question and could now understand the discomfort. But, unlike her handler, it was a question she would answer.

"I decided to live," she said.

That wasn't the whole truth. Really, she wasn't completely sure why she didn't become a multicolored splotch on the rocks below. As well as she could remember, it was more a feeling *to live* than a conscious thought, and if she'd learned anything from this place, it was not to argue with such feelings.

Michael stared at her again. His face was a mixture of confusion crossed with disbelief and a dash of strained comprehension. Carmen didn't think that what she said was strange or too hard to understand. That was her reality almost every day of her life, though. In that moment, the mere inches separating them seemed as unbridgeable as the widest chasm. He seemed to give up the effort after a couple of minutes. He also moved slightly away from her.

Carmen didn't think that was a good sign. "Why are you here?" she asked. Her tone wasn't accusing; it was asked in the same way she'd ask why the sky is blue when she was younger. "I thought the normals are afraid of Clairvoyants? You do know I'm a Clairvoyant, don't you?" she continued.

"Yeah, I know," he said sheepishly. "But is that what Clairvoyants call us? The normals?"

"No," she muttered, realizing that calling people names wasn't the nicest thing to do. "I guess that's just me," she lied.

But that was neither here nor there. Kali was right: she needed more practice at this. She moved away herself and then looked down at the ground. Carmen began thinking as she waited for Michael to get up and leave. Her thoughts didn't mine the most comforting reaches of her mind. Really, she'd be hard-pressed to come up with *any* comforting thoughts. It would only be a few short years until she had interactions like this every day to more than likely the same result. Just thinking about it made her want to jump off the bluff again and reconsider her choice.

"I'm not afraid of you," he said.

Carmen hadn't been paying attention to Michael. If anything, she was surprised he was still here.

"What?" she asked, turning to face him. He had moved closer to her than before.

"I said I'm not afraid of you." She gave him a hard look. He laughed nervously. "All right, maybe I am just a little. But my parents say Clairvoyants are dangerous—that you could kill us without a second thought. They would be really mad if they knew I was talking to you. The only reason I'm at the party at all is because it's mandatory for staff to bring their kids. My parents are janitors here."

"Okay," she muttered after a couple of nods.

She couldn't say she was surprised by the sentiment. The only people she had met thus far that weren't unnerved by Clairvoyants were the citizens of the town she flew to during her first flight.

Carmen looked at him. "I won't hurt you."

"Good. Good to know," Michael said with a smile.

She smiled as well and allowed it to hold a little longer than normal. Still, he hadn't answered her question.

"So, why are you here again?" she asked casually.

Michael shuddered like he was struck by lightning. Carmen found the reaction odd. It was a simple question.

"Well…. Well," he stammered, "I just got tired of the party and wanted to leave." She didn't believe him, and her face reflected as much. Michael noticed straight away. "Oh, well, I mean," he started, but his new explanation made even less sense than the old one.

She didn't say anything throughout. That didn't stop Michael from trying to come up with a reason that sounded at least halfway truthful. After just a couple of minutes, she got tired of waiting for the right answer and decided to just read him. She had barely started her exploration when she stopped short. *Oh*, she thought, surprised. She blushed and then looked away sharply. She didn't know why, but she was so embarrassed that she wouldn't be surprised if a flag was sticking out of her head to announce as much. Michael didn't notice. He just stammered on. Carmen figured she'd save him the trouble.

"I think I understand," she said after taking a moment to gather herself.

Michael looked at her, and she blushed again. *What's the matter with me?* she wondered. She looked out over the water and tried to avoid his gaze, at least until her Dark got more sensible. Michael said nothing else, and she could only assume he was looking out over the water with her.

"Well, I'm happy you got tired of the party," she said after a few minutes of silence. She still didn't look at him, though.

Michael said nothing but smiled and then nodded. Carmen preferred it that way. Words usually ruined everything. It wasn't like she didn't know what he was thinking or feeling anyway. After her brief glimpse into his mind, she went on longer strolls. She'd sampled more people than she cared to count. Each was unique in their own way, though usually not worth remembering. If pressed, she'd be the first to admit that Michael wasn't special or significant in that measure. Nevertheless, being around him now produced an odd tickle. She liked it.

He looked down at the water. "You jumped off here?"

"All the time," she said, her voice more energetic than normal. Michael couldn't tell, but the difference made Carmen smile.

He stared at the churning water below and slowly nodded. She watched him over her shoulder. Her smile transitioned to an even rarer smirk.

"Do you want to try it?" she asked.

"No, no, no," he said firmly. Then he leaned back as an exclamation point to the sentiment. "I can't fly."

"As I said, it's not hard to do," she replied.

"Well, maybe for you it's not—"

"You never know till you try," she cut off. He stared at her hard, and that same look of disbelief once again graced his features. Carmen laughed. "Here, let me help," she added with a giggle for good measure.

All it took was a gentle telekinetic push to send him over the edge. He screamed, and Carmen watched him go down with an unabashed grin that spread from ear to ear. Undoubtedly, he was reconsidering what his parents said about Clairvoyants killing people on a whim. That, however, was not her intention. She'd *catch* him or fly after him or something before he reached the bottom. He was too cute to let go splat.

14

IN THE CLOUDS

Carmen stared at the sky and couldn't help a small smile. It made no sense, and she loved it.

"Michael, Michael, Michael," she muttered quietly to herself.

It was admittedly a rather unremarkable name. She didn't know where Carmen or even Edge fell in that measure, but she could close her eyes, throw a stone, and hit a Michael—that was, when she was out of the facility. Michael himself wasn't that remarkable either. She told herself that over and over again; nonetheless, she couldn't stop thinking about him.

They had talked last night with gleeful abandon for hours. After, of course, she finally convinced him she wasn't trying to kill him when she tipped him off the bluff. Really, she had no idea how long they talked—she had no sense of time and wasn't allowed a watch. Michael didn't have one either. But when they returned to the party, together but separately, it was long over. His parents were terrified that something had happened to him. Kali simply asked where she had been.

Carmen didn't say much. She was unable to suppress a small giggle with each non-answer, but that was all she let go.

She wanted to keep Michael to herself. She shared everything with Kali whether she wanted to or not. Her every minute of every day, if not spent directly with her handler, was certainly reviewed by her handler. It felt nice to have something that was her own. She had never seen Kali so furious, but she didn't punish her for her evasiveness. Kali didn't even say much of anything. It felt like she wanted to tighten her grip but knew she was holding water.

Ultimately, she didn't think about it much. Kali was mad and Carmen wished she wasn't, but it had to happen some-time. Besides, she was staring at clouds! A couple assets stared at her as they walked by. It wasn't common for an asset to simply lie on their back and sky gaze, but Carmen didn't think about them much either. Her smile got a touch bigger.

"Michael, Michael, Michael," she muttered again.

She'd read stories of people seeing shapes in clouds. It seemed like a whole bunch of nonsense to her. Those amor-phous blobs resembled nothing other than amorphous blobs. Perhaps, if she were crazy, she could make out a dog, a mountain, or a face. Perhaps—but she wasn't that far gone yet. No, she wasn't crazy. Not completely, anyway.

She abstained from saying his name yet again and took a deep, contented breath as her thoughts refused to turn from him. She closed her eyes as she tried to recall both him and last night fully. She couldn't really remember much of anything specific, strange as that was. *I have to be crazy*, she thought with a wry smile.

She sighed and then opened her eyes to watch the clouds that looked like nothing but clouds. Kali stood over her.

"What are you doing?" her handler asked.

Carmen stopped smiling. She'd been too distracted to sense her approach as she usually did. She stood up abruptly and brushed herself off with a hand. Kali looked at the act with a thinly disguised sneer. Carmen rolled her eyes and cleaned her now dirty hand telekinetically. Her handler did have a point.

"Nothing," she said quickly.

It was now Kali's turn to roll her eyes. "I can see that," she remarked. "When I leave you alone, you're supposed to be socializing with the other assets. Not...doing whatever you were doing."

Carmen looked around the courtyard of the facility and surveyed her peers. The vast majority stood in general proximity to each other and appeared from a distance to be engaged in casual conversation. She had played that game just last night and knew the act well. Handlers were annoyingly good at sniffing out the ruse, though. A few other assets stood very close to each other and talked in animated fashion but in hushed tones. They were probably organizing a game of Knock Out. The rules were basically the same as tag, but *tagging* meant trying to knock the player down in four moves or less.

No one ever wanted to play with her. She didn't really mind it. She never heard of anyone wanting to play with Artemis either, but Artemis was only rarely let out anyway. In any case, Carmen did enjoy watching the matches, seeing a dozen or so Clairvoyants dart around the courtyard before the quick exchanges developed. The handlers hated it. Assets weren't supposed to fight each other, even in play.

Carmen looked at Kali and shrugged. "Sorry," she said simply.

It seemed like she was going to say something, but she took a deep breath and shook her head instead. Finally, she asked, pointing, "Is that it?"

Carmen glanced at the bag that had been lying next to her. She had been quite serious—she did want to torch the party dress—but Kali had said setting rented property on fire would be…impolite. Carmen nodded.

"You ready?" Kali asked.

She nodded again, and the two of them began walking, Carmen holding the dress under one arm.

Her thoughts stayed on Michael as they walked. Really, she couldn't stop thinking about him even if she wanted to. It caused her lips to tease a certain question several times, but she kept herself from giving voice to it. She desperately wanted to know what the answer would be, but she also didn't want to breach the subject with Kali. There was no telling where things would lead in open air. So, Carmen bit her tongue and said nothing. She and Kali had walked in silence before, but she had a hard time remembering when it was ever anxious. As her handler signed the paperwork for them to leave, however, it was quite obvious that the anxiety only flowed one way.

Kali looked at Carmen when she was done. "You have something to say?" she asked. Her charge's mouth had the look of an overfilled balloon. "What's with you? Why are you acting so strangely?"

Carmen vigorously shook her head and then groaned softly when she realized it made her look just as crazy as she felt.

"I'm fine," she said quickly. "What are you talking about?" she added, trying her best to make it sound like nothing was amiss.

"Edge?" Kali questioned.

Her tone wasn't harsh. It wasn't even annoyed. But it was the tone she used to warn that she *could* be harsh. Besides Michael, that tone was the only other thing ringing in Carmen's head. She had to have heard it about a dozen times last night when she was being questioned. She swallowed hard when she heard it now.

"When is the next party?" she finally asked. She wanted to see Michael again, badly.

Kali exhaled loudly. "Edge, I know you hate parties, but it hasn't even been a day since the last one," she remarked.

Carmen looked at her handler in mild shock. Kali often said she didn't know everything, and Carmen understood that intellectually. The reality of their four years together, however, regularly proved otherwise. This had to be the first time Kali got her intentions wrong. But before Carmen could make up her mind on whether to correct her, her handler spoke again.

"Well, you don't have anything to worry about," Kali continued. "After the little altercation between you and Artemis, all future parties have been postponed until there's a full security review. They may never be reinstated. If they are, they probably won't include non-Clairvoyant participants. There were several complaints."

Kali spoke simply, matter-of-factly. She was totally unaware of the significance of the words that just left her mouth. Carmen's eyes grew wide as she listened. Her hands shook.

"We didn't even do anything!" she protested.

"Yes, but imagine if you did," Kali pointed out. "Artemis is one of the most violent, aggressive Clairvoyants anyone has ever seen. And you two have fought before. I don't know why you seem so bothered by it. As you tell me ad nauseum, you hate parties."

Carmen paused as she noticed the bear trap she was about to step in. "Yes, yes, I do hate parties," she said, folding her arms. "I'm not bothered. Thank you, I'm glad to hear it," she added.

Kali looked her carefully up and down with a raised eyebrow. Carmen swallowed nervously, knowing she oversold herself on both sides of the argument. After a time, Kali slowly shook her head and then rolled her eyes.

"Right," she remarked under her breath. Her charge swallowed again. "Come on, let's go."

Kali didn't wait for a response and began walking. Carmen was glad for it. They walked in silence as before, but now Kali glanced at her from time to time. She could feel her soul freeze whenever her handler's eyes neared her direction. Nothing more, however, was said between them. Carmen pursed her lips as her mind roamed. She had no idea why this was such a big deal. Kali would probably be happy about Michael. She went on and on about how assets needed to learn how to socialize, and she had spent an entire night doing just that.

But then she gamed out how the conversation would go. Kali would dissect her every second with Michael as if she were a lab animal. Her every action, no matter how mundane, would be ruthlessly critiqued on what she did "right" and, more annoyingly, what she did incorrectly. As they walked, Carmen considered what her next few hours could entail and came to the same conclusion. She'd keep Michael to herself.

They got on the same bus they had boarded hundreds of times by this point. The bus driver was still terrified of each of his passengers. Carmen always found that odd. If Clairvoyants were as dangerous as he thought, surely he should be dead by now. Nevertheless, she was able to ignore him. They sat in their usual seats, and Carmen looked out the window as the facility grew farther and farther out of view.

"You're going to be released in two years," Kali said nonchalantly. Carmen looked at her and noticed the faraway look in her eye. "Have you given any thought to your future?"

She thought of Michael, turned to look out the window again, and smiled.

"No, not really," she lied. She thought about it all the time.

"Liar," Kali remarked teasingly.

Carmen smiled again. If her handler didn't know everything, she certainly knew most things.

"I don't really know," she said, getting closer to the truth.

She thought of Michael. She wondered if they could have a life together. The idea was utterly ludicrous. She'd only known him for a few hours, maybe. Ludicrous or not, it didn't hurt to dream. After all, most of her nights were filled with nightmares.

"Really? Nothing at all?"

Carmen shook her head. Then she thought of her handler. "What about you? What happens to you after I'm released? Do you get another charge?"

"If I want," Kali said.

"Do you?"

She looked at Carmen, who was now looking back at her. Perhaps it was something in her voice—maybe a facial expression, subtle but there all the same—or maybe, on some level, Kali could actually read her charge. Either way, she gave a knowing smirk before she answered.

"You're a tough act to follow, Edge," Kali said. Carmen smiled shyly and then looked out the window before the expression reached its fullest extent. "I could go through a hundred charges, but I'll never forget you. As it is, I'd like to take some time off. Maybe another charge later, or maybe not. Maybe I'll just do administration. But enough about me.

You should think about it—about what you want. Two years will go quickly."

The bus came to a stop in Haven City, their destination. Everywhere one could see, there were people, industry, and commerce. The two Clairvoyants didn't get up to leave as Carmen considered her handler's words. She considered the future…her future. Her thoughts strayed toward Michael in that future, though not completely.

"I'd like to be happy," she replied, looking at Kali. She considered the matter further and her eyes fell. "I don't really think I know what that means," she muttered softly.

Kali looked at her. She had to have heard her, but she offered no advice, not even a comment. She stood, and Carmen stood with her, dress in tow. They stepped off the bus and into the maelstrom of Haven City.

Today wasn't really a field trip. Today, they had purpose. Field trips were never focused on any specific task. The bus dropped them off in front of a large mall. They had been there before, even before they rented the dress.

New Earth wasn't as cosmopolitan as Earth or Evonea. Carmen had never been off planet, but she had read about it. Kali even mentioned it in passing here and there, regretting that she wouldn't have much of a chance to interact with "non-terrans," as Kali politely put it. She was curious about aliens—had read about them casually and wondered how different they really were from everyone else—but could ultimately care only so much. It was more interesting how much attention Kali got from bystanders, despite being a Clairvoyant.

Asians were an exceedingly small minority group on New Earth, and Kali wasn't even a New Earther. They walked along the crowded sidewalk, causing a small bubble around them of people trying to avoid their path. Kali was often the recipient of a curious backward glance. Carmen sometimes found the reactions humorous, but her handler didn't seem to notice. If she did, she certainly didn't care.

They entered the large glass superstructure of the mall. The majority of its bulk actually extended underground. She remembered getting lightheaded when Kali first told her that. The above-ground floors were no easy survey. The material wealth of Earth, the Great Colonies, and alien trading partners flowed to this grand shopping complex, and every inch reflected as much. Besides the local cuisine, there was food sourced from hundreds of cultures from more than a dozen worlds. It was much the same for fashion and almost anything else one could buy, sell, or trade. In the end, it didn't really mean much to Carmen. She had no money. But she spent all of her first day here and still didn't see everything. Subsequent trips still left many secrets to uncover.

"You go ahead?" Kali more said than asked.

Carmen looked at her curiously. "Alone?"

She nodded, and Carmen nervously licked her lips. Kali had never let her venture here alone before. She wasn't really worried about anything specifically; it was just unexpected. No fanfare, no preamble, just "Go off by yourself."

"How do I contact you?" she asked.

She was never given a PDD. Kali had one, but she was quite certain the only reason she did was to phone a suppression team if need be.

Her handler shook her head and rolled her eyes. "You're a Clairvoyant, silly. If you really need to contact me, do so telepathically. If not, wait for me outside the shop. I'll meet you there."

"Okay," Carmen replied, feeling slightly stupid.

Nothing else was said, and the two went their separate ways. Carmen glanced over her shoulder just before she moved out of sight. Her handler hadn't moved from where she watched her intently. Kali didn't seem apprehensive or expectant. She just watched. A second or so later, Carmen turned a corner, and Kali was gone.

The young Clairvoyant, for one of the first times in her life, knew exactly where she was going and why. How to get there, however, was still a bit of a mystery.

"Now, where is Idiotatopia?" she said to herself with a wry smile as various advertisements vied for her attention.

One service offered large cash rewards for people to resettle on off-world colonies. She didn't recognize any of the names. Another mentioned a new breed of genetically massaged cat. It quite proudly stated that the new cats were more responsive to commands than unmodified cats. They even had a pair of cats to demonstrate the new revelation. A crowd of maybe twenty or so people gave commands and requested tricks, to the delight of everyone. Carmen was a little tempted to join but thought better of it. The crowd was having too much fun for her to ruin it with her presence.

There were also the usual recruitment offices and posters for Space Force and New Earth SDF. Some of the posters even depicted glorified images of the Terran-Sorten War. She took a quick glance to see if Eli's battle on the moon was one of them, but it wasn't. Then something did catch her eye. It wasn't a dress burning service, as she hoped, but it did strike close to home, literally. It wasn't a shop or even an advertisement, just a small booth asking people to sign a petition. The petition asked for the termination of forced internment and training of children to be Clairvoyants. In all her field trips, she'd never seen anything like this.

She walked toward the booth and telekinetically retrieved a pamphlet, just to make it completely clear what she was.

The two middle-aged women staffing the booth looked at each other when she approached.

Carmen looked over the pamphlet, but it didn't really say much of anything. It was simply filled with uplifting images of children, contrasted with horrible images of beaten and injured children, presumably from the facility. She didn't know much about the functional goings-on of the place, but she doubted they allowed cameras there. Consequently, she assumed the images of the beaten kids were fabricated. They didn't do a very good job. She had suffered much worse than anything the pamphlet showed.

She put the pamphlet back and looked at the two women. "How many signatures did you get?" she asked, curious.

"You're one of them, aren't you?" one asked.

Carmen nodded. "How many?" she repeated.

"A lot less than we would have liked," the other woman said after a sigh.

"Why do you think that is? There have been protests at the facility. People want it to move, right?"

"Facility?"

Carmen looked at the woman, curious as to how she didn't know what the facility was. "The facility…where I'm from. What your pamphlet is about?"

"Oh, the training center," the first woman said.

"Everyone calls it the facility," Carmen pointed out.

"You call it the facility? I guess 'training center' sounds less ominous than 'facility.'"

Carmen shrugged. She'd never thought about it before.

"Anyway, it's real name is—"

"I don't really care," she interrupted politely. "My handlers have said that part of the reason for the facility is that some Clairvoyant children who weren't tempered turned violent against their parents or others. Is that true?"

The women leaned back in their chairs. They looked like they didn't want to say any more—like they didn't want to admit it was possible. But eventually they both nodded.

"Yes, yes, that's true. Just last week, an entire town was nearly wiped out by a four-year-old," one of them said. "The only reason he was captured was because he passed out. It caused new debate. Some are saying children should be interned younger than six. But you know better than us what they do in those training centers. The government doesn't like to talk about it, but a few details do leak out."

She went on, but Carmen largely didn't hear her. She thought of her time at the facility. For the first time, she wondered if it was possibly a good thing that she was taken there. Her parents had always been uncomfortable and sad around her, but she couldn't remember if she'd ever threatened them.

"If you don't mind," the woman continued, "I have my PDD here. If you can say a few things, it would certainly help us out to have a firsthand account."

Carmen waved the idea away. The thought of saying out loud what was on her mind made her knees shake. There was one thing, though.

"So, most people want us housed in facilities, and no one wants those facilities near where they live," she said more to herself than to them. If she wasn't monster, and if she didn't feel like a monster, she was sure treated like one.

"Oh, they do eventually let you out," the other woman said. Her tone was soft and gentle, like she was trying to cheer her up. "They can't keep you locked up forever. Just keep your head about yourself, that's all."

"What do you mean?"

"Oh well," the woman stammered. "Haven't been too many of you lot released. It is a new program after all."

Carmen nodded. "But the ones that have been released have had trouble. They have trouble adjusting. Trouble finding any work other than military or mercenary. It's near impossible for them to meet or keep romantic partners."

Carmen gave a quick shiver when she heard that. The feeling came and went in an instant, but it left her feeling empty all the same. She glanced upward, through the glass and steel pillars of the mall, and tried to look at the clouds. They were partially obscured by the skyscrapers of Haven City all around her, giving her the feeling of being sunk deep in a well.

"There have been a few suicides," the woman continued. "Hardly gets reported, but it certainly happens."

Carmen looked away from them. Once again, she thought of the future—her future. She couldn't help another shiver.

"I know I'll be released. We are told at least that," she remarked, her voice hollow. The two women were about to say something else, but she spoke first. "Thank you." Kali always told her to be polite. "I have to go." Then she disappeared into the crowd without waiting to hear their response.

Carmen held herself for a few seconds until the conversation with the women could be forgotten. By this point in her life, ignoring or flat-out forgetting the unpleasant was practically a reflex. Focusing on her mission helped. Unfortunately, the store where she needed to return the regal robes of Idiotatopia wasn't on this level. She couldn't remember exactly which level it was on, which prompted her to walk toward a large map. A crowd was already examining the map, but it dispersed when she approached. No screaming, no drama; they just all went away. It wasn't a new phenomenon, but this time it made her pause.

She didn't exactly look forward to when she was released, but she didn't fear it either. In light of her recent conversation, though, Carmen couldn't help but wonder. Before, it was just the daunting magnitude of choice she'd have when she was finally and truly on her own. Now, for the first time, she considered she may have no real choice at all. She couldn't even stand next to people without them shying away. How was she supposed to work with them? How was she supposed to find a place to live? Kali gave her etiquette lessons. They were silly, but it was better than nothing. Nevertheless, Carmen's handler completely glossed over the fact that, no matter how polite she was, people would only consort with her if they wanted to, and only a handful did. She thought of Michael and last night again. She must have dreamed it.

She shook her head and tried not to think about it. First, she'd return the dress. Then she'd worry about the very real possibility of ending up homeless and alone under a bridge somewhere. Carmen found what she was looking for without too much trouble and left immediately. After all, someone else may want to use the map, and obviously it was unreadable if a Clairvoyant was there.

Her destination was not down but up, to one of the shops on the upper floors. It was tempting, for a second or two, to just fly where she needed to go, but she decided against it. Kali never said anything about that, but Carmen learned that it's often better to not attract undue attention to herself. So, like every other normal person, she took the stairs.

At least the trip was a feast for the eyes. Most paths through the mall were designed to be serpentine, to get lost in, and the stairs were not a straight shot from floor to floor. The route wound and curved back on itself to give a quite impressive vantage point of the shops and Haven City itself. She looked over the side as she went and was able to see deep into the underground levels of the mall. At the bottom was a reflecting pool that gave her the impression of a kaleidoscope. Carmen was quite tempted to just stand and watch, much like she often did at the bluff, but she didn't want to get in the way.

Up and up she went. Advertisements were strategically placed to grab the eye, but so were holoprojectors, which won the battle for her attention. They were showing the news. She assumed she was deliberately shielded from everything that went on outside the small bubble that was her existence. Kali never mentioned anything outside of the facility—or even inside the facility if it didn't directly affect her. Carmen guessed that what happened in the whole wide galaxy didn't really matter for her day-to-day, but something new was something new.

"Today we are pleased to present you with the great experiment," the newscaster began. "Here with me are the Wiz Kids, as many are now calling them."

Seated in front of the newscaster was about half a dozen young men and women who looked not that much older than she was. Two of them were seated prominently side by side. All wore the black and silver of the Space Force Fleet Command uniform. They were in a studio with several other people seated all around them.

"Can you please give your name and rank for the audience?"

"I am Lieutenant Garvin Brook, and I'm very pleased to be here. Thank you for having us," one of the two seated most prominently responded.

He smiled for the camera and waved to the crowd, who gave applause. His manner was crisp and disciplined but warm. Carmen didn't know much about the military and didn't care to learn more; if she had a picture in her mind, however, of a young Space Force officer, she was looking at it. The newscaster returned the smile genuinely, and Carmen couldn't help a small smile herself. Lt. Brook made her forget about Michael, if only for a second or two.

"And you?" the newscaster said, gesturing to the other officer seated next to Lt. Brook.

It was a woman with light brown skin. She was somewhat pretty—not a knockout who could turn heads, but pretty. Her hair, trimmed to just above her shoulders, cradled her cheeks. It wasn't tied into a boring bun like her peers wore it. She looked slowly around the room with a wry smirk, commanding it as surely as any Clairvoyant. She was almost toying with them with her delayed response.

"I am Lieutenant Renee Brown. Don't take my colleague too seriously," she said, gesturing to Lt. Brook. "We're not all robots."

The newscaster spat out a laugh he couldn't help but reined it in quickly. "No, no, obviously not," he said. "And you?"

As Carmen walked past yet another floor, she ignored the responses of the remaining officers and focused on Lt. Brook and Lt. Brown. It was obvious why they were seated prominently; they were utterly fascinating to watch.

After her jibe, Renee looked at Garvin out the corner of her eye, on her face a smirk she failed miserably to hide, seemingly on purpose. It was like she had playfully kicked him in the shin and was daring him to kick her back. But he didn't. Instead, he muttered something that obviously made her laugh, despite her modestly trying to hide it with a hand. She then said something that made him smile before both turned their attention back to the newscaster.

"And, if I may ask, how old are all of you?"

"Twenty-two," Renee responded instantly.

"Twenty-two," Garvin said.

None of the officers gave a response older than twenty-four, though Carmen wondered why that even mattered. They were obviously young.

"So, most of you are twenty-two," the newscaster said. "A twenty-two-year-old Lieutenant is already unusual, though it has occasionally happened in Space Force. But please tell the audience what rank you will have when the Wiz Kid Program ends in four years, assuming it is successful."

"O-6, Captain," Garvin said.

Renee gave him a quick glance. "Captain," she said, though with far less confidence.

"Commander," the next one said.

The rest gave their answers, which all sounded similarly impressive, though Carmen failed to understand the significance.

"That sounds like a very big leap for all of you. So, what exactly is the Wiz Kid program? How is this possible?"

"Well," Garvin began, "it is, as you said, a great experiment. In my case, the average fleet captain has at least twenty years of experience. Or, to put it another way, they have been in the fleet the entire time I've been alive, bloodied of course in the Terran-Sorten War. Personal experience is, of course, invaluable, but the aim of the Wiz Kid program is to figure out and develop new ways and training methods to squeeze twenty years of experience into six."

"Amazing. How is that possible?" the newscaster asked, sounding just as astonished as Carmen was.

"With a lot of sleepless nights," one of the officers remarked.

Everyone in the room laughed, none louder than the Wiz Kids, though each, in their own way, adopted a knowing pained expression beneath their grins.

"It has to be remembered," Renee smoothly picked up where Garvin left off, "that the United Terran Empire and

Space Force are still very new. Earth and each Great Colony's Self-Defense Forces keep their own local security, but Space Force is responsible for policing the vast uncontrolled territory between the Great Colonies, as well as the smaller colonies that have no local defense. It is also the first line against xenomorphic threats, like the sortens. We are all very thankful for the service of the veterans of the Terran-Sorten War, but there are only so many of them, and only so many continue to serve. It's not just down to building the ships to take on this burden; they need crews as well. The Wiz Kid Program is an attempt to address the problem."

"So, you're tell me that, on the eve of your twenty-sixth birthday, you could be commanding from the bridge of a starship?"

"If we don't screw up," Renee muttered under her breath, which brought a few smiles from the audience. "But if all goes according to plan…yes, essentially."

The newscaster nodded, and Garvin began speaking.

"There is, for now, only one slot available as the commanding officer of a starship. There are other slots as senior positions of military spaceports and as executive officers aboard starships," he added.

"So, who is getting the slot as captain of a starship?"

Upon that question, Garvin and Renee looked at each other. Their gazes were friendly, respectful, and even had hints of admiration, but they were also challenging. Neither yielded to the other, and it seemed like it was but a small skirmish in an ongoing war. When they mutually broke eye contact by some unseen and unheard signal, both looked at the newscaster.

"Whoever is the best," Renee answered simply.

Carmen watched them, utterly transfixed. *They fly around*

in starships, and I get stuck in a hole for twelve years, she thought, wondering if she could trade.

She had long since reached her floor and stood by, waiting for audience questions. She had a few of her own and silently hoped someone else would think to ask them. But then she noticed that, while she watched, all traffic had stopped on the stairs. A queue was even forming at the bottom as people waited for her to leave.

Kali would want her to be polite and go on her way, freeing the path for everyone else. Carmen, however, found it hard to see how she was being impolite to anyone. She wasn't in the way; she was just there. A couple of young toddlers unaware of the apparent danger walked right by her, their parents hesitant to retrieve them. The scene made her let out an exasperated sigh and start walking. She was half-curious whether people would actually be surprised if she up and started murdering people for no reason. *A test for a different day*, she thought, smiling darkly. She put the idea fully to rest as she entered her store.

"Hello, may I…." the receptionist said before her voice trailed off.

Carmen tried to think nothing of it but couldn't help clenching her jaw. She could mostly ignore the thoughts or feelings of those around her now, but still, even without telepathy, she was well aware of what most people were thinking.

"Returns, please?" she asked.

The receptionist pointed to a large sign that said "customer service" in the back of the store. Carmen thanked her and headed toward it. She gave the other dresses and suits on display quick glances, but she was no student of fashion. The only thing she could think of was what had possessed her to pick the monstrosity she was currently holding. She should have gone with a potato sack. But she'd be rid of it soon enough. She got in line behind two girls around her age who didn't notice her whatsoever.

"Ava, hurry up. Cody is waiting," one of them said.

"If the stupid guy behind the desk would hurry up, we'd already be done, Taylor."

When the stupid guy behind the desk looked at them and then at Carmen, it seemed like he'd prefer to deal with the Clairvoyant. There was a first time for everything. The girls continued their inane prattle about some trip they were planning to take to the countryside. Carmen didn't really listen, but they did have her attention.

All three of the girls wore short sleeves. Carmen's arms were toned and athletic; theirs were skinny, flabby, and weak. Their hair, while not exactly pretty to her reckoning, was styled and colorful. It fell over their faces and was twisted in playful curls, while Carmen wore hers in a ponytail. Her clothes were the plain dull attire all assets wore. Their clothes were almost uncomfortably short in some places and plunged very low in others. Indeed, they constantly adjusted their outfits seemingly just to fit in them properly. Carmen didn't understand it.

"All done. Thank you for your patience," the stupid guy behind the desk said.

Both girls shot him a distasteful look but said nothing. They turned away without looking and almost walked right into Carmen.

"Ahh! What the fu—" Taylor started, but she stopped short.

They were about the same height, and Carmen looked her right in the eye. Taylor wilted under the stare. Ava wilted too, though the Clairvoyant didn't even look at her.

"Let's get out of here," Ava said under her breath, and the

girls left the store at a fast walk, cackling at how close they came to almost getting killed.

"May I help you?" the stupid guy behind the desk asked.

Carmen watched the two girls over her shoulder. She pondered over and over again what made them so appealing while everyone ran from her in terror. One of the girls even had a boyfriend or something. Carmen had tried for years. She'd acted polite, unassuming, and even meek, but it never made any difference. There was only her night with Michael, an impossibly foolish dream of a night.

"Yes, sorry," she said, approaching the desk. "I just have to return this."

"Is there any damage or stains?" he asked as he took the dress from her.

"I didn't kill anyone in it," she replied dryly. His eyes grew wide. "No, it's fine," she added, wishing she hadn't made the quip.

"Oh, all right," he muttered. "Do you want me to send you a receipt?"

"Yes, please," she answered, though the receipt would be going to the facility, since she had no money.

"Okay, all done. Anything else?"

"No."

"All right, have a nice day." Then he leaned a little closer to her, which made her look at him curiously. "But if you could kill those two, I don't think anyone would mind."

Carmen smiled, failing horribly to conceal it. It was all that needed to be said, and she left after giving him a nod, which he returned. *Maybe not an impossible dream after all,* she thought as she walked out of the store.

With her task complete, she considered what to do next and came up with nothing. So, she sat on a nearby banister and people-watched. Her attention was focused on the lower levels of the mall. She didn't look at any particular person or thing; her gaze merely drifted as her thoughts turned to Michael. Then her eyes found Ava and Taylor.

Presumably, Cody was one of the boys with them. The group was a level below her and in easy view. The boys loomed over the girls, playfully grabbing or caressing their shoulders, backs, and for the bolder, waists. Ava and Taylor made a mighty show of hating the attention, but mysteriously they never moved out of reach. Although they were around Carmen's age, they seemed much older...but also much younger in other ways.

She thought of last night. Michael touched her hand by mistake and got a painful shock from her bioelectric field. He made very sure not to get too close after that. She remembered being disappointed and feeling weird that she felt that way.

"What are you looking at?" someone asked.

Carmen turned, and it was Kali. She looked back at the group and motioned toward them with her head. "Those kids," she answered.

Kali stood next to her and watched as well. She gave an amused knowing smirk before she instantly became more serious.

"After the deed, those boys will forget about them in a month...if that," she remarked.

Carmen looked at her handler for a moment. "Maybe," she said. "Maybe not," she added, thinking of Michael again.

Kali stared at her with narrowing eyes, but Carmen just watched the young girls playfully toy with the boys. She wondered what it would be like to be them. To have people run toward her instead of away. To be able to have someone touch her without having to consciously make sure she didn't injure them. To have someone love her, if even for just one night and even if they didn't remember her a month after. She wondered all those things and more, but above all else, she wondered if such simple pleasures were completely out of her reach and whether she'd be a fool to try.

"Tell me about last night."

Carmen looked at her handler with a start but said nothing. Kali's eyes narrowed again.

"Edge, tell me about last night," she commanded. "Tell me what happened between you and Michael."

Carmen's blood turned to ice when she heard her say his name.

"You told me you couldn't read me."

"I can't, and I didn't," Kali replied. "A suppression team observed the two of you together."

"I didn't sense them," Carmen pointed out, but she also noted that she never sensed suppression teams, even when they were standing right in front of her.

"They wouldn't be very good at their job if you could sense them. Now, tell me what happened," Kali said firmly. "I gave you last night and all morning. You're starting to disappoint me."

Carmen swallowed hard and finally noticed she was trembling. She wished Kali wouldn't make her go through this. She obviously knew everything already.

"Nothing happened. He was just a boy from the party that followed me to the bluff. We just talked," she said quickly.

"Why didn't you tell me this when I first asked?"

"I, um…" Carmen stammered.

Kali took a deep breath and looked at the sky while rolling her eyes. At the moment, at least, she seemed to have more patience for gum stuck to her shoe.

"To answer your earlier question, Edge, I don't know when the next party will be, but unfortunately I had to order that poor boy's parents to be removed from the facility. They no longer work there, and you will not see him again."

Carmen's mouth fell open. "We didn't do anything!"

"No, you didn't," Kali agreed. "Yet your mind is obviously stuck in the clouds you've been watching all day. Now I find you here, watching a pair of idiot girls laughing and flirting like whores with idiot boys." She took another deep breath. "Tell me why."

Carmen grinded her teeth. She really didn't want to say, but a small spark lit a flame inside her that had plenty of fuel.

"Because I wake up when you tell me to. I eat what you tell me to. I go and do what you tell me to," she said in a rush. "You always watch everything I do all the time. Then it's 'Try harder. Don't do it that way. Be more polite,'" she said, trying to imitate her handler's tone. "I just wanted something you couldn't touch—something that was mine," she said softly, knowing that wish was now dead and could never be fulfilled.

Kali's eyes narrowed, but she didn't appear to be angry. "Edge, I'm your handler. Your wellbeing is my chief concern and always has been. Do you know what the difference is between this Michael and the boys down there?" she asked, motioning to them.

"No."

"Nothing," Kali said simply. "And you can't do what I need you to do—what you need to do for yourself—if you're worrying about him. Do you understand?"

Carmen took a deep breath and swallowed hard. "I understand," she said, her eyes falling as she spoke.

"Good. Let's go."

She watched Ava and Taylor leave hand in hand with a boy, laughing and flirting, as she guessed, like whores the entire way. Kali didn't offer her hand as she occasionally did, though it was becoming an increasingly rare event. Carmen wasn't sure she'd take it if it were offered. She simply followed her handler as she usually did. They walked in silence, as happened from time to time. This was the first time, however, that it wasn't because they had nothing to say or because she was too nervous or confused. No, this was the first time that they didn't talk because Carmen was too angry with her handler to want to speak.

15

THE ARTEMIS INCIDENT

Subject: Artemis Age: 18 Status: Prerelease

As it was often commanded to, the pen described that which its master had never seen. The walls of the dorm where she was kept were covered in similar drawings. Her first, from when she was a child, was a makeshift window when it became obvious she would never be let out.

She had grown up in the city, but it hadn't strained her imagination too much to envision what life was like in the country. In her drawing, the sun was shining—the sun had to be shining, of course. To her six-year-old mind at the time, that was just how the world was. Now she simply pondered why it went hand in hand with the idyllic. There were also clouds but no houses and no people. There was, however, one solitary cow. She vividly remembered debating whether to draw the cow behind a fence. At first, it made perfect sense for the cow to be fenced in. Then, for whatever reason, she decided to erase the fence. Now the lone cow remained, corralled by a ghostly fence that both was and was not there.

Artemis looked at the picture, as she did every day, and then got back to work. There was that drawing and many others from that time. She didn't draw much for a period after. It was hard to remember exactly when she stopped, as time was difficult to measure here, but she did know exactly when she started again. It was after her first flight. She just felt the urge for some reason, and from then to now, not a day passed without her placing pen or pencil to paper. More often than not, it was because she had nothing else to do.

She usually drew one thing and one thing only now: people. They had a variety of expressions and poses, and she drew whatever suited her fancy at the time. Young, old, pretty, ugly, man, woman, almost anything she could think up, except for one taboo. She never drew herself. Not anymore. For one, it was hard to completely know what she looked like, since she was only rarely afforded a mirror. She used to draw herself, though, more than any other subject.

She drew herself alone in the dark. She drew herself, in countless motifs, being tormented by her handler, Ramses. Eventually, images of herself in every imaginable expression of pain, despair, and anguish covered her walls like plaster. She always found it odd that Ramses never commented on her art. At some point, she could take no more and burned every last picture.

Today, now, she drew her father. She had never known him. Her mother had said her father died in the Terran-Sorten War, but Artemis wasn't sure that was true. Many potential *fathers* had come and gone out of their small apartment; none had seemed noble or self-sacrificing enough to do anything like fight in the war. Ultimately, it was irrelevant. She didn't and would never know her father. She did like drawing him, though.

She liked to imagine what he looked like. Her pictures had started as what she wished he looked like: tall, strong, handsome, and always welcoming, always with a smile. In time, she admitted that the drawings, which she still kept, had to be far from the truth. Now, they were often her best guess, working backward from her face and her mother's to fill in the missing details. But between the idealized and the more probable, one thing remained constant. In her drawings, her father always smiled. He always seemed eager and ready for her to bound into his arms. She wondered what that would feel like, though she knew she would never know.

Her grip on the pen tightened just then, but she was able to keep from narrowing her eyes. Ramses was coming. She only saw him rarely, but she loathed every moment of it, especially when he interrupted her drawing.

Nothing about her handler could be described as confident. She sensed him on the other side of the door steeling himself to open it.

"Artemis," he called through the doorway.

She didn't move and instead continued working, though this time she couldn't keep from narrowing her eyes.

"Artemis," he called again.

She raked her fingers through her brown hair and took a deep breath. She had to get the smile just right or the entire picture would be ruined. She leaned back when it was done, but she didn't stop working.

"So, I see you haven't forgotten about me," she remarked. "Are you finally going to let me go out again?"

She heard—felt—Ramses step into the room. He rarely did that. It prompted her to drop the pen and turn around.

"Most assets go out every day. You have only yourself to thank for the fact that you don't," he replied.

She thought back to her last field trip. It had been short. After several weeks, she guessed, of being stuck in her dorm, Ramses had decided to take her to a beach. They never arrived. She got in a fight with one of the assets before they could even leave the facility. She didn't know who the asset was, as she didn't get many chances to mingle with anyone, but he'd stared at her when she walked by. She got enough of the normals staring at her; she didn't need it here. He didn't stop when she almost politely asked him to look elsewhere. After that, he'd looked at the dirt with a broken jaw. The suppression team had been on her in seconds.

It got her wondering. Artemis stood and tried to get a look down the corridor.

"No suppression team today?" she asked in a tone that was just as teasing as it was filled with venom.

Ramses visibly stiffened. "We won't need that, will we?" he asked, his voice even and steady. His charge said nothing. "You will be released in a week. When that happens, you can threaten and fight people to your heart's content…till you're finally put down. But until that time, I am still your handler, and I need you on your best behavior."

Artemis crossed her arms and was tempted to just sit back down and finish her picture. "Why?" she asked.

"Your prerelease interview with New Earth SDF and Space Force is today. Perhaps, if you can show some restraint, one of them will recruit you and you can finally put all that bloodlust to good use."

Her eyes narrowed. As usual, she couldn't help it. "I didn't force myself to fight Constructs," she said icily.

"But you never needed much prodding," Ramses retorted. Her eyes narrowed again, but she gave no response. "Come. It's best that you're not late."

He extended his arm toward the door but didn't start walking. She noticed long ago that he hardly ever showed her his back. She wasn't let out all too often, but when she was, she was also quick to note that no other handler acted in a similar fashion toward their charge. She dipped her head to him, smirked wickedly, and began walking.

Ramses followed her out and stayed behind her the entire time. She glanced back at him here and there, but nothing was said between handler and charge. They entered the elevator, and it was half-surprising that he let his guard down enough to press the button. Artemis leaned against the elevator wall.

Usually, her mind was completely blank till something or someone aroused her attention. The skill was so well practiced that she hardly noticed the effort. Today though, for whatever reason, her usual trick of getting through the day without ripping her own head off was failing her. Ramses had mentioned before that she had a mandatory prerelease interview. She didn't care much for it then and still didn't now, but it made her think of the sum total of the past twelve years. In a week, it would all be over.

The elevator doors opened into the long corridor that led to the courtyard. There was already a handler and their asset present. The handler looked at her with alarm but said nothing. She did take a few unknowing steps away, though, which prompted her asset to turn to see what had alarmed her. Artemis looked at the girl. The girl looked back at her. The skinny little thing looked terrified. She seemed barely able to defeat a stiff breeze, let alone the hundreds of Constructs that had surely been set against her during her stay thus far.

"Ramses, why didn't you place the facility on lockdown?" the girl's handler asked. "Why wasn't I informed that you were moving Artemis?"

Artemis narrowed her eyes. She was quite annoyed by the habit. She assumed the girl was going for her first flight and tried to think of some sort of advice to offer her. It was hard to think about just how long ago her first flight was. She had flown back to the facility in hysterical tears after observing a family quietly eating dinner together. Her mother never ate with her; she'd kept her in a room where the door locked from the outside. Every night and every morning, she simply opened the door, dropped a plate of food for her daughter, and closed and locked the door again. At least the doors at the facility didn't make a sound when they locked. Artemis remembered how she'd shuddered every time she heard that sound.

In the end, she could think of nothing to say. She tried to force a smile, for the girl's sake, but couldn't manage it. She continued walking and looked at the girl's handler just as Ramses started muttering a reply. Her eyes glowed a whitish-blue, and sparks arced along her neck and throughout her short hair while she pursed her lips. The handler's breath caught in her throat as she began to raise a guard. Then, just like that, Artemis blinked and it was over. She stepped outside and basked in the sun.

She rarely got to enjoy it, both during her time at the facility and with her mother. She hated the woman. She distinctly remembered how glad her mother had been when Ramses came to collect her. When Artemis glanced back at her handler, it was quite clear that he wanted to say something about her prior display, but no words came forth. She ignored him and continued walking.

The sun was shining brightly indeed with not a cloud in the sky. It was almost idyllic. Other assets were outside as well, and they all froze when they noticed she was in their midst. Whenever she glanced at them, they looked away.

Then she noticed *her*. The blonde one was hovering in the air with two other assets. The one-percenters were a short distance from each other. Artemis looked directly at her, in the eye, yet Edge didn't shy away as everyone else did. Artemis's eyes narrowed and she balled a fist. From Edge's position, it looked like she was giving some sort of silent judgement over everyone, especially her. Eventually Artemis sighed, realizing how ridiculous that idea was. Then she saw someone else who annoyed her almost as much.

The boy she had gotten into a fight with saw her at almost the exact same moment she saw him. His entire body trembled. Until today, she never thought a Clairvoyant could show such obvious signs of fear. But Ramses did say, when he wasn't yelling at her, that there was really no difference between Clairvoyants and normal people.

Artemis brought an upturned palm to her lips and blew the boy a kiss. At first, he looked like he was struck by lightning. Then he just stared at her, utterly confused. She glanced at her handler, who looked just as shocked.

"Do you want me to do this part too?" she asked casually but with an annoyed tone, gesturing to the gate.

Ramses pressed his lips together hard and groaned but said nothing. He either disciplined her all the time or not at all, though it was quite obvious he wished he could do the former more often. He walked past her and approached the gate guard.

Artemis raised an eyebrow. "Wow, such bravery," she mocked, making light of one of the few times he showed her his back.

Ramses realized his error with an angry frown. He glared at her but still said nothing.

"Shall I call for a suppression team, sir?" the gate guard asked.

Artemis glanced at the man with an ounce of respect. He showed none of the terror that regularly possessed both her kin and normals whenever she was near.

"No, don't do that. I'll miss my prerelease interview," she teased icily.

"Artemis!" Ramses roared. "Keep it up and you'll miss much more than your interview! That is enough."

Handler and charge stared at one another. It was not a battle of wills nor a game of dominance; it was simply a measure of how long a week was compared to twelve years. Eventually, Artemis relented by folding her arms and looking away with a huff. Ramses took a deep breath and then turned back to the gate guard. He would never know that he and she came to wildly different conclusions.

"As you can see, that will not be necessary," he said confidently.

The guard nodded, processed the paperwork, and then waved them on.

"Come, Artemis," Ramses said, beckoning her on toward the bus that waited for them.

She offered no protest as he took the lead, his prior timidness gone. She did give him a sneer and a middle finger behind his back, though. The gate guard chuckled lightly when he saw it. She glanced at him and blew him a kiss as well. She *liked* him.

"Where is this interview?" she asked.

"You have some place to be?" Ramses asked back sharply.

Artemis sneered at him again. She wasn't trying to be difficult with her question. He must have saw her out of the corner of his eye, as he stumbled for a second when she made the expression.

"It's in the Crystal Palace Mall," he finally answered.

Artemis nodded as they prepared to board the bus. Every other Clairvoyant got out of the way when they saw her approach. A few handlers and assets were on the bus already, but they all got off. She sneered at each in turn when they walked past her. Ramses made no comment and simply stepped onto the bus when it was clear. She was right behind him when she paused.

The bus driver was staring at her. She could know everything he was thinking—everything he ever thought—but she didn't need to. His eyes, full of dread, told her everything already. Her face took on a particularly ugly expression.

"It's been six years and no one's harmed a hair on your head," she said calmly. "Maybe I should just kill you and save you the suspense."

The bus driver made a noise best described as a frog being stepped on as he melted into a quivering puddle of goo in the seat.

"Artemis!" Ramses roared again.

She looked at her handler sidelong through narrowing eyes. Then she turned and looked at the crowd of handlers and assets too afraid to get on the bus with her. She swallowed angrily but kept her reaction to just that.

"Get this fucking bus moving. No one else is going to get on," she said as she went to her seat.

She sat down next to Ramses just as the bus started on its way. Her handler stared at her. She could feel his fury bore into her.

"Leave me alone," she said softly.

If he said something, she never heard it. She was lost in herself for the moment. Annoyingly, the nervous bus driver's shaking hands made the trip just as erratic. She regretted saying that to him, but it was only a small misstep compared to the grand magnitude of them all.

They arrived soon enough, and she promptly got off the bus. She wanted to feel it. She closed her eyes and soaked in the short moment—the few seconds before the people outside knew there was a Clairvoyant among them. The feeling was disjointed harmony as dozens and dozens of individuals streamed to the mall with their own agenda and objective but ultimately the same purpose. And then it ended. Artemis felt the sting of their apprehension at her mere existence as thrown daggers. She blocked out the feeling and opened her eyes. People walked a little faster away from her, giving hesitant backward glances. She sighed softly.

As usual, Ramses had her take the lead. He could never keep it up for very long. She walked into the mall and took a minute or so to admire the exquisite glasswork of the superstructure. She was rarely let out, but she enjoyed whenever she was. It was a busy day indeed. People of all types buzzed around, mostly families. They were so preoccupied with whatever they were doing that they only noticed her when they got close. She smiled at a few of them; none were returned.

"Your first interview is with New Earth SDF. Their offices are on the upper levels," Ramses said.

She began walking as he was mid-speech. At first, he was heartened, until he realized she wasn't walking toward the grand, winding stairway that led patrons to the upper levels.

"Artemis?" he questioned.

She ignored him as she headed toward the railing that prevented people from falling deep into the many floors below ground level. Ramses said nothing else, assuming she just wanted to look around. But then she turned to look at him and smiled. He watched her curiously before it happened. She flipped over the railing and fell into the bowels of the mall.

The Clairvoyant glided down slowly, as if she were supported by air currents like some sort of kite. The sight caused several normals to watch and marvel and children to excitedly point. She happily waved back, completely oblivious to the shouts and curses of her handler.

She stopped to hover just over the reflecting pool at the

bottom of the mall. She'd always wanted to do that. Artemis looked up and, from this vantage point, the sheer scale and impressive craftsmanship of the mall almost took her breath away. Unfortunately, Ramses floating down after her in pursuit spoiled the view. When he drew level with her, she noticed his hands were shaking with rage.

"I hope you enjoyed that," he said, his voice in a forced monotone, though his lips couldn't conceal a snarl. "I will have no more out of you—"

Artemis smirked and shot upward at impossible speed. She then gracefully arced and spun to land softly on the level she just vacated. People hesitantly backed away from her until she smiled and curtsied as if it were all a big show. Then she disappeared into the crowd before her handler could follow.

Ramses landed with a distinct thud, which made several people nearby gasp. But his prey, slender and nimble, could not be seen. She could be sensed, however, if imprecisely.

Artemis moved at a fast walk with an unabashed grin. If she'd known it would be this fun, she would have done this years ago. Ramses was right behind her but gained no ground. She slipped by people too fast for them to even register what she was and moved aside those directly in the way with a soft telekinetic thrust. She soon realized, though, that her handler quite easily followed in her wake. She grinned again as she thought of the optimum countermeasure.

It started with a rather large woman who was paying attention to nothing at all. Artemis telekinetically pushed her right in front of Ramses, and the two collided with a definite crash. The woman shrieked from the pain of touching his bioelectric field as she fell down, but she was otherwise unharmed. The scene caused several around them to run, though. All they knew was that someone was screaming around a Clairvoyant, which meant it had to be bad. Yet somehow their feet were redirected to run right into Ramses. He wasn't a particularly powerful Clairvoyant, but he was a Clairvoyant. Agile and quick, he dodged the people coming at him from multiple directions, almost as if it were a dance.

"Artemis!" he yelled when it was done.

His voice was so loud that she could feel the glass of the superstructure vibrate. It only made her grin wider. She had reached the stairs that led to the upper levels. By this point, there was nothing she had to do to impede his progress. The main floor was complete chaos to the point that he had to abandon his chase and attempt to restore order. Several security guards, after realizing he wasn't a crazed Clairvoyant, also helped, but it was futile.

"Ah," she said softly when she reached the floor she wanted.

She knew exactly where she wanted to go since the beginning. Several of the workers of the dress shop were standing outside.

"What's going on down there?" one of them asked her when she got close enough.

Then the attendant paused a moment. She had been so interested in the commotion on the main floor that she didn't comprehend at first that she was talking to a Clairvoyant. Artemis paid it no mind.

"Nothing important," she answered simply as she walked into the store.

It was near empty, as almost everyone was watching what was going on down below. She figured she didn't have much time. She quickly scanned the latest fashions. Once, Ramses was nice enough to allow her a PDD so she could browse clothes for fun. That was, until he destroyed the device in front of her for some offence she could no longer remember.

She found her way to the Evonean section like a heat-seeking missile. Earth fashions were too conservative for her taste. She felt twenty years older just looking at them. New Earth wasn't sophisticated enough. It was basic and functional but drab. Her eyes eventually found exactly what she was looking for. The dress was a deep purple and managed to keep the difficult balance of being provocative without being suggestive. She was never allowed to wear anything like it at the parties at the facility. But she was no longer allowed to go to them anyway.

She retrieved the dress telekinetically from the rack and laid it against her body as she looked in a mirror.

"Yes, yes, perfect," Artemis said softly.

She heard Ramses scream something down below but ignored it. She was already heading to the dressing rooms. Her eye estimated almost perfectly; the dress slipped on as if it were made for her. She smiled, but the expression was dropped when she looked at her clothes from the facility. Dull and plain, they never fit her well. Sure, her dress would be torn to shreds in a fight, but what difference did that make? She left her old clothes and gave them no further thought as she walked toward the cashier.

"Clairvoyant?"

"Yes," Artemis responded. "Please bill the facility. They owe me a lifetime anyway," she said.

The cashier didn't really know what she was talking about but nodded anyway. "When will you be returning the item?"

"On no, this isn't a rental. This is to keep. Add on a fifty-credit tip as well."

After a short pause to get over her shock, the cashier uttered, "Oh, thank you. Is that all?"

"No, not all," Artemis said as she began to walk away. "It's just the beginning."

She left the store and went to her next destination, a chocolate shop right next door. It was a small store with only an elderly gentleman to mind the place. He swallowed hard when she entered but was able to force a smile. She smiled as well.

"How may I help you?" he asked.

She slowly scanned the store but didn't see what she was looking for. "Do you have any Earth chocolate?"

"Yes, a new shipment just came in this morning. I haven't had the time to put any out yet."

Artemis licked her lips in anticipation. Unfortunately, she had no money, and she doubted the facility had an account with this store. The idea of just stealing the chocolate came and went almost as quickly as she could have killed him, if she so wished.

"I don't have any money. Can I have a free sample…please?"

The man couldn't manage to look her in the eye. She didn't begrudge him that. She simply pleaded silently to the best of her ability.

"Oh, all right. I've got it in the back. Wait here."

"Thank you!" she squealed, clapping her hands.

He returned with a small piece, which she popped in her mouth immediately. She let the chocolate slowly melt while she closed her eyes. She sighed blissfully when she swallowed. Though she didn't fancy Earth-style clothing, their food was another matter. Having a several thousand-year head start on the Great Colonies helped.

"Thank you," she said as she opened her eyes.

The old man nodded as she started toward the door. "Tell your friends about me," he called casually.

Artemis stopped in place. She didn't have any friends. She didn't even have anyone who would talk to her without yelling. She figured that was all too much to explain, though, and simply nodded in response. Feeling slightly dour, she considered where to go next.

She heard Ramses calling for her. He didn't even attempt to conceal the wrath in his tone. She sighed again, feeling the exact opposite of bliss. Then Artemis saw a makeup store two levels above her. She flew to it and, upon landing, let the dress wash seductively over her legs. She did, however, hold it in place telekinetically so that no one watching from any angle could get a glimpse of what they weren't supposed to.

This store was quite busy. Scores of women buzzed about, excitedly arguing about and sampling lipsticks, perfumes, and other products from a dozen different worlds. Artemis had never tried makeup before. The lesson completely escaped Ramses's attention. She smiled as she watched the women work, curious if she could ever get so interested in something seemingly so simple.

"May I…" the greeter started but then trailed off.

"Yes, I need help," Artemis finished for her. The woman nodded slowly. Artemis didn't think much of it as, compared to some, it was a relatively mild reaction. "I've never done this before," she admitted. "…I'm going to need someone to show me how." Her cheeks reddened as she realized how inept that made her sound.

The greeter nodded again, this time more confidently. She turned around. "We can do that, but—"

"I can wait my turn," Artemis said. "Treat me like a normal person," she added after reading her.

"Okay. We'll be with you as soon as we can."

She nodded and then began walking slowly through the store while she waited. Eventually, she came upon a young girl and her mother seated in front of a mirror. The girl was maybe seven or eight. The mother was ostensibly trying on makeup, but she was far more focused on playing with her daughter in front of the mirror.

"Mommy, I want to try that one," the girl said.

"All right. Let me show you how."

Artemis watched silently from a little ways away, just behind them. She could never imagine her mother treating her like that. At this point, she could barely remember her mother. They had so little contact that it was like she was a ghost. This girl's mother put some glitter in her hair, which made her laugh. Artemis smiled drily. When she was that age, she was cleaning blood out of her hair.

"You!" someone yelled behind her.

She knew it was Ramses and didn't even turn to look at him. The store went completely quiet.

"You fucking bitch," he said. He moved to stand next to her, but she didn't even glance in his direction. "Forget your interview. We are going back to the facility right now, even if I have to drag you, kicking and screaming, by your hair!"

Artemis took a few steps forward and then knelt to the girl's level. "Aren't you so pretty?" she said softly. "I wish I had a mom who cared about me like yours does. You're very lucky."

Ramses continued to rant. She ignored him. The girl looked at her but said nothing. Her mother, however, whimpered softly as she grabbed her daughter in a hug, worry and fear drenching every action. Artemis stood up and backed away. She didn't intend to cause that reaction, and her eyes fell as she frowned.

"You will fucking acknowledge me, you crazy bitch!" Ramses barked.

Artemis's eyes narrowed, but she didn't turn to face him.

"I don't care what you are or what you can do. One week! You couldn't last one week, you demented psycho!" he continued. "You are going back to your hole at the facility, and if it were up to me, you would never be let out! Feeding you scraps through the door would be too good for you! I remember what you are, Artemis. I remember you thanking me—thanking me with tears in your eyes when I came to collect you. It was pathetic."

In one fluid motion, the young Clairvoyant turned and punched him in the throat, crushing his windpipe. Ramses fell to one knee and clutched at his neck as his eyes bulged and he struggled for breath. Countless people screamed. The greeter ran out of the store, shouting, "She killed! She killed him! She's a monster!" over and over again. Most everyone in the store joined her, except the half-dozen or so people right next to Artemis who were too afraid to move a muscle.

She stared down at her handler as he died. "Why do you look so surprised, Ramses?" she mocked. "I'm crazy, aren't I?"

He wheezed out an answer that no one would ever know. She took a deep breath, and it felt like hate was filling her lungs. She exhaled it bitterly.

"All I wanted was for you to love me. That's all I ever wanted. You knew that ever since you took me from a horrible place and put me in a worse one. I would have done anything for you," she said, her voice trembling.

Handler and charge looked each other in the eye for one long moment. She could have read his thoughts, but she didn't. Then, at last, his eyes rolled into the back of his skull and he sank to the ground. She turned and saw the little girl, now screaming and crying into her mother's quivering breast.

Artemis sighed softly. "…Shit."

16

DARKENED FUTURE

Subject: Edge Age: 18 Status: Prerelease

"They're letting her out. Edge, look! They're actually letting her out!"

Carmen looked at her younger counterpart and smiled weakly. She was casually floating in the air with two other assets who were only a month out from their first flight. They often squealed about all manner of nonsense that wasn't worth an ant's attention, but this time their excited panic made Carmen moderately interested. She turned to look down on whoever they were talking about and saw Artemis staring back at her. The fellow one-percenter seemed none too pleased to see her, and Carmen was quite certain she saw her clench a fist. After only a few seconds, though, Artemis seemed to no longer care and paid her no further mind.

"Yes, it seems that they are," Carmen said as she watched the girl at the gate.

Artemis had some sort of altercation there—really, she should have been named Altercation instead of Artemis—but it passed quickly. After that, she and her handler went on their way.

"Did you see the last time they let her out? She knocked what's…what's-his-name's block off. She's crazy, isn't she, Edge?" the other one asked.

Carmen hadn't been paying attention to them. She rarely if ever did. She was mere days—a week, really—from being released. She was only eighteen, but that made her an old lady, at least for this place. She had named these two Pip and Squeak. She couldn't remember their actual names. For the past couple weeks, they became a constant if sometimes annoying entourage. A few of the other, more approachable, assets around her age had their own hangers-on as well. None of the handlers encouraged it, but they didn't object either.

The two girls patiently watched Edge for a few seconds while she silently looked off into the distance. One of them coughed when it was obvious she wasn't going to answer.

"Yes, she is crazy," she said simply, content to leave it at that.

Everyone knew the two of them had fought once. It was practically a legend by this point. Everyone also knew it was a subject she wouldn't speak of, and no one talked to Artemis. Pip and Squeak had learned the lesson mere minutes after they first met her. In any event, the girls continued on with some inanity she paid no attention to. She sometimes humored them, but not today. She was in no mood.

The finality of her impending release pounded into her skull like a nail. It was all she thought about every day and all she dreamt about every night. Her counterparts who were also about to be released said the same. They, however, all said they were going to join Space Force, a planetary self-defense force, or even do mercenary work. She was nowhere near as certain. The last punch she threw was in her fight with Artemis, and she preferred to keep it that way.

"Edge, Edge, Ed—" Squeak said with increasing volume. The name was well earned, as far as Carmen was concerned.

"What?" she spat, rolling her eyes. The girls shuddered slightly upon hearing her tone, and she rolled her eyes again. "Yes?" she asked more pleasantly.

Pip and Squeak glanced at each other with a sly grin before they looked at her. *What is it now?* she thought. But she felt a soft pinprick on her consciousness right when they opened their mouths. She raised a hand to hold them off and looked to see what it was. When she saw it, she smiled as well.

Carmen fell from the sky like a stone. She landed right in front of her handler and stopped short of hugging her.

"Thank you for rescuing me," she said.

Kali looked at her charge with rising eyebrows until she saw Carmen's entourage floating after her. She smiled evilly.

"Your prerelease interview is today," she said.

Carmen nodded. "I know," she said, not realizing the trap she just stepped into.

"Prerelease interview? Can we come?" Pip and Squeak asked together.

They were standing behind her and couldn't see her eyes grow wide with horror at the question. It made Kali laugh lightly. Carmen mouthed, "No," several times.

"I'd have to speak with your handlers to sign you out. But it could be a good learning experience…. Edge, what do you think?"

If there was any time Carmen ever seriously considered murdering her handler, it was now. "It will be pretty boring. I don't think so," she said.

"Oh, we don't mind. Please?" Pip and Squeak said together.

"Well, girls, if you don't seem to mind, I don't see why not," Kali replied.

Carmen felt like she was on fire. "*I* will *kill you*," she spoke to her handler telepathically.

Kali laughed again. "Well, on second thought, it wouldn't really be appropriate," she said. "The interview is for Edge's benefit and no one else's." Pip and Squeak were about to protest until she flashed them a look. "That's final."

The two girls shuddered, much like how they did earlier, and said no more. Kali motioned with her head, and the two started walking. When they were safely out of earshot, Kali stopped and turned to look at her charge.

"…Would you have really killed me?" she asked, curious.

Carmen folded her arms and stretched to her full height. "Sometimes handlers deserve it," she said, punctuating the comment with a smirk.

Kali slapped her playfully, and they started walking again. Some commotion was going on outside the gate that could be heard even now. Carmen figured it was a protest of some sort. They were relatively rare, but she had been witness to a few on occasion. The gate guard paid them completely no attention.

"She was very snide, but not anything extreme," he said to whomever he was talking to on the phone. Kali sighed and retrieved the appropriate paperwork telekinetically when it was clear he was too preoccupied to give it to her. "I asked her handler if he wanted me to call a suppression team, but he said it wouldn't be necessary," the guard continued.

"What's going on?" Carmen asked.

Kali glanced at her. "I don't know," she said as she handed back the paperwork. The guard didn't even look at her when he took it. "Let's go."

Carmen nodded, and handler and charge exited the

facility proper. There wasn't some sort of mass protest as she expected, just Clairvoyants waiting for the bus as they always did. They were, however, arguing amongst each other and quite loudly. She'd never seen anything like it before.

Kali stepped forward. "What's going on?" she asked no one in particular. "What happened?"

The handler closest to them looked at her. "Artemis. Artemis is what happened," he responded. Kali looked at him hard. "She threatened the bus driver," he said after a sigh. "Now he and every other bus driver in the company is refusing to serve Clairvoyant passengers. The facility is trying to find another company to fill the contract, but this happened only a few minutes ago."

Kali nodded a few times as she turned away to think. The other handler nodded as well and then returned to arguing about what could be done.

"We can do the interviews a different day," Carmen pointed out.

Her handler held very still. She heard her—she had to have—but the words didn't seem to register. Then she looked directly at Edge, her mind clearly made up.

"Let's fly," she said simply.

Carmen shook her head slowly. "To the Crystal Palace Mall? That's too far. It's too tiring."

"The interviews aren't at the mall. I'm tired of going there. It's actually a little farther than that."

Carmen shook her head again. "You can't be serious."

Kali smirked. "Are you a one-percenter or not? Afraid you can't keep up?"

She didn't even wait for her charge's response. The Clairvoyant shot into the sky like a missile and was a small dot in the distance in a matter of seconds. A sonic boom marked her ascent. Carmen couldn't help a wry smile; obviously Kali was being serious. She streaked after her handler seconds later. Their example served as inspiration for the other gathered Clairvoyants. A few seconds later, everyone else flew off two by two, handler and charge.

Kali slowed her pace dramatically, as it was a difficult speed to maintain. She dropped her altitude as well, and Carmen could see her now. Her handler was flying backward, splayed out as if she were sitting on an invisible sofa with her arms crossed. The challenge was clear.

"Well, Edge, let's see what you're made of," she spoke telepathically as she turned to face forward again.

Carmen made no reply other than to purse her lips. Kali flew at treetop level or sometimes lower. She also flew in anything but a straight line, always arcing or curving, darting here and there, making it trivially easy to cut her off. Yet when Carmen tried, her handler turned to face her to wave a finger and shake her head. Then she increased her speed to spurt ahead before returning to her normal pace. After the third such exchange, Carmen realized Kali did want her to catch her, she wanted to be chased.

And that was precisely what she did. Handler and charge streaked just over the heads of pedestrians on the sidewalks. Kali shot between and sometimes even under aerocars, daring Carmen to also try for the impossibly narrow and always changing gaps. They climbed over skyscrapers, seemingly like a vault, clearing the summits by mere inches just to free fall back to the street below. Kali would land roughly and run for a moment along the ground, jumping and flipping over obstacles and even people, before she took to the air again. Her charge was more graceful, touching the ground like a stone skipping over water and returning to the air almost in a dance.

In due course, Kali slid to a stop in front of a modest

building. She kept her balance perfectly throughout, ending the maneuver with her hands on her hips, as if she just stepped off her stoop. Not to be outdone, Carmen landed high on the building itself and slid down its concrete frame to land next to her handler.

Her breath came in exhilarated pants. She'd never flown like that before. She had never even thought to do it. When she looked at her handler, though, Kali giggled lightly and did a terrible job of covering it with her hand.

"What?" Carmen asked, curious.

"Your hair," Kali answered, giggling louder.

She had no mirror. She brought a hand to her head and was surprised to find that, not only had she lost the tie for her ponytail, but also her hair was a frizzed mess. She always wondered why several Clairvoyant women, including Kali, made it a point to keep their hair short.

"Come here," her handler called softly.

Carmen stepped closer to her. Kali licked her hand and gently slicked down her charge's hair. Carmen allowed herself to be comforted by Kali's touch.

"This is the place," she said. "A Space Force recruiting station to be more specific. It's important you look your best."

"I don't want to join the military."

"We've talked about this, Edge. At least hear them out. They have a lot to offer." Carmen nodded glumly. Kali leaned back and looked her charge in the eye. "It's amazing to think we only have a week left. Six years with me. Doesn't feel like it." Carmen hugged her, and they stood there for a moment, holding each other tightly. "You ready?"

"I don't think so," she muttered.

"Only one way to find out," Kali remarked as she made for the entrance of the building.

Carmen swallowed hard and followed her in, though not immediately. She rested a hand on the doorframe while she took a breath. It was then that Carmen noticed Kali's legs were wobbling.

"Not all of us are one-percenters," she remarked.

Carmen smiled wryly. Kali did as well, though with a pained expression. Then she took another deep breath and walked inside. Her charge was right behind her.

The foyer of the building wasn't very big and was dominated by a large recruitment poster. She recognized the Wiz Kids right away, especially the two most prominent, Garvin Brook and Renee Brown. They were front and center, with the other Wiz Kids at their flanks. The background of the poster was a starfield that was more an artist rendition than actual reality, but it was quite pretty to look at. There were also starships in the distance. Underneath was the tagline, "Space Force, Go Far." Carmen studied it as they walked toward reception.

The receptionist was a short blonde woman wearing the black and silver of Space Force Fleet Command. She smiled warmly as they approached.

"Ms. Grey, I presume," she said.

Carmen nodded. The woman, who looked about her own age, wasn't a Clairvoyant. Nevertheless, she could sense no fear in her whatsoever. Carmen was so used to the normals being terrified by her presence that the lack of even apprehension caught her off guard. Also, it had been years since anyone referred to her by her non-Clairvoyant name. The last time she could remember was with Michael. She tried not to think of him, though. It was too painful.

"We're pleased you can join us," the receptionist continued. "Lieutenant Commander Santiago has been expecting you. You may enter when you're ready."

Carmen looked at her handler, who waved her forward. She sighed softly and then walked into the building proper. The next immediate room wasn't very large, but it was very open. It was quite obvious that not all of the personnel who worked here were part of Space Force, as they didn't wear the uniform. Moreover, their bearing was completely different. Whereas the civilian contractors were just normal people, every Space Force officer and enlisted walked, spoke, and even seemed to breathe with a quiet confidence that was more a part of their person than any sort of arrogance. Indeed, not one of them walked by her without giving some sort of pleasant greeting. She could sense no fear in any of them, much like with the receptionist.

A man, tall and well built, walked toward her. She knew he was here for her as she always knew such things. He stopped in front of them and nodded in Kali's direction before he spoke.

"Ms. Kali, we thank you for allowing us to speak to your charge," he said. She nodded in acknowledgement. "I am Lieutenant Commander Santiago. Ms. Grey, if you'll allow me, I'd like to speak to you about your future."

Carmen looked at her handler. The Space Force personnel may not be apprehensive, but she was. Kali gave a reassuring smile in response and waved her on. She followed Santiago with no more preamble. The Space Force officer moved quickly and directly, almost like a Clairvoyant. Before she realized it, they were in his office and he was gesturing for her to sit.

He said nothing and allowed her to look around the room. On the walls were pictures of starships, presumably where he had served before. There were also pictures of what Carmen guessed were friends. On his desk was a picture of his wife and two children. She studied it for a moment. They all seemed happy.

"Before I start, do you have any questions?" he asked.

Carmen looked at him. "Why do you call me Ms. Grey and not Edge?" she asked.

He smiled. "It's your name, isn't it?"

"Yes, but no one calls me by my name."

"Do you prefer to be called Edge?"

"Not really," she said without having to think about it. "But you refer to Kali by her Clairvoyant name," she pointed out.

"Yes, that is true," he said after a sharp nod. "Your handler, however, and other Clairvoyants of her generation don't have names. The sortens never gave them that luxury. Space Force respects the tradition of Clairvoyants naming each other, if that's what you choose. If you decide to join, though, you are not merely an *asset* to us. You would be an individual, but one that is part of a team. Do you know anything about Space Force?"

"Not really."

"Have you spoken to New Earth SDF yet?"

"No."

Santiago nodded slowly. "With respect to my counterparts in SDF, Space Force is a cut above. We accept volunteers and volunteers only. Only the best. Each planet's SDF is responsible for that planet alone. We are responsible for everyone. No one planet or citizen is above the other. When we become part of Space Force, we are no longer citizens of New Earth, Earth, or Evonea, or what have you. Our allegiance is to the United Terran Empire and to it alone. We are part of nothing and everything at the same time."

"Kind of sounds like being a Clairvoyant," she said.

"Yes, you could say that," he said, nodding again. "However, a Clairvoyant is one individual. We're more than a million strong. On my desk, you saw a picture of my wife and children, but they are only a small part of my family. Out there," he said, pointing to the door they entered through, "to starship crews defending us from the sortens and other threats, everyone in Space Force is also my family. Ms. Grey —Carmen—you can be part of that family too."

She sat and thought about it. Nothing he said caught her out as wrong or bad. She even had to admit that some pieces of it were even appealing. Nonetheless, she felt as ready to jump for joy as if she were stuck in cement.

"What would I have to do?"

"Well, we are always looking for recruits of your talents," he began.

Nice way to say Clairvoyants, she thought.

"You would receive a ninety-thousand-credit signing bonus. You wouldn't have to go through the same basic training as new recruits. We train the best. However, nothing...nothing compares to the training you've already received," he said. Carmen swallowed hard. "The basic you would go through is designed for Clairvoyants and meant to acclimate them to life in Space Force—"

"But what would I do?" she interrupted. "I don't want to fight anymore," she said softly.

Santiago opened his mouth to respond but closed it after a second or so. He leaned back in his chair as he considered her statement. She considered it as well. She didn't know what she wanted—she never really did. But she had always known she didn't want the constant battle that seemed to define her existence. She had no problem personally with Space Force. In another lifetime, maybe she would even be interested. But here and now, she doubted that this soldier, no matter how well-intentioned or capable, could give her what she wanted

—she didn't even know what she wanted—while not giving her exactly what she desperately sought to avoid.

He opened his mouth to answer her question when his phone beeped. "I'm with Ms. Grey. I said not to disturb me," he said, annoyed.

"Sorry, sir. Her handler is quite insistent on speaking with her," the person on the other end of the line said.

"Very well," Santiago said after a groan. "Carmen, Kali wishes to talk to you."

She nodded and went to the door. Her handler was waiting just outside of it.

"Edge, we have a situation. You're needed."

17

THE MONSTER'S LAIR

Kali walked quickly and with a startling lack of elegance through the Space Force recruitment office. She moved people out of the way roughly with no apology and telekinetically pushed aside a desk without putting it back into place. Carmen was right behind her, glad there were no walls between them and the exit, because Kali would have surely walked right through them.

Her handler said nothing to give credence to her haste. Carmen wondered what could possibly be going on but could think of no scenario dire enough to require all of this. Yet, when they exited the building, she stopped, frozen in place.

Soldiers lined either side of the walkway leading to the street. Several police and military aerocars were waiting for them. Bystanders curiously watched the scene behind nearly shut doors and out the corners of windows. Carmen looked into the faces of the soldiers, all heavily armed, and their eyes betrayed tense, grim fear. She slowly shook her head in disbelief.

"Kali? What's going on?" she asked.

Her handler hadn't stopped walking. She said nothing but

briskly waved for her charge to join her in one of the aero-cars. Carmen swallowed hard and did just that. The soldiers joined them in a rush. Orders were shouted, and the entire congregation moved as if a second wasted was a death sentence.

Kali took a deep breath and glanced at Carmen. "Artemis."

Carmen looked at her handler sidelong. "What about Artemis?"

"She did something. Something terrible."

"What do you mean?" Carmen asked, her eyes narrowing.

"I…I don't really know. No one does," Kali responded. "She killed her handler and is holding up in the Crystal Palace Mall. There are people trapped in there with her. We don't know how many, but there are families—children."

Carmen nodded solemnly. "Did she hurt anyone…other than her handler?"

Kali shook her head slowly. "We don't know. We have no access to the building. Probably, though. It's Artemis. I'm surprised her handler was confident enough to take her some-where so public in the first place."

"She's never been to the mall before?" Carmen asked, curious.

She didn't know much about Artemis's day-to-day life. No asset really did. But everyone went to Crystal Palace.

"She has, but as we can see, it was tempting fate," Kali replied.

Carmen nodded again. "Where are we going now?"

"To the mobile command center just outside of the mall. The police set up a perimeter, but they aren't really equipped to deal with a situation like this. The local SDF has been acti-vated, but it will take time to fully mobilize." Her handler took a deep breath before she continued. "Space Force can't legally handle security matters of this sort unless requested by the planetary government. Even so, it will take several hours —days maybe—for the closest starship to arrive. For now, the facility is lending our suppression teams to help."

The convey of aerocars arrived outside the mall just as Kali finished speaking. The soldiers ran to join the police barricade, but no one spoke to or seemed to even care about them. Carmen watched the troopers for a moment and then looked at her handler. For nearly the first time, Kali didn't return her gaze. She looked away sheepishly. It seemed like she wanted to say something but didn't want to utter the words.

Carmen felt suddenly cold. She mouthed what she was going to say several times before she actually spoke.

"You want me to fight her," she said quietly.

Kali took a deep breath and let it out slowly. "I don't *want* you to fight her, but I…we…the people trapped inside need you to." Carmen shook her head faster and faster with each word. "Edge, there's no one else. You're the only person powerful enough to challenge her."

"If I fight her…" she said, swallowing hard. "Clairvoyants fight to the death—"

"Artemis does, always has," Kali finished for her.

Carmen looked away and couldn't stop her mind from wandering free. Ultimately, when finally faced with it, she didn't care all too much about Artemis killing her. She didn't want to die, but she wasn't terribly afraid of the prospect either. There were worse things than death. She rubbed her hands as she reflected on the fact that the last one she killed was Mikayla. Before that, it was scores and scores of Constructs. She'd never told anyone—she could hardly even admit it to herself—but there was a time, maybe once or maybe in every instance, that she felt a distinct emotion when she killed. It rarely entered her life, but she knew what it was: pleasure. After Mikayla, she never wanted to feel it again.

"It's so simple, isn't it?" she said more to herself than to her handler. "Kill Artemis and save everyone in the mall. She probably even deserves it."

"She wouldn't hesitate if the situation was reversed," Kali pointed out. Carmen offered no argument and only nodded glumly. "I can't force you, Edge. This is the one time—the one and *only* time—I'm asking you to do something that is not in your best interest. I don't want this any more than you do."

Carmen looked at her handler, and they sat in silence for a long second until, at last, with words failing her, her eyes fell and she got out of the aerocar. Kali got out a few seconds later, and the two of them walked toward the command center. Kali tried to grab her hand, but Carmen didn't want it. She instead stared at the entrance to the command center, her mind in a fog. She eventually took a deep breath then walked inside.

"Our current scans show—" a man in the center of the room said, but he stopped for a moment when the two Clairvoyants entered.

Everyone turned to look at them, specifically her. There was utter silence as dozens of eyes studied the asset with the utmost scrutiny. They examined the clothes she wore, how she stood, and her every breath and glance. It didn't take Carmen long to realize each and every member of the team had spent decades training on how to put her down if necessary. She felt like a little girl compared to their serious focus and even shied back toward the entrance. She stopped when she felt Kali's reassuring hand on her shoulder.

"That the asset has not moved from her position on the seventh level," the man in the center of the room continued.

Everyone turned to watch his briefing, but she could feel their attention still fixed on her. "Scans also show that there is at least a half-dozen souls with her, all in close proximity."

Next to the man was a three-dimensional depiction of the mall. The large, pulsating red dot, she assumed, was Artemis. As he said, there were about a half-dozen smaller green dots right next to her.

"There are at least forty other souls holding in place throughout the mall. They have not moved since the asset began her attack, but considering their position, they had no direct contact with her," he continued.

"Can they be evacuated?" someone asked.

The man shook his head. "That has been discussed and deemed too risky. Even if we had enough TC2s for ourselves and the team performing the evacuation"—Carmen had no idea what TC2s were, but she filed it away for later—"the asset would sense immediately if anyone was removed from the mall, which could prompt an attack.

"That brings us to our next problem," he said after a short pause. "Where the asset positioned herself is close quarters. We can't fire in there without risk to the hostages. We have to lure her out in the open. Here," he said, pointing. "The main foyer. Most of Crystal Palace is glass, so she will see us coming. It will have to be weight and angle of fire. I previously mentioned our Clairvoyant support," he said, glancing at Carmen. "They will be the second line."

They? Carmen wondered.

"Is there a dead man's switch?" someone asked.

"Not this time. The threat to the surrounding population and property is too high. No birds this time."

"How do we lure her into the foyer?" another person asked.

"Good question," the man replied. "Artemis," he said,

voicing her name for the first time, "has been at the facility for almost twelve years. We have all read her psychological evaluation cover to cover more than once. This is not our first encounter. She's belligerent, aggressive, and arrogant. …We ask her to come to the foyer."

"Ask her?" someone muttered in disbelief.

The man nodded. "It's quite likely she'll take it as a direct personal challenge and will choose to confront us without harming the hostages."

"We'll have her right where she wants us," Carmen heard someone say under their breath sarcastically.

The man looked slowly around the room several times but said nothing. No one else said anything, and eventually he gave a sharp nod.

"Gear up. Undoubtedly she knows we're here and is waiting," he said.

The group stood hesitantly but with quiet resolve. The man who had led the briefing gave several members of his team pats on the shoulder while saying words of encouragement. He walked right toward Carmen as he did. She took a step forward, all thoughts about Kali or anything else dropped.

"Edge, I'm glad you decided to help us," he said. "I am Captain Logos."

He wasn't much taller than her, making him somewhat below average height for a man. She was surprised to see streaks of silver in his hair. She rarely interacted with the members of the suppression teams; the only time they had been used on her was when she attacked Janus. She certainly never talked to any of them. She had always assumed they were the youngest, fittest, most foolhardy brave men and women that could be found. He was quite fit. She didn't know if he was foolhardy. She could sense fear, but it was controlled. She never would have guessed, however, that any of them were middle-aged. The other members of the team were also older. In his eyes, however, she could see the serious focus of experience, and it began to make sense.

All the same, she noticed something else about him. Now that he was away from the rest of the team, his fierce confidence seemed to erode. It wasn't worry, at least not personal worry, nor was it worry for his team or even the hostages, but there was a mounting concern that she wasn't able to place without reading him.

"What's wrong?" she asked. She didn't like reading someone if she didn't have to.

His eyes grew wide as he looked at her. She couldn't stop herself from rolling her eyes in turn. Even people who trained to fight Clairvoyants were surprised when a Clairvoyant was clairvoyant.

"There's something you didn't say in the briefing," she elaborated.

Captain Logos took a deep breath. "You're right. There is," he began. "There are aspects about this attack that don't fit the pattern."

Carmen looked at him quizzically. "Pattern?"

"We've been training Clairvoyants for about twelve or thirteen years. When an asset runs away or kills someone, they are usually random events, like an outburst." She nodded slowly as she thought of when she flew to the forest, as well as when she attacked Janus. "Assets have killed handlers before. It's not uncommon. But if this attack fit the pattern, she would have left the mall. She knows we would hunt her and would have tried to escape."

She considered it for a few seconds but could come to no definite conclusions. "So, what does that mean then?" she asked.

Logos took another deep breath. "She killed her handler in the mall. Most assets kill or attempt to kill their handlers in the facility. They even had an altercation when he was signing her out this morning, but she did nothing. After she kills her handler, she doesn't leave and even takes hostages. If she didn't have hostages, it is very likely we would just kill her by destroying the building."

"I don't know what you're implying," Carmen said.

"I think she planned this," Logos explained. "As I said in the briefing, I think she wants to confront us directly. I don't know why, but it's the only thing that makes sense."

She thought about it and agreed with a nod. She looked at Kali, and her handler's features were grim.

"It's just a guess and not really worth much. Anyway, there are two people I want you to meet," he said, changing the subject and waving her forward.

Carmen nodded again and immediately saw who he was referring to. Both people were devastatingly ugly. Their hair was trimmed to just above their scalps, and unlike the members of the suppression team, they were wearing civilian clothes. Tattoos just peeked out from their shirt sleeves, and they had small ones on the side of their necks. It was only after a time that she realized they were women.

As they sat, quietly talking amongst themselves, they seemed completely out of place compared to the suppression team loading rifles and cross-checking equipment. These women, by contrast, looked like they were waiting for a parade. But they were both Clairvoyants. They noticed Captain Logos and Carmen approaching and stood. They dwarfed almost everyone in the room.

"Edge, this is Lt. Kennedy and Lt. Ridley of Space Force," Logos said.

"I thought you said Space Force couldn't be here for hours or days?" Carmen remarked to Kali.

"We were on leave here and found out about the situation," Kennedy said. "We offered our services and the mayor accepted."

Carmen nodded.

"I can trust her to your capable hands?" Logos asked the two Space Force officers.

Kennedy nodded respectfully.

"Kali?" Carmen muttered softly, glancing back at her handler.

"Edge, this is out of my realm. Stay safe. I'll see you after," she replied.

Carmen said nothing but swallowed hard when she looked at the two women. They eyed her up and down several times. She didn't like their collective gaze. It made her feel like a piece of meat.

"The equipment you requested is in the next room. You can change in there," Logos said.

"Thank you, Captain," Ridley said back.

The three women then walked into the adjoining room. Carmen gave her handler one last look before the door closed. Kali returned her apprehension with a calm, determined nod. Kennedy and Ridley nonchalantly walked to the center of the room where a table had clothes piled on it. Carmen could only lean against the door. *What am I doing?* she wondered dismally.

"You're a mousy little thing," Ridley said, noticing Carmen. The woman already had her shirt off. "They told us you were formidable."

Kennedy laughed lightly. Carmen said nothing and walked toward the table as they continued to undress.

"What is this?" she asked as she picked up one of the sets of clothing.

It was a bodysuit dark blue in color. It had nothing to cover the head, but it did encase the hands and feet. As she held the suit in her hands, she noted it was a little heavy.

"Body armor for Clairvoyants. Heat resistant mostly, with some bullet resistance. We can't be hurt by lasers; our bioelectric field makes them bend right around us," Kennedy said.

"I've never been shot by a laser," Carmen remarked softly.

"And I've never been prom queen. Hurry the fuck up," Ridley snapped.

Carmen pursed her lips but gave no reply. She turned her back to them and began undressing. She could feel them watching her. She didn't long for the attention.

"Hey, San, remember that girl they asked us to put down on that cruise liner a while back?" Ridley asked.

Kennedy laughed again. "Yeah, the whole place was covered in shit and entrails. Half the trooper squad behind us threw up. When it was all over, she was lying there, dying, crying for her mother. Dumb bitch…. That was the first person she took out! All that over a fucking cookie."

"They should make normies take classes," Ridley said. "If your brat is a Clairvoyant, give them whatever they want. It's like that punk…."

Carmen no longer listened to them. She closed her eyes and took a deep breath as she slowly put on the body armor. *Why am I doing this?* she wondered again. To her considerable surprise, the suit fit her perfectly, almost as if it was made for her. Its weight went unnoticed after only a few seconds. She rolled her shoulders a couple times and did a quick low kick. The suit didn't restrict her movement whatsoever. Air was more encumbering.

"Shit, it's too small," Kennedy groaned loudly.

Ridley walked over to her and made a show of trying to force the suit on.

"Ow, that hurt, bitch," Kennedy said after playfully slapping her counterpart in the face.

"Told you you ate too much cake," Ridley said back. "Forget it. I'm surprised they were even able to find these suits."

"Easy for you to say," Kennedy muttered as she hastily put back on her civilian clothes.

Ridley ignored her and walked closer to Carmen. "I can burn your hair off, if you'd like. Don't want hair like that in a fight."

Carmen looked at the two of them watching her intently and then looked at her hair. "I'll keep my hair," she said softly but firmly.

Ridley shrugged the comment away and walked back to Kennedy, who was finished dressing. They held each other by the shoulders and looked each other intensely in the eye.

"You ready for the fight?"

"You know it!"

"You ready to get nasty?"

"Absolutely!"

Then they roared loudly before ending the ritual by smacking each other hard in the face. Neither flinched. Ridley then walked toward Carmen with her hands held wide, presumably to do the same with her. Carmen's eyes narrowed slightly before she raised her chin and walked to the door.

"Priss," Ridley muttered, easily loud enough for Carmen to hear. The one-percenter ignored her.

Carmen was first into the next room. The suppression

team was waiting for her. Their battle dress was a little more elaborate than hers, but it was nothing she hadn't seen before. She saw no foam cannons this time. Every member of the team was armed with rifles. She also didn't see Kali.

"Everyone move out," Captain Logos commanded when all three Clairvoyants were ready.

The suppression team broke out in a slow run. They were out of the makeshift command post in seconds. She was right behind them, and Kennedy and Ridley were right behind her.

"Oh, I see them now," she heard a newscaster say. "It's the suppression team from the local training center. They are joined by two Clairvoyant officers from Space Force who were luckily on leave in the area. There is another Clairvoyant with them. We don't know who she is; we will check our sources."

"Eyes front, Priss. Pay attention," Ridley said.

Carmen did as she was told, though not without rolling her eyes. That wasn't the only newscaster, though. They ran by a gaggle of them before they could even see the police barricade. News aerocars floated in the sky. Curious civilians were everywhere she could see, but when they saw the team, their reaction was not what she expected. They actually cheered, and the roar of the crowd drowned out all else. Carmen could feel it in the pit of her stomach. She didn't know about anyone else, but the insanity of the moment struck her with all the intensity of a bolt of lightning. For the first time ever in her young life, people were actually happy to see her. Not only that, but they also cheered her on like she was their savior.

She thought back to her time in the Space Force recruitment office, to now, and to every other period in her life. If she was well and truly a monster, and there were many times she was quite certain she was, the only difference she could see between being cheered for today and reviled every other day was that here, now, she wasn't just a monster. She was *their* monster. Carmen remembered what Janus said. She was a monster meant to give other monsters pause. She didn't know what he meant then and wasn't completely sure now, but she finally had to admit that perhaps her time at the facility had more purpose than she ever before realized.

The cheers were near deafening at this point, and as she heard them, the idea of joining Space Force or whoever seemed more and more appealing. She dug her fingernails into her palm and tried to ignore the praise.

"I won't forget," she whispered softly to herself.

The team was at the barricade now. The police made way, and the team entered the parking lot of the mall. Logos dramatically slowed. Then he gave a hand signal that made the team spread out with the selfless unity of a school of fish.

"TC2s switch on," he said.

One by one, she could no longer sense the suppression team. She was looking right at them, but they may as well not even be there. She no longer wondered what TC2s were.

She could still hear the crowd at her back as the team bunched up at the glass doors of Crystal Palace. They moved past the obstruction quickly and entered the mall proper. Other than some soft background music that the mall always played, but which she never noticed till now, there was silence.

Carmen had never been in an empty mall before. Her footsteps, and the rest of the team's, echoed throughout the establishment. She could sense people, but they were nowhere to be seen. Food still left in ovens and on grills smoked and smelled terrible. Clothes that patrons had been sampling before the incident were left on the ground. There were shoes left here and there that had fallen off in the mad rush to escape. Indeed, there were some spots of blood from unfortunate individuals who had gotten trampled. So silent was the din that the sound of water from the fountain far below could be heard even on this level.

She looked at the level where Artemis was supposed to be. She could sense the wayward Clairvoyant, but there was nothing to be seen.

Captain Logos gave several hand signals, and the suppression team broke into multiple smaller units. They quickly but quietly ran to strategic positions on their current level and several above. Logos and Carmen watched their progress, though she did so more out of curiosity than anything. Kennedy and Ridley paid the team no mind. The Space Force officers casually scanned back and forth, periodically pausing for a time. Carmen knew they were looking at the hiding spots of the mall patrons who were unable to get away. None of them could be seen. Their fear, however, hung in the air, almost thick enough to walk on. Carmen was unable to ignore it, despite her best efforts.

Eventually, the pitter patter of the members of the suppression team moving into position stopped. Logos didn't give away their positions by looking at them; he simply took a deep breath and gripped his rifle more firmly. Then he looked at Kennedy and Ridley.

"Priss," Ridley started. Carmen hated her new name but came to attention nonetheless. "Pick a spot out of sight. We'll take her first. Then you attack when she's off guard."

Carmen nodded and then began running. A holoprojector store caught her eye, and she made a beeline for it. It was as much a fortress as it was a starship, but the entire front of the store was glass, giving her an unimpeded view of the foyer. She ducked down behind a store display to put herself out of view and waited.

Once again, other than the soft music of the mall and her own quickening breath, there was silence. Logos quietly discussed something with the two Clairvoyants before they moved off, but she paid them no attention. Something else caught her eye.

"I know this," she said softly to herself.

The holoprojectors were silently demoing several movies. She didn't know them—she was never shown any at the facility—but this one was different. It was old. There is a ball at the castle. The prince grabs a servant girl's hand seemingly by mistake. Both the prince and girl are surprised, but they start dancing anyway.

"I know this," she said again.

She knew it another lifetime ago. She could barely remember it—she *didn't* remember it—but it was still part of her all the same. As she watched, she began to move in time with the dance. She didn't miss a step.

"Artemis," Captain Logos called loudly, breaking Carmen of her reverie. He stood valiantly in the center of the foyer, all alone. "Artemis," he called again.

At the sound of his voice, there was a soft whimper from the back of the store. Carmen walked toward it with an eyebrow raised. She sensed someone was close but didn't think to look till now. She searched with her eyes and Clairvoyant senses, and both came to rest on the cashier's counter. Two young women about her age shrieked when she peeked over it.

"I won't hurt you," she said softly. The girls looked oddly familiar, but she couldn't place them. "Is anyone else here?" she asked. She didn't sense anyone, but it didn't hurt to be absolutely sure.

The two girls were holding each, shivering in terror. Their hair was colorful and styled badly but styled nonetheless. If fell over their faces in a tear-soaked mess. In contrast to Carmen's all-covering body armor, their clothes plunged very low in some places and were uncomfortably short in others.

Just before they could answer, the lights started flashing.

"Why are the lights flashing, Ava?" one of them murmured.

"I don't know, Taylor."

Carmen involuntarily stiffened as she turned to look at the foyer. The holoprojectors shorted out and failed throughout the store, and the lights flashed with even wilder intensity.

Artemis was coming.

18
____

EDGE VS. ARTEMIS

It was all really very silly. Yet, for some reason, applying the nonsense was unexpectedly fun in a way she was never before allowed to experience. She puckered her lips and slowly turned her head from side to side.

"You're right," Artemis said. "This color does match my hair better."

"Glad you like it," the stylist said with a trembling voice.

Artemis ignored the stylist's quivering and examined her reflection again. She undeniably looked better with lipstick than without. Strange how such a subtle addition made such a drastic change.

"What's next?" she asked.

There was a response, though it was not one Artemis was expecting.

"What do you want from us?" one of the store patrons screamed in terrified frustration.

The lot of them were huddled together not too far from the Clairvoyant. Ramses's corpse was opposite them and to Artemis's back. She could see it in the mirror but strategically placed her head so it was out of view. The stylist next to her had stood perfectly still after the outburst, as did everyone else. There were whimpers and moans of fear when Artemis glanced in the direction of her unwilling company.

"I waited my turn," she said nonchalantly. "You can go after me if you want. I'm almost done. So, lipstick, blush… what's next?" she asked again, getting back to business.

The lack of response from the stylist, still frozen in place, prompted Artemis to glare at her with narrowing eyes.

"Oh, ah…mascara maybe," the woman said with a start.

"Okay, let's try that," Artemis agreed, still turning her head from side to side to examine her new look.

The stylist picked up the brush, but her hands were trembling so badly that she dropped it. Artemis caught the item telekinetically and brought it to her own hand.

"I can do it. Just tell me how," she said.

"Well, hold it like this."

"Mmhmm." She leaned closer to the mirror as she brought the brush to her eye.

"Just make sure you—"

"Artemis!" came an echo from the foyer.

Everyone in the room jumped, save for the Clairvoyant.

"Wish I was able to finish first," she said softly to herself. "I have to go. Sorry, but as I said, I don't have any money."

The stylist swallowed hard. "That's okay. I don't mind."

"Thank you."

She stood and posed one last time in front of the mirror. Then she walked toward the huddled people and dropped to her knees.

"Artemis!"

The call made her eyes narrow—she could never help it. But the feeling passed quickly when she looked at the little girl and her mother. The woman still held her daughter close and squeezed her tighter as the Clairvoyant drew near. The girl had long since abandoned any fear.

"Remember what's about to happen," Artemis said softly. "Don't believe what anyone who wasn't here says about it."

Then she stood and made for the exit, pausing briefly to sneer at Ramses's body. With that, she walked out of the store, a picture of total calm. Yet there was a spark along her arm as she began to descend the glass stairway to the foyer. Then there was another spark. Shortly thereafter, the lights of the mall developed an odd flicker that only grew in intensity.

Even the non-Clairvoyants awaiting Artemis knew she was coming and that she was preparing for battle. It took several seconds for Carmen to realize her breath was firing in rapid pulses timed to the beat of her quickening heart. Her mouth was dry when she first caught a glimpse of her.

The fellow one-percenter descended the stairs in complete casual disregard for the force arrayed against her. Indeed, she knew Carmen was here. Her glowing eyes looked right where she was hiding before she turned her attention to Captain Logos.

Logos stood in the center of the foyer, alone and without cover before one of the most powerful beings in the galaxy, completely undeterred. Carmen had never seen anything like it. She couldn't sense him with his TC2 switched on, but not one aspect of him seemed stressed in any way. Carmen felt the sweat on her brow and couldn't help feeling a small bit of shame in comparison.

The lights stopped flashing, and Artemis's eyes no longer glowed. She reached the main foyer and walked toward Logos, who was still a good distance away. Oddly enough, the Clairvoyant wore a dark purple dress. In any other context, she would look like just another young woman at the mall.

Logos slowly brought his rifle to his shoulder. It all happened faster than Carmen was ready for.

"Get on the floor, face down!" Logos commanded.

Artemis stopped in place. "Captain Logos, I hoped it would be you."

"Down on the floor, now!"

Artemis opened her arms wide, seemingly welcoming what was to come.

"All right, take her out!"

Every member of the suppression team had set their rifles to full power. The combined weight of their report was deafening. The glass of the store Carmen was in shattered. Ava and Taylor screamed, though even Carmen couldn't hear them. Hypersonic bullets that missed Artemis chewed into the floor where she was standing, kicking up a cloud of dust from the debris. Glass, plaster, and steel behind the Clairvoyant crumbled to bits from stray fire. Sparks and heat flashes from the pure kinetic energy of the bullet impacts reduced that small area of Crystal Palace Mall to a smoldering hell. Then every member of the team reloaded and unleashed a second volley.

Yet, when it was all over and the dust finally settled, Artemis remained standing in place, arms still held wide. Now there was a smirk on her face, as well as the sound of hundreds of bullets falling to the ground after mysteriously stopping in place before they hit the Clairvoyant.

Captain Logos and the asset looked each other in the eye. The brave captain remained resolutely in place, but the muzzle of his rifle slowly fell.

"Artemis!" Ridley yelled as she flew in on the attack.

Just as the young woman was about to raise her guard, she was kicked in the side by Kennedy, who attacked unseen from her flank. The one-percenter tumbled end over end across the foyer from the force of the blow before she came to her feet. Ridley was on her instantly, kicking her hard in the chest. Artemis groaned as her body wilted. She lay on the ground in the fetal position, gasping for air. Kennedy unleashed a heat beam, and Artemis only just managed to avoid it. She took to the air and Kennedy's beam followed, cutting large swaths out of the mall.

Carmen's lips trembled. Some of the people she sensed since they arrived—the people unable to get of out of the mall —were no longer there. Kennedy's beam killed them. *They don't care about the people!* she realized in horror. The suppression team hadn't been reckless with their fire. They made sure there was no one behind Artemis when they attacked. Kennedy and Ridley didn't seem to have the same concern.

Carmen turned around and ran toward Ava and Taylor. "You have to get out."

The girls looked at her with mouths agape. "Are you crazy? We can't go out there!"

Both shrieked as Carmen ended the argument by telekinetically snatching them off the ground. She ran toward the exit of the store with the girls floating after her. She then slid them on their butts toward Captain Logos.

"Get them out!" she shouted.

Logos had been watching the ferocious battle with his rifle raised, waiting for an opportunity to take a shot without hitting Kennedy or Ridley. He jumped slightly when Carmen called out to him.

"Right!" he said after looking at the two trembling girls. Then he spoke into the communicator built into his helmet, giving new orders.

Carmen shot across the foyer toward the next closest group of people.

Ridley and Kennedy alternated their attack on Artemis. The young Clairvoyant's psychological profile stated that she was unstable—that, while reasonably intelligent, she was unable to focus on any one task for extended periods. Yet, for all that, she was a measured, disciplined fighter in battle. Her technique was picture-perfect in form and millimeter-accurate in execution. She was easily more powerful than both of her opponents, but she was also more efficient as well. Kennedy was able to hold her own on the defense but unable to translate the defense into any offensive momentum. Ridley attacked recklessly, though not stupidly. Her style left her horribly open, but Kennedy's pressure kept Artemis from counterattacking.

Carmen slid to a stop in front of a hotdog stand. She sensed an adult and a child hiding inside of it.

"Come on out. You need to get out of here," she called.

There was no reply, save one from the middle of the foyer.

"Priss! Priss, we need you! Get her!" Ridley cried desperately.

Carmen ignored the summon. "Come on," she tried again, her attention completely fixed on the hiding normals.

"We're coming out," she heard a man say. A few seconds later, an older man and a young boy emerged from the booth.

"Get to the suppression team," she said, pointing at Logos and his team. "They'll get you out." The man looked at the battling Clairvoyants in the center of the foyer. "You can make it. Don't worry about them," she added when she saw his reticence.

The man nodded and scooped the boy up in his arms. Then he started running as fast as his aged legs could carry them.

Carmen flew to a higher level. She sensed about ten

people, but just then a heat beam—she didn't know who shot it—blasted right above her. The people were all right, but glass rained down on her. She flinched, though she didn't actually need to; her bioelectric field made the shards flow around her. She did, however, hear a groan from down below. She turned and saw the old man getting pelted by the glass. He hunched over, sacrificing himself to protect the boy. Shards stuck in his back, shoulder, and arm, but remarkably he was able to keep his pace. Logos grabbed the man and took the boy himself before giving Carmen a thumbs-up. She nodded sharply and went back to her task.

"Come out," she called. "I'm here to get you out."

"It's about fucking time," someone who had yet to emerge said.

Eventually, all ten came into view. It was a group of boys and girls only slightly younger than herself. If she didn't know better, they looked like a school group. At the sight of their rescuer, they paused. Carmen ignored their expressions and instead gestured for them to follow her as she ran to the railing.

"Whoa, look at that!" one of them muttered upon seeing the devastation to the mall and the battling Clairvoyants.

All ten started pulling out PDDs, which made Carmen to roll her eyes. She crushed two of the devices telekinetically before the group got the point that this was no time to take pictures.

"Jump," she said, looking over the railing to the foyer below, where Logos's team was ready and waiting.

"We can't jump. It's better to stay here than to jump."

Carmen rolled her eyes again. "I'll catch you telekinetically. Jump. Trust me."

The teens looked at each other and then, one by one, jumped over the rail. True to her word, each of them slowed to land softly on their feet just before they hit the ground. The suppression team took them from there, and she flew to the other end of the mall.

Both Ridley and Kennedy breathed hard. For their part, Artemis's clothes were torn to shreds, and she had a bloody lip and a burn on her arm. Neither Space Force officer was injured in any way, but in this brief battle pause, they looked on their adversary with eyes wide. Artemis wasn't even breaking a sweat.

The girl's eyes narrowed just before she took a step forward. Ridley went on the attack first, as she always did. This time, however, Artemis didn't try to match force for force, as she had thus far. Instead, she fell back from the attack, drawing Ridley into a deeper and deeper commitment. Kennedy rushed to join the battle but was somehow always out of position. Eventually, both women realized Artemis was inducing each frustration on purpose.

When engaged with roles reversed neither of them was as fluid. The defensively-minded Kennedy was unable to mount the required aggression to intercede on Ridley's behalf. Ridley's over-aggression soon turned against her. Every attack she made was countered with sharp punches or kicks from Artemis. After a few more exchanges, she was reluctant to attack, pushed to be totally defensive. In that uncomfortable state, Artemis was able to completely neglect her own defense and attack with hard, dominating strikes. A strong punch to the mid-section dropped Lt. Ridley to the ground. Artemis then turned to face off against Kennedy as Ridley spat blood.

Carmen slid to a stop in a makeup store. She briskly walked inside and then stopped when she saw Artemis's dead handler, Ramses, on the floor. *This was where it all started*, she thought. About a half-dozen people were huddled in the back of the store, and she went to them at a rush.

"Come on," she said, helping a few to their feet.

"What happened to the lady?" a little girl asked her. "She was doing makeup."

It took Carmen a moment to realize she was referring to Artemis. Carmen looked at the counter next to her and, sure enough, used lipstick, blush, and mascara were strewn about. It was the exact last thing she expected to see.

"She didn't hurt anyone?" she asked no one in particular with a small degree of amazement.

"Just that man," the girl's mother said, pointing at Ramses on the floor. "They had a terrible argument."

Carmen nodded. "Well, I have to get you out of here. It's not safe while they're fighting."

The group ran toward the exit with her in the lead. But she sensed and then heard someone trip and fall behind her. She turned to help the fallen person just as the group reached a railing that overlooked the foyer. They all screamed at once in horror.

The despairing cry, "Sandra!" reverberated throughout the mall.

Carmen ran back to the ledge to see what had happened. She arrived just in time to see Lt. Kennedy fall to the ground, dead. A hole was burned right through her.

"Damn you! Damn you!" Ridley screamed, blood dripping from her mouth.

She charged Artemis, abandoning any idea of self-protection. Carmen also flew at her. Artemis raised her hand and pointed it at the charging lieutenant.

"Artemis! Artemis, don't!" Carmen shouted.

The girl's first heat beam ablated Ridley's body armor and made her wail in pain, yet she kept coming. The second burned her arm off at the shoulder and caught her hair on fire. Carmen hesitantly raised her own arm to fire, but it was too late. Artemis's third attack hit Ridley in the face. She screamed for a moment, and then there was nothing as the Clairvoyant fell to the ground, mangled and broken, to slide to a stop at Artemis's feet.

Carmen landed near Kennedy's body and could only watch as Artemis slowly dropped her hand. A million thoughts and a million emotions went through Carmen. In the fog, there was nothing—nothing at all that could avail her.

Artemis stood still with her back to Carmen. She looked at Ridley's charred remains and then half-turned to look at Kennedy's. There was a quiet second of nothing. Then, all at once, her body slackened like a marionette with its strings severed and her eyes fell.

Carmen had no idea what to make of the expression. She stood transfixed as Artemis seemed just as confused and unsure of what to do. Slowly, the other girl gave her a hesitant glance. Then she looked up and shot into the sky after a pause, breaking through the glass roof of Crystal Palace.

Carmen followed immediately, unsure if she would be able to keep up. She hovered over the mall as she tried to sense which direction she'd gone before she realized Artemis hadn't gone anywhere. She looked down to see the Clairvoyant sitting on the roof, legs dangling over the ledge much like how Carmen often sat at the bluff.

She landed behind her and raised her guard. Artemis didn't even turn to look.

A small stream of blood ran down one of Artemis's arms. Her short hair was beaded with sweat and caked in a few places with blood. Her breathing came deeply and evenly, though at an elevated pace. She swallowed hard and then took a deep breath.

"They ripped my dress," she said, as if her mind was far away.

Carmen looked at her adversary and subconsciously dropped her guard. "...It didn't look very good anyway," she remarked.

Artemis glanced at her over her shoulder and rolled her eyes. "What do you know of style?" she scoffed. "I remember that pink monstrosity you had way back when."

Carmen smirked slightly but gave no reply. The other one-percenter also said nothing, nor did she change her position.

The sun was just beginning to set. The night was calm, tranquil even. Down on street level, however, the crowd and police were still waiting...and not quietly. Their din could be heard from up here. A few police aerocars eventually spotted them and hovered a safe distance away. Carmen ignored them.

"Are you going to kill me?" Artemis asked simply, without fear or threat.

"Do I have to?" Carmen asked back.

"I don't know," she said after a short pause. "I would fight you if you tried."

Neither of them said anything else for a long while. Carmen looked at Artemis, but she still had her back to her. The girl took a deep breath again but this time let it go with a shudder.

"Until today, I've never killed someone Ramses didn't tell me to kill," she said. "I was only defending myself. I didn't want to hurt anyone. I didn't even attack the suppression team or Captain Logos."

"So, Ramses told you to kill him?" Carmen pointed out.

She couldn't see it, but Artemis's eyes narrowed. "He had

it coming," she said, her voice sounding harsh for the first time in their conversation.

"That doesn't absolve anything."

"No, it doesn't," Artemis agreed, her eyes dropping again. "…I don't care. So, are you going to kill me?"

Carmen looked away from her and took a deep breath herself. "I don't know," she muttered.

"And what's the cause of your mercy?" Artemis asked, some sarcasm bleeding into her voice.

"I never wanted to fight you. Ever," Carmen said as she slowly looked away. "I never wanted to fight anyone," she added softly.

The comment made Artemis turn her head slightly. "Then why are you here?"

Carmen shrugged weakly. "Someone had to be. They said you went crazy and killed people."

"Of course you believed them," Artemis remarked bitterly.

"Why wouldn't I?" Carmen retorted. "Why would anyone who knows you not believe that?"

Artemis sat silently for a long while. It seemed like she was considering what Carmen said, though not completely. Whatever went through her mind, she sat still and stiff until, at last, her eyes narrowed while she took on a particularly ugly sneer.

"But you don't know me," she finally said.

"You're right," Carmen said after a pause. "I don't. Never had the chance. But since I don't know you, I need to know why. Why did you do it? Our group is going to graduate in a week. Why did you do this now? Why didn't you try to escape? Why…why did you stay just to do makeup?"

"I had to do it," Artemis said, her words firm and even. She turned to look at Carmen fully as she spoke. "I had to let them know. Twelve years," she added grimly. "Twelve years of it. I had to let them know they couldn't hold me in that room forever—that they couldn't just make me what they wanted and then release me when they wished. I had to make them know I could have escaped anytime I wanted to, and there was nothing they could do to stop me."

Carmen nodded slowly. "So, what now?" she asked.

"Now?" Artemis questioned. "Now I don't know," she said, looking away. "I'm not going back. If you expect me to go back, you should just kill me. Whatever my future is, I'm going to live according to my own will…wherever that leads me." She looked at her fellow one-percenter again. "You should come with me."

Carmen shook her head. "I can't."

Artemis looked at her with utter disbelief. "You'd rather go back to that shit? I don't know what we'd do or where we'd go, but come with me. Anything is better than going back."

"I can't," Carmen said again, shaking her head once more. "I didn't know you, and you don't know me. I…I'd fight you if you tried to stop me from going back."

"Why?" Artemis shouted.

Carmen shook her head for a third time. "I have to go back. I have to let them know that, after twelve years of doing everything they could to make me what they wanted. After doing everything they could to break me. After doing it all, that in the end, I'm still able to smile."

Artemis heard her words, and when they reached their conclusion, her eyes fell. "Edge, you're stronger than I am," she said mournfully. "We should have been friends. …I think I'll hate them most for that."

"We still can be," Carmen offered.

Artemis looked at her peer and then stood. The two girls

embraced each other then. No words were said. They held each other fully, deeply, and with eyes closed. They felt no pain from their bioelectric fields. Eventually, they let each other go and took a step back.

"What are you going to tell them?" Artemis asked.

Carmen shrugged. "Whatever. It doesn't matter. What else could they do to me?"

Artemis nodded slowly. "I'll see you around, Edge."

"I'll see you around, Artemis."

They embraced each other again, and then Artemis shot off into the distance. Carmen watched her go until she could no longer be seen. It only took a few seconds. Then she sat on the ledge herself and watched the sun set over Haven City.

19

THE BEGINNING OF HOPE

Carmen lay awake in bed. She hadn't slept all night, and she guessed it was roughly morning.

No one would be coming for her. Not Kali—not even Janus. She stared at the ceiling as she had for the past twelve years, her mind blank. Today would be the last. At least, the last day she'd ever lie in this bed, staring at this ceiling. She was sure the nightmares would stay with her, no matter where she slept, but some things did in fact end.

She sat up and looked around her soon-to-be former home. The place seemed to wrap around her like a blanket that was both ugly and uncomfortable.

She went to the set of clothes folded on her table. She'd been allowed one set of clothes of her choice for this day. The attire the assets wore was no longer appropriate. Prior events inspired her to pick a deep purple skirt and matching top. Kali said the choice didn't really suit her, but they fit Carmen perfectly nonetheless.

She looked at herself in the mirror that had been provided for this day. Something was missing, though. She didn't look bad—well, she didn't think so anyway. And despite Kali's opinion, what she was wearing was as much her as her left foot. She rolled her eyes when the obvious dawned on her. The issue wasn't the clothes. She retrieved the tie for her hair and put it up in a ponytail as she had countless times before.

"There," she said softly to herself.

She was tempted to smile but couldn't bring herself to. Instead, she turned to face the door and walked toward it with short, tentative steps. The door opened easily. She'd been told she would be able to open it from the inside, but the process was dramatically more anticlimactic than she expected. Perhaps her door had always been unlocked; she never tried to open it before.

Another asset stood in the corridor. His idea of how to dress himself was a bit grander than hers. He wore a dark grey suit that made him look like he had just stepped away from a dinner party. He looked at his door and seemed just as amazed as she had been at how easy it was to get out.

He gave her a nod when he noticed her presence. She returned it before looking toward the elevator at the end of the corridor. She gestured for him to join her, and the two began walking. They said nothing to each other. Everything was a little too surreal to shatter the perception by speaking. For what it mattered, she was somewhat sure she'd never seen him before, but she could be wrong.

When they got into the elevator, only one button was lit. He pressed it, and they went on their way. In not too long, they were deposited into the long corridor that exited the indoor part of the facility. He took the lead this time, but Carmen had already forgotten about him.

He entered the courtyard of the facility and then stopped for some unknown reason. She was a few steps behind him, and when she saw what he saw, she stopped as well. Maybe two dozen or more assets were already there, all dressed in spectacular array. In contrast to the dull sameness assets always wore, not one color or style was repeated.

She shook her head and was no longer mesmerized. Then, with no aim or destination, she walked into the courtyard as she had countless times before. No handlers were present. Carmen took to a quiet spot in the courtyard and waited.

Over the next few hours, the assets of her release group slowly exited the facility in the same dazed fashion as she had. Eventually, their number could not be easily counted. They all waited, for what they did not know, but none felt prompted to leave. Then the door opened again with an entirely different group. Slowly, all the handlers marched into the courtyard in double file. Carmen looked for Kali and didn't see her, but she could sense her.

The handlers made their way to one of the gates in the wall and walked through it. All the assets looked at each other. Some were also dressed like they were going to a dinner party, some like they were going to take a walk in the park, and others in a...less dignified manner. One of them made the first move, though Carmen didn't see who. After that unsaid cue, all of them followed the handlers out the gate. No one stopped them. No one required that they be signed out before they left. There was a gate guard, but he only smiled and nodded at anyone who looked in his direction.

The handlers were waiting for them on the other side. They formed two columns, one on each side of the gate. Their attire was all in the same general style, but it was not the uniform normally worn by handlers of the facility. The clothes were ugly to the point that they didn't even look terran in origin—like whoever made them had contempt for the terran form. Moreover, they were dirty and well-worn in places. Some were too small for their wearers and others too big. All had distinct numbers on their chests.

The handlers' expressions, however, were not anywhere near as homogeneous. A distinct majority seemed to have no more care for the event than when seeing an ant make its way across a sidewalk. There were a few, however, who, for lack of a better description, actually came across as proud. A couple others clapped as the parade of assets walked by. She didn't know handlers could have such countenances. Once again, she looked for Kali, but she couldn't be seen.

The assets walked on. At the end of the columns, a man stood on a large stage.

"Such as it was then, such as it is now, Clairvoyant releases and welcomes Clairvoyant into an unknown world," he said. "You are not the first. You will not be the last. As it was then, the galaxy trembles in anticipation of your will. Now and for the first time, you are able to act on its own accord. Of this, I offer one last bit of counsel. We, servants of the Dark, are not creatures of it. Meet insult with temperance and wrath with discipline but violence with the inevitability of reprisal. Hell—all hells—are prisons locked from the inside."

He said nothing else. Carmen and every other asset slowly looked away.

"Just like that," she said softly to herself, "it's finished."

Smiling wasn't the first thing that came to mind, though nothing did. The others seemed just as confused as she was. In turn, each of them, including Carmen, looked at the handlers. The handlers did nothing but stare back with arms crossed.

She didn't see Kali; she didn't need to. The point the handlers made came across clearly to everyone. She swallowed hard as the familiar dread of not knowing took hold.

But this time, it wasn't off in the future to be feared later. It was all around her.

It was then that Carmen noticed some of the assets were wearing Space Force or Sol SDF uniforms. That group flew off toward Haven City when it obvious they need not stay for anything else. Some of the other assets, lost and alone though traveling together, simply started walking. They looked back at the group a few times, and then they were gone.

She watched them go but had no mind to join them. For whatever reason, she couldn't bring herself to. Her first instinct was nothing of the sort. She began walking and was the only asset who went in that direction. She could have found the bluff with her eyes closed. When she reached the edge, Carmen looked down to the churning water below. Then she sat down and looked at the town far away on the horizon, the destination of her first flight. She knew she was still technically on the grounds of the facility, and that seemed fitting.

"I knew you would come here," someone said behind her.

It was Kali. Carmen didn't turn to look at her.

"I thought you weren't supposed to talk to me?"

The woman sat down next to her. "You're just not my charge anymore. No one said I can't talk to you."

Carmen nodded glumly. She glanced at Kali, who was unsurprisingly dressed like all the other handlers.

"Why are you wearing those clothes?"

Kali looked down, as if she had forgotten what she was wearing, and then looked at her former charge. "This was what the sortens had us wear. These are the same clothes I wore when…."

"When what?" Carmen asked when she trailed off.

"When I and a group of other Clairvoyants escaped the compound the sortens were holding us in." She looked away, her eyes becoming glassy and distant. "I remember when we stepped out of that place. We killed all the sortens—most of them, anyway. We were alone and had to fend for ourselves for the first time. I'd never been so scared in my entire life."

Carmen looked at her. Right as she was about to say something, Kali shook her head, and the memory seemed to pass.

"You figure out what you're going to do?" she asked.

Carmen frowned, feeling a small taste of what Kali had felt way back when. "No," she said. "I have no idea."

But just then, she thought she heard someone call her name. Not her Clairvoyant name, but *her* name.

"What was that?" Kali asked with a start as she turned around. There were still several handlers and assets in the area, making it difficult to see anything.

"Carmen!" came the call again.

"I don't know," she said as she stood.

"Carmen!"

She began walking toward the sound, and Kali followed. It was hard to make out who it was with this many Clairvoyants around her. But there was exactly one individual present who was not a Clairvoyant, and the direction of the voice and that individual seemed to coincide.

Almost painfully slowly, the crowd in front of her cleared enough to catch a glimpse of who it was. She stopped in place, as if she were rooted to where she stood. Kali's mouth fell open. When the rest of the crowd moved out of the way, Carmen's heart skipped a beat. There was a feeling—it started in the pit of her stomach and spread outward from there. Her toes curled, and her fingers tingled and went numb. The sensation rushed up her neck like flowing lava. When it reached her lips, they broke into a smile that gave no evidence of just how long it had been since they were last graced with pure joy.

"Michael!" she said, more in shock than as a call to him.

She hadn't seen him since that night and had tried not to think of him since Kali fired his family the day after. Yet here he was, among Clairvoyants who could crush him with a mere thought, his eyes only looking for her. He looked exactly how she'd dreamed.

They moved toward each other at a rush. She grabbed him and kissed him hard on the lips. It was her first, and part of her worried she could wake before she got the chance to. Michael stiffened at first, surprised by the action, but then he submitted to it and held her close. The feeling that had started in the pit of her stomach now began at her lips and flowed the other way, every part of her body responding like before.

They moved apart, and Carmen looked the impossible in the eye. She felt a tear form. She wiped it away with a finger, shocked it was actually possible to cry from happiness. Kali looked at the two of them. For a moment, it seemed like she wanted to say something, but no words came forth. She instead shook her head and smirked pleasantly. Carmen smiled back. The exchange was the last goodbye between handler and charge.

After that, Carmen embraced her future, still able to smile.

EPILOGUE

Subject: Edge Age: 19 Status: Released

"Carmen, Carmen, slow down. I can't keep up," Michael said.

She smirked and only half did as he asked. She wasn't really holding the box she was carrying; that was only a formality. Unfortunately for Michael, he had to struggle with only sheer muscle strength. They couldn't afford drones to move all of their belongings—well, mostly his belongings—to their new place.

He only got a few steps before she alleviated him of the burden telekinetically. As they waited for the elevator, her box and his box floated together side by side.

He looked at her, breathing hard. "Why didn't you do that before?" he asked.

"You didn't ask," she said, shrugging, as they got in the elevator, her tone light and cheerful.

"...Stupid me."

She smiled but could think of no reply to keep the joke going. When the elevator opened, they started toward their new apartment. Their new neighbors were in the hall, talking, and they looked Carmen up and down as she approached. Then they hastily went back into their room. Michael didn't notice. He usually didn't, and she wasn't in the habit of telling him.

"Now, where's that key?" he said to himself as he rummaged through his pocket.

Carmen opened the door telekinetically and stepped inside before he retrieved it. She'd soon learned, after she was released, that mechanical locks were no barrier to her. This was an older, cheaper apartment and still used physical keys. She'd read about them in history books.

"I know it's not much, but—"

She silenced him by placing a finger on his lips before she kissed his cheek. "Don't worry about it," Carmen said softly.

Financially, at least, their relationship was rather one-sided. It was difficult for her to find and keep a job. She just wished he could hold her when they slept. He said that, almost every night, she fidgeted and made noises like she was having nightmares. But he'd get shocked by her bioelectric field every time he tried to touch her. She couldn't control it while she was unconscious.

Carmen moved into the room and gave it a quick once-over. Then she turned around to see what Michael thought and was surprised to see he was still at the door. In fact, he rested against the door frame, still breathing heavily. There was even sweat on his brow.

"You all right?" she asked.

The box wasn't that heavy. She'd never tell him, but she partially supported the box even before she took it completely from him.

Michael wiped his brow and tried to stand up straight, but he only coughed roughly. "I'm fine," he said.

Carmen's eyes dropped for a second. Even when she

didn't read him, she always knew when he was lying. She often wondered why he even bothered. She played along anyway by forcing a smile. It probably was nothing.

"Why don't you set up the holoprojector?" she said. "I can get everything else."

He nodded and then sat down on one of the boxes. She walked toward the door slowly, watching him as she went. He eventually noticed her concern and gave her a reassuring smile before he beckoned her to go on. She smiled as well and then left the room.

She came back after a few minutes. The biggest issue was figuring out how to get everything in the elevator with only one trip. The train of boxes floated after her when she returned to their room. Michael had set up the holoprojector, as she had suggested, and now started at it intently.

"What is it?" she asked as she gently moved to hold him from behind.

His body made no reaction to her touch, such was his focus. He said nothing too, which prompted Carmen to watch the projector.

"We are here with an exclusive interview with Captain Renee Brown," the newscaster said.

Carmen thought she looked familiar. But *Captain* Brown looked like she hadn't slept in a few days.

"There's very little I can say," Renee began, "but I can confirm that there has been an engagement with a new alien race that call themselves the arkins."

"And, if I understand correctly, you yourself were involved in this battle?"

Renee nodded. "Yes, but I can speak of no more than that."

"We understand. But can you confirm reports that, following a declaration of war by the arkins, that sorten and

Eternal fleets have also begun mobilizing? And that Space Force and every SDF is now at full alert, preparing for, quote, 'Massive counterattack by possibly overwhelming forces,' unquote."

The captain hesitated. Her face reflected a growing dread before she was able to catch herself. "I am unaware of such reports."

Carmen had never met her before, and she couldn't read a holoprojection, but she was quite sure Renee was not lying. "Ignore that. It doesn't matter," she said. "Help me unpack," she added, letting him go.

She went to the first box, but just before she could open it, he grabbed her wrist and pulled her close.

"I love you," he said.

"I love you too," she said back.

They then leaned forward for a kiss.

ABOUT THE AUTHOR

Yup, I'm the evil guy keeping you up all night to read, "Just one more page." A storyteller from birth, it was inevitable that I'd find my way to writing books. All of my works have a very strong focus on character and believable worlds.

Other than books, I'm a licensed pilot and certified jet nerd. I'm also interested in motorsports and a lover of the "sweet science."

Check my latest updates and join my newsletter at ktbeltbooks.com